Dear Reader,

I fall in love with all my heroes and heroines. I don't think a book would work if I did not. But in the case of *Her Vampire Husband*, I fell so madly in love with Creed and Blu that I wanted to hug them and squeeze them and kiss them and take them home and call them George. This couple is absolutely my favorite fictional couple so far. I wish I could go visit them and see what they're up to now that I've put them through hell and brought them back again. I bet they're languishing somewhere in Paris, wrapped in a snuggly embrace, unconcerned for the world save each other.

This story is actually the third in my WICKED GAMES series. Each of the books stands alone (you don't have to read one to understand the other), but if you are interested, look for *The Highwayman* and *Moon Kissed*, too!

For a complete listing of my books, and to learn of future releases, stop by my website, michelehauf.com, or my blog, www.dustedbywhimsy.blogspot.com. Or you can follow me on Twitter, twitter.com/michelehauf.

Michele

MICHELE HAUF

HER VAMPIRE HUSBAND

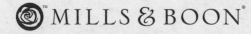 MILLS & BOON®

First published in Great Britain in 2010
Harlequin Mills & Boon Limited,
Eton House, 18-24 Paradise Road,
Richmond, Surrey TW9 1SR

© Michele Hauf 2010

ISBN: 978 0 263 88779 2

89-1010

Harlequin Mills & Boon policy is to use papers that are
natural, renewable and recyclable products and made from
wood grown in sustainable forests. The logging and
manufacturing processes conform to the legal environmental
regulations of the country of origin.

Printed in Great Britain
by Clays Ltd, St Ives plc

A Minnesota native, **Michele Hauf** lives in a Minneapolis suburb with her family. She enjoys being a stay-at-home mom with a son and a daughter. Michele writes the kind of stories she loves to read, filled with romance, fantasy and adventure. Always a storyteller, she began to write in the early nineties and hasn't stopped since. Playing guitar, hunting backyard butterflies and coloring (yes, coloring) keep her creativity honed. Research for her Mills & Boon® novels has yet to see her stealing jewels or racing cars on a high-speed chase, but…she can pick a lock or bake a mean chocolate cheesecake (with a file inside) if duty calls. You can contact Michele at: PO Box 23, Anoka, MN 55303.

To Jeff: Because I know you would slay a dragon for me. You are the only knight I will ever desire. Love you.

But really? Because that dragon carcass in the front yard could get just nasty, not to mention you'd always complain about having to mow around the tail. And do you think I'd let you hang the dragon's head on the living room wall? I don't think so. Though we could have a grand backyard BBQ. And just think of the money we'd save on the grocery bill, not to mention our new dragon leather attire.

CHAPTER ONE

"I WOULD RATHER BE home dyeing my hair."

Blu Masterson peeked between the heavy red curtains that stretched two stories high. She searched for her groom, but no particular man stood out amongst the huge crowd on the first-floor atrium of the Landmark Center. The room was ninety-percent male. The few females were vampires.

She saw that the room's inhabitants had divided, as if magnetic filings to opposite poles—vampires to the right, werewolves to the left.

The dais toward the back of the ballroom had been decorated with a ridiculous white pergola tucked with red roses, and a string quartet played an adagio entirely too upbeat for her heavy heart at this, her wedding.

"But your hair is such a pretty color tonight." Blu's best friend, Sabrina Kriss, smooshed her friend's thick bob with both hands and delivered her a glitter-frosted wink. "You're just nervous."

"Nervous? Is that what you call it? I'm marrying a freaking vampire, Bree. A vampire I've never met. A vampire I've been told is nine hundred years old. And in case you still missed the point—he's a *vampire.*"

Bree rolled her violet eyes. She was sidhe, so did not relate to Blu's ingrained disgust for vampires. Faeries got along with pretty much all the various paranormal nations. Werewolves did not.

As far as Blu was concerned, vampires were vile, blood-hungry creatures. They flaunted aristocratic snobbery that manifested as entitlement, and were possessed of an inhumane fixation on mortal man. They *needed* mortals for survival, while the species wasn't worth her time.

Bree asked gaily, "What do you think Ryan—"

"Don't say his name. Please, Bree. It'll only make the night more difficult to get through."

Blu bowed her head and wandered to the window. Tugging aside the curtain, she looked over the dark street outside.

She'd agreed to this idiotic farce of an arranged marriage to appease her father and pack leader, Amandus Masterson. "To show the werewolf nation we are capable of putting aside our differences and embracing the vampire nation," Amandus had proclaimed, but not without a wink.

Yeah, but he wasn't the one being forced to marry a vampire.

And it was force.

When presented with the marriage proposal, Blu had staunchly refused. For weeks. She was a princess; no one told her what to do. That argument held little weight within her father's pack. Blu hated all the Northern pack members. The only one she could tolerate was Ridge, her father's right-hand man.

And Ryan.

Don't think of him.

After the engagement had been inflicted, Blu had pleaded and pouted and even went on a hunger strike for two days, but she did love to eat, and self-denial was not her strong suit.

How she wished her mother was still around. Someone to stand on her side. Someone Blu could tuck her head against and sniffle out a few tears to. At the very least, someone who would nod encouragingly as Blu walked down the aisle tonight.

The door opened and a man poked his head inside the room. Blu stiffened and clasped her fingers together.

"There you are." Amandus Masterson crossed the room to her. The standard proud-father smile was absent from his long, drawn face. Blu would have been surprised had he shown her any sign of pride. He inspected her hair. "What is that ghastly color?"

She looked down, eyeing Bree surreptitiously. The faery had retreated to the wall, arms across her chest and eyes seeking anything but Amandus.

"I should have expected nothing better," he said grumpily. "Why must you always challenge me, daughter?"

"Challenge? I haven't said a word since you stepped in."

Blu had tried every trick in the book to convince Amandus she wasn't marriage material, until her father had threatened to have Ryan removed from her life. She should have protested more. But she never could find her strength in Amandus's presence.

And she knew what *removed* meant. Blu didn't want her lover harmed because she was too stubborn to play along with Daddy's game.

No doubt about it, this fiasco was a game.

She had her orders. And now the dread night had arrived.

"Here." He dropped a heavy ring onto her palm. "The jeweler delivered it moments ago. Don't lose it. And don't give me your disdain. Tonight you will not act as your mother so frequently did. You will do as you've been told."

Startled, Blu shook her head minutely. So rarely did he mention her mother. She wanted to grab him by the shoulders, shake him and ask him for more information. Her mother never did as she was told? Had she irritated Amandus, as well? Why had she left?

Persia Masterson had disappeared when Blu was eleven. No trace left behind, no trail to follow, completely vanished. And with the father/daughter relationship as impersonal as it was, Blu would never have the chance to learn the answers to her aching questions.

"The wedding march begins in five minutes," Amandus stated. "You've your instructions, Blu. Don't let me down."

"Yes, Father."

Jiggling the ring in her cupped palm, she waited until Amandus exited and closed the door before she exhaled and caught her shoulders against the wall behind her. Her heart raced and she winced to realize how quickly her anxiety had shot through the roof.

"Remember," Bree offered as she approached. "It may seem the most awful thing to marry a vampire, but with your vows tonight, you will be leaving your father's house."

"Thanks, Bree. I knew you'd be the one to point out the good in this disaster. Tuck this somewhere for me, will you?"

The faery took the ring and sought Blu's bouquet among the tissue paper crumpled in the florist's box.

Clasping a palm about her neck, Blu couldn't decide which was worse—marriage to a vampire or remaining at the pack compound. Neither offered the freedom she desired.

So she would seek a third option, when the time was right.

With a brush of her fingers, she confirmed the three-inch-wide choker was still in place at her neck. Though the gemstones resembled diamonds, they were cheap cubic zirconia. Blu had bought it as a treat for succumbing to her father's demands—and for protection. She didn't want any vampires getting ideas at the sight of her neck. It was a futile defense, but it did provide reassurance.

Tonight she needed all the support she could muster.

She wasn't afraid of vampires. Not that she'd been around many, or had held a conversation with one.

And she wasn't afraid of a creature because he or she was different. She'd accepted Bree; the faery was her best friend. Years ago she'd had a few witch friends. And her father had once dated a chaos demon; she'd liked her.

Moving in and playing wifey to a vampire? Bring it on. Just because she would sign the marriage contract did not mean she had to like him or go to bed with him.

She would go through the motions. Until her father determined those motions proved successful. But would compliance then see her back at the compound? That was not her ultimate goal.

"It's time," Bree said.

The faery hugged her from behind, snuggling her cheek on Blu's bare shoulder. Her violet-and-blue wings tickled along Blu's arm, warm with tenderness. "You look gorgeous, honey. There's not a wolf in the house who won't shed tears over losing you."

"You think?"

Female werewolves were rare. Which was why this whole arranged-marriage thing was expected to mean so much and be the catalyst to bringing the two nations together. If the wolves could sacrifice one of their females to marry a vampire, then they could surely stand back and allow peace to reign.

Peace was a long time coming, she had to admit. For decades, probably centuries, the two nations had been at odds. The vampires were the cruelest; they'd hunted and slaughtered her breed without mercy.

And what were the vampires sacrificing? Nothing, as far as Blu was concerned.

Sure, this man she was to marry was some revered vampire lord who belonged to Nava, one of the oldest tribes around. He was called an elder, and there were supposedly but a handful of his ilk walking the earth. That meant little. Only that he was old. Old, old, old.

"Chin up," Bree whispered.

"It is." Blu lifted her chin and turned to her friend. "How do I look? I may attract all the male wolves but do you think I can bring a longtooth to his knees?"

"You're going to have to quit using that word. I don't think it'll go over so well with the new hubby."

"Whatever. Longtooth, bloodsucker, flesh-pricker." It felt good to rattle off the epithets one last time. "So do I pass muster?"

Bree shimmied her gaze over the tight black sheath Blu wore.

Her bridal shroud, Blu had named it. She'd had it specially designed. It plunged low in the front, clinging and only covering half her high, full breasts. The black silk was slit high on both thighs, clasped at her hips with tiny rhinestone chains. The back…well, there was no back. It plunged to her derriere, and revealed the intricate tattoo her lover—former lover, she amended—had etched into her flesh along her spine.

Ryan had claimed her as his own after her father had grudgingly agreed to consider their engagement. As the pack's scion, Ryan was the next in line as principal should Blu's father die. But Amandus thought himself immortal. No whelp was going to wrench away his command.

That had been a year ago. Amandus had reneged on their engagement when presented with a grander, more delicious proposal.

Her lover had been shattered, but that hadn't kept them apart. They had been together 24/7 until two days ago when Amandus had sent Ridge to retrieve Blu from Ryan's home.

"Do you think Ryan will ever have me again?" she asked Bree.

"Of course he will."

"But I'll be tainted. I'll smell like nasty longtooth."

"I thought you weren't going to let the vampire touch you?"

Blu lowered her lashes and looked aside. Her reflection in the night-dark window pouted.

The marriage contract the Council had drawn up stipulated that the alliance was not considered consummated until she had accepted the vampire's bite. It was supposed to be the ultimate bonding in the vampire nation.

If a werewolf wore a vampire's bite, the stigma would be unbearable. Not to mention the wolf would develop a blood hunger it had never known before.

Blu smirked. "Hell, no. It's all for show, Bree. Don't forget that."

"You won't let me. Hey, will you let me bless you?"

"I'd love it."

Blu closed her eyes as her friend drew her fingers lightly down her cheeks and traced over her shoulders and to her hips. Calm and a tingle of joy infused Blu's pulse. In the wake of Bree's motions, a fine sheen of faery dust glittered onto Blu's flesh.

"Blessed be," Bree said, and kissed Blu on the cheek. "May the stars guide your nights and the sun your days."

"Thanks." For a moment she almost dropped a tear. But it passed quickly. "Now, where's that bouquet? If I'm going to do the bride thing, I intend to be the best damn bride out there."

She grabbed the posy of black roses tied with a long red velvet ribbon. She sniffed, but the flowers offered no perfume. Pity. She had wished for a distraction from the vampire's scent, which she dreaded taking into her senses.

"YOU FIND OUT which one she is? Shouldn't be too difficult to spot a female werewolf in this crowd," Alexandre said.

"I think they've got her secreted away until the ceremony starts."

Creed Saint-Pierre tugged at his shirtsleeves and traced one diamond cuff link with a finger. He looked over the crowd from his position on the dais. His best friend and best man, Alexandre Renard, stood at his side.

A female wolf should stand out amongst the female vampires, who all, he'd noticed, had decided black was the color for the event. Interesting how the two nations had divided, keeping to their respective halves of the ballroom as if the aisle of red carpeting were the proverbial line drawn in the sand.

While he had led the Nava tribe since the late eighteenth century, and had endured pomp and ceremony of all sorts, Creed did not care for fussy events. Strategy and the hunt were his mien. And when not serving his tribe members, he was a private man, and chose his pleasures carefully.

The very fact he stood upon this dais now represented a three-sixty-degree shift in his thinking. Whether or not he was actually being true to his nature remained to be seen.

That half the crowd milling here in the Landmark Center were werewolves put up his guard. They smelled wild and earthy, and were easily roused with the most innocent of glances. Creed was impressed a fight had not broken out yet. But then, only the trusted few had been invited to the ceremony.

The Landmark Center had been marked a neutral zone for the evening, but he didn't trust the dogs not to start something. It was so like them. Though he should be more relaxed knowing half the security force were vampires.

Because so many wolves were present, the room was

overwhelmingly male. With lots of testosterone floating about, anything could happen. Which was why it was necessary for posted sentries outside and along the inner hallways hugging the ballroom.

Creed never let down his defenses.

"All the dogs in the room," Alexandre said over his shoulder, as he scanned the crowd, "gives me that aching hunger feeling, you know?"

His second in command never turned his back on a werewolf, for painful reasons. It had been less than a year since Creed had rescued Alexandre from the blood sport.

"I feel like Henri of Navarre on the night of his wedding to the de Médicis bitch," Creed commented uneasily. He'd been in Paris in the sixteenth century during that event. Nasty memories.

"The Saint Bartholomew's Day massacre? So what does that make us?" Alexandre asked. "Catholics or the Huguenots?"

"Catholics, most definitely." Creed had never sided with the losing team.

"You're actually doing it." Alexandre's tone held a smirk. "Never thought you'd go through with it, old man."

Creed shoved a hand in his trouser pocket, ensuring the ring ordered specially by the Council was at hand.

"I did not believe the wolves would actually put up

something so valuable as a female. But they have, and so I am no man to back from a commitment."

He prayed she was not hairy. Male wolves had hair in abundance on their head, arms, legs and chests. In all his centuries, Creed had never seen a female werewolf, but he could guess she would be hirsute, as well.

Gods, what had he gotten himself into?

For nine centuries he'd walked through this thing called life without once getting involved with any particular female for more than a few months. Only one time had he begun to consider a woman more than a mere plaything and, well—he did not think about her if he could prevent it.

He did not like to be beholden, or to share. Emotion was easy enough, but love? It was not to be dallied with.

He was safe from the falling-in-love part. What vampire could love a werewolf, princess or not? He couldn't do it. He would simply go through the motions, make the marriage appear real.

A celebratory banquet was planned in a few weeks. The Council would parade them before the same crowd as tonight to demonstrate they were getting along; all would witness a happy couple. Whether or not the woman agreed to the charade, Creed would see she had no choice.

Quite a bold idea the Council had by proposing the

vampires resolve their differences with the werewolves by joining a couple together to prove they could accept one another.

Thankfully, love was not a requirement.

After discussion with his tribe, and various other vampire tribe leaders across the United States, it was agreed this match was the thing to do. Creed would be their representative. He was the only choice, for the position required a great sacrifice. He was one of few elders who possessed witch magic. A rarity amongst his kind, he was valued, as well as respected.

The things he had done to obtain such magic would turn the stomachs of most, he felt sure.

More than anything, though, Creed had made a personal vow to himself. This marriage would serve as a means to atone for his past indiscretions.

Sounded magnanimous and honorable, but could he keep such a vow?

A violet-winged faery stepped up to the dais, clutching a bouquet of red roses. She smiled warmly at both Creed and Alexandre. "I'm Sabrina, the matron of honor."

Creed nodded congenially. Alexandre muttered close at Creed's ear, "Nice."

A fine-looking woman, but Creed and Alexandre both kept their interest vague. Faery ichor was an addictive drink, as meth was to humans. Besides, Alexandre already had a gorgeous girlfriend.

"The bridal march is starting," Alexandre noted.

Creed set back his shoulders and assumed a modicum of hopeful expectation.

Make it look good.

He'd say the vows, kiss the new wife's cheek and then get the hell out of here. A bottle of whisky waited at home, the good stuff, imported from Scotland. He was going to need it.

"Oh, hell. Really?"

Alexandre's remark prompted Creed to scan the red aisle to the end of the massive four-story room. The doors closed slowly, having emitted one person.

"Look at that body," Alexandre whispered appreciatively. "Always thought a female wolf would be more butch. But what in the world? What's with the hair?"

Creed observed the tall, lithe woman dangling a tight bouquet of black roses at her side. She sauntered down the aisle, long, slender legs catching the eyes of all the werewolves in the room. The wolves all bended one knee and bowed, deferring to her high rank in the pack.

Some vamps even nodded approval. Creed understood their awe.

The dress, what little there was of it, clung to narrow hips, a sensual waist—look at those breasts. There wasn't much fabric to cover them. Full and round, they twinkled with glints of something…faery dust?

Full red lips parted as she glanced about, taking in every face, every sigh, every wanting lick of lips. Bright eyes, rimmed in dark shadow, fluttered. A diamond choker at her neck glittered.

But the truly startling bit was her hair.

"Green?"

Lime-green. The color of glossy neon plastic. Of irradiated spring buds. Of a spoiled, saucy werewolf princess who didn't meet his eye as she stepped up the dais to stand alongside him.

Standing as tall as he—thanks to some killer high heels—the reticent princess stared ahead to the officiant in a red robe. She smelled sweet and dark—like candies rotting in the box.

Creed stopped himself from saying hello and turned to face the officiant. If she were not going to acknowledge him, then neither would he.

She stood there. Intensely. The room had melted away and only she existed beside him. How strange. The two of them alone, reluctant symbols designated to save two struggling nations.

Creed shook his head to clear the weird notion from his brain.

Still she did not regard him. Of course it may be dif-

ficult for her to cast him a friendly glance. She must be
nervous. As he was.

No, not nervous, but expectant. So far things were
going far better than he'd expected. She was gorgeous.
That, at least, took the sting out of this humiliating event.

As the officiant began to speak, Creed could not focus
on the dry words.

She is gorgeous.

Her body is killer.

*And those lips and eyes! Not to mention breasts he
could suckle at for hours.*

But what's with the hair?

Feeling something he'd not experienced in years—a
fine sheen of perspiration—Creed forced himself to
listen and not play the fool by missing a prompt.

Such determination lasted a few seconds.

So this was what the werewolves would sacrifice to
gain peace? Creed exhaled. A tilt of his head caught the
flutter of her thick lashes as she looked over the black
roses now clenched to her breast. A fine prize, she.

For a werewolf.

But for a vampire?

"And in joining together a marriage recognized by the
United Nations of the Light and Dark, the two of you seal
a pact, a promise of peace between the werewolves and
vampires," the officiant recited.

No priest for this ceremony. Creed did not put stock in the human religions, though he did believe in the existence of a God. He wasn't sure what the werewolves believed in. Didn't matter.

"Will you, Lord Edouard Credence Saint-Pierre, take this woman as your legal wife, protect and secure her, honor and provide for her, love and cherish her?"

Sounded reasonable enough. Though the love and cherishing part may prove a challenge. Hell, he'd no intention of submitting to either.

Creed smiled at his bride, who did not look his way, and said, "I will."

The officiant nodded, and asked the same of the princess Blu Adagio Masterson.

Creed wasn't sure why the word *obey* was not included in her vows. Should be in there. Without question, the man was the leader and master of the household. How modern times had distorted the positions of power between a man and a woman. He still struggled with it.

When prompted for a reply, the princess suddenly looked at Creed. Soft gray eyes widened at sight of him. Red lips parted. Such white teeth, bright as the diamonds at her neck. She searched for something. Did her eyes water, perhaps to tear?

Glancing over her shoulder, she sought the masses. Did she look for a means to escape? For one strong soul

to step forward and rescue her from what she surely felt
a horrific fate?

Until now, Creed had not considered her personal sacrifice. The wolves branded vampires with the vile invec-
tive *longtooth*. She could be no different. It must appall
her equally as it did him to enter this marriage.

"Princess?" the officiant prompted.

Give your answer, he persuaded calmly. *Do not make
a fool of me or you will regret it for generations to come.*

Turning her gaze to Creed's, her bright eyes told him
his persuasion had not permeated her thoughts.
Vampires never could persuade wolves—or any paranormal, for that matter. Creed wasn't sure why he'd
even tried it. Now was no time to institute his magic,
either. Not when a couple witches from the Council
were in attendance.

Her gaze slid down his neck, skipping along the jet
buttons of his Armani suit, and averted to the faery at her
side. The faery nodded encouragement.

When the princess took Creed's hand in hers, the heat
of her flesh startled him. Like his, her skin was a little
moist. She was nervous, too.

With the slightest twitch, one side of her red lips
curled, she silently promised him she was in for the ride.

"I will," she declared boldly.

A rousing hoot from the crowd could not have come

from a wolf, Creed decided. But the resulting applause was immediately hushed.

Creed nodded acknowledgment to her. The werewolf's smile slid from her red lips, and she dropped his hand. Contact had been so brief, he wondered if it had even happened.

"You've the rings?" the officiant prompted.

Creed drew the ring from his pocket, sized especially for his new wife. He held it up for the crowd to see. Subtle whispers clattered through the room. All knew the meaning of the gift.

He slid it onto Blu's finger.

Blu? For a woman with green hair? And who wore body-revealing silk and clutched black roses on her wedding day?

What in hell was he stepping into?

"Titanium for strength," the officiant announced, describing the ring. "And in the glass chamber, witch's blood. A sign of the vampires' willingness to cede to the werewolves."

And a deadly weapon, Creed thought as he let go of the ring. Witch's blood from *before* the Protection spell had been lifted. Which meant one splash to a vampire's flesh would burn the average vampire alive, reducing him to ash.

Of course, the werewolves had overlooked a pertinent

detail regarding Lord Creed Saint-Pierre. Though he wouldn't dismiss the blood could have its damaging effects on him. Or perhaps not. Might it actually aid him? He couldn't risk finding out.

His bride plucked a ring from the petals of her bouquet and held it high for all to see, before taking Creed's hand. She fumbled with the bouquet, not sure how to hold it and put the ring on at the same time. Finally, done with it, she tossed the bundled roses out to the crowd.

She offered Creed a had-to-do-it smirk and shrug, and slid the ring onto his thumb. A perfect fit.

"Titanium for strength," the officiant again announced. "And filled with liquid silver to show the were-wolves' willingness to cede to the vampires. I now pronounce you lord and lady Saint-Pierre. Please kiss your bride, Lord Saint-Pierre, and begin the path to peace."

Quite a profound demand: *Begin the path to peace.*

It was all on his shoulders now. Hers, as well. But she merely had to stand there, shifting on her feet and sneering those glossy lips, defying him to dare kiss her.

He would not, no matter that her lips were thick and soft and wouldn't they be the most exquisite to kiss? He could prick them and suck the blood for an evening treat.

Creed leaned in and, keeping his head tilted before the crowd, brushed her cheek with a kiss. His shoulder-length hair concealed their connection. No one would know if he'd kissed her mouth, save he and she.

She. His new wife.

A wife who flinched as his lips brushed her skin.

How dare she?

She was no better than he. She had walked the aisle, willingly entering into the marriage. There were certain expectations to be upheld. And he would not allow her to dodge them.

Gripping Blu's bare shoulder, Creed pulled her to him and captured her soft lips against his mouth. She mumbled a protest.

He kissed her harder.

The kiss was not at all distasteful, as he had imagined. Much better than most kisses, actually. And her efforts to push him away only fired his desire to pull her closer. To mark her before all, so they would know she was his.

Only when his fangs descended, and he feared accidentally cutting her, did he relent.

Yet he could use this moment. And he did.

Fangs bared, and wicked smile growing, Creed turned in triumph to the cheering crowd.

CHAPTER TWO

AS THEY ARRIVED at the end of the aisle, Creed felt Blu slip away from his side. He let her go. There were more important things to do right now.

He would always have more pressing matters than tending to a wife.

"You did it, man!"

He received a congratulatory handshake from Alexandre and manly busses to both his cheeks.

"By 'did it,' you mean jumped off a high cliff and am now free-falling to my death?"

"Close, I'm sure. But what's up with the chick's hair?"

"She's young," Creed tried.

It was more a consolation than an excuse for her. Young and alarmingly sexy, she embodied vitality. Creed had felt truly ancient standing next to her.

He'd been transformed to vampire when he was a

mere twenty-seven years old. He still looked it. Okay, so perhaps a handsome thirtysomething. But there were days Creed felt every one of his centuries like a weight upon his mind, shoulders and flesh.

"Her youth will serve you well," Alexandre said on a sly whisper. "The younger ones are the most open to trying new things."

His second in command winked.

"New things," Creed muttered. Could this old vampire be taught new tricks? Without the innate need to simply steal them?

He hoped the werewolf could get beyond the naiveté of such youth. If she were to be his wife, she must be able to relate to him on an intellectual level. He would not babysit for a spoiled princess.

"Lord Saint-Pierre." A tall, gangly gentleman with gray hair and veiny hands stepped forward. The pinstriped suit reminded Creed of a gangster, but the gentleman's hooded eyes exuded genuine warmth.

Creed slipped his hand into Amandus Masterson's. Though his new wife was called a princess, the father was not considered a king, merely the alpha, or leader of the pack. So he addressed him accordingly. "Principal Masterson, I am honored."

"You should be. My daughter is a prize, in more ways than mere beauty."

"I understand. She is a rarity. You have my promise I will protect and respect her."

The pack leader nodded acceptance. "It would be foolish of me to ignore the fact she's a feisty one. She's a mind of her own, and is very stubborn. That awful hair."

"She's lovely. I can only hope to win her admiration."

"You say all the right things, Lord Saint-Pierre."

Indeed, he did.

"Now, let's go have a drink with the Council and get the final negotiations settled. The marriage contract must be signed."

"It would be a pleasure." Yes, like pounding a nail into his coffin. "After you."

THE COUNCIL had gathered in a small room off the main ballroom. The dull lighting blended the red carpet into the red-arabesque-papered walls, and cast a sickly sheen upon flesh, yet Creed could make out faces with ease.

Vampires were considered the Dark by witches. They, in turn, had labeled themselves the Light. Werewolves landed somewhere in the middle, depending on who was doing the labeling. It was all rather superfluous, Creed felt. He had no need for labels.

At least three vampires currently served on the Council. Creed had been asked decades ago to serve, but at the time had no desire to involve himself in the politics of the Light and Dark nations.

Yet here he stood, at the center of the most political move the vampires and werewolves had made in centuries.

A faery, a demon, two witches and a selkie rounded out tonight's Council representatives. Depending where the meetings were held across the world, various members showed in different numbers. The Council was about fifty members strong, and new members were only inducted when a previous one had died.

Their mission was simple: to keep the peace among the paranormal nations. The key purpose was to keep mortals in the dark. Mortals did not believe in the myths and legends their books and movies touted. And that was the way it must remain. The Council went to great lengths to keep that silence, yet they rarely interfered violently.

Some days Creed wondered if violence were not the only way to make the opposition see the point. He had never subscribed to the whole violence begets more violence theory. A good bloodbath tended to weed out the weak and make the strong rethink their motives.

Or so he had learned earlier in the past millennium.

Don't forget your vow, he reminded himself. *Atonement, remember?*

He shook Nikolaus Drake's hand. Taller than Creed by half a head, the Kila tribe leader's bald scalp advertised a havoc of twisting black tribal tattoos. He was the gentlest vampire Creed knew. A former brain surgeon, if rumor held truth.

Drake was also a vampire who had magic himself, though it had been obtained by a witch during the Protection, which made his powers much weaker than Creed's.

Nikolaus was liked by most, and Creed figured it was because he'd only been a vampire for three decades. He still retained much of his human morality.

Creed had morals. It was just harder to recognize them as the centuries stretched them further from immediate access.

"Drake," he said. "I understand there's paperwork and such to sign."

"Yes, the marriage contract is right over here." He directed Creed to a rosewood table and handed him a pen. "The princess signed it before the ceremony. This is a good thing you're doing, Saint-Pierre. I think it'll go a long way toward enacting the peace amongst the nations."

"I sure as hell hope so." He scribbled his name at the bottom of the first page that was marked with a yellow highlighter. There were two more pages to sign. "I would have loved to be a fly on the wall when the Council decided this was the way to solve the unrest."

Nikolaus chuckled and leaned in close to Creed, putting his palms to the desk and shadowing the papers. "You will do us proud, yes?"

The vampires had a lot riding on this marriage. They expected the sporting warehouses—a bane to the vampires' existence—would be shut down upon the werewolves' acceptance of their enemy.

Creed desired that, too, beyond any other good thing that should come of this.

"I always give any task my all," he reassured him. Straightening, he again shook Drake's hand. "Has Principal Masterson handed over the same olive branch?"

"He has. He's hopeful for the results. Which can only be measured by the princess taking your bite."

Creed lifted his brows and sighed. Biting a dog was not tops on his list. But the kiss had gone over well, so he wouldn't rule anything out.

Amandus Masterson joined them and said, "And what exactly is the sacrifice the vampires are making that is equal to my daughter being bitten?"

Both Creed and Nikolaus silently summed up the pack leader. The old wolf had once been known to ruthlessly retaliate against those he'd marked as his enemies. He'd aged and grown gentler, though the jury was still out on whether or not he'd embraced wisdom.

The Northern pack did not engage in the sport that saw

vampires tortured relentlessly and then caged to perform for the wolves until one was literally sucked to an agonizing death. But there was something about the old man that put Creed off.

What sort of man would offer up his only daughter as Amandus had?

"The mere fact I allow your daughter into my home, my very life," Creed said, "is a sacrifice you cannot begin to understand, Principal Masterson."

Yet even as he said it, it felt like an excuse.

What, indeed, was his sacrifice? The wolves assumed the vampires were offering up their eldest and most revered. That was true.

"Doesn't seem balanced," Amandus muttered.

"The Council approved the terms a week ago," Drake explained. "If you had a disagreement you should have spoken then."

As should have the werewolf representative on the Council, Stephen Severo. Creed was aware he showed up irregularly at Council meetings, and wasn't even sure the wolf had been part of the agreeing quorum.

"You mustn't feel you are being cheated, Principal Masterson," Drake continued. "What your daughter is doing will have a resounding effect upon the nations of Light and Dark for centuries to come. I'm proud of your sacrifice."

The old man nodded and, slapping both arms across his chest, nodded toward another wolf in the room, and wandered off.

"You're very good at that," Creed said to Drake.

"Smoothing over the differences?"

"Actually, I was going to say bullshitting, but I suppose your explanation is better. So I'm off to find the new wife. Any words of wisdom before I do?"

"My wife used to be my enemy," Drake said. "She's taught me not to judge a person from the outside. Our hearts can be more alike than different."

Creed nodded and smiled. It sounded good in theory. But Drake wasn't the one taking a dog home with him tonight.

BLU SHOVED AWAY the chocolate martini Bree tried to get her to drink. "For later," Bree had coaxed, "when your husband tries to bring you to his bed."

She didn't need a loosen-up drink. "Bed is the last place I'll follow that vampire tonight. Ugh. Do you think he sleeps in a coffin?"

She'd heard some longtooths engaged in the practice, though it was unnecessary to their survival. The novelty, or something stupid like that, was their reasoning.

"No coffins, sweetie. Don't think things like that."

"Thanks. Call me soon, okay?"

Blu did her best to control a tear when hugging Bree goodbye. A stroke of her friend's wings showed her love and gratitude.

Outside the back door was where the vampire had said he'd drive up to get her after he'd spoken with the Council. Blu shrugged a palm up her arm, but before she could wonder if the shiver was from the cool breeze or nerves, she squeaked at the hard pinch to her upper arm. Spun about, she stifled a defensive scream at the sight of her lover.

"Ryan, what are you doing here?" Shadowed by his overwhelming bulk, he still held her tightly. She struggled, but that only made his grip go tighter. Normally she wouldn't react defensively, but tonight was not a normal night. "Father said you were not to come near this place. You risk too much."

"I had to see you, Blu. I've been kicking the wall all day thinking about you and that longtooth in the same room together. Promise me you won't share his bed."

When he released her, the pinch at her shoulder stung. He was never aware of his strength, and always went too far.

"It's an easy promise." She leaned in and kissed him quick on the mouth, but he grabbed her by the neck and forced the kiss longer, harder. She mumbled against his mouth and pushed his chest, forcing him to the wall.

"That's enough. I don't want to mess up my makeup and have the vampire suspect. Get out of here. Now. Before he sees you."

"Maybe I want him to see me."

"Ryan."

"Fine. I'm gone." He toyed his fingers along the ends of her green hair. "But don't forget the sacrifice I'm making for you, Blu. Soon it'll just be the two of us."

She gave him a small smile and nodded. Tugging her wig back into place, she kept her back to him as he loped off down the alley.

In theory his plan sounded too good to be true. But it was all she had to hope for, so she subscribed to Ryan's plan for her freedom. For now.

A black BMW 7 Series pulled up from the opposite direction Ryan had left. No streamers or shaving cream announcing the newlyweds decorated the classy vehicle. Thank the goddess. The vampire lord stepped out and opened the passenger door for her.

Blu stood clutching her arm where Ryan had squeezed her and took in Lord Saint-Pierre. About as tall as Ryan, which put him a head taller than her, yet more lithe, not so bulky. Streamlined muscle did stretch beneath the fancy suit. Charcoal hair spilled onto his shoulders. She liked dark hair on men, but not vampires.

She did not like vampires. And that was all that

mattered. He may be the most handsome and stylish man for miles around, and still he would not turn her head.

Sliding inside the car, Blu did take note of his manners. No man had ever held the door for her. It wasn't entirely offensive.

They drove in silence for what seemed forever. Away from the rush of the ceremony and in the quiet confines of the BMW, Blu moved her hands up her bare arms, mining for warmth. The air-conditioning blasted.

What to say to one's new husband whom she'd known less than ten minutes?

"Turn that down," she blurted. "You want an ice cube for a wife?"

"Sorry." He grimaced. Flicked the control knob to Off.

More miles of quiet followed. Creed tapped the steering wheel, but didn't offer conversation. The radio was not on, which Blu would have preferred, and the interior was soundproofed from outside noises.

Blu could not stand uncomfortable silences. Life was to be lived, loud, proud and wild. "Up all night, sleep all day" was her motto.

But now she appreciated the sharp silence.

Never mind he was her husband. Her *vampire* husband. That creeped her out on so many levels.

How to converse with someone she had no interest in?

She tangled her fingers in the glossy strands of her

wig. Maybe ask him how he dared to kiss her like that in front of everyone? So brazen. So freakin' dominant. Hadn't she suffered the alpha males enough? This little foray was supposed to be a vacation away from all the testosterone she literally breathed daily living at the pack compound.

Thinking of testosterone...

She could still taste the vampire on her mouth. It wasn't like blood—she wouldn't know that taste—but it wasn't like her lover's taste either. This taste was different. In ways that shouldn't intrigue her but did.

"You spoke to my father," she stated. Okay, so the silence was beginning to grate on her.

"Principal Masterson is a fine man. The leader of the Northern pack?"

"Since Severo stepped down." She looked out the window. Raindrops spattered the glass.

Severo. The former principal of the Northern pack who had stepped down to become a lone wolf. He'd married a vampire last year. He had been the one to suggest this idea to the Council and to encourage her father to put her hand in for this ridiculous scam.

Why could they not use his marriage as an example?

Blu recalled something about Severo's wife being changed to vampire only after they had fallen in love. Supposedly it wasn't the same situation.

It was a good thing Severo had not been at the wedding. Blu knew exactly how hard she'd swing a fist at him when she did see him. Hard enough to draw blood. A loose tooth would serve the icing on the cake she hadn't gotten to taste this evening.

"So," she said, "what are we to do with ourselves? You're taking me to your home?"

"Yes, I live at the edge of the suburb, but more in the country."

"What are your intentions?"

"You are my wife. I had assumed we would do the married thing."

"The married thing." She tapped the rain-streaked glass with a knuckle. "What does that imply exactly?"

"Living in the same house. Appearing to others as a couple. Conversation."

She waited for him to summon further examples but he did not. Because he could not? He was not so pleased with this arrangement either, she bet.

At least they had one thing in common.

"Sex?" she prompted.

"Of course."

"You wish."

"The marriage must be consummated."

"The Council's idea of consummation is not sex."

"You would take my bite?"

"When hell freezes over."

The car swerved sharply, shoving Blu roughly against the door. She sensed her husband's smirk as he pulled through an automated gate and onto a cobbled driveway that curved before a three-story brick mansion.

Supposedly her new hubby lived in France during the summer months and wintered in Minnesota. He'd moved back to the States a few months early after agreeing to the marriage. What a freak. She'd take the glamour of Paris all year if given an opportunity.

The estate fronted by climbing vines initially impressed Blu until she decided it wasn't so grand. Her father's compound covered more acreage, and the pack probably owned more surrounding land—no thanks to the greedy vampires.

"Big mansion," she remarked. "You must have servants."

"Gardener and Housekeeper."

Short, to-the-point answers. Wasn't he the one who'd suggested marriage implied they converse?

"Has anyone ever told you you're a real conversationalist?"

The car abruptly stopped and he shifted into Park. Blu jammed her heel into the floor mat to keep from lunging forward.

Twisting and leaning his forearm on the steering

wheel, Creed turned to her. "Let's get things straight between us, shall we? I can assume we are both uncomfortable with this arrangement."

"Hallelujah."

"Yet while I have vowed to myself, and my tribe, that I will do everything in my power to make this work, for the sake of both nations, I suspect you have made no such personal vow."

"Vows are so medieval. I'm just here for the show, Credence."

"It is Creed," he corrected.

"Creed," she tried. "So alpha. Shouldn't you have a vampire name like Damien or Lucien or—"

"Or something inane like a color?"

Blu gave him her cheek, peering out at the increasing rain. Bastard.

"Our first fight," he said. "I suppose that falls onto the list of what is expected of married couples, eh?"

Despite herself, Blu smirked.

"Let's go inside and I'll give you a tour. I understand your luggage was delivered earlier. I've ordered it placed in our room."

Our room? She closed her eyes and bit the inside of her cheek. Since puberty had struck, and she'd become a kind of beacon to male wolves, she had been fending off testosterone like a vaccine-resistant plague.

She didn't need it from a vampire.

"Could you please leave me alone a bit?"

"Here in the car? But it's raining."

"Please, Creed," she said softly. "I need a few minutes to myself."

He didn't reply, and instead opened the door and got out. Unmindful of the rain, he strode to the front door and left it half-open to expose the soft golden light shining within.

Blu pressed the side of her head to the passenger window. Her reflection wavered in the glass; green bob smooshed against a cheek, and dark eye shadow smears. Tears streamed down her cheeks, falling more swiftly and harder than the rain.

"Creed Saint-Pierre," she whispered. "Don't hurt me like the others have. Please."

SHE SAT IN THE CAR for fifteen minutes before Creed wondered if he should go out for her. Was she pouting? More likely trying to prove she would not listen to his authority.

It wasn't difficult to guess she would be obstinate to a fault. She was so young and inexperienced. He would teach her manners and respect. It was the very least he could do—send her back to Daddy more respectful and submissive.

Because he would send her back eventually.

Creed paced before the glass-and-stone-tiled bar that curved along the wall in the main room. This mansion had been built in the seventies and retained much of the original design, only now he could pass it off as retro.

He liked the massive fieldstones set into the floor and the open three-story entertainment and living area. It was a sort of landing, a place to relax and order his day, before venturing outside or to his office in the back. Once or twice he'd held parties, and the guests usually convened in this spacious room or outside by the pool.

He glanced up the curving red-carpeted staircase. He'd had her things—three large traveling trunks—delivered to his bedroom. She hadn't liked that.

Resisting a smile, he decided she would have to get used to answering to a new authority. Surely she must have practice. Packs revered their females yet would never allow them to step out-of-bounds. They were also fiercely protective of the rare female wolf.

How had Creed managed to simply drive away tonight with a valuable female without bringing the wolves upon him?

Could this peace thing really work?

"I'll be damned if it does."

When the door opened and a sodden green-haired werewolf stepped inside, Creed sucked in a breath.

The thin fabric that had barely covered her breasts was now wet, revealing the gorgeous shape of them, erect nipples and full, delicious volume. He did love to caress a woman's breasts. To lick at them. To nuzzle into them and suck her to climax. Heaven.

"You keep staring like that, vampire, I'm going to have to punch you."

Or hell, depending on the woman.

She strode past him and dropped her shoes and purse on the damask sofa. With the same nonchalance, she plopped onto the sofa and put up her feet on the Brazilian ironwood coffee table. The wood wasn't supposed to get wet.

Creed went around and shoved her feet off it with his heel. "Your manners are lacking. But what should I expect?"

"From a werewolf? I suppose you expect me to romp about on your furniture and tear it apart with my teeth. I probably better not wash or comb my hair either because that would destroy your mental picture of me. Should I stop shaving my legs and do the whole hairy thing?"

Creed paced to the bar and poured two fingers of whisky. Putting it back in a tilt did little to curb his annoyance. Irritating as she was, though, he couldn't deny curiosity. He had expected her to look much different. Distasteful.

Not like a colorful and very sinful dessert.

"Let's do the tour and get you situated," he said, leaning over the back of the couch.

She stood before he could slide his gaze down her dress. "Can we save the tour until morning? I'm tired. I just want to shower and hit the hay. You have a stable out back? Wouldn't want you to have to board an animal in such a fine home."

"Your things are upstairs in my room. *Our* room."

"Yeah, I heard you out in the car."

The green chin-length hair bobbled as she strolled around the end of the couch. A fire he couldn't imagine being ignited in such cool depths flamed in her quiet gray eyes.

"Our room?" she reiterated.

"You are my wife."

"You expect me to sleep with you before I know anything about you?"

"You *will* sleep with me?"

"Didn't say that."

How infuriating she was to raise his hopes so easily, and then dash them. But at least she was talking to him. And looking at him. And weren't those lips devastating? Could he have one more kiss before he tucked her in?

Tucked her in? Hell.

Could he get beyond the age thing? Creed had never

discerned age before, because if he did then he'd always end up the old man to the young women he'd pursued. Nine centuries was hard to beat.

"I want my own room," she said, and started toward the stairs, strappy shoes dangling from a couple fingers. "It would be cruel of you to force me into your bed, vampire."

Cruel, but wicked fun to watch her squirm to think he would try to take her only hours after meeting her. But, to his disadvantage, he was not that kind of man. Women must be pursued and seduced. Their favor must be won.

"You can take the room at the top of the stairs," he said, following her upward. "Housekeeper keeps it made up for guests. It's not as elaborate as my room, but until you're comfortable with our situation it should serve."

She strode to the door and turned, pressing her palms and hips into it, while leaning forward in a slinky come-on. The front of her wet dress clung to her breasts, exposing the dark curve of an areola.

Was she teasing? Or was it his heightened attraction to something so new and utterly baffling that had him seeing the sensual in her every move?

"Situation," she pronounced precisely. "Is that what you call a marriage?"

"I'm sure it's a much better word than you would choose."

"You're right. I call it a farce."

He could not deny the word hadn't crossed his mind a time or two.

"You did agree to the terms. And you said vows before a healthy number of representatives from both nations. And you signed the contract."

"As did you. But do you really think this is going to work?" She patted the bottom of her hair with a palm and pouted coyly. "That we'll fall madly in love and set an example that will bring the werewolves and vampires together in some kind of freaky lovefest? Come on, Credence."

He did not care to hear his name spoken that way. The memories it stirred would only hamper his need to remain staunch and in control.

"Madly in love?" He pressed a hand to the door over her shoulder and leaned in. The move put her off, which pleased him. *Come on, princess, you're not allowed to tease without retaliation.* "At this very moment, I can't imagine that happening unless hell turns to ice. You, Lady Saint-Pierre, are standoffish, spoiled and contrary."

"And you are an aristocratic bore."

"Uneducated," he countered.

"Old."

"Uncouth."

"I'm not sure what that means."

He smiled. "Ill-mannered."

"Ah. I'll take that one. And I'll counter with dull and uninteresting."

Did she really want to play this game? Because he'd show her how far from dull he could get.

Creed slid a hand over the sparkling choker caressing her neck, fitting his fingers up under her chin. Her eyes flashed defiantly. A bit of the faery dust had nestled at the corner of her eye, glinting mischievously.

"Tease," he countered softly.

"You like it though."

That glint in her eyes would be his undoing. It challenged, bedeviled and defied with a knowing he thought her too young to possess.

"I prefer my women to follow through with their promises."

"I've promised nothing," she said.

"You promised to honor and obey me."

"*Obey* was not in the vows. Trust me on that one, buddy."

Now he smoothed his hand under her jaw. The jut of her chin was sharp. Every bone stood out, defining, creating remarkable dimensions to explore. Her flesh was soft, warm, alive. And beneath the flesh, her blood smelled darkly sweet, a wicked perfume.

"You had better not be thinking what I think you're thinking, longtooth."

The demeaning curse should not go without a swift slap.

Though he wasn't taken to harming females, some could only be controlled with physical coercion. Like witches. And others. He'd once worked with a female vampire bounty hunter in the fifteenth century. She'd liked it rough.

But Creed had made a vow. And he had meant it when he'd promised her father he'd protect his daughter, and ensure no harm came to her. Some things in war and love were never fair game.

So instead, Creed leaned in for a kiss.

She was quick, sliding her fingers over her lips before he could make contact.

Creed tugged her hand away. She struggled, and because he didn't trust his strength, he conceded, flinging back her arm and stepping away.

Pacing before her, he looked to the carpeting, not wanting to show her his defeat.

"You've already stolen one kiss from me," she said, defiance brightening her tone. "The rest should be earned. If you can earn them, I'll be more than willing to give them."

And she slipped inside the guest room and slammed the door.

Creed fisted his fingers at the door. A nasty condemnation slid across his tongue, but he gave it no voice.

Turning and stomping down the hallway, he threw open the door to his bedroom.

"Green-haired wench," he muttered. "Thought I'd had to deal with the last of your kind in the sixteen hundreds."

CHAPTER THREE

BLU TRACED A FINGER along the stainless steel kitchen countertop. Cold, precise, engineered for maximum inhospitality.

Much like her new husband.

The glass-fronted cabinets displayed many crystal goblets, snifters and shot glasses—and only a few plates. The wine fridge was as big as the regular refrigerator. She peered at the labels on the wine bottles. Some bottles had hand-printed labels and the years were from the seventeenth to the nineteenth centuries. She was no expert, but did know some rare wines sold for tens of thousands of dollars.

"Nice. Bet he'd throw a fit if I tapped into one of those."

Much as she'd like to witness a vampire conniption, wine didn't interest her; she needed food. Sustenance.

She hadn't eaten since yesterday noon. Her prenuptial nervous stomach hadn't allowed her to do more than nibble. Now her stomach growled like a banshee.

She opened the fridge door and gaped at the bleak interior. "What? You have got to be kidding me."

"*Bonjour,* my new wife."

She spun to find Creed leaning against the counter. She hadn't heard him enter. *Bad werewolf.* She should have smelled him the moment he came down the stairs in the other room. Vampires had a vivid scent, earthy and yet refined, perhaps a little sweet.

Damn, she was off. It was the house. It was filled with new and odd smells. And it was so open and vast. She couldn't acclimate.

Or it might be nerves still.

"You've no food," she complained.

"Never had a need for it." He stared at her head, a curious grin toying with his expression.

"Yeah? Well, I require food to survive. I'm famished."

"I'll send Housekeeper out for something. What do you like?"

"Anything edible. Preferably meat, fruits and veggies. A nice porterhouse steak would fit the bill. You seriously don't eat? Must save on the grocery bills. Please tell me you don't have a fridge with bags of blood in here somewhere. That would so make me retch."

"Wouldn't want to see that. Though now that you've put the unsavory image in my brain it's stuck there."

"You're welcome."

She closed the fridge door and turned to face him, crossing her arms over her stomach. Now she scented him strongly. Dark, spicy, brewed together with some kind of masculine musk.

"And just so you know," he added, "I don't do bagged blood. It must be warm and have a heartbeat."

"Peachy. Thank *you* for that image."

That pleased him enough to grant her a lift of brow. "Turnabout is fair play, and all that."

She'd give him the point. But only because he wasn't so awful to look at during the day, even though the shades were pulled on all the windows, reducing the daylight to a dim mire. Hair blacker than the dress she'd worn last night feathered about his face. Eyes equally dark studied her curiously.

"What's wrong, vamp? You're staring again."

"Your hair." He gestured, his fingers tracing a loose circle between the two of them, but gave up trying to figure it out. "Yesterday it was…and now it's…"

"It's called violet. You like it?"

Head tilting, he seemed to search for something nice to say, but decided silence was best.

A shake of her head swung Blu's shoulder-length

violet bob. The long bangs that dusted her eyelashes tangled in the silken strands and she blew upward to disperse them.

"I think it's one of my better colors," she said perkily. "Goes with the skirt, too."

He studied her plaid pleated miniskirt, drawing his eyes the length of her legs, where she twisted the ball of one foot on the floor. She was barefoot, the only way to go when not out partying.

"You're quite a loud dresser, aren't you?"

"Loud?" Blu chuckled heartily. "This is but a whisper, buddy. And it's me, take it or leave it. I like to play with my looks. You don't like it? I don't much care. Now where's the housekeeper? What's her name?"

"Housekeeper."

"Yeah. What's her name, and I'll go tell her what kinds of food I like."

"Housekeeper," he stated again. "That's what I call her."

"You're not serious?" Blu did air quotes, and repeated, "'Housekeeper'? Poor chick. Doesn't even garner a name from her employer? Bet you're loads of fun at the office Christmas party."

"I don't celebrate Christmas."

"Of course not. Because you've banned fun, right?"

"And I think you've fallen into the fun barrel, gotten stirred up and tumbled out the other side."

"If that's a comment on my clothes, I'm not biting. Color is my thing. I don't like to blend in."

"One would think a wolf would prefer more natural camouflage, or an understated look."

"So you're all up on my breed now, are you?"

"Not at all. I know only a little."

"Which is obviously less than nothing. So! I'm heading out for a jog after I find the housekeeper with no name. Where are the best places to run around here?"

"I don't think that's wise."

"I didn't ask your opinion. I need some directions. You got a computer? I'll check the neighborhood on Google. We are at the edge of a city suburb, yes? I think I saw some houses last night. Kinda far off though. This is like Green Acres to me."

"I mean, you shouldn't go out alone. In fact, I insist you do not. It's not safe."

Blu swung a look at the man. He was serious.

"Dude, I'm a werewolf. If some mugger tries to take me on, I'll give him what for. Not like anyone would be out here in the boonies, anyway."

"There are wolves and vamps camped outside the estate."

"What?"

"I'll show you on the security cameras if you must see. I checked this morning. I suspect both factions will be keeping a close eye on the two of us."

"Well, that's unfair sportsmanship."

"I agree. And I suspect if you go out alone they may not simply observe. The vampires might threaten you and the wolves, well…"

Yeah, she knew what to expect from the wolves.

"Ever hear a wolf do a catcall?" She winked. "Those guys are randy as hell, always."

And a very good reason for her to stay nice and safe tucked inside. Yet seclusion here with the enemy was not going to be a day at the park.

"I had assumed so. And you being the lone female wolf in the vicinity… Well, your safety is my concern."

"You say that like you love me *so* much," she mocked.

"I—"

"I know, I know, you promised my father. You take those marriage vows so seriously, like some honorable knight's vow to protect and serve."

"I've served under three French kings and various vampire tribes. I'm accustomed to taking vows and standing by them."

"Whatever." She peered out the window. The estate's west side backed up to a lush forest. "You've a lot of acreage. Is it all marked off with the fence I saw out front last night?"

"It is."

"Bet I can run around the property awhile. I have to run, you know. I need the exercise. It's my nature."

"A werewolf thing?"

"Exactly."

"And what about when the full moon arrives?"

She tilted a sultry gaze at him. She knew when he discerned that she was flirting because his eyes lit up. But he didn't understand it was all in fun, and the confusion on his face pleased her.

So now he was getting to the questions that mattered. One in particular that must be burning a hole through his uptight brain. He had married a werewolf. What the hell did that mean?

"What do you think will happen when the moon is full? Think I'll wolf out and attack you?"

"Blu, please. I know enough about werewolves to avoid them, or to catch them by the throats with a blade if they charge me, but I'm not up on everything. Besides, I've stood before my share of werewolves in my day."

"I bet you have. Slaughtered many?"

She read so much in his condemning gaze. He wasn't going to answer the question, though Blu suspected the answer was *more than many*. Rare did a vampire and werewolf encounter one another without bloodshed. At least, she'd never known differently.

"I've only ever encountered the male of your breed. They are formidable during the full moon when they are in shifted werewolf form. But I know little about the female."

"Then you've some learning to do, buddy."

She tapped him on the nose and breezed past him, determined to exit before she decided a punch would serve better than a mere tap.

The audacity of him to assume she would wolf out because the moon was high in the sky. She wasn't like her male counterparts.

She was much more dangerous.

And the sooner the vampire learned that, the better off they'd both be.

CREED EMERGED FROM HIS office after making phone calls to the major tribe leaders in the Minneapolis/St. Paul area. He confirmed the werewolf princess was in his care and that things were running smoothly. Whatever that meant.

His perception that things were running smoothly was hindered by his vacillating notions about werewolves: befriend them or kill them. Centuries ago, such would have been an easy call. But now, he struggled to find the answer that would serve him best.

Another phone call checked with Alexandre on the Rescue Project. He liked to be kept abreast of all happenings with the project. If a new sporting warehouse was located or if a lone vampire had been reported missing, he would send out the team.

All was quiet on that front, but the information did not put him at ease. The whole calm-before-the-storm thing was an accurate measure of anything the werewolves did.

Leaving his office to walk off his anxieties, Creed padded barefoot through the living room. An awful stench teased his nostrils. "What the—?"

He followed the odor to the kitchen, and wandered in and caught Housekeeper as she was tidying up.

"She doesn't like it rare?" he asked.

"Yes, rare."

"Smells like you grilled a cow to oblivion. And you did it inside?"

"There is the special grill on the stove, my lord."

He'd never paid any mind to the appliances. "Gods, I hate meat."

"I enjoyed the opportunity to cook, my lord." The woman bowed to him and slipped by.

Creed preferred his help obedient. This one should have asked him first before firing up the grill. On the other hand, they never did stick around long enough for proper training.

He opened the fridge. It was stocked with a colorful array of fruits and vegetables. The freezer held cuts of beef, pork, chicken and—he thumbed a plastic-wrapped package—buffalo?

"Ghastly."

He could barely remember what it had been like to eat so long ago. The flavors and smells were too distant to recall, but the *knowing* it had satisfied still remained within him.

Admittedly, he envied Blu for her appetite. While blood satisfied now, he wouldn't mind the occasional taste of truffle, oven-warm bread dripping with butter or even steamed fish. Food—beyond a lick or nibble—would make him sick, though.

He was just thankful he could consume wine and whisky with no more effect than a dizzy head. He liked that he could get a little drunk off alcohol. Not drunk, actually, but looser. Relaxed.

He imagined Blu would be a sight drunk. She was already so colorful and in-your-face. A few goblets of wine might see her dancing on the tables.

Not a horrible image, when he considered those long sexy legs. They grew up to her armpits. And those hips would rock so sensually….

But then, she was now his wife. Decorum must be learned. He wasn't about to appear in public with the foulmouthed brat until he'd polished her up a bit.

Make that a lot.

Summoning a simple wind spell, he waved his hand and conjured the wind through the window screen and curled the breeze about the kitchen. The air hooked into the scent molecules and carried the officious smell out with it.

He'd have to watch his usage of magic. He felt sure the wolf would have questions. Which would then lead to accusations. He preferred to avoid the conflict. The best defense was always to pick and choose the battles worth fighting.

Centuries earlier he'd made a promise to the Council—the witches foremost—that he would not use his magic skills. It was either that or be magically shackled to prevent him from doing so. He preferred living without being bound by a spell.

Wasn't as though he used it in large amounts. About eight hundred years ago, the spell had been put in place to make witch's blood poisonous to vampires, and to prevent the vampires from enslaving witches. Though he could drink from a Protected witch simply because he'd been drinking from them since before the spell, and had obviously developed an immunity.

Didn't matter now. The spell had been demolished a couple decades earlier. Though he had no need for magic, he did find it made life easier and he hated to lose it completely.

Strolling through the living area, he noticed movement out on the patio. Violet movement.

"Those wigs. I wonder what her real hair color is?"

He snagged a pair of sunglasses from the cupboard beside the patio door and, checking skyward to make sure the mechanized sunshades were drawn over the vast patio, went outside.

She had tugged a lounge chair off the tiled patio and onto the grass, which was not protected by the massive canvas shades that rippled in the breeze.

Having purloined a pair of his sunglasses, her eyes were hidden behind the black lenses. Her long lean body stretched along the slatted wooden chaise. The bikini did not cover much territory.

But a thin strip of pink fabric covered her obviously shaved mons. She was tan there. Creed decided she must lie out often. Probably in the nude, because he didn't see any trace of pale skin around the edges of the small strip that didn't cover more than the most important parts. No clue as to what her natural hair color was there, either.

Bemused, he glided his eyes along her shapely skin. Equally small triangles stretched over such perfect breasts, Marie Antoinette would be jealous. Perfect globes, high and proud.

"You have this thing with staring at me, you know that?"

Creed realized he leaned over her, as if he were a mortal inspecting fruit displayed on the grocer's counter. He straightened and stepped back onto the patio tiles.

He could withstand indirect sunlight for ten, fifteen minutes tops, before it began to burn his skin, though he could go about in the day if the sky was overcast. There was no magic spell that would make him impervious to the UVs.

"I see you've made yourself at home."

"This *is* my home now. And since I'm not allowed to leave the property without an armed guard, I figure I'd make the best of it. Why don't you join me?" She patted the grass beside the lounge chair where the sunlight beamed strongly. "Oh, right. Burn, baby, burn, eh?"

"It's why I spend a lot of time in Minnesota. Not much sun here in the wintertime."

"So that's why the vamps are thick as blood here. Pun intended."

Creed pulled a lounge chair to the edge of the tiles and sat in the shade, stretching out his legs. They reclined parallel to each other, she a goddess of the brilliant day, and he ever a slave to the night.

"I envy you," he said before he could stop himself.

"What for? My ability to soak up the UVs without dusting to ash?"

"No, your reckless abandon. You're very free."

"I don't see any shackles on your wrists."

"I mean inside. Underneath that violet wig. You don't care what anyone thinks, and that's refreshing to me."

"Yeah, I bet you think about everything before you say it. Wonder how your words will make others react."

"Not at all. I've been around long enough. I say and do as I wish. And I have certain expectations—"

"You expect to have met."

She flipped to her stomach and propped her chin on her forearm. The backside of the bikini bottom was but a string.

Creed suppressed an appreciative moan. A man could bounce a quarter on that ass. And look at that tattoo. It was a tribal design, but delicate, flourishing up her spine in a gorgeous arabesque.

"Look all you like," she said.

"Don't mind if I do. You don't normally sunbathe wearing a swimsuit. Why today?"

"So you've been looking for tan lines. Naughty vampire. You think I'm going to give you a peep show? Now you're starting to sound like the wolves in the pack."

"Don't ever compare me to a wolf."

She smirked. "Dude, don't worry. That would be too flattering."

The chair creaked when he leaned abruptly forward. "Do you purposely mean to offend, or is it your nature?"

"I think it's a little of both. Hey, you don't have to talk

to me. There's a whole big yard—oh, right. Pale boy needs to stay under the protective covering. My bad."

She was right; he didn't have to suffer this abuse. But to reach over and admonish her with a swat to that sexy ass might convince her he wanted to touch her.

He did want to touch. What man could resist such a tantalizing display? But he wouldn't give her the satisfaction of knowing she'd won this round.

"You like to swim?" he tried.

"Nope."

The violet hair splayed across her face and the dark sunglasses. Surely she could still see him, but he didn't care. He couldn't look away from that incredible ass. Softly rounded, so firm, and taunting him to stroke his fingers over the sun-heated skin.

Damn, was he getting hard looking at a werewolf? Of all the absurd—

"Penny for your thoughts," she cooed. The tip of a pink tongue lashed out to stroke the underside of her upper lip. "But I bet they're worth a mint."

"You've a great ass," he conceded. "Nice tits, too." Leaning back and stretching an arm behind his head, he tilted up his sunglasses. "You're the complete package, Blu. Why on earth did you agree to this marriage when you could have been married off to a fine werewolf, most likely a pack leader?"

"I was promised to the scion of the Northern pack." She tucked her head into her creased elbow, away from him. "Tattoo is from him."

Interesting. What little Creed did know of pack politics was that a scion either had to kill the current principal or wait for his death. In this case, Amandus Masterson's death. So how would the principal putting his daughter forth for this marriage screw with the scion's plans?

"You loved him," he guessed. "Sorry."

"I didn't love him. I loved having sex with him and being his girl. He was my lover. But I'll never fall *in* love. It's not in my nature to give my heart over to a man. Remember that, vampire. It's all an act. That's all it can ever be between us."

Creed closed his eyes behind the sunglasses.

Indeed, an act. He wasn't stupid. He'd entered this marriage with eyes wide open and his brain working all the angles. But there were so many variables he hadn't anticipated.

Like being attracted to his wife. Physically, that was. So far their exchanges had only reinforced to him that she was spoiled and most likely unwilling to put forth as much effort in this marriage as he would.

What he did know for sure was this conversation didn't need to happen. They were only required to play their parts before observers.

Though he couldn't be sure the vamps and weres camped outside the perimeter of his estate weren't using telephoto lenses to take pictures. They could have the damned yard bugged, as well.

But they wouldn't get past his security. Should a werewolf breach the fence by means other than the front gates, silver darts were set to find the target all around the perimeter.

As for vampires, he didn't fear challenge from any.

So why was he sitting here trying to converse with the obstinate one? Logic determined they would need to get to know one another, to make it look good. She seemed amenable to that.

Or was it that the view was so spectacular? Before last night he'd thought it impossible to consider kissing a werewolf, let alone get a hard-on from looking at her body. Yet right now he sported some serious wood from the visuals she broadcast.

What was wrong with him?

Mon Dieu, he needed to take blood. It must be nearing the end of a fortnight since he'd last taken a donor. He could go as long as a month without sustenance, but two weeks was best. If he considered stroking the heat-softened flesh of a woman who should be his greatest enemy he wasn't at the top of his game.

"Besides," she added, "love wasn't a requirement."

"No, it was not. Quite a relief, eh?"

"Tell me about it."

He caught her gaze for a nanosecond before she looked away. Caught. He could smell the longing on her. He was sure of it. Or, at the very least, interest.

"Do you swim?" she suddenly asked.

"Every day."

A dip in the cool waters would serve to chill his insubordinate lust. But he usually dove in wearing nothing. He wasn't sure he owned swim trunks, though he could dive in wearing his skivvies.

Why the hell not? If she was going to flaunt her sexy curves before him, he shouldn't be prudish about stripping before her.

"That's what I came out here for, as a matter of fact."

He stood and felt her gaze upon him as he strode over to the pool. A woman's regard was a fine thing, but more so when she wished to deny that interest.

Peeling off his shirt, Creed tossed it aside onto another chaise. A stretch of his torso flexed his tight abs. He retained the physique of a warrior even though his battle days were long behind him. And though sword, ax, bullet and fangs had entered this ancient body, he retained no scars.

"Stare much?" he volleyed at her.

She turned her head into her arm. "Nothing to see, pale vampire dude. I prefer my men hairy anyway."

He may be pale, but he was nothing to sneeze at.

Stepping from his pants, Creed snapped the band of his black boxer briefs. She was looking again. He could feel her curiosity as a tangible wave through the air. Felt great. Felt…different.

Closing his eyes, he whispered too softly for even paranormal ears, "You do prefer me."

Out his peripheral vision he saw Blu lift onto her elbows, as if she'd heard something. A whisper only he could make audible through air magic.

Take that, snotty werewolf princess.

Diving, he hit the water with a sharp cut and swam the entire pool length before surfacing on the other side. When he flipped back his hair and swiped the water from his eyes, the violet-haired goddess knelt at the pool's edge.

"Thought you said you didn't swim?" he asked.

"I don't. I just… Did you hear something?"

"Like what?"

"I don't know. A whisper?"

"Did they wed me to a mad princess?"

She snapped her fingers, dispersing droplets of water. "Whatever. Hey, you know what cold water does to a guy's dick?"

"The water isn't cold."

"Yeah, I noticed."

Starting a backstroke, Creed was amused he wasn't the only one who couldn't avoid looking.

BLU DIALED BREE'S NUMBER and slipped into the guest bathroom attached to the room she was staying in, locking the door behind her. Bree rambled on about how sexy her new husband was and how daring of him to kiss her in front of everyone like that.

"Yeah, whatever. He's sex with fangs. Not. So did you talk to Ryan after the ceremony? Did he say anything to you?"

"Haven't seen him. But you know I only see him if he stops into the bar."

Bree danced strip at the Goddess in St. Paul on weeknights. She was an amazing dancer with a body Blu envied. And the wings rocked, too. Blu had always wanted wings. Instead, she got stuck with the hairy wolf stuff.

"He was there last night, waiting for me outside the Landmark. I had to be quick with him because I didn't want the vampire to see. You'll call me when you talk to him, right? And you'll ask him about me?"

"You know I will. Even though it's only been a day, I'm sure he misses you to death, Blu. But tell me about your first night? Did you and he...you know?"

"Miss I-Take-My-Clothes-Off-For-Strangers can't say

the naughty words? Please, Bree. I slept in the guest room. You think I'd have sex with a strange man?"

"You have done it on occasion."

"Yeah, but they weren't vamps." And don't remind her of those disastrous stranger sex encounters. "I hate thinking that I'm sitting in a vampire's lair."

"It's your lair now, too."

"I'd prefer a cave. Doesn't feel friendly, whatever you call it. Would you come over, Bree? I don't have anyone to talk to and he won't even let me go out to jog."

"Sounds kind of Neanderthal."

"He hasn't dragged me around by my hair yet, but I wouldn't put it past him. There are vampires and were-wolves camped at the end of the property, spying on us. He thinks they might do something to me."

"Protective fellow. How romantic."

"Whatever."

She swung her legs up onto the vanity and leaned against the wall. Mr. Romance had been hoping she'd look when he'd stripped to go swimming. Sexy muscles had cut through the water with precision and unnatural speed. Pale as he was, he didn't need a tan to highlight the tight abs and delts.

She'd only looked to make him feel good.

That was her story and she was sticking to it.

"All right, I'll give you one thing," Blu said. "He does have a great body."

"So you did peek!"

"He went for a swim. Couldn't avoid the browse over his abs."

"All muscles and brawn?"

"I suppose. Nothing like Ryan, but nothing to sneer at either."

"Ryan's a freak of nature. He's got too many muscles."

"Yeah, but I love to lick them. I miss him, Bree."

"You need to not think about him. He's your past now, Blu. Why don't you stare into your hubby's eyes for a while? You might find something interesting in there."

"Yeah, like bloodlust." Blu palmed her throat. "It's going to be so gross if I see him drink someone's blood. He's not coming near me with those fangs."

"Fine, but will you let him prick you with something else?"

"There's my nasty girl."

"That's me. Always eager to hear about everyone's love life. Please promise me you'll give him a chance, Blu. You're both in the same situation. Doing something for an entire nation you don't even know. You should be bonding over this, cleaving to one another. It'll make you stronger, I promise."

"Bree, you do know cleave has two opposite meanings. I'll take the prying-apart definition."

"I meant the clinging-to-one-another definition."

"Yeah, I know. You, Bree, are always too positive about everything."

"It's the faery dust."

"Will you slip me some of that stuff next time I see you? My supply is running low."

"Sure! Now quit hiding in the bathroom and go get to know your hubby."

Blu smirked. Leave it to Bree to know she was hiding out.

"It's getting dark. I think he's gone hunting, or whatever it is they call stalking mortals for blood. Pulling a Dracula. Yeah, that's what I'll call it."

"That gives you time to shower and slip into something sexy before the count returns. Try a little flirtation on your hubby."

"Yeah, but flirting will mean a promise to him."

"Nothing wrong with that. Woman cannot survive for more than three days without sex. I know you agree with me on that point."

Blu rolled her eyes. She was not going to agree, much as she did. "Goodbye, Bree. Talk to Ryan for me, and call me back."

"Love you, Miss Blu!"

Blu snapped her cell phone shut and tucked it beneath her chin. The faery was entirely too cheery and centered for her own good. If such a thing as Zen Sidhe existed, Bree was the poster fey. The girl needed a good shake— like being forced to marry her complete opposite—to give her a dose of reality.

What was the opposite of faery? Hmm…maybe a demon.

But Blu couldn't begrudge Bree the positive vibes. Bree was the only one who actually believed this marriage had a chance.

Sliding off the vanity, Blu tugged the bikini strings loose and stood naked before the walk-in shower tiled in polished river stones. She slid her palms down her stomach and hips. It always made her feel apprehensive when a man stared and hungered after her.

Creed couldn't keep his eyes from her. It had made her nervous so she used her snotty comebacks to disguise it. Living at the compound, she'd learned a few sharp words sometimes proved more effective than a slap that could be construed as rough foreplay.

She smoothed her palms up to cup her breasts. A glance over her shoulder studied her body in the floor-to-ceiling mirror on the back of the door.

Let the vampire look. She was the one who would decide if a look could turn into a touch, and a touch into something more. It was high time she took control of her life. It was not something she'd had at the compound.

Peeling the wig from her head, she shook out her hair and flicked on the shower.

Flirting with her husband?

She did need something to keep her from getting cabin fever. And if it put her in control? All the better.

CHAPTER FOUR

THE DONOR FELL AT Creed's feet and collapsed, arms and chest folding over her legs. Creed swayed against the rough cement wall, catching his palm against it, as the swoon shimmered through his body.

After nine centuries, taking blood still never failed to satisfy. Nothing near a raging orgasm, but a sweet tease similar to it. And with age, the high all vampires called the swoon lasted longer, fixing to his veins in a lingering shimmy of sensation that he could draw out for hours. Of course, that was due to the blood magic he'd gained from a witch. And since that little exercise of magic didn't harm anyone, he wasn't about to give that up, vow or no vow.

He licked his lips. The blood wasn't as tainted with beer as he'd expected. Perhaps haunting local bars should not be marked completely off the list.

Normally he invited a select clientele to his home

when he needed to drink. But he couldn't do that now. It didn't feel right with the wife at home. He didn't want to answer any questions she would have.

Besides, if she were going to withhold information about her change during the full moon, then he would keep his stuff private, too. Most especially the magic. If the wolves discovered his usage of it, they'd go straight to the witches, and then the war between witches and vamps would be renewed.

Creed had enough on his shoulders with the werewolf princess prancing about his home.

After unlocking the BMW, he climbed inside and headed home. All he wanted to do after taking blood was lie back and enjoy the mellow ride.

THE HOUSE WAS DARK, save for the light at the end of the hallway, which told Creed that Blu had found the theater room. The loud music was an even better indication.

Tonight should have been his movie night. He liked viewing movies on the plasma TV, sitting in the dark with a sexy woman draped in his arms. After a long drink of hot blood, he usually had a driver escort her home because his persuasion stole her memories for the evening.

Who said drinking blood had to be all horror and chills? He'd done enough of that in the Middle Ages. Flash the fangs, freak 'em out and suck them dry.

That was so gauche now. A man must possess style, decorum.

"Hell, you really are an old man," he muttered. "You don't bother with the scare anymore, just popcorn and sex. *Dieu.*"

Erratic sound blasted from the room. The wolf must have turned the volume to eleven. He wanted quiet tonight, to enjoy the lingering blood swoon.

"Silly wolf. This vampire can still do the scare."

Marching down the hall, he fisted his hands and had achieved a tight anger by the time he pushed the double doors open. Prepared to march in and flash some fang, Creed paused.

The lights were on. Poufed pink feathery stuff bobbed in the air two rows down. The room touted six rows of four seats on each side.

On the screen, Mick Jagger pranced and rasped through "Sympathy For The Devil" as Keith Richards ground out a solo.

Tucked on one of the wide theater seats—rather, draped—Blu grooved to the beat, her long legs hooked over the seat before her. Those pink feathery things were some kind of high-heeled shoes Creed had only seen in black-and-white romance movies.

The pink hair bobbed in time to the music.

"Pink?" Anger dissipating, he strode down the aisle.

A see-through sweep of black fabric dashed across her legs and part of her stomach. The rest of her was clad in black lace providing only a little more coverage than the bikini had earlier.

"Loud enough?" he shouted.

She hadn't noticed him yet. Why should she? Her eyes were closed and she beat the air with delicate fists in time with Charlie Watts's drum kit. Weren't wolves supposed to have excellent smell?

Creed leaned over and glided his fingers up her smooth calf.

She startled, her legs sliding down and her shoes hitting the floor. "Whoa! Dude, way to go for the creep."

He reached for the remote tucked in a cup holder, and muted the noise. "You discovered the sound system."

"Oh, man, this so rocks. Surround sound in this little theater? I could *live* in here."

"I see you've made yourself comfortable."

She sat up on the chair arm, the gossamer robe sliding away and exposing maximum flesh. She looked like a high-priced hooker in her bubblegum pink hair and push-up black lace bra. Add the spiky heels and she was dressed to earn a pretty penny.

Not that he would know anything about hookers. Not from this century, anyway.

Creed sat on the chair arm across the aisle. Her exotic

perfume, which could be suntan lotion with its tropical coconut aroma, carried across the aisle, prodding at his blood swoon. *Just relax, and sink into the sensation....*

"Is it okay I'm using this room?" she asked. She made no move to tug the robe over her flat, tight abs. Not that the sheer fabric would conceal anything. Those legs were so long. They could wrap around his back and hang on for the ride. "I didn't know when you'd be home. Were you...out?"

"Out?" He could play the innocent as well as she could.

"Well, you know."

"I'm not sure. What *do* I know?"

She sighed and pointed to her neck. "You know. Pulling a Dracula."

"Pulling a—?" Was she really going to insult him with a reference to a fictional character?

"The sucking thing."

"Ah. You mean the part where I answer the call of instinct to survive?"

"Yeah, whatever. So what do you do? Stalk hookers in the night or something?"

"Look who's talking. You appear as though you tickled one and she sneezed her attire all over you."

Affronted, she sat straighter. The move pushed up her breasts so they strained against the black lace.

Creed sucked in his lower lip. Mercy, but the wolf had a nice pair.

"I'll have you know there's probably not a hooker on the streets who can afford this bit of black lace. It's from Paris."

"Ah? As am I, or thereabouts."

"That's right, my hubby the Frenchman." She leaned forward, propping her elbows on her knees. The position did amazing things with her breasts. Creed could see the rosy circles surrounding her nipples. "Always had a thing for Frenchmen."

"Is that so? You could have fooled me."

"Frenchmen who don't bite," she said with a scratch at her neck. "So what's the deal with you going out? I should think a rich guy like you can afford to have your bites shipped in."

She was so gauche and, yet, entertainingly so. Tonight's wig matched the pink marabou and it bobbed sexily against her porcelain-fine jaw as she nodded to the muted beat.

"Normally I entertain donors here at the house. I didn't want to disturb you though, so my hunting habits had to change."

She shrugged. "I don't care. So long as I don't have to watch."

Creed stretched an arm along the plush velvet cushion and propped an ankle across his knee. No harm in marveling over her. Drawing in her delicious scent. "You know, some *do* like to watch. Taking blood is a sensual act."

"Yeah? Maybe for the vampire."

"For the donor, as well."

"Donor? You mean victim."

"They're not victims if I don't harm them."

"You don't consider a bite harm?"

"I use persuasion to erase their memory of our transaction. The bite heals overnight and they wake with only minor soreness."

"Donors? Transaction? Okay, that's enough." She pressed the off button on the remote and stood. "You've thoroughly creeped me out."

"And you continue to intrigue me, Blu. Did you intend to seduce anyone in particular tonight with that clothing choice?"

"This little thing? Dude, this is what I wear to bed."

He rubbed his throbbing brow. "I am not a dude. Your language skills impress me little."

"Oh, that's right. You're an old man who's lived it all, seen it all, and must be so cultured and refined. Ha! I can actually mean it now when I talk to my girlfriend about my old man."

"Do you speak of me?"

"Hell, yeah. I told Bree all about our skyrockets-and-lightning wedding night."

"Blu, do you ever tire of this front you put on constantly?"

"Don't know what you're talking about."

Sex incarnate had no idea how hot she made him merely by standing there, one leg out jauntily and twisting on the heel of her shoe. Or maybe she did.

Yes, she must be aware of every single move she made, and how best to move for the optimum impact on the opposite sex. And yet—

"You keep people back with your blasé attitude and your snotty comments. Why is that? Are you afraid to allow people close to you?"

She stepped across the aisle. Legs spread and hips high, she bent over him. Her breasts were level with his line of vision, but he instead looked into her eyes. There in the depths glittered a sadness Creed was beginning to realize may have been there a very long time.

Why he realized that, he did not know. Because she came off as hyperfun, sexy and all about the flirt. Truly, was it a facade?

"I let a lot of people close, Creed," she said precisely. "The ones I trust."

"How does one go about cracking your exterior? If you won't accept the trust I offer, then I've no means of winning this game."

"That's your problem. You think this is a game."

"And you don't? You've played the Tease Card yet again. I've known you but a few days, but already I've learned that's your favorite one."

"Is not."

"Prove it."

The pink wig bopped at a jaunty angle as she cocked her head, considering. She had to know she played him. The sexy clothing was a dead giveaway. Who wore an outfit like that to listen to music? No, she had been expecting him.

Blu leaned closer, the tips of her pink hair dusting his wrist. Red lips hovered near his and her breath played over his mouth, his chin. Coconut air surrounded them. Beyond that scent though, something darker and sweeter lingered. *Werewolf blood.*

Creed's heartbeat slid across the plate and hung suspended, waiting for the next play.

"I like to tease," she whispered, her eyes dazzling across his.

"That is apparent."

He would not reach for her, though it killed him to remain aloof and uninterested with her warm, enticing flesh so close.

No. Werewolf blood interested him little. Let her have this hand. Let her see she could trust he would not always need to be in control. That was how the masters gained enemy ground.

But it was difficult to restrain himself. Her breasts were right there, barely enclosed with mere wisps of black lace. A flick of his fingers would splay them across that luscious, tan flesh.

"You've been drinking blood?"

He nodded.

"Thought so. No kisses tonight, husband."

With that, she strode out in a sweep of flowing sheer fabric and bouncing pink marabou.

No sympathy for this devil tonight. Creed eased a hand over his erection. Each time, her teasing play made him harder. The werewolf princess was getting under his skin.

And he liked that just fine.

But no man was a rock. Nor could any sane vampire avoid the lure of the exotic. Damn, but her blood smelled delicious. A dark sweetness he would know, and soon.

BLU CLOSED THE BEDROOM door and tugged off her wig. Sliding a hand down her neck, she traced her fingers over the warmth between her breasts and down her stomach where she absolutely flamed.

"Insufferable vampire."

That man—that *vampire*—had gotten her hot. And he hadn't even touched her.

It was the way he had looked at her. Those dark irises, surrounded by impeccable white. Focused. Delving. Promising. And maybe bemused. Like, if she had touched him, he would have touched back. And that touch would have so been worth the effort of waiting in the theater room for two hours before he'd finally found her.

And when had she ever been turned on by a man's voice? Creed's was calm and measured, but had a burnished edge of darkness that vibrated at the base of her throat. Mercy, he could fuck a woman with that voice.

"This is so wrong."

And yet, she'd set out this evening on a quest to gain control. And strangely, she'd earned some. He now knew it was she who would set the pace between them.

Maybe.

She turned her cheek against the wall. It was papered in old-fashioned flocked arabesques, and whispered against her skin. Sighing, she eased a finger down inside her black lace panties. She was wet. For *him*.

"Wrong, wrong, wrong!"

But while flirting with a vampire should be disgraceful, it didn't stop her from satisfying the ache that yearned for appeasement. She stroked herself, slowly, steadily.

The image of Creed's sexy stare haunted her. Let him look. Let him hunger for her. Let him…make her hot and horny.

She didn't need a man to feel good. She could take care of business by herself.

And she did, bringing herself to a climax, clinging to the wall, yet wanting it to be a man's broad shoulders she clung to instead.

CREED PAUSED AS HE PASSED the guest bedroom door. Whimpers, moans, a huffing sigh. The sounds inside were unmistakable. She was...

"Pleasuring herself?"

Had she been turned on just now in the theater room? Had the saucy pink princess gotten as hot as he had?

"Oh, my sweet, wicked werewolf."

He turned to grip the doorknob but stopped himself.

A smile crept onto his lips. The werewolf had gotten hot for the vampire.

Nodding, he stepped back and crossed his arms. "Nice."

OVER A MIXING BOWL of Cap'n Crunch, Blu drowned her morning blues. She had never been a morning person. And though she'd yet to tip the night into dawn since the marriage—and had been getting to bed far too early— she still didn't have to like the new day.

A few taps checked her cell phone. No messages. *Come on, Bree, I need contact with the real world.* And Ryan was being strangely silent. Had he already found himself a new girl? No, he was probably busy with the Western pack.

Blu spooned in a load of sugary sweetness. Milk

trickled down her chin and she swiped it off with the back of her hand.

This time she sensed his arrival before the kitchen door swung inside.

"Morning, darling," she offered coquettishly.

Blu admonished her inner flirt. She'd come so close to kissing him last night. If he hadn't smelled like blood, she would have.

Good save. Way to stay in control.

Mostly. The dude didn't have to know what had gone on behind closed doors.

Dressed impeccably, as usual, Creed wore another Armani suit, unbuttoned to reveal a slice of shirt that matched the whites of his eyes. The shirt, too, was unbuttoned, exposing a patch of pale flesh. Diamond cuff links advertised his wealth.

Blu had no idea how rich the man was, but much richer than her family was, she felt sure. The pack compound might be larger, but this mansion had all the luxury goods. Marble floors, gold faucets, high-thread-count sheets and plasma TVs.

A girl should take advantage of her new bank account. She was his wife, after all. And didn't wives have access to all of their husband's cash?

"Sleep well last night?" he asked.

"Blissful," she answered, then caught his knowing smirk.

What was that about?

Morning paper in hand, Creed eyed the massive bowl of cereal. "Why don't you pour the milk in the box and eat it that way?"

"Oh, ha-ha. The vampire made a funny."

He sat before the table, across from her, and smoothed the paper neatly before him. "You eat a lot."

"Worried I'm going to get fat on you?"

"I suspect you run it off. How far do you run every day?"

"I'm guessing I'm getting about ten miles doing your estate five times in a circle."

"I could get you a treadmill."

"Oh, right. Why don't you get me a leash, too?" She chomped a huge bite, milk trailing down her chin again. "And while you're at it, a special room with all my chew toys and a doggie bed."

"I didn't mean to offend, Blu. Though you seem to take offense at the drop of a hat," he muttered.

Blu sneered mockingly.

He looked up from the paper and zoomed in on her chin. He made a brushing gesture over his own chin.

Blu tried to lick away the dribble of milk but in the process sprayed out a pink kernel of cereal. It rolled across the paper and landed near Creed's finger.

The vampire stared at the cereal and the wet trail drawn across his immaculate paper. Blu could sense his anger;

it smelled acrid. Bet the man had never had his life upset. Bet he called all the shots. Tribe leaders were like that, all in control and in charge. Or so she imagined.

On the other hand, the leaders she was accustomed to liked upset, chaos and mayhem. Hmm…well, if he was of that nature, the guy hid it well.

He flicked the cereal piece and it pinged the bowl and soared onto the floor.

"No points for you," Blu said. "Want to go for a goal?" She displayed a pink puff between her fingers.

That got a smile from him. Pleased with her attempt to crack his hard armor, Blu popped the cereal into her mouth.

"So what do you do for fun, Creed? If we're going to do this marriage thing right we have to *do* things. Like go out dancing or clubbing."

"I abhor the raucous scene and find the stuff that qualifies for music nowadays considerably lacking."

"Figured as much. I suppose a game of chess at the local fencing club is more your speed?"

"How about sailing?"

"Seriously?"

"No. I'm not keen on open water."

"Nor am I. But you had me for a second there. One point for the vampire. So what *have* you done, in all your centuries, to have fun?"

He folded the paper and set it aside. The white shirt

enhanced his European bone structure. He was not overtly handsome, but every time Blu looked at him she saw something new to wonder over.

Today it was his chin, darkened with fine stubble. The slightest cleft drew her eye. The indentation was as wide as her smallest finger, a place a girl could dip her tongue for a taste.

If the girl wanted a taste. Which she didn't. Not at all.

"Fun?" He crossed his arms and leaned back in the chair. Then, he leaned forward, moving himself into her space. Was that enthusiasm in his expression? "In the fourteenth century I used to steal armor from the opposing troops then set their barracks on fire."

"And that was fun?"

"It was. At the end of the sixteenth century was the St. Bartholomew's Day massacre. Killed a good number of Huguenots in that." He settled back and eyed her narrowly. "You feel a bit like a Huguenot after that charade of a wedding ceremony?"

"I'm not following."

"The Catholics and the Huguenots—or Protestants, if you prefer—came together for the marriage of Henri of Navarre to Marie de Médicis. Two opposing forces wed in hopes of uniting the religions. Much like we were wed."

"Right. But you said it resulted in massacre?"

"Yes." Creed tapped the paper absently. "Catherine de

Médicis, along with her son King Charles IX, ordered the Huguenots slaughtered."

"You think that's what will come of our marriage? A slaughter between the nations?"

"I hope not, Blu." He looked aside, then dismissing the dread topic, offered gaily, "I've had plenty of fun. In the eighteenth century there were the opera and salons. Salacious gossip was bantered about. Lives and destinies were created, changed and destroyed with a mere word or an exquisitely biting twist of phrase."

"I've always had a passion for the eighteenth century. Paris. I like the big poufy dresses and the sexy frock coats the men used to wear. Man, do I love a fop!"

"Really?" His eyes softened and he spread his fingers on the table, not far from the milk trail. "That was a comfort time for me. I used to wear damask and velvet frock coats. Alençon lace and diamonds at my wrists and jabot. Nothing but the finest to attract the ladies."

"I bet you attracted them far and wide."

"I shouldn't say so, but...well, yes. This fop had his choice of women."

"You're not so foppish now."

"I've worn many costumes over the centuries. I find my current situation the most comfortable, though I often long for the medieval times when battles were fierce and bloody and wenches were, well...submissive."

"You men and your attraction to a submissive woman. Ugh. So much testosterone." She stabbed her spoon into the cereal. "Were you ever in love, Creed?"

"Never."

"Come on. Not even a little bit? You've had, what, nine centuries to fall in love?"

"As you have said, love isn't real. It's only for losers of the game. I prefer lust and instant gratification."

She could so get behind the instant—and self—gratification.

"Sex, too?" she prompted.

"Lots of it. With the most beautiful women."

"Did you bite them all?"

"Not always."

"Huh. So vampires can have sex without biting?"

"We can control those urges, yes. Did you expect we were nothing but lust-crazed blood-hungry creatures?"

"No." She sat back, her appetite fulfilled after half a box of cereal. "Yes. Maybe. I've not spent time with vampires. I can only go by what I've been taught. Living with the pack, you can imagine the talk I overhear about longtooths."

"I hope to change your mind. And to remove that horrible slang term from your vocabulary."

Longtooth? Yeah, it was horrible. But so was a vampire calling her breed *dogs*.

"Fair enough. And maybe I can change your mind about werewolves."

"You already have, Blu."

"One point for the werewolf!" She lifted the bowl and tilted it back, swallowing the pink milk. "I love cereal."

"I noticed."

"I think I'll go for some Count Chocula next time, what do you think?" She waggled her brows at him.

"If it gives you a twisted thrill, do as you must. You've—" He brushed his chin again.

Blu slurped her tongue out to lick the sweetness. "Love me or leave me, Creed, this is how I am. Messy and colorful."

"And turned up to eleven."

"You know it."

When he nodded, as if to grudgingly accept her, she decided that was better than she'd expected of him. At least he wasn't telling her what to do. And that gave him more points than the scoreboard could handle.

"So about those diamonds you used to flash for the ladies," she said. "Betcha they cost you a pretty penny. You think you could front your wife some cash to go shopping? What's yours is mine, yeah?"

"I don't see a problem with that. I'll call my accountant and arrange for a credit card in your name."

Pleased with the snag, Blu wiggled appreciatively on

the chair. "That was easy. I promise I won't go overboard. I mean, I'm not into diamonds. The choker I wore at the wedding was rhinestone. Good enough for me. But I do like shoes."

"Do as you wish with it. Buy an entire rainbow of wigs, if you must."

She pumped her fist triumphantly. "Score."

"Back to your idea for us to do something together. What do you say to a night on the town?" he proposed. "A fine restaurant and then a walk in the park?"

"Sounds far too romantic for this old married couple."

"Sounds like the perfect means to get to know one another better. We should learn our lines for those who wish to observe our progress. Shall we say seven?"

"I suppose it's the closest I'll get you to letting your hair down and living it up. Should I dress up?"

"I did say a fine restaurant. Which may mean not quite so colorful."

"You don't like orange?" she said of her latest wig selection.

"It's not one of your better colors."

She pouted.

"I prefer the violet." His smile was so charming that Blu was inclined to believe him.

CHAPTER FIVE

HALFWAY THROUGH HER JOG around the estate, Blu paused at the fence and shoved aside the overgrown hornbeam vines. She'd not shifted to wolf form this afternoon—her usual running shape—because she needed to do something.

Her wolf could only stay cooped up for so long. She needed the wide-open fields beyond Creed's estate. As well, the wolf was drooling for a lope through the nearby forest. And something might come up that would require she leave the estate on more than two feet.

By observing the crews of wolves and vamps camped out front, she'd learned they took breaks on alternate shifts. Around four in the afternoon, both factions were trading shifts, which left the estate unwatched for about twenty minutes.

She'd always wondered what it would be like to be a

celebrity for twenty-four hours, having the press drooling over every tidbit of her life. Now she'd changed her mind. This was plain ridiculous. Who cared what she was doing? And could they actually get shots of her with those cameras?

She didn't need to avoid the snoops; she just preferred doing this out of their interest. They couldn't sight her at the back of the property. She hoped.

Pushing aside the wide glossy leaves, she grabbed the cool iron fencing. A weird vibration hummed through her fingers and at her wrist. Not like electricity, but almost like the vibrations Blu felt when Bree used sidhe magic.

Something mechanical clicked.

Blu startled, releasing the fence. Her T-shirt tugged across her stomach, as if someone pulled it from the side. The hot burn of metal grazed her skin.

Stumbling backward, she landed on her butt, legs sprawled and arms catching her from a complete backward body slam into the grass.

"What the hell?"

Lifting her shirt, she studied the torn fabric. A red burn mark slashed across her stomach. It hadn't cut skin but the abrasion stung. Something had come close to doing some serious damage.

"Damn, that stings. Feels like…" A substance she didn't want to consider.

Crawling forward, she cautiously searched the grass, being careful not to get too close to the fence again. Touching the fence had activated something. She'd thought it sidhe just moments ago, but that made little sense.

A ward? Possible. The vampire would very likely have his land warded as a means to security.

"Would have been nice if he'd told his wife about that."

Though they could do physical harm, wards were usually invisible. Yet she'd felt something solid touch her. And it had burned her flesh. Inspection of her stomach showed an abrasion, though the skin hadn't been torn.

A glint of silver on the ground attracted her. She reached for it but pulled back before touching it.

"A silver dart? Is that some kind of joke?"

No wonder, despite it not opening flesh, it burned liked a mother. She'd have to douse the abrasion with alcohol to see that no trace of silver remained on her skin.

She prodded the deadly thing with her running shoe.

"Silver. Which means this ward is specific for were-wolves. Lovely. Forget Green Acres, I'm a prisoner at Stalag Vampire. The hubby is so going to hear about this one."

THE WEREWOLF PRINCESS of the wild hair colors and revealing clothing could do subtle well. Almost too well after she'd trained him to look forward to her sexy exposed curves.

The clingy black velvet dress rose to the base of Blu's neck and plunged to her knees. Her arms and lower legs were the only part revealed. Even the back was covered. Unfortunate. Creed would enjoy a lingering study over that tattoo.

Tonight's wig was snow-white. She preferred the chin-length style that emphasized her fine bone structure and sensual red lips. Was it the thick lashes or the dark eye shadow that kept his attention straying to those gorgeous gray eyes?

All in all, understated glamour, he decided. The only thing she needed was a string of pearls to fit with the silver-screen Hollywood types. But this was Minnesota, and she would stand out, silver screen or not.

The restaurant was so exclusive he'd had to offer the maître d' a large tip to secure a table on short notice. It was worth it. Creed had not accrued billions to let it spoil in a dusty bank vault.

Blu hadn't surprised him this morning by asking for money. It bothered him little to give her a credit card. Again, why let it rot in a bank? Even if the princess could shop a blue streak, she'd never dent his finances. And if she brought home more of those sexy next-to-nothings like he'd caught her in the other night, then all the better.

They were served; Blu had actual food, and he a snifter of Armagnac. Blu questioned the waiter about the silverware. No, it was not real silver, he apologized dourly. The answer pleased her. Though Creed noticed she then pressed a palm over her gut and winced. Hmm...

The waiter pulled the gauzy white tent closed to conceal their booth from other tented booths in the airy dining room. Kissing booths, they were called. The restaurant was famous for surprise wedding proposals and, as well, notorious for dramatic breakups, all within the not-so-private-as-one-would-wish gauzy tents.

A swallow of brandy warmed Creed from the inside out. In keeping with the theme of the restaurant, he intended to earn a kiss by the end of the meal. This marriage, sham that it was, had best start making progress sooner rather than later. He had no intention of failing the Council's expectations—until it was necessary he did so.

Kisses were not required, only a mutual companionship—and a bite—but he felt a kiss now and then certainly couldn't hinder their effort to compromise.

"You're sure you don't mind watching me eat?" she said, a forkful of lemon chicken lingering near her bloodred lips.

"Not at all. I don't think I've ever met a woman who so heartily attacks her food. It's exciting."

"Don't tell me my gluttony turns you on."

"Maybe a little."

"Okay, you're just weird, vampire. But I can dig it. Watch this." She forked in a piece of chicken dotted with capers and closed her eyes to savor.

"I remember capers," Creed said. "A Greek delicacy. Very tart. Do you know they are actually unopened flower buds?"

"I do. Imagine that. Eating pickled flowers. So decadent."

"You like decadence."

"I do, but I don't get nearly enough of it. The pack compound was more redneck beer and bruisers than nightclub fun, you know?"

Another forkful of dinner passed her lips. A drop of lemon sauce dribbled down her chin, which she skillfully mastered with a dab of napkin.

"I bet," she said, "despite your need to appear refined, you have some very decadent moments."

"I've been known to debauch and indulge with the best of them. That eighteenth century was a good one."

"But no longer? Now you've retired from the raucous and prefer to wither away in your big old estate?"

"Your presumptions of my social life are all wrong, Blu. If it is decadence you crave, I can give you that."

"Really? But that would require…"

He waited for her to summon the truth of them. Five

days married and they were still no closer than they had been that first night. Perhaps more comfortable around each other, but the divide between them gaped.

"That we get along?" he provided.

"We do get along." A sweep of crusty French bread through the lemon sauce occupied her. "Much better than I expected we would." She stroked her stomach again, making a sour face, but dismissed it quickly. "I still barely know you. To do so I need some basic details."

"Such as?"

"Hmm, okay, basics. Let's start with some fun get-to-know-you questions. What's your favorite car?"

"BMW, all the way. Though I've a Bugatti in Paris."

"Hmm, you like to go fast, spend the big bucks and be recognized for your taste."

"All that just from my choice of vehicle?"

"Yep. I like Hummers. They're so masculine."

For a woman who claimed exhaustion from the alphas in her life, she surprised him. Perhaps the redneck lifestyle, as she'd put it, was ingrained in her.

"Who's your favorite singer?" she asked, followed by a loud crunch of bread.

"A tie between the castrato Farinelli and Frank Sinatra."

"A castrato? Dude, you are so strange. I'm not even going to analyze that one." Munching constantly, she queried further, "Favorite color?"

"Black."

"Black is not a color. You're treading emo territory, Creed, except without the angst. Though I'm sure you can brood with the best."

"What is emo?"

"It's too difficult to explain to the older generation. So—"

"What is your favorite color?" he asked. "I've seen so many on you."

"It changes daily. The whole rainbow is my favorite. Next question." She eyed him discerningly. "How'd a French guy end up with a name like Creed?"

"You don't think it sounds French? Perhaps not. My full name is Edouard Credence Saint-Pierre."

"Now that's a mouthful."

"Indeed. My mother was English, so I assume that's where the middle name came from, though I never asked her about it. It's a mystery to me. She always called me Creed when my father wasn't around. And as a man who has lived so long, it is necessary to change my name every century or so. I rotate between some form of Edward or Creed." Elbows to the table, he clasped his hands before him, forefingers to his mouth. "My mother would have appreciated my use of her nickname for me. I miss her, even after all these years."

"That's sweet."

"Or it could be pitiful. One of the disadvantages of immortality is that one tends to outlive their family. Soon they are left with no blood relations. Friends wither and die. It's one of the things I envy about the wolves, actually. Their packs are true family."

"You've the tribe."

"Yes, and they are close to family, but it's not the same. Though I do claim Alexandre Renard as a sort of pseudobrother."

"Did you create him?"

"No. I've never made another vampire."

"In all your centuries? Wow. That must have required restraint."

"Not really. I've never believed I've the right to change a person's life through such a drastic means. I've enough to atone for as it is."

"That's why you're so kind about not insisting I take your bite."

He shrugged. "It's not kindness. I would bite you the moment you showed sign of lowering your aversion to it just to taste the sweet darkness that runs through your veins."

She tucked her wrists close to her chest, hiding the undersides of her arms from him, and the veins. "That sounds gross."

"Trust me, Blu, it is heaven. Orgasmic."

"Really? So you come every time you bite someone?"

"Not unless it's a sexual situation. Which it isn't always."

A bite of bread dispersed flaky crust across the front of her velvet dress. Without thinking, Creed swept his fingers over the fabric. She clasped his fingers tightly. "That wasn't an invitation to touch."

He relented and she brushed away the crumbs. Sitting back, she patted her mouth with the cloth napkin, then tapped the silverware. She wasn't sure what to do with her hands now.

So she was unsettled at his little touch. Score one for the stodgy old vampire.

The waiter swung by and Blu ordered dessert. He left them, closing them in the gauzy tent.

"When *will* I get the invitation, Blu?"

"You're waiting for *me* to make the move?"

"Perhaps. Normally I would take what I want, but we are so opposite, and you haven't given me any signals yet, so I don't want to offend. On the other hand, the black lace last night could be construed as a signal."

"It wasn't." She looked aside. A lie. But he knew that already.

Blu played a game, writing the rules as she went along, and forgetting those rules as quickly. He'd never faced an opponent quite like her before. The challenge appealed on so many levels, most especially the sexual.

Creed slid his hand across the tablecloth, parallel to hers. Her dinner forgotten, she seemed to wait for something. Was she wondering if she could make a dash out of here? Or deciding what her next move would be?

"Okay, we've done cars, colors and names," she said. "What's your favorite means of dispatching werewolves?"

"What?"

"Silver darts?" she snapped.

What could she possibly be getting at? Her attitude had quickly turned cold— Oh, hell. Creed's heart sank. He slapped his hands on the table. "Blu, you didn't? The fence?"

"I almost took a dart to my gut this afternoon. Well, in fact, I did. The burn mark just faded before we left tonight. Lucky for you I found aloe in the first-aid kit. Nice way to start the peace brigade, vampire. Slay your wife before the week is up?"

"Is that why you've been clutching your stomach?"

"It still aches a little. Silver burns me, Creed. Had it cut my skin and entered my bloodstream I'd be pushing daisies."

"If I had known you were going to poke about the fence like that I would have warned you. I thought you were running the grounds. My security is there for a purpose. The wards have been in place long before the peace talks began. What were you doing?"

She toyed with the end of the fork. "I need wide-open space. I thought to dig a hole under the fence. There's a huge forest behind your estate. And I wouldn't go anywhere near the spies camped out front."

"Dig a hole?" The image of her getting those long slender fingers dirty—ah, perhaps it would be *paws.*

There were so many things he still did not know about his wife. Did he want to know about them all?

"Blu, why didn't you ask? There's a gate at the east end. It's hidden behind vines and trees, but it's there. If you promise to stay away from the spies, I'll give you the remote tomorrow."

"A remote? Cool."

He stroked her arm lightly, still overwhelmed at her confession. "You could have been seriously hurt."

"Or dead. Silver kills wolves dead, buddy."

"I know. Damn it, I would have never forgiven myself."

"Seriously?"

He nodded.

Now she patted his arm tenderly but didn't linger. "It's cool. I should have told you or asked. Any other booby traps on the grounds I need to beware of?"

"No. The fence is warded against werewolves, faeries and vampires. If anything else gets beyond it, then it probably isn't dangerous to me."

"How can you ward against faeries? It almost felt like faery magic to me."

"It's difficult, but I used my—er, I employed a witch when I moved in. Don't look so surprised. I'm sure your pack's compound has equal safety measures."

"I never asked. But I suppose." She shoved her plate aside for the waiter to retrieve. "So, what questions next? Favorite movies? Favorite songs?"

"I want to kiss you, Blu."

Reaching for the wine bottle, she poured a full goblet of Cabernet, and tossed back half of it. The woman could certainly consume the alcohol. A means to hiding from the truth perhaps?

"Rather, I want you to want to kiss me," he challenged.

Sipping the wine, she looked aside and down.

"Will you ever desire me?"

She smirked. "You think I don't?"

"I think you deny the feeling the moment it comes up. If it does come up at all."

"It does," she answered quietly. "You actually desire a wolf?"

He shrugged. "Wonders never cease, eh?"

"Yeah." Lashes dusting her cheek, she still couldn't look directly at him. "You going to finish your brandy?"

"Go ahead."

Their proximity was about two feet. They sat in a

curved booth, so he could easily slide next to her. But Creed wasn't sure how to bridge the distance and to take what he wanted. She was so different from any woman he'd known. Not delicate, and yet so fragile he could cut her with but a word. Not demure, and yet right now he'd silenced her with a confession of his desire. And not at all his type.

What *was* his type?

Beyond A, B and O negative?

He had always favored a confident woman, one who could stride through a room turning all heads and smiling triumphantly as she did so. Blu was that sure woman. To a degree. She liked to turn heads, but she wasn't quite sure what to do with the attention once she got it.

He also liked learned women, those he could have meaningful conversations with over a bottle of wine. Blu insisted on calling him dude, and playing the tunes loud enough to wake the neighbors. She was unpolished, ill-mannered and utterly unconcerned about it.

Yet he couldn't stop watching her. Every sensual movement. Every purse of her lips as she sipped the Armagnac. The glide of white hair dusting her long slender neck.

And there, the pulse of her life beat beneath the silken sun-bronzed skin. Dark treasure coursed just below the flesh. Pulsing not too fast, but more rapidly now than it had been before he'd suggested they kiss. The scent of her overwhelmed the Armagnac's oaky perfume. And like a fluff of pink marabou, it teased at him.

So that was it. He desired her blood. Nothing more. She was simply sustenance. Not so different than any other female.

And yet, had the silver dart cut deeper, he felt sure he would have mourned her loss.

"What's going on in the Catholic's brain?"

"Hmm?"

"You're thinking too hard, Creed. I can see your brain groan. Plotting to overthrow the Huguenots?"

If she only knew. But she must never know. Just because he called her wife did not imply he trusted her.

The waiter delivered her dessert and Blu dug into it.

"Try this," she said after a few bites, offering him her fork. Chocolate sauce glinted on the silver fork tines. A drop splattered the white linen tablecloth. "Hurry."

"I don't eat."

"It's not eating. It's barely a lick. The chocolate is out of this world. It's spicy and hot. Have you ever tasted chocolate?"

"A nibble once or twice. Chocolate was the rage in the eighteenth century."

"Your favorite century, obviously."

"Yes, you've picked up on that?" He smiled. It had certainly been a time of decadence and debauchery he would never forget. "The women would drink it so bitter."

"This is silky and sweet."

Mmm, like her blood?

"Go on, I dare you."

There were far better dares to receive from a ruby-lipped stunner such as Blu. Her eyes sparkled in anticipation and her lips parted to reveal gorgeous white teeth.

Creed never refused a dare.

Sliding closer, he parted his lips. She touched the fork to his tongue. The chocolate, sweet and smooth, dispersed across his palate. The small taste heated his tongue. It possessed a bite, a surprising piquant sharpness.

In truth, he'd only ever enjoyed the sweet treat from the mouths of his lovers.

"Neat, isn't it? It warms your whole mouth."

"Interesting. Must have some spice in it."

"Chile peppers." She drew her fingertip through the sauce on the plate and offered it to him. "Just a little more."

How could he resist those expectant gray eyes and anticipatory pout?

Creed tongued the tip of her finger, and he closed his lips over it, sucking, teasing the whorls of flesh with his tongue. Gods, but he'd love to suck at her breasts, lick down her stomach to the apex of her thighs. To feel her soft and smooth on his tongue. Finer than any chocolate, surely.

Her lids grew heavy—then she flashed her gaze wide. Tugging her finger from his mouth, she ended what could have become delicious folly. Poking it into her mouth, she cleaned the fiery sauce—but of course, there was no sauce on her finger. Interesting.

"Mmm." Those brilliant eyes dazzled. "Do you wonder what it would be like to kiss me now with our tongues on fire?"

"Blu."

"Go on, Creed. You were the one to bring it up. So do it. Kiss me."

So she would turn the challenge back on him? "You're teasing me."

"If I were, I'd be sitting farther away."

She had somehow slid closer. With little space between them, the tips of her hair skittered across Creed's shoulder. Her knee nudged his. Perhaps the heat he felt was also from the hug of her shoulder against his.

Creed leaned in, eyeing her sparkling grays carefully. The tease in that twinkle could prove dangerous for both of them.

He touched his mouth to hers. She did not flinch. She took his kiss. And so he pressed firmly, indulging the sweet fire lingering on the center of her lips.

First kisses were always awkward. This one flamed

with welcoming adventure. It wasn't really their first. Yet it was the first they'd both agreed to.

She was the one to dash her tongue across his, blending her fiery chocolate heat with his own. He had never tasted a finer kiss. A kiss so wickedly hot, and capable of melding two mouths that would normally never touch.

"I like that," she said against his mouth. Her lashes fluttered. "The chocolate, I mean."

"Right, the chocolate." He kissed her again, more chaste, a finale to something that could become much more were the gauzy tent not so sheer.

"Thank you," he said. "For teaching me to experience new tastes."

"No problem, dude. Er, I mean Creed."

"I like the way your mouth moves when you say my name. Makes me wish you had more chocolate sauce to share."

They glanced to the plate. Not a drop remained.

"You're richer than God, aren't you?"

Now where had that question come from? "I like to think God has no need for money. But I do have a substantial amount."

"Then you should be able to hire the chef to come make this dessert for us some time."

"An excellent suggestion. You ready for a walk in the park?"

CHAPTER SIX

CRICKETS CHIRPED IN the tall grasses behind the line of poplars demarcating the edges of the park. A cicada intermittently joined the chorus with its long rattling buzz. Tall hedgerows muted the rush of a nearby freeway. The scent of gasoline took a backseat to the lush perfume of myriad flowers.

The taste of chiles and chocolate tingled on Blu's tongue as they strolled the well-lit sidewalk in the small horticultural park.

The taste of Creed also persisted.

It was a good taste. A powerful one. Manly, yet not too controlling. It hadn't been brisk and rough, as she was accustomed to. He hadn't kissed her until she had first invited him to. That went a long way toward his chivalry quotient.

It was easy to think of him as some ancient knight who

made vows and fought for rights and wrongs now that she was getting to know him better. The muscles straining at his sleeves and across his chest could swing a sword to chop off heads. But the guy would probably bless the fallen afterward, that was how honorable she suspected he was.

Not that a blessing from a vampire would be all too welcome. Gothic good fun, as far as she was concerned. She could so get into the fantasy.

Blu tugged her arm from Creed's and swung both of them. *Okay, enough of that,* she remanded her inner thoughts.

All this closeness stuff was getting to be too much. A few kisses had seemed appropriate. They *were* married. But she wasn't about to fall for seduction and all that chivalry stuff. Fantasies were just that, not meant to become reality.

Most men took what they wanted. What made her believe this man would be any different?

The peonies lining the walk perfumed the air. Huge bushes hung heavily with thick fuchsia blooms as big as cats' heads. One of Blu's favorite flowers. The peony won over the rose every time with its lush bloom and frothy petals. She didn't even mind the ants nestled within the petals.

Dragging her fingertips over the bloom heads, she fell out of step with Creed. From the back he marked an imposing figure. Tall, lean, yet broad-shouldered. Broad shoulders were the best. They gave a girl something to cling to when…

Well, whenever.

She wasn't going to start fantasizing about having sex with the man. It would never happen. Vampire or not. She had her principles, and if a girl didn't stick to them, then she had nothing. Three-day sex rule be damned.

Thinking of clinging to him brought up Bree's comment. She would not cleave, unless it was to wrench herself *away* from the man.

Creed paused, wondering at her with a glance over his shoulder.

Snapping off a bloom, she waved her hefty prize at him. "I love these."

"I bet the park patrol will have something to say about that."

"You know, Creed," she said as she plucked the petals one by one and dropped them to the sidewalk, "for a vampire you're much too inhibited. I mean, you are a tribe leader. You're like a big kahuna. Don't you ever do the daring?"

"The daring? Of course I do. But I am not the official tribe leader at the moment. Alexandre Renard, my best man you met at the wedding, is acting in my place while we get this marriage thing going."

This marriage thing. Yeah, that was how she felt about it, too. Just another…thing.

"Perhaps I've done enough of it already," he added. "I am, as you so callously put it, an old man."

"You're only as old as you think you are."

"That would be nine hundred seventy years." He sighed.

"And still looking like a thirty-year-old." She hooked an arm in his and relished the warmth spreading over her bare arm. Funny, she'd expected vampires to be cold. "Are you dead?"

"You ask the most out-of-the-blue questions."

"That's because they are out of the Blu." She chuckled. "Oh, sometimes I *kill* myself." A toss of half the petals landed a fuchsia explosion on the sidewalk behind them. "But what are you? Dead or alive?"

"Do I look dead?"

"No, but I've always heard. Not from anyone in the pack, but I've read books."

"Ah, the remarkable accuracy of the fiction novel. I'm surprised how those from our nations still form opinions from the mortal fictions and entertainment shows. I never died to become vampire. I simply transformed after being bitten. I'm immortal now."

"Only a stake will do, eh?"

"And perhaps that precious little ring of blood on your finger."

"Yes." She stroked the ring. It was heavy and didn't go with any of her outfits, but she would never remove it. The blood glinted under the park lights as she tilted her hand. It gave her peace of mind. "Will it really work? The Protection was dropped years ago."

"That is blood taken from a witch before the spell was dropped. It will eat through a vampire's flesh and bone within seconds, and reduce them to ash in minutes—unless they've an immunity."

"What a gross thing to witness. So it'll kill you dead?"

"Well…"

"Well what?" Her heart suddenly pounded. That *well* had not been a good well. "You're immune? Wait, you have magic because you're an elder. What's the deal with that? You had to have gotten it from a witch, right?"

"You know about the elders?"

"I'm not stupid, Creed. Bree told me. She said there are ancient vampires who used to steal magic from witches before the Protection spell was even created."

"Your faery is very knowledgeable. I do have magic."

"So does this ring mean anything at all? It won't kill you, will it?"

"I'm not sure what it will do to me, Blu. It may drain what little magic I have remaining. It may enhance it. For all I know it could be tainted with a poison that would take me out, no matter my immunity created centuries ago. Nothing good, that's for certain."

"But it's not a sure death like the silver in your ring promises me." She squeezed a fist. "I knew you longtooth bastards weren't on the up-and-up."

"Blu. The Council requested an elder step forward to take the vows, and I did so. I am considered an equal sacrifice to the wolves handing over one of their females. But I cannot know if that blood will have a deadly effect on me. And I prefer not attempting to find out."

She sighed heavily and plucked out a few more petals. "Is there some way to test it on another vampire? I mean, suddenly I feel at a disadvantage."

"You should not. Besides, I took a voluntary vow not to use my magic centuries ago. It was a means to atone for the harm I've done to the witches."

"Honorable. But let me guess, those witches you did harm are dead, so no one is really going to feel the effects of your atonement."

"Blu— Ah, I shouldn't have said anything and you would have been assured the device granted some kind of safety. But do either of us really want to use the thing against the other?"

"No. Well…maybe. I'm not into violence. But if you are—"

"Never would I use violence against women. If I can prevent it," he said with a noticeable wince.

What was that about? she wondered. Blu moved a palm up her arm, feeling a shiver. If he had stolen magic from witches…and he'd said he'd harmed them.

"Your ring is a symbol, as is mine," Creed offered. "I would never think to use this against you."

"Promise?"

"I do, I promise."

Blu sighed and tapped the decimated flower head against her chin. "Fine. For now. So show me some of that magic."

"I just told you I've sworn not to use it."

"I won't tell any witches." She eyed him sweetly, thinking to soften him with kindness. "You must slip up and use it once in a while."

He sighed. "There have been occasions. And I'd appreciate it if you'd also keep that information from any werewolves. With that secret in hand a werewolf could go to a witch, and I would be in big trouble."

"How big?"

"I would be bound by a spell, shackled from using my magic. It's not a pleasant experience. And I shouldn't wish to sacrifice my freedoms because I've used it for insignificant means over the years."

He eyed her fiercely. Blu knew what he was doing, trying

to intimidate her. So he'd given her a secret? Stupid vampire.

"Show me your magic, and you can consider the secret kept," she challenged.

"I'd rather not in such a public place. There are couples all about tonight. And as I've said, my magic wanes."

"Creed, the reserved one."

"Are you any less reserved? You can dress up and put on a show behind the walls of my home. Yet you are no more than a sheltered princess who's not been out in the big bad world all that much."

"You think? I know things, vampire." Who was he to decide what she was like? "I used to go to the clubs with my lover. He's a fighter. Loves to start a ruckus."

"A ruckus starter. Such a fine quality to possess. I bet he's into stirring up brouhahas, as well."

The vampire put himself so much higher than a wolf? Superior asshole. Who was possibly immune to her little ring. *Damn.* This was something her father needed to know about. As well, should she tell him the secret Creed had just trusted her to keep?

She'd consider her options later. "You should see my lover. He's amazing when he's wolfed out."

"You love him."

"I told you I didn't."

"You did, but sometimes we speak differently than we

think. I can hear reverence for him in your tone. I only wish to earn such admiration from you."

Blu toed the flower petals, then twisted the ball of her shoe into them, releasing a pungent fragrance between them.

"You don't want me to feel the way I do about Ryan toward you. It's just sex, Creed."

"I'd take just sex from you any day."

"Seriously? You really have taken a one-eighty. I assumed your sacrifice was taking a wolf into your home. I can't imagine you allowing one into your bed."

She strode ahead a few paces. Glancing over her shoulder at him, she tapped the decimated peony in the air. "Sex and decadence? You did say you were going to give me decadence tonight."

"Good food and fine brandy. Chocolate that makes your kisses fiery. Those are decadent. And sex?" He gained her side and murmured at her ear. "I'm all for that, Blu."

She pressed the decimated flower head to his chest, holding him off from getting too close.

He plucked the stem from her. "But you continue to tease. If we're going to fool the Council we've to make a go at it sooner rather than later."

"A go at it? Is that how you term sex? How utterly unromantic."

Not that she expected romance from a vampire. Or

from any man. Blu had never been romanced. She wouldn't know romance if it bit her on the neck.

Please, no bites.

"The Council merely wants to see I've been bitten," she said. "They couldn't care less about the sex."

"My bite is accompanied with a certain degree of intimacy. The Council will ask us both if we've been intimate."

"They will? That's so…personal."

"Intimacy bonds the couple."

"So does superglue."

He crushed the flower head in a fist. "We're under the looking glass, Blu."

"Yes, the crews camped outside your home. And you want to perform for them? Bend me over the bed and let them watch so they'll be appeased?"

"That's crude, even for you."

"But it's the truth."

To her left in the parking lot, a streetlight beamed across the BMW's hood. Dusting her nose with the single flower petal she held, she drew in the aroma. Something sweet to disguise the sour odor of this conversation.

She didn't want anyone to tell her what to do. Not now that she'd gained freedom from the compound.

"We can make any truth we wish." Creed clasped a wide, strong hand about her fingers, crushing the petal so it bled pink in the whorls of their flesh. "You have to be strong enough to make the leap."

"Listen to you, all self-sacrificing and motivational-speaker guy."

"Blu, I like you."

"Yeah? That's probably a good thing to say to your wife."

"Yes, but can you return the same compliment to me?"

She glanced aside, wishing she'd fled to the car when she'd had the thought. This conversation tugged at things inside her she didn't want to unravel. It was easy playing the game. Making nice on the outside. Sharing a flirtatious kiss here and there.

But in reality, things had changed. Drastically. And she wasn't sure how to deal with it all. Especially when the vampire she'd been determined to hate was looking at her with such hope.

Who could hate a man who liked to watch her stuff her face with cereal? A man who hadn't attacked her when he'd seen the black lace and marabou number? A man who endured her nasty comments about his species?

He wasn't like any man she'd ever known.

And that put her off her game.

High in the sky the waxing moon warned in less than a week it would be full. Then her husband would know exactly what he'd gotten into by vowing to love and honor her. Could he be the chivalrous knight then?

Would it be better to surrender to his expectations before then? Soften him with agreeableness and hope for the best when she revealed her true colors?

She did have his secret to use as a bargaining chip. And she'd keep that chip handy.

He opened his hand and the crushed fuchsia petals sifted down the front of her dress. Catching one, he traced it over her mouth. The silken glide tickled her lips. Closing her eyes, she surrendered to the sensation. And when she opened her eyes, it was not the petal, but Creed's mouth that brushed her lips.

Blu spread her hands over his chest, thinking to push him away but unable to do anything but pull him closer. Unable and unwilling. How was that for split personalities? Blu Masterson was always willing, and ever able—for the wrong guy.

Clinging to his shirt, she held him in her world, on her mouth, invading her breath, her life. Her better senses.

The faintest trace of Armagnac sweetened his tongue. She wanted to taste the truth of him, to gauge the darkness and decide if she were willing to step a little closer to the edge—into Creed's shadow.

She'd stepped so far away from reality in the past few days, Blu felt she was entirely surrounded by shadows. Some were merely remnants of her expectations; others stoked with mystery lured her.

A man shouldn't be such a good kisser. A girl might start liking him, even start desiring more of his kisses. She might also find herself wanting to spend all her time with him.

Kissing him more, longer, deeper.

Touching him across his tight abs, up and down his strong back, discovering all the hard places on his body.

Knowing he could have her if he wanted her.

"A kiss in the moonlight," she whispered. "Maybe you are romantic after all."

He stroked a thumb along her cheek and glided it across her lower lip. Had any man ever looked at her so intensely? Yes, but never with such obvious care in his eyes. It was disturbing—but in a good way. Creed's shadows grew less menacing.

Blu dashed out her tongue, licking his thumb imbued with the peony oil.

Creed sucked in a restrained moan. The sound of his want rippled over her skin, tickling at her throat, and lower, pricking delightfully at her breasts.

Her husband slid a hand over the black velvet, glancing a finger over her hard nipple. Like a shot of chile-laced chocolate, the touch ignited her desires.

"What if they're watching?" she whispered.

"Who?"

"The crews that have been lurking about the estate."

"I'm sure they are."

Oh, really? Suddenly she got it. Sometimes she could be so naive!

"So this is just a show? Take the wife out and put her on display. Give her a few kisses to make it look good?"

"It's not like that," he said against her ear. "I don't want to share these new feelings I have for you with anyone. Let me take you home and kiss you until the moon leaves the sky."

Blu scanned her periphery, but didn't see any watchers in the trees. She sniffed and scented wolves, perhaps five hundred yards off. They were watching. And Creed had known. She should hate him for that, but…she should have suspected as much, too.

Kiss until the moon was gone? Was that what he'd said?

"Just kisses?" she sought to confirm.

"Until you ask for more. You wanted decadence?"

Yes, and what could be more decadent than making out with the enemy?

If Ryan found out he'd howl for hours and rip up anything that wasn't nailed down.

But he wouldn't find out; Blu would be sure of that.

They clasped hands and slipped through the darkness to the car. Blu became aware of the werewolves at the park perimeter. Three of them. Watching. She couldn't smell vampires until they stood right before her, but she sensed other eyes watched.

If she and Creed's flirtations kept the weres and vamps from going at one another, she guessed that was fine. But it was merely a bandage.

Blu knew this marriage would never produce the results the Council desired. Because the werewolves had ulterior motives. And she was merely the decoy.

HE COULD SEE CLEARLY IN the foyer without the lights on. And he knew from experience during a few medieval sieges that werewolves had excellent night vision.

Creed didn't pause to turn on the lights as he and Blu crossed the threshold. Instead, he landed on the bottom step, which was a huge worn fieldstone. Blu stood on the top step, putting herself face-to-face with him. He wrapped an arm around her back and swept her into a kiss.

She didn't protest. And for some reason he'd lost all hesitation regarding kissing a breed not his own. She was perfectly female, wondrously luscious. From her lips answering every kiss he gave, to her breasts hugging high upon his chest, to the long legs tangling between his.

Easing a hand down her hip, he squeezed her ass. The damned dress was too tight and too long to shimmy it up. He wanted her bare as she'd been out by the pool.

"Why such a reserved fashion statement tonight?" he murmured against her lips, which continued to seek his for kisses. He splayed a hand over the black velvet that went all the way to her neck.

"You said fancy. I didn't want to shock."

"Blu, the princess werewolf, did not want to shock? You do not cease to astonish me."

"You like me better shocking?"

"Hell, yes. I don't think I could imagine you without wild hair and some sexy skin showing." He glided a palm down her bare arm. "So soft. I like it when you bare this skin."

Turning her in his embrace, he put his chest to her back and kissed her shoulder at the edge of the fabric. Cupping a hand under her breast, he massaged the nipple. She glided a foot along his ankle, the hard spike heel doing strangely erotic things to his cravings.

All he could think about was hard things piercing soft tender things.

Licking a trail, he lifted her arm to glide his tongue to her elbow. There the skin was softer and sensitive, for she gasped as he painted lazy circles on the flesh. The vein pulsed under his lips. He'd taken blood days ago so did not need to feed, yet she smelled so tempting.

...*piercing soft tender things.*

There were times he could not control what his body desired to do, such as getting an erection—or dropping down his fangs. He'd freak her if he flashed his fangs at her, so he was careful, but arousal had a way of controlling him.

"I'd like some wine," she said. "Some of that fancy stuff in your fridge."

"More wine?" He was about to argue she'd had a whole bottle and Armagnac at the restaurant, when a jingle at her hip stopped him.

She dug a cell phone from her purse, and signaled to him with a finger she was going to talk. "Bree, what's up?"

Those provocative spike heels carried her through the living room and out the patio door. "You heard from him?" Closing the door behind her, she gave Creed no regard.

Standing there on the bottom step, his heart racing with arousal, Creed crashed. The denial from her brisk exit plummeted his heart a few notches. He slapped a palm over his chest.

Plunged back to reality.

You heard from him.

That could only be the lover they were talking about. Ryan. A man who had marked Blu with a tattoo.

And yet, she would refuse to take her own husband's bite.

His neck muscles tightened, as did his fists. The gratifying image of clenching his hands about some bastard werewolf's neck lured his heartbeat back to a normal pace. He'd like to twist the dog's head from his shoulders and kick it across the floor.

Creed exhaled. "Ryan," he muttered acidly.

What the hell? Here he was, getting jealous over his wife's lover.

When had he stepped over the edge of "playing the game" and into possessiveness? He shouldn't care less if Blu had a lover.

Had a lover. She certainly couldn't be seeing him now. Could she?

No, she'd not been off the grounds without his knowledge. Not for lack of trying. She'd intended to *dig* under the fence? He'd better adjust the wards. He didn't want to risk harming her. More magic. It was truly the one vow he couldn't keep, despite his efforts to do so.

Even if Blu did get off the property to go rendezvous with her lover he'd smell the male wolf on her when she returned.

He must see to this Ryan fellow. Gather information on him in the event it was necessary. He'd delegate the task to Alexandre.

And he'd see to giving Blu the fence remote. His concerns for her safety aside, he couldn't afford a dead werewolf on his hands when the relations between the two nations were so tenuous.

Heading to the kitchen to retrieve a bottle of Burgundy, Creed busied himself with the corkscrew.

Had the lover seen Blu in all her vibrant incarnations? Did he marvel over her colorful hair? Gaze adoringly upon lips softly thick and kissable? Had he seen her in those sexy black lace underthings?

Likely the dog had seen much more than that.

The idea of another man looking at *his* wife, touching her, having sex with her— The cork split out and wine spilled over Creed's cuff.

"*Sacrebleu.*"

He tugged a towel from the oven handle and dabbed at the wine, but the rich maroon liquid already stained the white silk. Then he noticed the spatters down his front.

"I've become some kind of bumbling idiot if I cannot open a bottle of wine."

Tugging out the diamond cuff links and unbuttoning the shirt, he removed it and tossed it into a heap on the table. Housekeeper would see to it, but it was a loss anyway.

A glance at the spilled wine and the bottle resulted in a sneer. No more treats for the princess. "She's ruined the evening anyway."

Leaving his shirt and the mess, Creed wandered from the kitchen.

Blu met him at the door, a blaze of white tresses glowing in the midnight darkness. Two spots of desire glinted in eyes that had fallen from the sky.

"Gotta say, this is a sexy look for you." She pressed her palm to Creed's bare chest. "But you're moving too fast for me, buddy."

He sucked in a breath at the searing contact, but was in no mood to play anymore tonight.

Gripping her wrist, he stopped her from leaning in to kiss him. "What did your friend have to say? Something about your lover?"

Even in the darkness he could plainly see her coy pout. "Can you hear through glass doors, vampire?"

"I don't eavesdrop, but you were excited about the call and I can make conclusions. Have you seen him since we've exchanged vows?"

"No." She twisted her wrist from his grip. Stiffening her shoulders, she heeled the floor with a spike. "But what if I had? Would you be angry with me?"

"Of course I would. You are my wife. You belong to me."

"Oh, I don't *belong* to anyone. What is it about men that they believe a piece of paper with signatures on it gives them right to lay claim to a person?"

"Marriage vows are a promise to honor and obey."

"Way to beat a dead horse, buddy. I didn't hear the word *obey,* and you know it."

Neither had he, and he wished damn well it had been included. "Honoring one another means being faithful and exclusive."

"Does it?" She strode toward the stairs, glancing over her shoulder. "I'll give you that. But exclusivity would hold true only if the vows were not a sham."

She waggled her ring finger at him. It happened to be the middle finger. "Sham," she repeated.

He should have never brought up the fact that he wasn't sure what the witch's blood could do to him or his magic. No matter what, he didn't want to find out. And then to tell her he'd used his magic? Fool vampire.

He hastened to match her pace up the stairs, and beat her to the top, where he wrangled her into his embrace. She struggled and beat a fist on his bare chest. It was a powerful blow and set him back against the wall.

Stunned, Creed stared at his seething princess.

"That's right, vampire. Not a woman you can push around. Strong." She flexed a bicep muscle. "And owned by no one."

"I didn't mean it that way. I don't want to own you."

Perhaps he did. Why did he care? He'd never wanted to own a woman before. Yet never before had he been bound in a relationship with one either. Was that it? He'd taken the marriage vows to heart?

"If this marriage is to work I have to trust you, Blu."

She hooked a hand at her hip, powerful and proud. "And I you."

"You can. I've no designs on other women."

"What of those you bite? Don't you seduce them? Touch them? Lure them into your arms? You think I'm not jealous of that?"

"There's no reason to be so." She was jealous? That nugget of information gratified. "The seduction required for donors is merely a means to an end."

"Then start drinking from men."

"Whatever for?"

"To prove to me I am the only woman you wish to touch."

"Preposterous." While he did drink from men on occasion—rare occasions—he preferred women because some level of seduction was involved. "You don't know what you ask."

"Chicken."

"Ignorant," he countered.

"Not so sure of your manliness, eh?"

He lifted a finger to come back with another retort, but realized this banter would get him nowhere. When engaged in combat one always discovered the opponent's weakness. And he guessed hers.

"If I agree to such an inane thing," he tried, "then you must hand over that precious pink cell phone and refuse to have any contact with the lover."

She pouted, but it was an act. The wild and colorful spoiled princess had broken free of the restraining black velvet. He liked her better this way.

Creed held out his hand. "Hand it over, and I will make the effort."

"But I've other friends. And I haven't spoken to him. Bree gives me reports."

"Blu. Please."

She tugged the cell phone from her purse and caressed it to her lips, a cherished object.

Put those lips upon mine. Speak to me as you speak to your friend. Give me that part of you, that focused regard.

"But you'll snoop."

"Me?" He shook his head. "I've no interest in your friends. I've no idea how to even turn one of those high-tech things on. You've noticed I've but landlines in my home."

"So you would deny me all my friends?"

"Just the lover. But it seems your only means to that information is your precious little phone. You ask a lot of me in return."

"You've never taken blood from a man before?"

"I have, but it's uncomfortable for me."

The coy princess looked up through thick lashes he could easily imagine dusting across his bared abs. "Sexual?"

"It can be."

"Right, you said it can be orgasmic." She thrust out the

phone, but when he grabbed it, she tugged, unwilling to relent. "I want to watch."

"What?"

"Next time you take blood—from a man—I want to watch."

Creed exhaled. She did not cease to challenge. He loved a good challenge. And the defiance in her tone prodded him to accept.

Yet he feared her watching him drink from anyone would scare her off him for good. Their intimacy was still fragile. They were only just learning each other. And then to witness him in so awkward a situation as taking blood from a man?

"If you give me that trust," she said coyly, "I will relinquish this piece of my world to you. No more chatting about the lover. I won't even think of him."

"Instead you will shudder to recall your husband taking blood?"

"Why do you think it will disturb me? It may turn me on. Two men, breathing heavily? Each wanting something from the other? Closely entwined? Creed." She approached, the cell phone tapping her chin. "If you want to take this marriage to the next level, I insist you show me a part of you you've never shown another. Do you dare?"

He snatched the phone from her. "Tomorrow evening we'll go out together."

A lick of her lips and her wide-eyed flicker of lash promised tomorrow night would be an erotic adventure they would both either regret or relish.

CHAPTER SEVEN

ALEXANDRE ARRIVED THAT afternoon and Creed greeted him with his usual cold bottle of Michelob. He kept a stash in the crisper drawer of the fridge for his friend. They headed down the hallway.

"I'll never understand how you tolerate that piss water," Creed said as they entered the office.

Alexandre downed half the bottle and smacked his lips. "Gods' mead, my man." He strolled to the sliding glass door and opened it, leaving the screen closed. "It's hot in this house. Don't you have air-conditioning?"

"Having a new system installed next week. The old one broke over the winter while I was in Paris. Bunch of icicles fell into the mechanism and damaged the blades. The waiting list for home installment is insane."

"Something even your money can't buy. Such a domestic life you lead. Must be marriage, eh?"

"It's called being responsible. You should give it a try sometime." Creed slapped him across the back.

He only teased. Alexandre was responsible with the tribe's affairs, and if any man deserved to let loose and abandon responsibility, it was Alexandre. He'd suffered at the hands of the werewolves. And in proof, he still bore a long thick scar along his left forearm from having his vein stripped out. Vampires rarely scarred, save for emotionally.

Creed's heart held a few scars from wolves. There were reasons he worked the Rescue Project beyond what had happened to Alexandre.

"You know I'm taking responsibility seriously now with Veronica in my life," Alexandre said. "I love her."

"I'm glad you were able to find someone you can love again."

Alexandre nodded, a tilt of his head. He'd lost his wife a hundred years ago in the most vicious way. He'd met Veronica a year ago while on retreat in Paris. The man deserved love. Veronica was good for him.

"As to business..." His second in command tossed a brown file folder onto the desk. "Here it is."

Inside the folder Creed found a few pages detailing phone records and GPS surveillance notations. And a color photo.

"Ugly sucker, isn't he?" Alexandre commented.

The werewolf pictured was talking to someone out of the frame, pointing a beefy arm as if giving directions. His muscles bulged grossly out of a shirt that barely covered his oversize pecs.

"Do wolves do steroids?" Creed asked. "That is just hideous."

How could Blu favor something so overtly muscle-bound? The wolf was bald, which lent further credence to possible steroid use. Hadn't she said she liked her men hairy?

"I verified he's with the Northern pack," Alexandre commented, tipping back the rest of his beer. "But here's the freaky thing. A new pack out of the west has been creeping toward the Twin Cities area. Headed by Dean Maverick. Ryan has been very close to them. Packs don't usually shake hands and play buddy-buddy."

"Much like the vampire tribes," Creed affirmed.

"Right, so why does the information track Ryan to the Western pack six times over the past month?"

"You put someone on him to continue the track?"

"Yep."

Creed read the information page. Ryan was a last name. His first?

Oh, this got better and better.

"Eugene?"

Alexandre confirmed with a smirk.

"I didn't think packs are interrelated," Creed said. "Blu mentioned Ryan is the pack's scion, next in line after her father. If Amandus Masterson knew his scion was chumming up with the Western pack he'd have the dog's head in a vise."

"From the little I know about pack politics that chummy situation would be a rarity. About as rare as the females. You sure she said she was promised to the guy? Maybe she was going behind daddy's back, having an affair?"

"Maybe." Had he heard Blu wrong? Possible. She cooed so sweetly when she talked about the lover.

The bald, beefy, 'roid-addicted lover.

Creed had stood before many a man who'd towered over him and mastered him in physicality and bulk. Yet he rarely lost a battle when properly armed both physically and mentally.

But wolves were a different foe. When in were form—shaped as a man—the vampire and wolf were an equal match. But should his opponent shift to werewolf form—half man, half beast—all bets were off. Then the vampire had to utilize cunning to enhance his lacking brawn. And pray he had a good supply of silver. The silver needed to enter the wolf's bloodstream to do damage.

Thank the gods, or Blu would be dead right now.

Creed made a mental note to alter the wards this evening to accommodate his wife.

"You ever consider she could be a spy?"

Creed's head shot up at that question.

"I'm just saying, man. We have our spies. They could have theirs. And what better way to infiltrate a tribe than by putting a spy right next to their leader."

"I...don't think she is. I always find her either out sunning herself or listening to tunes in the theater. Clothing and chatting with her friends are the princess's pastimes. She is incapable of espionage."

"Could be an act. It's something to keep at the back of your mind. Be careful, Creed."

"You know I always am. So how are things with the tribe?" Creed tossed the file onto the desk and leaned against it, crossing his arms over his chest. "I feel so ineffectual having to step down for a few weeks while I settle into this marriage."

"Chill, man, I have everything under control. I've got Revin Parker keeping an eye on the sporting warehouses. And the dissention in Russia with one of our splinter tribes has already been contained. We're replacing Novachek with that German guy, Einer."

"Fine choice for a leader. Good work, Alexandre. Will I have a job when I wish to return?"

Alexandre smirked and waggled a brow.

"That's what I thought. When the cat's away… And the rescue operation? No word of any forthcoming blood matches?"

"I've got my man Revin on it. Haven't heard a thing, but as always, we're prepared to move at the drop of a hat."

"Good. Don't hesitate to call me when you learn of a match."

"You know I won't. So where's the wifey today? Thought I'd get a glance at that wild green hair."

"She's sunning herself, as usual." Creed nodded toward the patio door, but Alexandre was already there, peeking out and around the corner. "You stare too long and I'll have to throttle you. Out of principle, of course."

"Of course." Alexandre stepped inside. "Because a vamp shouldn't care less about a werewolf, right? Her hair's blue today."

"You haven't seen the violet wig. It's positively lush."

"Lush? Creed, my man! Doesn't sound like a word a man in hate would use. You falling for the dog?"

"She's not a dog," he answered too quickly. Alexandre's brow lifted in disbelief. "At least, I haven't noticed any wolfish behavior from her. She's quite humane, and not at all hairy." He delivered Alexandre a smug grin.

"Yeah, but wait until the full moon comes."

"Did you come up with details about that?"

He'd asked Alexandre to find as much information on the female werewolf as possible without going to the Council. He didn't want them thinking he was uneducated about the wolves, though he was, regarding their females.

He hadn't avoided werewolves over the centuries, but all contact had resulted in drawing their blood. A man couldn't take the time to study them when always engaged in combat with one of them. He did know their methods of battle, however. They liked to herd away the weaklings and slaughter them first.

But that was all medieval knowledge. Though the wolves hadn't evolved much over the centuries, there were now no full-out battles or wars like in the good old days. Pity.

And after the hunts in the 1950s the vampires had expected the wolves to become extinct. But they were a hearty breed, no matter the challenges the vampires pressed upon them.

"There's little information about the female," Alexandre said. "And we lost our pack snitch right after I got the info on Ryan for you. Sorry. But I think I have a good lead on a new one. Why don't you ask the wifey for information?"

"I've tried. She likes to dance around things. Never gives a straight answer. And when she does, it's usually a lie. She's still nervous around me. I'll give her time."

"Moon's full soon. You should prepare if, well, preparation is necessary."

"Right. Do try to establish that new snitch, will you? The information the former had been giving us was invaluable. What the hell happened to him?"

"Er…" Alexandre eyed the floor.

"Again?"

If anyone had a good reason to hate the werewolves it was Alexandre. It had only been nine months since Creed had rescued him from a blood match. Made it difficult for him to work with the snitches. A single withheld bit of evidence or sarcastic comment, and Alexandre liked to rip out the wolf's heart through its chest.

Blood directly from the heart was quite delicious. But again, rather medieval.

Hell, who was he to judge? Had a week of domesticity already softened his bloodlust?

"I hope you burned the body."

"Taken care of," Alexandre replied. "Sorry, man. It's hard to forget sometimes."

"No apologies necessary. So I've been thinking we need to contact Truvin Stone's wife. Lucy is her name. She heads a paranormal debunking agency out of Venice."

"What for?"

"Because they do excellent public relations and work with the mortal news stations. I want to expect peace, but know to prepare for chaos in the coming weeks. If anything untoward should occur between the werewolves and vampires we're going to need spin in place."

"Good thinking."

"That is why I'm the leader, and you're not."

Alexandre conceded with a smiling nod.

WITH HER BACK AGAINST the mansion's outer wall and one foot propped on the stucco, Blu listened outside the screen door. The men's voices grew softer as they walked down the hall toward the front of the house.

She'd seen Alexandre gaping at her from around the corner. He was the vamp who'd stood next to Creed during the wedding ceremony. Another male who wasn't blatantly handsome but irrepressibly sexy.

And he liked beer. One point for that vampire.

Sliding the screen door open, she slipped inside Creed's office. She'd wrapped a blue gossamer sari around her waist after sunning herself, and now the fabric caught on the doorknob, jerking her backward.

"So stealth, Blu."

She unhooked herself and tiptoed into the room.

She didn't have to look long or hard to find something of interest. A plain brown folder lay on a desk that was bare except for a closed MacBook. *Thought the vamp didn't do technology?*

Briefly, she wondered if her cell phone was in his desk drawer. She wouldn't look. It had been a fair trade.

She touched the corner of the file folder with one finger, sliding it to face her.

Glancing toward the open door leading into the hallway, she listened fiercely. The front door closed.

She must be quick.

Inside the folder was a photo of Ryan. "Not a very flattering shot." He looked like a nightclub bouncer whenever he wore those shirts with the sleeves cut off. She did attempt to get him to dress more subtly than his usual redneck garb.

But who was she kidding? Ryan would never get into manscaping.

Closing the folder, she shook her head. "He's checking up on me. What did I expect?"

All was fair in… "War," she muttered, feeling the venom muster.

Strolling the room, she eyed the shelf of books on the wall near the door. History, mostly, save the volume of *Men Are from Mars, Women Are from Venus*.

"Seriously? Why, Lord Saint-Pierre, you do surprise."

Twisting her hips to shimmy the skirt—it was weighted around the hem with beadwork—she savored the sweep of fabric across her bare legs. She then noticed the massive battle sword hung on the wall opposite the desk.

"Interesting. I wonder if it's his."

The handle was wrapped with worn black leather. There were symbols etched along the blade and inlaid curlicues of— Blu hissed as a touch burned her fingertip.

"Silver," she said, and sucked on the tip of her finger.

And the weapon had definitely seen use. Against werewolves?

"Snooping?"

At the booming voice, Blu jumped and let out a chirp.

Creed stood in the doorway. Filled the doorway, actually. Those broad shoulders made her wonder if he'd wielded the sword on the wall. The stubble on his chin had darkened and grown up below his bottom lip, darkening the sexy cleft. He'd also started a mustache. It added a rugged macho touch she couldn't deny.

He entered and she stepped back, fearful of what he might do, having caught her out. His gaze swept the room and landed on the file folder—not in the same position he'd left it.

"I was tanning, and thought to explore the property. Your door was open, so—"

"So you decided to snoop."

She shrugged. "Just gathering information on the husband. Kinda like you're doing with the wife." He tracked her gaze to the folder. "Nice sword."

"It's a battle sword."

He took it from the hooks, swung an arc behind him and brought the tip under her chin. Blu chirped again.

"When I was mortal," he said, "I served the Capetian kings. Two of them. They were my feudal lords. I went into battle at their command, and in turn received land to plow."

"D-did you have a family?"

"My lord had decided I was more valuable swinging a sword than tupping a woman and chasing after younglings, so I was denied that privilege."

"You mean the feudal lords could tell people what to do back then?"

"Oh, yes. They owned the entire village, and every man, woman and child in it. So I fought, because I enjoyed it."

"And your lord gave you this sword?"

"Oh, no. We were forced to procure our own weapons and armor. The set I owned was dented and rusting, a hand-me-down from my father. During one particular battle, I strayed from the vanguard and ran across a werewolf. Never seen one of those before. It wielded a sword—this sword.

"I fought for my life, not knowing what kind of hell-forsaken creature dug its talons into my flesh. Somehow, I ended up defeating the thing."

He met her eyes. Blu cast him a wondrous gaze.

"I still look back and wonder how it happened. Dumb luck is the only answer I can come up with. I cut its head off with this sword."

She dropped her fascination. "The wolf's sword had silver in it?"

"That was something I added later." Creed reverently smoothed his fingers over the inlaid design. "There were vampires in the woods watching me that night. It was less than a fortnight later that I joined them. And not by choice."

"I see. They saw in you a wolf slayer and weren't about to lose that prize."

"Exactly."

"Tough luck, sounds like to me. But you got to keep the sword."

"I wielded it in battle through six centuries. Wolfsbane."

"Wh-what?"

"The name of my sword." He glided the tip along the bottom of her blue wig. "Wolfsbane."

"No kidding?" She pressed her fingers over the blade and shoved it away. "You kill many more wolves with that thing?"

He relented. "Hundreds."

"Yeah, I bet you savored every bloody cut, too."

"I did. The act of swinging this blade and spilling wolf

blood onto the ground is in my very DNA. It is the most natural thing."

Reality crashed upon Blu with daggers to her heart. And she had begun to think this pairing would actually work?

The man had slain hundreds of her kind. No matter how long ago it had been, or how refined he appeared now, inside Creed Saint-Pierre's blood flowed with the kind of vengeance that would allow him to take another man's life.

Another wolf's life.

She couldn't look at him. A horrible yet familiar pain twisted in her gut. He was like all the other testosterone-laced bullies she'd thought she had escaped.

Stupid werewolf princess. Did you think you could really be free?

When Blu made to leave he thrust the flat of the blade against her stomach. "We're not done talking. I asked if you were snooping. Did you look in the file?"

"Of course I did. Spy much?"

"Merely ensuring all enemies are accounted for."

Like some kind of battle lord. She'd discounted his mettle too quickly. And she was beginning to think she was in over her head. "I thought we were doing the peace thing here?"

"You tell me." Sweeping the sword around his back,

Creed stepped into her personal space. He towered over her, a formidable presence who could command with a look. "Let's establish a truce, shall we?"

"Like you don't spy on me and I won't snoop on you?"

"And seal it with a kiss."

Kiss the enemy? Surrender to the one who wielded a freakin' sword named Wolfsbane?

Blu glanced aside. Her hands shook and she clutched at her skirt to hide it. The pack relied on her to play this through. And much as she hated her father, she had equal determination to get away from his control. *The control all men wished to force upon her.*

But most of all, she was no quitter.

"Put the blade away first," she said.

Creed drew up the sword and inspected the blade down the center, a master of battle checking the blood groove for remnants of lives taken. With a satisfied nod, he replaced it on the wall.

Blu stood in his arms before she could realize he'd taken her from her feet. She stubbed a bare toe against his shoe, and wobbled. A firm hand across her back secured her. The string on her bikini top slipped high. It wouldn't take much to pop the small triangles of fabric from her breasts.

"Truce?" he prompted, his eyes taking note of the tiny bits of fabric. Blu recognized the lust that hungered there. She was too nervous to toy with it though.

Pressing her hands to his chest, more to stabilize her weakening mien, Blu nodded. "Truce."

They kissed urgently, the killer of werewolves claiming his battle prize with a masterful stroke of command. And even as the sword glinted in her peripheral view, Blu could not deny him the spoils.

His mouth opened to invite her and she slid her tongue against his. *Crash. Take me deeper.* Following the race of her heart, Blu's breaths quickened. He crushed her body to his, and she stood on tiptoe to stay there.

With his thumb, he brushed the side of her breast, teasing at the bikini string. She prayed it would not come undone. She hoped it would.

Blu liked to feel overpowered. Controlled. Taken.

Rather, she was used to the feeling.

But it was different when Creed held her. Though he did overwhelm her, she felt a certain safety in his arms. She needn't fear harm from him, or a raging tantrum. He would master her as he saw fit, but he would not force her to submit.

The realization sparked a wondrous sigh from her.

"You are happy with a truce?" he said against her mouth.

"Momentarily."

"I'll take that."

CHAPTER EIGHT

FOR THE EVENING'S ADVENTURE Blu chose an appropriate bloodred wig. It was shaved short and bouncy at the back with long chunks that veed to points at the corners of her jaw in front. Bettie bangs finished the bloodsucker look.

A punky black leather corset dress hugged her body. Dozens of buckles gathered down one side and along the tight suede skirt.

The spike-heel boots were her favorite. So kinky. They were fashioned entirely of black leather buckles from knee to ankle, à la the gladiator look. It took her ten minutes to fasten them all.

She examined her reflection in the floor-length mirror. "All I need is a whip to complete the look. Wonder if Mr. Decadence is into kink?"

She admonished her image. "Nah. Fangs to flesh is kinky enough."

Thank the gods she had seen no flash of fang since arriving here. Blu had always thought when a vampire kissed someone that the fangs came down automatically. It was good to learn her assumptions weren't all true.

She'd surprised herself with this request to watch Creed take blood. Blu couldn't bear to watch if the victim were female. It would be too intimate, and she would feel jealous.

But to watch two men embrace? Even if it did merely serve a need for Creed, she took a thrill from knowing he would be uncomfortable with this. And that was worth giving up contact with Bree.

Besides, if she got desperate, she could sneak into his office and use the phone.

"The vampire so didn't think this one through. One point for the girl in the red wig."

The BMW honking out front clued her he waited.

Impatient? Well, then, she'd have to recheck her lipstick before she left. Another coat of the glossy red appropriately named Bite Me would finish her Watch My Husband Suck Another Man's Neck look.

"Now I just need to get beyond the bloodsucking part."

Because if anything would turn her stomach, that would.

"HOLY CHRIST ON THE CROSS," Creed said as Blu slid into the front seat. "That getup…"

"Turns you on?" she wondered sweetly.

Instantly aroused, Creed could but gape. Parts of him were getting hard so fast he feared an injury.

The glossy red lipstick emphasized her thick lips, but Creed couldn't take his eyes from her cleavage, pushed high and exposed to the rosy areolas. The tight corset looked as though it offered her little breathing room. About as much room as he had in his pants right now—which was less than nothing.

And those boots. What he'd like to do with those buckles and his teeth. *Sacrebleu.* How long before they returned home? He could not conceive of allowing the woman to get by without tugging a few of those buckles free.

"Where we headed?" she asked.

"There's a club in Minneapolis I know you'll like."

"I thought you didn't do noise?"

"I don't. But with all the visual stimulation you're sending my way right now I'll need the noise to distract me."

She wiggled on the seat. "You like the look? I call it steampunk vampire."

Crass, but somehow not ridiculous. And, oh, so sexy. Her lips were the color of fresh blood. Mercy.

"You would make a lovely vampire, Blu. Fangs would become you."

She smiled, revealing pointed fangs.

"Fuck. Put them back up or you'll make me come

right now." He'd forgotten werewolves could bring out the fangs at will. "Do you know what that does to me?"

"That turns you on? When I let down my fangs? I suppose so. What if I bit you?"

He breathed in and out, concentrating on driving. *Focus, man. It's just another tease.*

"Wow." She put a foot on the dashboard, the pointy black toe scraping the windshield. "I thought it would take another vampire to get you off that way. But seriously? If I bit you?"

"Being bitten ranks right up there with orgasm."

With her one leg up, he could see all the way up her thigh. But from this angle he couldn't determine if she wore panties or not.

No panties, please.

"But that's not going to happen, is it?" he said. "If you won't take my bite, then I shouldn't in turn take yours."

"Yeah, but sounds like it'd be more fun for you if you did let me nibble on you. Not that I'm into blood."

"Please, Blu, I'm unsettled enough about this night. Don't give me more to run through my thoughts. I want to get this done with."

"I don't want you to think of it as a task."

"All challenges require focus and careful strategy."

"Have fun with it, Creed. Save the strategizing for the tribe. Haven't you ever had someone watch?"

The things she would see if she could browse through his past catalog of sexual depravation. Of course he'd been watched. Had watched. Had participated in orgies of fangs, orgasms and wild climactic moans. Ah, that decadent eighteenth century.

But he'd never cared about those random limbs, breasts and necks before. Blu he cared about.

Yes, it wasn't so hard to admit—he did care for her. The werewolf princess had pierced his armor and tickled his humanity as much as his desires. How remarkable was that?

Fool. You know how this will end. If you care even the slightest for her you won't be able to pull it off.

Yes, he would. He must. For the sake of the entire vampire nation.

BLU HAD BEEN INSIDE the club Violet before but not for any length of time. Ryan hadn't liked the feel of it. He preferred pool tables, baskets of week-old peanuts and NASCAR playing on half-a-dozen big-screen TVs in his bars.

She loved the atmosphere. Trance music pulsed through her veins. The purple lighting and violet fabric walls murmured all things sensuous and decadent. The lights turned her hair and lips a strange bruised color. All eyes followed as she sashayed down the hallway toward the purple dance floor lit from below.

Yeah, she could so work a crowd.

Before she gained the crowd's edge, Creed's hand slipped in hers and tugged her right.

"Dude, I was working it," she sputtered, but not loud enough for him to hear over the growly music creeping through the air. It was a heavy metal remake of "Send Me An Angel." She loved that song.

Hand in hand, they wandered the labyrinth of hallways and rooms designed for dark and dangerous liaisons. Slick violet satin coated the walls. The floors glittered with pinpoints of purple light illuminating no higher than her ankles.

Creed navigated the darkness with ease. He wore a crisp black shirt and pants and, with his dark hair, he blended into the shadows. But the diamonds at his cuffs glittered intermittently, giving away his position like a flashing GPS sensor.

At each corner, more purple beams of light shimmered up the walls. The entire hallway sparkled as if a violet Milky Way. Musty incense perfumed the air. Blu suspected Creed had been here before because he did not pause at any turns, merely walked with purpose.

A man with a dark destination. She did get off on that.

An amethyst crystal chandelier topped the large but private room just off the dance floor. The space wasn't lit enough for the average human to see more than shadows and shapes of bodies, but she and Creed had excellent night vision.

He curled an arm around her waist, and she clasped her fingers in his hand over her hip. Warm breath spilled down her neck. Whisky. Had he needed a loosen-up drink?

His nose nudged her hair and prickles of desire raced up Blu's neck—until she imagined him nudging about for her vein. She flinched from the heat of him.

"You nervous?" she asked.

"Not much."

"Listen to the music. 'Send me an angel…'" she sang. "'Right now.' You want me to be your angel, Creed?"

"An angel? You? The heavens must have pushed you out."

"That's me. I didn't fall. I was pushed. But you like me still?"

His breath warmed her lips. "I do."

His close regard tickled her dangerously. The brush of his crisp shirt along her bare arm heightened her sense of touch. His deep voice mastered the noise and rumbled in her bones. And he smelled darkly wicked. It all worked for her right now.

Bobbing her head to the music, she scanned the room.

A couple clad in black leather passed. The man, not seeing Blu clearly but obviously drawn toward her, brushed the back of his hand across her cheek. The sensual touch switched her sensitivity from Creed's voice to the sounds of moans and kissing in the room.

"Why don't you select the one?" her husband whispered.

"Really? Cool. Any dislikes?"

"No drunks."

"Definitely not. No drugs, either. I can smell an addict, and they're all over this room. Would you get drunk or high from their blood?"

"Yes. And it would not be pleasant."

Prowling forward, she took in the room. Faces moved in and out of the shadows. Violet light flashed on body parts, skin brushing skin, mouths open in surrender. The whole scene enchanted her darkly.

"Something tall, dark and ripped will fit the bill," she said.

Creed's fingers still entwined in hers, he caressed her hip and slid his hand along the side of her torso, toying with the buckles on the corset. They were just for show, but she wouldn't spoil his curiosity.

She paused to observe a couple kissing on a chaise. Half-naked, they cared little if anyone watched. That was the room's purpose—to be watched.

Blu wondered now if it would be dark enough to conceal her husband's wicked needs. They'd acclimated to the subtle light, and she guessed even the mortals could make out faces and body parts. Could Creed drink from a mortal without allowing others to know what he was doing?

"Is this safe?" she asked over her shoulder. "For you?"

"Never. But isn't that what you desire, my fallen one?"

"Don't forget, I was pushed."

His other hand slid around across her stomach to caress her breasts. The leather did not allow much sensation, but when he skimmed her nipples, Blu sucked in a breath. She arched her back to signal she wanted more of his touch.

"You like to push beyond boundaries," he said. "Challenge the norm."

"I'm sensing this isn't so much a challenge for you," she replied. "You've been here before."

"Only with women."

She nodded toward the short blonde with one breast exposed. Her tattooed lover with a chain streaming from nose to ear kissed her deeply, their tongues lashing out to taste lips, flesh and the incensed air. "Do you think she's pretty?"

"When compared to you?" Creed answered. "Simply plain. But why are you looking at the women?"

"Just wanted to get an idea of your type. We can't include me because I don't fall on the correct species list."

"I don't discern by species."

"Liar."

"Assumption."

"True," she said.

"Very well."

"Kiss me, Creed."

His mouth skimmed her bare shoulder. A tickle of tongue. A gentle suck at the base of her neck. If he were to bite her, it would feel amazing, she knew that. But the wound would scar and she would be shunned by her pack—all werewolves, actually—for allowing a long-tooth such intimacy with her. As well, she'd develop a blood hunger no werewolf would ever desire.

How dare her father force her into this situation.

The peace pact was a dream. Only a dream.

"I like the ones who have been pushed," he said at her ear. A kiss at the base of her jaw scurried luscious tickles up her scalp. Thoughts of nasty and admonishing paternal figures fluttered away. "Remind me to check you for wings sometime soon."

"No wings," she cooed. "Even lost the halo on the way down."

"Goodie for me."

"Did you say goodie?"

"Hell. I do believe you're starting to rub off on me."

A strong arm brushed her shoulder and Blu followed the man's lingering gaze. He wasn't looking exclusively at her, but taking in both her and Creed. Dark hair, shaved military short. Lots of muscles. He didn't wear a shirt. Probably bi, she figured. And he smelled like Old Spice.

Unoriginal.

"His cologne is too strong," Creed said. "I would be sick from it."

"Me too." The music changed to Madonna's "Frozen," and Blu swayed to the beat, shimmying her shoulder against her husband's buff chest. "How about the one sitting on the velvet chair at the back? He's watching everything. Handsome."

"Handsome isn't a requirement. Clean is."

"He's got a Guy Pearce thing going on. I like him."

"I don't know that name."

"He's a movie star. Sexy in a gaunt, muscled kind of way. I pick him. You going to go for it, or do I get my phone back?"

He smiled against her jaw and nipped gently. "Your wish is my command, Princess."

"Goodie."

VAMPIRES ENTHRALL THEIR victims to believe they want the dark stranger approaching them to touch them, hold them, kiss their neck. Blu knew that much. So she wasn't surprised when the man rose to meet Creed and, without a word, allowed her husband to slide an arm around his back.

She couldn't hear what the vampire whispered as he

slid his fingers up the man's bare chest and tilted his chin aside. Her husband was as tall as the stranger but his broad shoulders gave him the advantage.

He was quick, as she expected he would be, but that didn't keep her from enjoying every small detail of the embrace.

The stranger shivered as Creed's fingers stroked up the center of his chest. Blu took it all in: the murmur of Creed's mouth so close to the man's skin, the spill of the vampire's dark hair over his ear to dust his jaw, the scent of arousal sweetening the salted, sweaty air.

The stranger's shiver manifested as her own. Watching Creed's fingers slip under the man's chin, moving his head as if a lover putting the flesh before him. *Here. Here is where I want to touch you. Lick you. Taste you.*

Enter you.

Blu hushed out a sigh. Yes, to be entered by him. Invaded and filled by a part of him he kept concealed from the world. She traced fingertips over her breasts. Arousal both hardened and softened her flesh.

Creed leaned into the man's neck, his nose venturing along his stubbled jaw. For a moment, he lingered, as if drawing in his scent, deciding where he'd like to place his lips.

Kiss him, Blu thought. *On the mouth. Pretend it's me. Or don't pretend and make me jealous.*

Creed looked to her, his mouth slightly parted to reveal the tips of white fangs. He silently asked her permission.

Blu stepped closer, fitting her hip against the victim's thigh. The man groaned, a wanting sound that pleaded for connection, and he muttered, "Please."

She stroked the side of his neck, and the vein but inches from Creed's mouth bulged like a bruise under the wicked purple lights. Creed's breath hissed across her fingers. She traced her husband's lips, avoiding the slick white fang that stirred a chill in her breast even while their proximity made her wet with desire.

"Kiss him," she whispered.

His reply entered her pores like a lover's hot tongue. "As you command."

Creed kissed the man's neck, softly but sure as he swept the tip of his tongue over the vein. The man's gasp hushed over Blu's lips like a stolen prayer.

Creed held the man by the chest. Blu wanted him to move his hand lower, to brush it over the erection she knew the stranger had. Imagining the erotic act was exquisite enough. Any minute now her vampire husband would take the hard, pulsing vein with a different type of penetration.

"Do it," she whispered. "For me."

Mastering the stranger, Creed clenched his grip and

locked his mouth over the victim's straining neck muscles. The man cried out, but it was desirous and blended with the moans and hushed climaxes around the room.

The scent of blood tinted the air. Blu pressed her cheek beside the man's open mouth, intent on her husband's exploits. Fangs pulled from the flesh, rising into his gums, and he began to suck. To draw out the man's life and revitalize his own.

The man moaned loudly at her ear. Blu cupped her palm over his mouth, unconcerned for his pleasure now and a little irritated with his display. It was all about Creed taking sustenance. Her husband's eyes were closed and his mouth sucked at the stranger's flesh.

Make it her flesh, she wished. Not her neck, and with no fangs. Just Creed suckling at her breast like that, feeding, needing the connection, the aliveness, the exquisite pain and pleasure.

It mattered little they were so different, not supposed to be getting along, much less married. The sensual experience was not prejudice.

The stranger shuddered and climaxed. His gasp heated Blu's palm. The swoon was always good to the victim.

Creed pulled his head back, parting from the flesh and blood—the life. He dropped the stranger onto the chair and stumbled backward against the satin wall, struck by a scintillating thrill.

Blu followed, fitting herself against him, studying his swoon.

His entire body was tense, as if at the peak of climax, but he made no sound. Eyes closed, he parted his mouth, the fangs down and glistening, but showing no blood; he'd licked them clean.

She traced his arm, feeling minute shudders strafe the hard muscle. The blood must be rushing through his system, she assumed. She didn't understand the mechanics of it, but it didn't matter. Extreme pleasure held him captive in darkly glamorous surrender.

She glanced her palm down his taut chest, and over his pants, expecting to find him hard there, as well. He was not. Good. The bite hadn't turned him on sexually.

But then he did become hard, quickly growing firm beneath her touch.

He pressed her palm to his erection. "Good enough for you, Princess?"

"That was so erotic." She kissed his jaw, but would avoid his mouth. A squeeze of her hand and his body tensed in reaction. "Turned me on. Did you come?"

"No," he gasped, then chuckled softly. "Something close, but never like that. Not with a man. But you. You cannot touch me like this and expect we'll walk out of here unchanged."

"We'll never be the same," she agreed. "I desire you, Creed. Watching you take blood was a gift. Thank you."

"Christ, Blu, harder," he said, directing her hand over his cock.

She moved her hand, rubbing the front of his trousers over the hard shaft. Even through the fabric she could feel the pulse of the thick vein on the underside, the heavy, smooth head of it. She wanted to unwrap it and glide it along her warm skin.

He kissed the crowns of her breasts, hard, demanding. A lash of his tongue behind the leather corset targeted her nipple. Blu stretched back a shoulder, which lifted her nipple above the leather. He sucked at it as fiercely as he'd taken from the man's neck.

"Oh, yes." This was what she'd wanted. And she hadn't realized it until now. "That's good. Take me."

As she tilted her head, her hair brushed against another person. A hand caressed her ass. It was not Creed's.

He turned her around and slammed her against the wall. "Not this way for us," he growled. He worked his hips, grinding his erection against her thigh. So hard and thick. She wanted it in hand, bared, bold and ready. "Just the two of us. Has to be."

"Yes," she said with a throaty pant. "Yes."

THE BMW'S FRONT SEAT wasn't designed for comfortable sex. Blu fit herself onto Creed's lap, straddling him with those crazy-sexy boots. He adjusted the seat all the way back so the steering wheel wouldn't dig into her.

She'd taken the keys from him and stashed them in the glove compartment. Tucked at the back of the parking lot, and well away from the security lights, who was he to argue against a car make-out session?

"You make me so hot," she said, skating down his neck with her tongue. "Feel me, Creed."

While he wanted to kiss her, to pierce her mouth with his tongue and taste the wet heat there, he would not. He didn't want to turn her off after he'd drunk blood, though the vodka he'd thrown back as they'd exited the club had cleaned his palate.

She directed his hand up her thigh and he curled his fingers past a few buckles, under the suede skirt and into her sex. Mercy, she was so hot there, slippery wet. He moaned at the chile chocolate heat of her.

She, a werewolf, hot for him? It was like gliding through a surreal dream.

"Make me come," she directed. His shirt unbuttoned, she pressed kisses down his chest, and bit not too softly at his nipples. "Please, I need it."

Head against the seat and still riding the blood swoon aftershocks, Creed slid a finger inside his wife. Every woman was different, shaped individually and designed as if a snowflake, no two alike. The discovery of what could bring her to climax was always an excursion he enjoyed.

It didn't take long to learn Blu needed direct and rhythmic contact. Slow and then a little faster. She rode his fingers, grinding the sweet spot.

A metal buckle rasped across his chin. The pain was small compared to the pleasure of Blu's whimpering moans. She bowed to his manipulations and begged for more.

Tonight he would tame the wolf.

"Yes," she gasped. "Harder."

He pressed harder, stroking the inner shaft of her clit that controlled her pleasure. The heat of her drove him mad. She wanted so desperately. She needed. And her lack of fear, of discretion, enamored him.

"Faster, please."

Her whimpering pleas dizzied him. He loved it when a woman asked for exactly what she wanted, what she needed. He wanted to give it all to her.

"Right there. Oh, my gods." Her thighs tightened. She tensed. Gasps warmed his neck. "Yes."

Her climax was loud, joyous and unabashed. She arched against him, her body stiffening as shudders shook her thighs against his. The red wig dusted his eyelids, his nose and mouth. The call of her wild nature curled her nails into his shoulders, but he took the pain gladly.

One exposed nipple grazed his mouth. He sucked at it, sparking another exquisite peal from her parted lips. Her pleasure put him over the edge. His erection still firmly tucked inside his trousers, he came, spilling into the fabric and bumping his hips against her shuddering thighs. He gripped her hips, not allowing her to slip away.

Her body wilted upon his. She tucked her bewigged head aside his shoulder and curled one leg against his torso. She jutted the spike heel into his thigh, but not deeply. They panted together, deliciously spent.

She stroked his crotch. "You came, too? Good."

The scent of her, like exotic flowers crushed against the flesh and salted, was the most exquisite perfume.

She laughed deeply, her breasts crushing against his beating heart. "That rocked."

"I have to agree."

Creed slid a hand up her arm, hot and sticky with perspiration. He pressed his fingers over her neck. The vein pulsed madly. Life soaring beneath his fingertips. Thick red corpuscles and platelets and sexy plasma.

His fangs lowered. Sweet darkness lingered but a bite away. An after-sex suck never failed to bring the donor to orgasm again. She would know what it really meant to be *rocked,* and that this vampire was all about the decadence.

Creed twisted his head to the side. Fighting the compulsion, he willed his fangs back up. A wistful smirk dismissed the desire to bite his wife's neck.

Not yet.

Not without her permission.

CHAPTER NINE

IT WAS RAINING BY THE time Creed pulled the BMW up to the front door. He didn't park in the garage, which was not attached to the house, and sat a hundred yards to the east near the front fence, because he didn't want Blu to have to run through the rain.

"We can wait until it stops raining," he suggested, drawing a finger along her thigh. He slid it down between her thighs, and Blu sucked in a breath. "Is that a don't-touch-me-anymore noise?"

"Actually..." She opened the door and held her palm out to catch the cold raindrops. "It was a catch-me-if-you-can noise."

She batted her lashes at him and blew him a kiss.

Spattered by tiny droplets, Blu raced toward the front door, but her high-heeled boots made the run treacherous. Didn't matter. The rain soaking into her pores felt great, but it didn't erase the sheen of perspiration produced from their amazing car sex.

Caught about the waist by powerful arms and swung around, Blu laughed. She twisted in the vampire's embrace when he set her down. Impatiently, she shoved his unbuttoned shirt down his arms.

"Out here?" he asked.

"Here's a tidbit about me, vampire. Rain makes me horny."

"And here I thought it was what we'd just done." He lifted her leg, tucking it alongside his hip, and found her bare bottom with his palm. His touch branded her.

"Mmm..." A kiss upon her clavicle licked away the rain. "What of the spies?"

"I didn't see any when we drove up," he said. "They must be tucked away from the rain for the night. Or else they followed us, and we lost them along the way."

"Works for me. The shrubs block the view of the lower front door and the step is carpeted."

"Oh, yes?" He nudged his foot behind her boot, forcing her knee to bend. As she went down, he cradled her and positioned her across the front step, which was carpeted, but with that scratchy, plastic outdoor stuff.

"Wait." He tugged off his shirt and laid it down so she could at least fit herself from ass to shoulders on something softer. Such a gentleman. Lifting one of her legs high, he bit a buckle and tugged. "These are insanely sexy."

"Maybe you should bite them off? One by one."

"It would take all night," he muttered as he moved to kiss up her neck and then at her ear. "I want you now. We only just got started in the car."

She wanted to continue, too, and yet what they'd shared in the car had been their first real no-holds-barred encounter. Blu wasn't quite prepared to give it all up just yet.

"More of what we did in the car," she said, bracketing his face with her hands and holding him but inches from her face. Dark and spicy, his scent did not preach patience. "Not full-on sex yet, Creed. I'm…not ready."

"Ah?" He nodded. "I'm sorry. I am rushing things."

"No, you're not." She wrapped her legs about his hips. "What we did in the car was amazing, and I want to keep doing it now, but I'm still not completely there yet."

"Trusting me."

She shrugged and blinked at the rain that spattered her forehead and eyelids. "Is that okay?"

A kiss to her breast lingered there. Creed glided his hand down to her thigh and then between her legs. He certainly knew how to play her to a screaming orgasm. She should reciprocate, but she worried that once she got his erection out from his pants, even she wouldn't want to stop. She liked the feeling that came with holding a man's penis: utter control.

"It is more than okay." He stroked her between the legs softly, a delicious change of pace from their previous frenzy. "You are not too cold? You're shivering, Blu."

"Mmm, it's a blend of ecstasy and a chill."

"I can do something about that." He kissed her quickly, then sat up, his legs straddling her hips, and spread his arms before him, as if to part a veil.

Suddenly the rain stopped. Creed leaned over her and studied her face, and then Blu realized the rain had not stopped. It had just stopped raining on them.

"Did you do that?" she murmured.

"Just one of those tricks one keeps up their sleeve."

"You're not wearing a shirt."

"So I'm not. Water magic."

"You said you weren't going to use your magic. Something about atoning?"

"I feel sure no witch will mind me keeping my wife dry and warm. As long as you don't tell."

"I won't tell," she whispered, crossing her fingers behind Creed's back.

Creed brushed his lips lightly across her eyelids, tasting the rain. Within moments he brought her to another deliciously muscle-twisting high. She didn't cry out so loudly as she had in the car. Instead she came softly, glancing into the realm of utter delight, and then landing back in the real world.

In the arms of her vampire husband.

THE FOLLOWING AFTERNOON Blu peeked in on Creed in his office. "I'm going for a jog."

He barely looked from the papers before him. Then, as if prodded to life, he dropped the paperwork and rose to meet her at the door. He stroked aside the pink strand fallen loose from her ponytail.

"You're gorgeous when you come," he said.

They'd stumbled, arm in arm, into the house last night, but a note from Housekeeper had sent Creed to the servant's quarters. Blu hadn't followed. She had gone up to shower and had fallen into a blissful sleep.

Brushing her cheek into his palm, Blu shrugged. "How's Malena?"

"Malena?"

She made air quotes. "'Housekeeper'? That's her name—Malena."

"Ah. She's no longer with us. Family emergency. A new housekeeper will arrive tomorrow."

"Wow. That was quick. So a new housekeeper. I dare you to learn this one's name."

He smirked. "Much easier not to. They come and go so quickly. So a jog? In a dress?"

She tugged the hem of the short sundress. "Uh-huh."

"All right. I know it's never wise to try to understand your inner workings. You have the remote?"

"Yep. Thanks for understanding."

"I adjusted the wards last evening. You should have no trouble passing through the gate."

"Thanks. More magic?"

He nodded.

"We're going to discuss you, your magic and the witches sometime. Soon. If you expect me to keep your secret."

"Yes, I do, and we will." He stroked her arm with soft, feathery touches. "Care to meet me later this evening for some—" a stroke strayed across her nipple and it hardened, which pleased him immensely "—entertainment? It involves chile chocolate sauce."

"You hired the chef? Nummy. Of course it's a date. Nothing can keep me away from chocolate." She kissed his temple. "Back in a few."

Aware he watched as she prowled away, Blu blew a flirty kiss over her shoulder before turning down the hallway.

"What am I doing?" she admonished as she hit the driveway outside and ran along the yard periphery to the back where she could slip out of her dress. "Flirting with my husband like that?"

As if she wanted him. When this whole marriage thing

was only a farce. A *situation,* as he'd callously labeled it that first night.

And the vampire! He wasn't supposed to fall for her. For a feral, wild animal, as he'd put it. He most certainly was not supposed to have sex with her.

"Must have been something in the incense," she decided.

But she knew differently. Last night had shot her theories of bad sex with vamps all to hell. Just thinking about his fingers inside her, moving over her, commanding her to a raging orgasm, made her wet again.

"Not cool, Blu. Not right now. Save it for later."

So she shoved the vamp from her mind, but not without a secret shudder. And a wonder. Was he thinking about her right now? About sliding his fingers inside her and feeling her come at his command?

"He should be."

That he had commanded the rain to part all around them was another wonder. If he could do that, what other tricks did he have up his proverbial sleeve? And just what would he do to ensure she kept that secret?

"Could involve Wolfsbane," she decided, with a shudder. She'd have to be very careful how she handled the information with which he'd trusted her.

Once close to the east wall of fencing, she clicked the remote and eyed the shrubbery to spy where the gate might be. Just ahead, she saw it.

"Nice. But why a gate at the back?" Maybe he owned some of the land that wasn't fenced off. It was possible.

Approaching cautiously as she gained the open gate, she decided to leap through, thus avoiding any possible trip wires. Better safe than sorry. Of course she knew wards required only magical intangible sensors. And he had said he'd adjusted them.

"Still. Just to be safe," she muttered.

Closing the gate, she then tucked the remote near a rock wedged in the grass.

Slipping off her dress, it shimmied down her legs and puddled on her bare toes. Tugging off her wig to toss it on top of the dress, she then shifted. She didn't jog as a two-legged creature, after all.

The shift was easy and always felt like a really intense, stretching, Thai massage as Blu's bones, flesh and organs reshaped. Her human mind segued with the animal mind. She still possessed some human thoughts in wolf form, but mostly her thoughts grew instinctive. So if she had a task to accomplish in wolf shape she had to focus.

The pores on her skin tightened, forcing out fur. Her skull squeezed, producing flashes of brilliant sunlight at the backs of her retinas. Teeth and claws grew.

As Blu made the shift, she concentrated: *three miles to the north.*

In wolf shape, she shook her body, ruffled her fur and let out a low howl that wouldn't be heard by the vampires outside the front gates, but probably the wolves would pick it up.

She raced away from the gates, across the edge of a plowed field. Her paws took the uneven ground swiftly, gliding through the air effortlessly. Corn stalks three feet high lashed at her muzzle and fur, but the wolf loved the freedom. Tongue lolling, she trotted from the field and along the edge of the forest.

Three miles to the north, the wolf spied a vehicle she associated with humans—but also her breed. Normally she would avoid human contact. But the scent on the van was familiar, a welcoming beacon.

The back doors of the black van opened, and she leaped inside.

A blanket was held before her. The wolf dodged her head into the olive-green wool and shifted. Her bones and flesh stretched, the fur and tail giving way as her limbs lengthened. The last change was claws segueing to finger-nails.

Blu tugged the blanket about her shoulders and made sure it covered her completely in front. It didn't cover her legs at all. They could have provided a bigger blanket.

"Whose idea was this to meet so far out? I so should have driven here."

Two werewolves in black camo gear sat in the back of the van, hands between their knees. Ridge, her father's bodyguard and right-hand man, was bulky and had no apparent neck. Blu felt comfortable enough around him to trust he did respect her. In a werewolfie-alpha kind of way. He'd never hurt her, and had once torn a horny pack member from her before he could rape her.

The other wolf she didn't know, but his ruddy skin and scruffy beard put her off almost as much as his menacing gaze.

Normally she was all about the hairy men. But lately, she'd developed a taste for a cleaner more aristocratic look. Hmm…

"You weren't followed?" Ridge asked.

"Not unless a bunny rabbit got curious."

She settled on the metal bench across from Ridge but kept her distance from the other, who was beginning to creep her out. She could sense his increased breathing and smell the musk on him.

Get a room and take care of it yourself, buddy.

"So what's up? Bree gave me the message I was to rendezvous here."

The last message she'd checked before handing her precious phone over to Creed. He'd won it fair and square. And she was definitely up for the next challenge if it ended as it had last night.

"Your father wants an update on you and Lord Saint-Pierre."

"Dirty vampire," the other muttered.

"Who are you?" Blu snapped with affront. "Who is he?" she asked Ridge.

"New recruit. Diaz, keep your trap shut. And don't look at the princess like that. Head down."

Diaz obliged, but Blu could still feel his leering gaze creep down her legs. She appreciated Ridge's respect, but tugged the blanket tighter across her chest. While they could satisfy their lust perfectly well with mortal females, male wolves were susceptible to the female wolf's pheromones, oftentimes against their own volition.

"Your father wants to know if you've been able to get close to the vampire."

"I'm working on it."

"I'm supposed to ask…" Ridge looked down, twitched his fingers in a loose clasp. "If the marriage has been consummated?"

"That depends on what definition you're looking for. The Council's definition or otherwise?"

"Have you had sex or been bitten yet?"

"Hmm, sort of and no."

Ridge's pleading gape gave her a chuckle. "What does that mean, Princess? I gotta have something to report back."

"What that means is, I'm making way in the intimacy department. We've made out. Kissed. Done—" she smirked and tucked a loose strand of dark hair over her shoulder "—things. But no official sex yet. And no biting. That's never going to happen."

"Your father feels it is necessary to show the vampires we've succumbed. The Council requires it."

"Succumb, my ass. This chick isn't going to let anyone bite her neck. Pact or no pact. Besides, it shouldn't matter, not with my father's plans."

She stretched a leg, and when Diaz noticed, she smacked his knee with the back of her hand, and said to Ridge, "Could you put a leash on him?"

"Princess, about the bite—"

"Sex should be enough. And…I'm working on that." This conversation humiliated her more than the idiot Diaz's lolling expression.

"I'll report back to your father."

"You do that. Anything else?"

"The banquet is in a few days. You'll be there with Lord Saint-Pierre."

"Of course. The Council wants to see how we've progressed. We'll attend and put on a show. My father doesn't plan anything for that night, does he?"

"I've no information, Princess. I'm sure you'll receive a call with information deemed necessary."

Which meant she wouldn't get the whole shebang. Or even half, if she knew her father. "I've broken my cell phone. There's no way to contact me."

"I'll see you get a new one. Have it delivered in a box from a clothing store so the vampire will not suspect."

"I'd rather you didn't. He keeps a keen eye on me." And she didn't want to lose the trust she'd already gained. Besides, they'd made a deal—kinky man-on-man skin-dancing for the phone—and she wouldn't go back on her word. "I'll find a way to call my father in a few days to check in."

"Very good, Princess. Would you like a ride back to the estate?"

"No, I'll finish my run. Thanks, Ridge."

She opened the door, but Ridge caught the metal edge before the sunlight entered. "Princess, you're not wearing the ring."

"Well, duh, I just wolfed out. Jewelry doesn't become fur."

Diaz growled low and warning. Blu rolled her eyes. The males always thought they could admonish a female when she spoke out of turn to them.

Ridge, thankfully, maintained his deference. "It's your only protection."

Really? Not according to what she'd learned. Though, Creed had intimated it could still do a nasty to his magic. Obviously, her father wasn't aware of that misleading detail.

And what was with the vampire's magic? What she'd seen him do with the rain last night was fabulous. But it was a pretty trick. Didn't seem as though he needed it to actually survive. Had she been traded to a worthless vamp? Someone his tribe could risk losing?

She should tell Ridge about the magic and the ring. But it didn't feel right. She didn't want to betray Creed.

"I wear the ring always in human shape, Ridge. Thank you for your concern. Besides, I think not wearing it to the banquet would be a tremendous signal to all that I trust my husband, don't you?"

"I'm not allowed an opinion in the matter, Princess. But I'll have to report this to your father."

"You do that. Oh, and let him know Diaz was leering at me."

Diaz gaped.

"One other thing, Princess. The full moon is in three days. Will you require an escort to a safe house?"

She hadn't thought about that. Didn't want to think about it.

Just sitting with Ridge, a connection to her pack and family, put her to odds. While he had a tight grip on his aggression, she could smell the wolf's desire. The feral need to grab the naked female and mate with her.

She much preferred to be home with Creed.

But she should think about what would happen when the moon grew full. Seriously.

"I'll call if I need assistance, Ridge. Goodbye."

This time, she shoved the door open and jumped out before the bodyguard could grab her back. Home was but a race across the field and through the forest.

"Home," she tried. And with a smile, she nodded. "Yeah, home."

Kneeling at the side of the van with the blanket over her body, she shifted again, and scrambled from under the blanket as a wolf.

FOUR THOUSAND DOLLARS to bribe the chef away from the Louis XIII restaurant for two hours this evening had been worth every penny. They hadn't needed a meal, only the rich chocolate sauce poured over a small piece of vanilla cake.

Blu made swift work of the cake.

Now Creed sat on the couch, legs stretched the length, back to the arm. Blu straddled him. The chef had left ten minutes earlier. She leaned aside, spooning a drizzle of chocolate from the plate onto her tongue.

He glided a hand up her bare thigh, loving that all her skirts were short and slinky. The violet hair bobbed about her shoulders as she swung to press her palms to his chest. She cracked an endorphin-laced smile.

"You've chocolate on your lip. After all the cash I laid out for the chef, it would be a crime to waste a single drop. Come here."

She obeyed, leaning in for a kiss, but he instead tongued her lip, licking the spicy chocolate. It heated his palate when he pressed his tongue upward. The kisses that followed were exciting and fervent. He licked and sucked at her mouth as if she were the dessert.

"Your mouth is so hot," he murmured. "And that's not from the sauce. Come here, violet lady. I think you dripped onto your breasts."

The low-cut dress was shocking pink and the fabric so thin he could see the darker areolas through it. Creed palmed a nipple, tweaking the hard jewel.

"Mmm, my mouth isn't the only thing that's hot," she said. Sliding the sleeves from her shoulders, she tugged down the fabric to expose her nipples. "Want a peek?"

"Tease. I want to see something else first."

"Oh, yeah?" She wiggled her hips, grinding her sex against his hard-on.

"Take off your wig."

She toyed with the purple hair, a pout plushing her chocolate-stained lips.

"I want to see your real hair. It must be dark." He traced one of her eyebrows. "Like this." He slid his other hand between her legs. "And like this. It's your disguise, Blu. I want to see the real you."

"I'm not sure."

It was just hair. He couldn't understand why she would be shy about it. Unless it was short and unkempt? Everything he'd expected this werewolf to be was not at all true. And how much did he enjoy that?

Immensely.

"You know I like to wear wigs for the color and fun. This is who I am."

She teased a fingernail beneath his pectoral, and flicked it across his nipple. He sucked in a breath and tensed his jaw.

She was not going to distract and redirect him this time. "If you're shy about it…"

"It's not that. It's just…"

Something deep inside emerged to soften her eyes. Her lashes fluttered as she looked aside, unsure. And sad? He'd noticed the sadness in her eyes before. That such an emotion even existed within this gorgeous woman troubled him.

He'd lost her. She'd separated from him and floated above their sexy embrace, his pushed angel trapped upon this hellish earth. What secrets darkened her gray eyes?

"Blu?"

A huff of breath blew up the violet strands caught in

one of her lashes. "If you must know, wigs give me control. And the bright colors seem to keep men a few paces back. Keeps them from wanting to grab it."

"Grab it?"

Her posture slumped as she sat upon him. Now unable to meet his eyes, she had moved inward, farther away from him.

How did he get her back? Could he find the halo and restore her glimmer?

"Werewolves are lusty and alpha," she said, toying with the button on his open shirt, tucked near his elbow. "I've had my real hair yanked and pulled and twisted about a fist too many times to count. It frightens me, that helpless feeling."

"Blu, I would never. I don't want to hurt you. You know I wouldn't hurt you, don't you?"

She shrugged. "Who can ever know something like that? Emotions are complicated. Even the calmest and kindest man can rage and rant and change into a beast."

"I'm surprised your father allowed his pack members to be so cruel."

"There are a lot of things you don't know about Amandus Masterson."

Evidently. He'd thought the old wolf ineffectual actually. So did the other vampire tribes with which Nava was currently allied.

"Can you trust me to tell me?"

She trailed a finger over his abs, toying closer to where the dark hairs began below his belly button. But arousal sat aside, deferring to this quiet moment. She had revealed herself to him, and he would respect it.

Drawing up her knees, she circled them with her arms and propped her chin on top, closing herself from him like a child protecting herself from pain.

"Let's just say I'm Amandus's favorite reward to give over when one of the pack has done something for him. You can imagine what a randy wolf will do with a female when given an opportunity."

"Blu, I—" Anger roaring to the surface, Creed clenched his fingers. How dare the old bastard use Blu as a sexual reward? "I don't know what to say."

"There's nothing to say. I've known nothing else. It is what I am, and I've taken some measures to protect myself, but it's just silly wigs."

"But you shouldn't have known such cruelty." She flinched when he touched her chin. "Please, don't be frightened of me, ever. I think it's despicable what your father did."

"Does, not did. You are just another recipient of his rewards."

"No, I— No."

Yet truly, he was. *Sacrebleu.* Creed swallowed his

heartbeat. The father was a monster. And Creed had unknowingly played into one of his twisted games by accepting the prize.

"I would never use you, Blu."

"I think I can believe that." A small smile didn't last more than a moment on her lips. She tucked her head, then looked over her knees. "You are different than the wolves."

He stroked the violet wig, being careful to do so gently. But Creed didn't have to think about tempering his touch; for him it was the way women should be treated. They were not prizes to be earned and used roughly. He'd learned much over the years, and looked beyond his distant past when he may have been overly rough with a witch or two.

Atonement. Had this woman been put in his life for that very reason? So he could treat her like the princess she was to make up for his past mistakes?

Damn, he needed to honor his vow not to use magic. He would. For Blu.

She looked aside. "Let's not speak of it anymore, 'kay?"

"No, if it makes you uncomfortable."

She shuffled her feet to bracket his hips, her knees hugging his torso. A discreet tug pulled her skirt down in front.

"I want to trust you, Creed. I feel like I already do. And that frightens me more than a lusty werewolf determined to mate."

"I will never force you to do anything. I would be no man if I did. And know I will avenge you to your father—you've only to ask."

She pressed two fingers to his lips. "You're a good man, Creed. Even if you do own a sword called Wolfsbane."

He clasped her fingers and kissed them as if the greatest treasure. "I haven't used it for vengeance in centuries. Promise." Self-defense was another matter.

"And never on females, right?"

"Never. Though my fingers itch now to take it after any man who has harmed you, or pulled your hair."

She tugged at the ends of the violet wig, wobbling it on her head until the bangs tilted across her brows. Then, she pulled the whole thing off and dropped it to the floor.

A coil of dark hair unraveled from the crown of her head and spilled free onto her shoulders. Lush darkness, like midnight unbound. It dusted her cheek. Caught in her lashes. Trickled to the tops of her half-exposed breasts. Dashed ink marks across the brilliant pink dress.

The fallen angel's halo. She'd had it all along.

Creed touched the ends curled at her breast. "It's gorgeous." He leaned in and nuzzled into her neck, the veil of her silken hair slippery across his nose, his mouth, his eyelids.

"It's the color of your eyes," she whispered. "So dark. I was afraid of your eyes that first night at the ceremony. That's why I didn't look at you so much."

"And now?"

"I want to dive into them, to discover what lies in the darkness. I think it'll be such an adventure. It has been so far."

"I could do the same with your hair." He splayed the lemon-sweet strands across his face. "A girl named Blu with the blackest hair, and a penchant to adorn herself with all the colors of the rainbow. My wife. My lover. My danger."

"I'm not dangerous to you," she whispered. "So long as the moon isn't full."

"And just what happens when it is?"

"You'll see."

He brushed her hair from his lips. "Will I?"

"Yes, I think so. I…vow it to you. You've sacrificed for me—I should sacrifice something for you."

"Taking blood from a man at a nightclub was hardly a sacrifice."

"It was an emotional one. You risked humiliating yourself in front of me. You couldn't know how I would react."

So true. "I thought you enjoyed it?"

"Loved it. Can't get enough of the kink."

"I guessed you like to watch."

"You'll know me completely when the moon is full, Creed. But I don't want to open that can of worms now. You've already tugged my most humiliating secret from me. Enough for tonight, yes?"

A humiliating secret? It ached in his heart she had to have secrets. Idiot wolves. He would make them pay, each and every one of them.

Creed kissed her hard on the neck, her hair billowing over his face. She surrounded him with flesh and desire and erotic need. So much trust she gave him. He winced to think he had not earned it.

For he yet possessed secrets.

But all he could do now was put his desires into touch. To give to her what she gave him.

Tugging down her dress, he palmed her breasts, massaging them, loving the weight of them in his hands. He could suckle the firm globes all night.

Spreading her hands through her hair, she spanned it in a gorgeous veil and let it fall about their heads. It spilled across his face, adorning him with her truths, surrendering her defenses.

His wife rocked her hips upon him, grinding against his erection. Both still clothed, they'd agreed before sitting down that intercourse was not in the terms this evening. They were close, so close to being one, but Blu was yet reluctant. And for good reason, as she'd just revealed.

He could wait. The wait would be worth it.

Blu traced his lip. He sucked in her middle finger, tickling the underside of it, then nudged her hand. She traced her moist finger around her nipple. He followed with his tongue, dancing behind her, taking direction, then mastering her with licks and suckles that stirred up throaty moans.

Drowning in her softness, he didn't pay attention to the hard slide of fang inside his mouth.

He leaned in to kiss her on the lips, and her palm slapped his chest.

"What?"

"Not like this." She scrambled to the end of the couch. "Your teeth."

Creed touched his mouth. Damn. Never before had he needed to struggle so much to keep back his fangs when aroused. "Don't worry, Blu—"

"I don't want your bite!" She stood and slid up her dress to cover the rosy dark nipples. "I thought you understood that."

"I do. It's just…" Hard to control? He'd always had a handle on it before.

"I'm sorry." She looked about, at the chocolate-smeared plate, her wig. "I uh…lost the mood. I'm going to shower."

"Blu, don't do this. It was an accident. I— It just happens with you. I can't explain it."

She double-stepped it up the stairs.

Unwilling to chase her, after her tale of abuse at the hands of her father's men, Creed remained on the couch. Staring at the ceiling, he cursed this bizarre inability to control what he'd mastered centuries ago.

Why was this happening now?

Was it really Blu who stirred his teeth to descend? And did that mean he needed her blood more than he could imagine?

CHAPTER TEN

CREED RECEIVED THE CALL from Alexandre just before midnight. With Wolfsbane in hand, he slipped from the house undetected. Blu was in the theater room listening to some music video station. Volume cranked, his secretive getaway was ensured.

Pealing the BMW from the driveway, he made the contact point with Alexandre in less than fifteen minutes. Creed hopped in the unmarked black van already rolling across the tarmac. From the passenger seat, he leaned over to nod to the three vampires in the back.

Revin, Fresno and Merce nodded solemnly. All were outfitted with combat gear and weaponry.

"My information was incorrect," Alexandre said as he navigated toward the warehouse district in Minneapolis. "I think the fight's already in progress. We may not get there until after."

"Damn it."

They always tried to show up before the blood match occurred. The goal was to waylay the transport van en route to the fight warehouse. That way they could rescue two vampires.

Arriving after meant only one survivor.

"The new snitch is still getting the hang of things."

"At least we've a new one. Good job, Alexandre." He slapped him across the back. "We got darts?" he called to the back, where the atmosphere was strung like a bowstring.

Revin cocked a dart gun. "Check. Silver-nitrate bombs, too. You going in, Saint-Pierre?"

He tapped Wolfsbane. "I'll lead the way."

THE MOST DANGEROUS PLACE for a vampire to venture was a blood match. They were held in privately owned warehouses in the suburbs and sometimes abandoned barns in the countryside. The fights were attended by dozens of werewolves, both from packs, and those lone wolves who were secure enough to stand next to a pack wolf without being intimidated.

The aggression and blood scent frenzied the wolves to their beastly werewolf shapes. Even as the fighters went at each other, the wolves clashed amongst themselves.

Creed had witnessed a match years ago, from behind

the safety of protective chain-link fencing. It had been an exposition of sorts, offered to the various tribe leaders by the pack principals to show them what they could do to their kind if they did not return the lands the wolves accused them of stealing.

Scare tactics never worked against Creed.

The matches were a vile form of blood entertainment. A horrific punishment to the innocent vampire who fell onto the path of a werewolf. The wolves strictly stalked those independent vampires who hadn't aligned themselves to a tribe. It was safer that way for the wolves, less risk of bringing an angry tribe upon them.

What they did was chain the vampire up for weeks in a cell lit by UV bulbs, starving it of blood and driving it mad with UV sickness. After about a month, the vampire was literally insane for blood. But usually after two or three weeks, the vamp—depending on his age—was in agony for blood. When two starving vampires were put in a cage together they went after each other, biting and draining, and finally punching their fists through muscle and bone to claim the greatest cache of blood—the heart.

It meant survival to the winning vampire. If only for a few more months of captivity.

They'd kept Rachel only three weeks before she'd succumbed. She hadn't been strong enough. The first fight had been her last.

That day Creed had vowed to take down all the sporting warehouses he could find, and make the werewolves suffer for their cruelty.

"They expect us to come to terms of peace?" Creed eyed the warehouse as Alexandre pulled up a block away. "They should burn every sporting warehouse in the country. Then, and only then…"

He didn't finish the statement. It sounded too hypocritical now with him married to a werewolf. *And nearly fucking her.*

What in hell had he been thinking lately? Mooning after a werewolf? It was idiotic. No vampire in his right mind would succumb to such foolishness.

He tightened his grip on Wolfsbane. Vengeance against the wolves he'd only buried shallowly upon accepting the marriage agreement now surfaced. Tonight he was going to take some wolf heads.

Muscle cars, Jeeps and SUVs pulled from the lot before the warehouse. Beer cans littered the tarmac and raucous rock music blared from speakers.

"They're dispersing," Alexandre reported. "Fight's done. The containment truck is being loaded. We'll have to take them on the road."

The truck would hold the winning vampire, sated for now. Blood drunk, surely. But no less a prisoner in chains.

"It'll be easier," Creed stated. "There are only two

wolves in the driver's cab. I don't think they keep a guard on the vamp after the fight. Unnecessary."

They watched the white truck pass by, and Alexandre spun the wheel to follow two blocks behind. The wolves would return to the pack's compound. Having no idea which pack had mastered this evening's blood sport, Creed and his men did not know where they were headed.

When the van took the 35E exit, Alexandre said, "I bet they're headed east toward Wisconsin. Might be the River pack."

"Overtake them now," Creed ordered. "As they enter the freeway."

He gestured to the men in the back, who prepared rappelling hooks, masks and dart guns.

The four-lane freeway wasn't abandoned this late at night, but they drove on a clear stretch for a few miles. The black van pulled aside the white truck. Alexandre was an expert behind the wheel, having spent some time working as a getaway driver during an armed robbery stint a few decades earlier.

Creed was handed a dart gun from over his shoulder. He rolled down the window.

The truck driver saw him, gaped—and took a dart to the neck.

"Now!"

At Creed's command, the back doors of the van

opened, securing to the vehicle sides with hydraulic latches. Revin speared the truck's steel wall high on the back quarter panel and attached a rappelling hook. Fresno followed him as Alexandre kept the vehicles parallel.

They'd honed this operation to a well-oiled mission that took less than three minutes. It was dangerous to do it on the freeway, where mortals cruised by in the opposite lanes. As long as no one tried to pass in the third lane, they were good.

The wolf driver struggled to keep the truck on the road. The dart wouldn't knock him out, but it would make him lethargic and blur his vision. Creed would not risk killing him—and a resultant crash—when the vampire was yet unclaimed in the back.

The other werewolf appeared from the passenger window and crawled on top of the truck's cab.

Expecting this, Creed levered himself up through his window and jumped atop their van. He snatched a row bar. His combat boots gripped firmly. A rappel hook would secure him to the van, but he didn't want to risk becoming entangled. His sense of balance was impeccable.

At the back, the vampires had already secured the fight's winner.

The werewolf, perched on the top of the truck, shot

Creed in the shoulder. It was a wooden bullet, he knew from the dull, piercing entrance. It wouldn't put him down.

Creed fired a dart that managed to skim the wolf's shoulder. The impact didn't even make the wolf jerk. Without a thought, Creed blew hard, utilizing his air magic. The incredible gust of wind sent the wolf stumbling backward. He toppled, but caught his fingers on the edge of the truck. He'd dropped the weapon.

Suddenly the werewolf, having shifted to beastly shape, lunged up and sprang for Creed. The hairy beast stretched through the air, momentarily suspended in an attack lunge between the two vehicles.

Creed did not vacillate between life and death. One sweep of Wolfsbane severed the werewolf's head and upper shoulders from the body. Both halves dropped onto the tarmac and tumbled toward the ditch.

The hooks were released from the back of the truck. The opponent's truck spun out into the ditch. Gripping the edge of the passenger door and sliding headfirst into the front seat, Creed righted himself. He swiped away blood from his face. Revolting to consider tasting it.

In the back, the captive vampire lolled, lethargic from a blood overdose. He reeked of sweat, fear and blood.

"Good job," Creed said to the team. He pressed two fingers below the wooden bullet stuck in his shoulder and eased it slowly from his flesh. "I'll call for cleanup to clear the body and debris from the road."

He flicked the bullet out the window. If it had landed in his heart it may have dropped him long enough for the wolf to plunge a thick stake into his heart, which could have killed him.

Vampires: one. Werewolves: zero.

BLU STUDIED THE WIGS she'd pulled from boxes this morning. The violet was Creed's favorite. She liked the green one. The white reminded her of that romantic night when they'd walked in the park surrounded by the heady scent of peonics.

And she'd thought to never have romance.

"Silly princess, some dreams do come true."

She touched the violet wig. Now it reminded her of the other night when she'd been so close to giving herself completely to her husband. She'd shared a dark part of herself with him. The secret that wasn't as much a secret amongst her father's men as a shared badge of honor.

Some honor. Not.

Creed had been so gentle and understanding, listening without judgment. At that moment she'd never wanted her vampire husband so desperately.

Until his fangs had flashed and had slashed through the mood like fangs through flesh.

Though Creed pleaded an inability to control them in her presence, rationally, she knew she would be safe. Irrationally, she wanted to stay at arm's distance from the potential threat of becoming forever marked.

She couldn't believe her father had sent the message through Ridge that he expected her to take the vampire's bite. He'd made it very clear before she set off on this adventure that she was merely to play the role, to convince the vampire she cared for him, but to never take his bite if she wished to return home.

Did Amandus no longer believe she would return to the pack at some point? And that if she were marked no wolf would ever have her?

Well, her father didn't have to know everything.

Couldn't the Council accept them having sex as a seal to the pact? It did represent an intimacy with one another no vampire or werewolf would take lightly.

Not that they'd completely had sex yet. They'd done everything but. She'd yet to take Creed inside her, to feel his thickness embody her. She wanted that. But not at the risk of being bitten.

Shouldn't a vampire nearly a millennium old be able to control his fangs by now?

Shoving the three wigs aside, she stroked her real hair forward. It hung to her shoulders and was the color of her mother's hair. A mother she missed with an aching soul.

Blu had been eleven when her mother, Persia Masterson, had disappeared from her life with no note, not even a goodbye. Her father had growled and said she'd gone off with another lover. That was the last he'd spoken of the enigma Blu wished was still in her life.

Was it true? Had her mother taken a lover? Why?

The *why not* was easy to rationalize. With a husband like Amandus, Blu suspected her mother had sought attention, perhaps even simple kindness from other men.

How could her mother abandon her like that? Truly, for a lover? And without word she was leaving? She tried not to think about her, because it simply brought tears.

They'd never been close, yet her mother had been the only other female werewolf in Blu's life. Left the sole pack female following her mother's disappearance, Blu had wanted to emulate her cool reserve around the males, but it hadn't been easy once Amandus had started giving her to his men.

Had she still been around, would her mother have protected Blu from the cruel treatment? It had only started after her mother was gone. Amandus had taken out his frustrations on his daughter, the spitting image of her mother.

Save the one time Ridge had pulled a drunk wolf off her, no one had ever protected Blu, so she'd developed her own methods of defense. She twirled a finger around the end of her hair. Creed had been so gentle with her hair. She'd wanted to cover him with it and linger in the safety of his embrace.

She did not hate the vampire. In fact, she might even...

She couldn't go there. Yet. Even though he'd taken her phone away, that didn't mean Ryan was not still on her mind.

"Rough, sexy werewolf that you are," she said with a sigh. He'd tugged her hair more than a few times, but he'd been more protective than rough. Most of the time. "That wolf never knows when he's gone too far."

Bruises on her wrists and hips were a common find after having sex with Ryan. But that was simply the way wolves were. Right?

And even after sex, when she lay sated and tousled, she could forgive Ryan his roughness. Because he was the only lover she'd known who didn't demand without then returning some kind of sexual favor. The other wolves had just taken and shoved her aside. And Ryan had promised to be her mate. To take her away from her father's men to another pack.

The new pack would never dream to use her as her father had. Ryan had promised escape, so she took the bad with the hopes of good.

Some good had come already. Escape of a sort had been achieved through an unexpected means. She was now another man's wife.

Ryan would rage if he were ever in the same room as Creed.

She wondered what Creed would do if approached by an angry werewolf who had been denied his mate? She'd never seen her husband in a fight. He was brawny and probably very capable. Hell, the way he'd controlled the sword had put her heart in her throat.

Could have been the name of it, too. Wolfsbane.

Blu shuddered.

But she thought of Creed more as a sensual lover than a fighter. And that kind of softer, yet still dominant, man was starting to appeal to her.

But come on, she wouldn't know a good thing if it slapped her.

"Creed would never slap me."

And instead of tears at the thought of her distant lover, she smiled a little. And then a lot. But the happiness was not because of Ryan.

Deciding to go wigless, she combed through the long strands of her mink-dark hair and pushed them over her shoulder. A red jersey dress slithered over her skin, resembling a swimsuit cover-up as it clung to all her curves and exposed a lot. Creed would like it.

But before she went looking for the hubby, she needed to check in with her father. Though she had decided not to tell Ridge about Creed's magic and the ring, she wanted to see if she could get any more info from Amandus.

The office was the only place she'd seen a phone, so she headed down the stairs. On the bar, a white envelope was propped against a full bottle of wine. Her name was scribbled on the envelope.

Blu tore it open. Out slid a black credit card with her name on it and a note. *Don't spend it all in one place.*

She knew the black card was only given to elite clients, and it had something like a million-dollar credit limit.

"Oh, baby. The vampire doesn't know what he's done. I won't spend it all in one place, Creed. That would be a crime, considering all the best stuff is spread out, and in Paris."

The man lived in France. So did that mean he'd take her to Paris someday?

"Christian Louboutin, here I come!" The designer shoes were on the top of her wish list.

Tucking the card back into the envelope, she went in search of her hubby to give him a hug that would probably become a kiss and then a lick, and then… Well, she was ready to go there.

The house was quiet. Housekeeper had left hours earlier after vacuuming and dusting. The new girl was similar to Malena. Young, Latina and polite. And she must know her employer was a vampire, because Blu figured there had to be blood on things occasionally. No vamp could be neat all the time.

On the other hand, he was taking his donors, as he called them, away from the estate.

She decided tomorrow she'd find out the new house-keeper's name and then relentlessly use it around Creed. She'd get the guy to warm to the hired help one way or another.

Her bare feet took the Berber carpet softly, but she slowed as she neared the office. The door was open a crack, and Creed's sexy, deep voice echoed out.

Pausing, Blu listened and got in on the middle of a phone conversation.

"The victim has been placed in the safe house? Good. I hope he survives. It wasn't the River pack? But I thought the Western pack— Hell, really? They were a long way from home. And headed in the wrong direction. Doesn't Dean Maverick lead that pack?"

Silence, then, "Seriously? Ryan has been seen with the pack?"

Blu sucked in her lip. Was he talking about her lover?

Ryan was supposed to be careful with his visits to Maverick. As scion of the Northern pack, it would not be tolerated for him to have contact with a rival pack. Her father would be outraged.

"Can we put a man or two on him? I don't want what

happened last night to occur any time soon. Especially with the peace pact under such scrutiny. Though don't get me wrong. Slicing that wolf's head from his body was gratifying."

Another pause. What had happened last night? she wondered. He'd killed a wolf?

Blu tilted her head and slid her hair behind an ear. Her hearing was good, but not acute enough to pick up the voice coming over the receiver. It had to be Alexandre, her hubby's second in command.

"It's going far better than we had hoped," Creed said. "No, no bite. But it may be unnecessary. Yes. Yes, I understand. No, I believe the werewolves will see their princess has accepted a vampire, and will surrender to the peace pact. I'm beginning to wish it were not a farce."

Blu stretched her shoulder along the wall, tracing the surface lightly with her fingertips. A farce? His conversation sounded so similar to the one she'd had in the van with Ridge.

"Yes, then when they're not looking, we attack. I'll be in contact. Goodbye, Alexandre."

We attack?

But that was— That could only mean—

Blu gripped her throat. The vampires were plotting against the werewolves?

No. Freaking. Way.

Blu kicked the door and stomped through the doorway. Fists forming, she couldn't immediately find words. But when she did, she shouted, "You bloody longtooth!"

Creed leaned over his desk, fists to the varnished wood. He had to know what she'd heard. "A good afternoon to you, wife. *Très bien?*"

"Ditch the French bullshit, longtooth. I heard what you said." She crossed to the desk and smashed a fist near his. "The vampires are plotting against us?"

"Now, Blu—"

"Tell me the truth!" Her voice screeched when she got angry. She hated that.

"Blu, I don't think it's wise."

"No, look at me. Tell me it isn't true." She beat a fist on his shoulder and when he turned to wrangle her wrists, she repeatedly pounded angry fists at his shoulders and chest. "You've been tricking me this whole time? That's not fair!"

She kicked his shin and broke from his grasp. Creed groaned at the painful placement of her heel but didn't race after her.

Stalking the other side of the desk, she hissed and let out a frustrated squeal. "I can't believe I was duped! I should have been smarter."

"Blu, this has nothing to do with my feelings toward you."

"Bullshit! It's all a lie. The intimacy. The kisses. The attention you've been showing me."

"No, it's not."

"You're a liar. I know it's all a farce because it's been so since the beginning. The wolves are doing the same thing. This was never to result in a peaceful ending. So there you go, the Huguenots are going to kick the Catholics' asses!"

He whipped her around, gripping her shoulder so tightly she winced. "What? The wolves are plotting, too?"

"Let me go."

"No. I want to hear this," he growled. "So you're telling me it's all been a lie on your part?"

She hadn't meant to blurt that out, but damn it, now she was angry. Was all this work to end because the vampires would beat the werewolves to the punch?

"A farce," she blurted out. "A lie to convince the vampires they could trust my breed. And then when they're not looking...?" She punched a fist into her palm.

"So you and I?" Creed shook her by the shoulders. The intensity of his ferocious gaze frightened her. The glint of Wolfsbane on the wall backed up his threat. "Has this been nothing?"

Through her anger, Blu had a momentary thought.

No, it's meant everything to me. But instead answered, "I guess so."

"I refuse to believe that." He swung her around and pushed her against the wall. Her shoulders hit roughly. The sword clanked on the hooks. "Tell me what you know. What is your father plotting?"

"I'll let you run me through with the sword before I'll tell you that."

"Damn it!" He shoved her and stepped away, pacing to the desk. There, he swept a hand across the surface. Papers and folders flew through the air and scattered.

"Do you think I wanted this?" she countered.

"Of course not, you were pushed!" he said mockingly. "You know nothing."

"And you know more than I could have imagined."

"Bloodsucking longtooth."

"Deceptive hound."

She hung her head.

"I didn't expect this," Creed said.

Blu chuffed. "No shit."

All this time the vampires had been plotting against the wolves? Had her father anticipated this? He couldn't have, or else he would have informed her to protect her back.

Then again, Amandus never told her everything she needed to know. Pack females weren't allowed to know any more than that they were in this world to serve and be used.

She had been a pawn.

"Blu, you don't understand." Creed turned to her. "I didn't expect to fall in love with you."

CHAPTER ELEVEN

BLU SUCKED IN HER lower lip. Why did it tremble at the sight of Creed's steady gaze? Of that sure promise in his dark eyes? Eyes she'd once been frightened of, but now only wanted to lose herself in.

Men weren't supposed to be true to her. To want anything emotional from her.

To say things like *I love you,* and mean it.

And this one! He had been betraying her since day one.

As she had betrayed him.

It wasn't in her nature to give herself to a man. They were simply big hunks of flesh and blood to be tolerated, appeased.

And yet, she could go there. Step up to the same dais Creed stood on, toss aside the stupid flowers and shout what she was really feeling. Because, in her heart, she believed what he'd just said to her.

She huffed out an exhalation. Damn it, there was no beating this man. "I love you, too."

Their breaths thundered between them. Two souls forced together, colliding against their differences and surfacing in a new and wondrous pairing.

She did love the vampire.

This had nothing to do with being secretive or betraying his trust. Blu loved Creed's gentleness. His austere simplicity. His chivalric need to protect her. His devotion to his tribe and the entire vampire nation. His darkness, and the clean lines of his body and face. His kisses and touches.

And his honesty in the midst of forced betrayal.

"Creed." Her voice trembled, as did her body. "Both sides want to slaughter the other. We're standing at the vanguard. I…I feel so small, so helpless to control the outcome. What will we do?"

He considered the question. Then, decisive, he offered, "We'll stand together. It is all we can do. Will you be my ally, Blu?"

"Yes." She nodded, knowing the answer could be nothing but. "Yes."

He rushed to her and the kiss was a collision of differences. Atoms smashing and rejoining in midair. The world dropped away. The war between the werewolves and vampires misted to nothing.

There was only them. The two of them stranded as collateral damage amidst a dangerous undertaking.

Blu moaned at the sweet pain of her lover's kiss. How desperately she wanted to hold it forever. To claim it as a war prize.

She tore at his shirt. Buttons popped and she fumbled with the diamond cuff links. The priceless jewels dropped at their feet.

She stepped into him, pushing him backward until his thighs collided with the desk. He pushed back. They hit the wall roughly. He slapped a hand to the sword to steady it and keep it from dropping. The red dress he pulled over her head, baring her to him.

Creed stepped back and she realized then that it was possible to look drunk with desire. The assessing look he gave her made her proud to stand in his gaze. Only for him.

"You are my wife," he commanded. "And I will have you now."

"Yes." She gripped his pants and unzipped him. His kisses trekked over her breasts and up her neck. A fine-pointed hardness skimmed along her jaw. His fangs had descended. "Creed, no."

"Yes." He forced her shoulders to the wall. Parting his lips, he revealed his fully extended fangs. "Look at them. See what you do to me? Arousal brings down my fangs, but I can normally control it. But you, Blu, you bring them down without volition. I cannot prevent it. You control me."

She was about to protest, but he opened his mouth wider. The deadly fangs looked so sharp one prick would open her vein and start the blood flowing.

She controlled him? It sounded ludicrous. Women couldn't control men.

"I know you don't want my bite. I will not bite you, Blu. I swear it. Not unless you ask for it."

"I would never. I don't want your mark. Or the blood hunger that would result."

"Understood. And you must understand, I desperately want to taste your blood, but I don't *need* to. Accept that I cannot control them going down."

"I make it happen?"

"Yes, you've such power over me." He kissed her softly on the chin. Her nipples skimmed his bared chest. "How does that make you feel?"

She hushed out a sigh, then gripped his shoulder. "Powerful."

"No blood drinking, I promise. Will you trust me?"

She nodded. She could trust him. More than she'd ever trusted any other male.

"Then prove it," he said. "Kiss me."

On his mouth? With his fangs proudly bared?

FREE BOOK OFFER

To get you started, we'll send you
a FREE book and a FREE gift

There's no catch, everything is **FREE**

Accepting your **FREE** book and **FREE** mystery gift
places you under no obligation to buy anything.

Be part of the Mills & Boon® Book Club™ and receive your favourite Series
books up to 2 months before they are in the shops and delivered straight to
your door. Plus, enjoy a wide range of **EXCLUSIVE** benefits!

- Best new women's fiction – delivered right to
  your door with FREE P&P
- Avoid disappointment – get your books up to
  2 months before they are in the shops
- No contract – no obligation to buy

We hope that after receiving you free book you'll
want to remain a member. But the choice is yours.
So why not give us a go? You'll be glad you did!

Visit **millsandboon.co.uk** to stay up to date
with offers and to sign-up for our newsletter

FREE book
and a
FREE gift

DETACH AND POST CARD TODAY!

T0JIA

Mrs/Miss/Ms/Mr _____ Initials _____

BLOCK CAPITALS PLEASE

Surname _____

Address _____

_____

Postcode _____

Email _____

MILLS & BOON®

NO STAMP NEEDED!

MILLS & BOON®
Book Club

FREE BOOK OFFER
FREEPOST NAT 10298
RICHMOND
TW9 1BR

NO STAMP
NECESSARY
IF POSTED IN
THE U.K. OR N.I.

If offer card is missing write to: The Mills & Boon® Book Club™, PO Box 676, Richmond, TW9 1WU

It wasn't the sight of his fangs that frightened her. Gods, hers were as long, but thicker, made for tearing meat. And she'd seen him bite the man in the club, and had found that erotic. Then the sight of his fangs had actually turned her on.

Could she kiss him now?

Reaching up, Blu slid a finger along one of Creed's canine teeth. He sneered, drawing back his lip, but allowed her the exploratory touch. It was pretty, monstrous. Yet she'd watched him take blood. It was his means to survival, his connection to life.

The longtooth was no longer repulsive. Because she had begun to understand him.

Her body was weak for him. Her heartbeat thundered behind her naked breasts. Despite the devastating discovery that the vampires were plotting against her kind, all that mattered right now was the two of them. Alone. Wanting to be complete with one another.

She needed her husband inside her. She craved the intimate claiming.

Blu plunged into the kiss. Fangs skimmed the curve of her lip but did not cut. She went so far as to tease her tongue along the hard column of one of them.

"Blu," he moaned into her mouth. "*Dieu,* that's amazing that you can accept me." Lifting her against the wall, he slid a hand between her thighs. "So ready for me."

"Come inside me, lover. Claim me." She shucked down his pants past his hips. "Take your wife."

She wrapped her legs around his hips and he entered in one forceful glide. So thick, he stretched her. Filled her. Impaled her upon him and against the wall beneath the sword that had slain hundreds of her kind.

Blu slapped out her arms, clawing into the wall.

"You are so tight," he gasped. "Made for me. I can't wait."

Already he shuddered against her. The delicious prelude to what would be a stunning climax. He moved quickly, his length dragging at her clitoris and tweaking her better senses with every inch that he gave her.

"Deeper, Creed. Lose yourself in me."

He moaned, hilting himself into her. The sharp canines rubbed her lower lip. She dashed out her tongue to touch the deadly weapons.

"Now," he groaned deeply. "Now you are mine."

Cleaving to him—yes, clinging—she released her tense muscles and surrendered as he cried out in triumph. A melty release wilted her against his chest, the slick muscles pulsing with his climax. Every part of him twitched and dazzled at their joining. He was alive and hers.

All hers.

"No regrets?" he whispered, breath huffing upon her mouth.

"Not a one."

They would have to face the reality of their futures soon. But not now. Not for this day.

"Take me to bed, husband."

"THIS ROOM IS HUGE."

Creed laid Blu on his bed and shrugged out of his shirt. But one button had survived her ravaging. Feisty princess.

"Told you you'd be missing something." Sliding off his pants, he kicked them aside.

"It's like a Parisian boudoir. But manly." Blu stretched her arms across the lavish bedspread and curved her body luxuriously as if a goddess demanding worship. "I can't believe I didn't peek in here earlier."

"You mean snoop."

"Don't throw stones, Secretive Vampire Dude."

"Admonishment taken, Undercover Werewolf Princess."

The things they had learned about the other, about their respective pack and tribe. Creed didn't want to think on it now. Not with a raging hard-on and the intense desire to nibble on his wife.

"So if you had snooped—er, *peeked*—" he said, "would that have seen you in my bed sooner?"

Climbing on the bed, he bent over her body. He melted his gaze along her stomach and bent to lick her nipples, hard, sweet jewels he toggled with his tongue.

"Maybe. It's all so detailed and rich. The tassels on the bed canopy, the paintings and the Aubusson rug. Is that an original Renoir?"

"Of course. A friend, actually."

"No shit? Oh, snap, this is a dream!"

She stretched her arms over the half-dozen goose-down pillows and sighed dramatically. "You know how to live large, I gotta admit that."

Creed pulled her hips up and nuzzled his face against her flesh to worship her. Pointing his tongue firmly, he traced her inner curves and explored her wetness. She squiggled happily and moaned those delicious throaty moans that rumbled in his heart.

Mon Dieu, he loved the sounds of her pleasure. He had taken a wolf to his bed. His wolf.

"You do that so well," she drawled as she slid her fingers through his hair. "Your teeth aren't down anymore."

Charmed at her awareness, Creed swiped his tongue across his teeth. She was right. He hadn't realized they'd risen.

Whatever it was about her that made his teeth react, he couldn't be concerned right now. The sexy, dark, sweet taste of her frenzied him. He had to have all of her. Deeply, sucking, teasingly. She whimpered hungrily as each lash of his tongue found new ways to please her.

Sheets gripped in her hands just to the side of his head,

he watched as his attentions slowly worked her fingers looser. Then she'd clutch again. And finally her fingers spread and slid over the bed.

Her climax sweetened his tongue. He drank her as he would at the neck. But this sweetness was a treat he did not need for survival, only pleasure.

As she cried out, he moved up alongside her and nestled his face into her long black hair. Blu tilted her head and bit down on his neck.

She did not break skin. Her teeth were not sharp enough. Yet the exquisite pain of it, pinching his vein, exploded within him. Taken by the surprising clutch, Creed's climax started first in his brain—she was biting him, giving him something he'd revealed was the ultimate in pleasure—and then he plunged himself inside her and filled her with his seed.

Her fingernails dug into his shoulder. Blu's teeth slid over his flesh. The pain of it heightened his orgasm, expanding it beyond the usual. He tremored, coming wickedly.

Nothing with his werewolf princess would ever again be usual.

HOURS LATER, Blu posed at the end of the bed. She gripped the bedpost and wiggled her derriere. Her lover, who'd taken a break in the bathroom, returned and clamped his hands to her hips to take her from behind.

"Mmm, I like it this way," she cooed as he entered her to the hilt. "I can feel all of you, deep inside."

He massaged his palms up her spine, slick with perspiration. "I could feel your teeth on my neck earlier."

"I didn't break skin, but it was a sort of bite. Did you like it?"

"Christ, Blu." His exhale, a guttural sigh, blended with a moan.

"I'll take that as a like."

"Don't ever pause should you want to bite me, just know that."

"I won't. I like to give you pleasure."

"This tattoo…" His fingers traced the intricate lines on her back as he pumped lazily inside her. "Tell me about it."

"It's just a design."

"That means you don't want to tell. Pretty girls like you don't put any old design on their bodies. It has to mean something. You said—"

"It's a symbol related to the pack." A claiming mark. "Ryan inked it." It meant little to her at this moment, so she didn't want to discuss it.

Creed drew his hand over her breasts and along her throat, directing her to stand against him, his cock still deep inside her. He dropped a kiss to her shoulder, and then he smoothed over her throat. "Someday you will wear my mark."

He said it as truth.

And Blu said the first words that came to mind. "Yes, someday."

"OH, SNAP, WILL YOU look at this shower?"

Blu's lover hugged up behind her as she stood at the massive shower entrance. His erection pressed into her derriere. She couldn't get enough of it and his need to always rub it against her skin, so she wiggled to encourage him to press harder.

"It's huge," she purred. "The shower, too. I think it's the size of my bedroom at the compound."

"Sea glass imported from Venice," he said of the indigo and pale green tiles.

"It seems to glow. Looks like pieces from a stained-glass window, with the sunlight captured in it." She stroked the smooth tiles. They were small, about two inches square.

Creed stepped inside and turned on the water, adjusting the complicated dial. "The pipes are stretched the entire surface overhead. I can make it like a rain shower, if you like."

"Sex in the rain?" She traced a finger up his thigh, and then higher. His cock bobbed expectantly. "You know I like the rain."

When the water fell in gentle droplets from the ceiling, she tilted her head to catch it on her face.

Creed kissed her chin. He slicked his palms over her breasts. The warm rain beat in rhythm to her heart.

"This is magical."

"It's just a shower." He kissed her, but she pressed him back. He gripped the steel bar overhead, groaning when she palmed his erection.

"It's us, Creed. We're magical, don't you think?"

"The wolf and vamp thing? I suppose something like that. But I didn't use my magic to coerce you, I promise."

"I know you didn't. I've never felt coerced with you. This is so much more than anything I can imagine. I feel so different in your arms. Like the world slips away and I've no worries. It's just the two of us."

"That is magical," he said. "I'll take that, and I'll raise you a wondrous."

"Remarkable."

Cupping her breasts, he leaned forward to catch the spatter of raindrops against his mouth. "Breathtaking."

She opened his mouth with her fingers and traced his teeth. "Dangerous."

"Danger can be erotic."

He followed her lead as she pressed down on his teeth and directed his mouth to her breast. The tugging and licking at her nipple zinged through her system. Every time his teeth grazed her flesh it rocketed her desire to orbit—yet also pricked at her fear.

Because he could bite her. With fangs. And Blu wasn't sure she'd deny him when it happened.

She'd not purposely bitten him earlier. It had been something done in the heat of the moment. And when he'd groaned to encourage her to bite harder, she had. But she hadn't used her fangs. Not yet. She didn't want to taste blood.

Maybe.

So much had changed since she and Creed had become intimate. She still knew little about him. What exactly did a tribe leader do? What were all the important papers in his office for? Where had he been the other night when he'd returned home with Wolfsbane, a sword he'd said he hadn't used for centuries? What about his magic? Would he ever think to control her with it? Would he ever take her to Paris?

But when he touched her, those questions fell away. It was as though he were reading her, learning her more intimately than any other had.

That meant a lot to Blu. That he was not rough. That her pleasure remained fore in his mind. That he loved her.

This man actually loved her. How incredible was that?

The intrusion of his fingers between her legs prompted her up on her tiptoes. She clung to his wet shoulders, not wanting to slip. Wanting to give him the best access to her.

"Hold the bar on the wall," he said.

So that was why that bar was so high. There were a few other bars, at varying levels on each of the three shower walls.

"You're quite the Casanova," she said as he knelt before her. She put one foot up on his shoulder. "How many women have those fingers explored? Anyone famous?"

He stroked her quickly, making it difficult to concentrate. But she was curious. "You've walked through history, Creed. I want a name. One name you've had sex with."

And then she gasped as orgasm captured her. He'd mastered her body this night. He could bring her to orgasm with a few flicks of his fingers, or guide her through a long and lip-biting session that had her screaming for more.

Shivering with the rush of pleasure, she bent forward to grasp her husband's back. Clawing softly over his flesh, she poked him with one nail. "One name."

"Watch the claws. Okay, okay." Holding her beneath the rain, he rose and stroked the slick hair from her face. "Marie Antoinette," he said. "Famous enough for you?"

"No way. Seriously? That's so cool."

He smirked. "She was young, and her ineffectual husband ignored her for much of the early years in their marriage. She was surrounded by a lavish and doting court, and yet, she was so lonely."

"You made her less lonely?"

"For a night."

"Were you sad when she went to the guillotine?"

"I was out of the country. On to new things, new adventures. But yes, I'm always sad to see an innocent punished."

"So she was the only famous one?"

He shrugged. "No. The only one worth remembering though, save a few vampiress lovers."

"I bet the blood flies when you have sex with another vampire."

"The mess is minimal. You don't want to discuss my old lovers while we've this rain shower to share, do you?"

"You owed me one. I told you about mine."

"Then we are even. No more talk of lovers. Mmm, that's the perfect grip."

She turned her fingers about the head of his cock and rubbed firmly on the underside where he was most sensitive. There, the thick vein pulsed. Blu knelt and took her lover into her mouth.

Above her head, he slapped his palms to the slick wall and growled. "Blu…" Her name whimpered out. Pleading her to control him as she wished.

She cupped his testicles and squeezed gently. It took only minutes to bring him to climax. The mighty vampire lord surrendered with a throaty cry.

He drew her into a hug. "I love it when you swallow me."

"I love it when you love me."

CHAPTER TWELVE

BLU LEANED AGAINST the bathroom wall, naked, wet from the shower.

"You know, Bree was the only one who ever believed this could work."

"The faery?" Creed kissed her stomach. A slick of his hot tongue licked the water droplets there.

"Yeah. That chick is so smart."

It was two days until the full moon and Blu was already beginning to feel the changes within her. Changes that manifested as being majorly horny.

Sex was important to a werewolf. More so for the female. During the full moon was the only time the female could get pregnant. Blu's body was preparing her for the event.

But she couldn't get pregnant by a vampire. The werewolf was *born* a wolf, whereas vampires were *created* from humans; the two didn't jibe. Sure there were some rare born vampires, but Creed had told her of his creation. So as a vampire's wife, she could embrace the need for sex heartily, with little fear of consequences.

She wasn't the motherly sort. Not yet, anyway. She had a few decades of partying to do first. Sex with no worry of getting pregnant? That so rocked.

Creed, slick and steamy from the hot shower, pressed his forehead to hers, their fingers entwined.

"What are we going to do?" he asked.

The question had nothing to do with the moon, and everything to do with the expectations of their mutual nations. Reality had a way of pulling the rug out from under all the fun.

"I don't know. You tell me, husband."

"I can't be the one to tell you to do something that may have an effect on your family and pack."

He was so kind that way. Any other man would have demanded she do this or that to make it all go *his* way.

Creed was as alpha as any wolf, and yet, he wielded power and strength much more humanely.

"What will you do?" she asked. "Inform on the werewolves?"

He smirked. "We've an incredible secret, don't we? I'm not so keen on reporting back to Nava with this info. On the other hand, I've never betrayed them before. As tribe leader I owe them complete honesty. Blu, I must tell you straight out. I don't want war. And yet part of me relishes the idea of drawing Wolfsbane against a pack of snarling werewolves."

She shivered, but not because of his honesty. She'd come to understand Creed. He was a man of intention and integrity. No man was perfect, hence his inability to keep a vow about not using magic. And that he was split regarding this issue only meant he was not perfect, and that like anyone else, he could see two sides to everything. Even if one side was not in favor of her breed.

"I don't understand my father," she said. "I've heard him rant about vampires over the years, but that's normal. Just his deal, you know? Never had I expected he'd want war. There's something about him I'm missing. The reason behind his need to send me to the vanguard, to, well…to sacrifice me for some greater cause."

He kissed her arm, his mouth lingering. The ends of his hair tickled her breasts. "Do you feel you've been sacrificed?"

"The night of our wedding I did. Oh, man, I felt like I was walking into hell to wed the devil Himself."

"Please, don't bring up his name. We don't want any unwelcome visitors."

"Sorry. But now, I find it hard to believe being forced into your arms was as terrible as I'd expected. Do you think we can change the minds of both the pack and the tribe? If they know we are in love? Do you even want to?"

"I do want to. For you. For us. The original plan—lie that it was—was to set the example everyone thought we were supposed to set, and both nations fall into hugs and kisses and sing peace, love and happiness."

"That'll never happen," she said.

"Yeah, I don't think so either. But love was never mentioned."

"It could be the thing to unite us all."

She stroked the side of his neck, knowing he loved any touch to his sensitive veins.

"But how do you think they'll react to seeing us happy together?" she wondered aloud. "Should we go to the banquet and be ourselves? Stop playing the game and show them we do love one another?"

"It could be dangerous. But that's what I want more than anything, Blu. For the world to know I love and honor you. *Mon Dieu*, I could never imagine doing harm to your family either. But this war exists no matter what we say or do."

"It's been going on for some time."

"Yes, but unless we can stop it, it's going to come to a bloody head."

"That's a lot on our shoulders."

"No shit." He turned and paced to the center of the bathroom.

The steamy room smelled like soap, heat and sex. His broad shoulders flexed and water glistened on his tight ass.

Blu licked her lips. Round four, anyone?

"Well, Mr. Tribal Leader, what do you suggest? You must have experience."

"Experience with a coup like this?" He wobbled his head side to side and made a face, a funny little motion Blu associated with Frenchmen. "Once only, in the twelfth century when I served Philippe Auguste in a battle against the Burgundians. We tracked the invasion along the Seine. After my war days I worked as a bounty hunter. Singular stuff that did not involve such a large tactical scale. It's been so long, Blu. Now my tribal duties involve reprimanding strayed tribal members and rescuing independents from blood matches."

"You rescue vampires from the blood sport? I didn't know that."

He splayed a hand before him. "Someone has to do it. Your breed is as bloodthirsty as mine. Only we do it for survival, not for sport."

Blu clasped her arms across her chest. She'd been to one blood match, and only because Ryan had forced her to "have some fun with him," as he'd put it. It had been the most despicable thing she had ever witnessed.

Creed really was the knight in shining armor she'd initially mocked.

Now? She would stand proudly in his shadow and watch him protect, as his mien demanded. She'd not known integrity before, and now it absolutely glowed at her.

"I'm proud of you," she said. "What you do, rescuing the vampires. It takes courage."

"Thank you. But you must know, when I told you I had not wielded Wolfsbane in vengeance for centuries, I meant just that."

She shrugged.

"Self-defense is different from vengeance. I had to strike a wolf dead the other night to save one of my own."

"I see." Blu winced. One of her own had fallen. For some reason she couldn't get as upset as she felt she should. If he had threatened Creed, then she was thankful the survivor was her husband. "You're still very courageous."

"I just hope to summon the courage to keep you in my arms forever. I could go before the tribe and talk to them," he said. "Feel them out. Tribe Nava has been plotting with Zmaj against the werewolves for years. This was an opportunity we jumped on. I'm as much to blame as the wolves."

"But you've changed your mind now. That's what matters."

"Yes. But, Blu, I'm not sure if I can change the minds of dozens of vampires, some with a blood debt for lost loved ones they believe the wolves must pay."

And to change the wolves' minds? They'd lost entire generations to the vampires. The very reason the females were so rare was due to the systematic hunt and destruction of wolves by vampires in the mid-twentieth century.

"Well, I'm no help. A female wolf could never tell the males what to do. It just isn't done." She sat on the vanity stool outside the shower and propped her elbows on her knees. "I wish my mother were still around. She'd know what to do."

"Where is she? Was she at the wedding?"

Blu shrugged. "She left when I was little. Daddy said she ran off with a lover. I think it was a lie. But I miss her, no matter what. It hurts to think about her."

Creed kissed her on the forehead. "Family is good."

"Not if your family is plotting to kill your new husband's family. Maybe if we moved to Russia and secluded ourselves away?"

Creed glowered.

"I know. I couldn't do the snow thing for long. And I'd stick out like a sore thumb amongst the babushkas."

"You and your purple hair. I think you should go purple here." He knelt before her and kissed her mons. His hot breath traveled her flesh, tickling up to her breasts.

"Really? On the landing strip? It'd be too much work. Wigs are easy."

"They did pubic wigs in the seventeenth or eighteenth century. I don't recall which."

"Wigs for the bush? Oh, that kills me. Besides, I like being natural for you. You like me this way?"

"I adore you this way. Here." He kissed her short hairs. "And here." He stroked the ends of her tresses spilled slickly over her breast. "This long black hair is magnificent. I like when it sweeps over my skin and sends tingles through me." He parted her legs and lightly thumbed her.

"How did you get started rescuing vampires from the sporting warehouses?"

His motion stopped, but he didn't remove his finger. "They captured a woman I felt very strongly about once."

"You loved her?"

"I couldn't say it was love, but probably if we'd had more time together it could have become so. I'd known her a few months. Her name was Rachel."

"How was she captured?"

"Not sure. I thought she was away with family, when Alexandre called me after a rescue mission. They'd rescued Rachel, near death. By the time I made it to her side, she had but a few breaths left." He pressed his cheek to her leg and met her eyes. "Rachel's death only fanned the fire I have held toward the wolves and their damned sporting matches."

"You did what was right." Blu stroked his cheek, and

he closed his eyes to her gentle touch. "What would you do for me?"

"I would kill for you."

"I don't want you to do that."

"It is in my blood, Blu. I am a man who solves problems by the swing of a blade."

"Yet you just said you wanted this to work. Us. The vampires and the werewolves. Can you…change? For me?"

"I want to. I have changed. I just need to stay on course."

"You said you wanted to atone."

"For the witches. That has nothing to do with the werewolves. Let's play it by ear, shall we? We'll go to the banquet, and let everyone see it's possible to join the two nations. And then…"

"Don't expect me to report to you with info from the enemy."

"Nor will I give you details of whatever comes of it all. Though I hate to keep anything from you." He slid his finger rhythmically in and out of her.

Blu tilted her head against the wall, relaxing her shoulders, devouring his lazy attention.

"Anything could happen. I don't want to lose you," she said. She bit her lower lip and her heartbeat increased as her body subtly shivered at his ministrations. "But I may yet. The full moon is in two nights."

"And yet you haven't told me what to expect. Should I leave you alone for the night? Do you need to be…?"

"Locked up?"

He offered a helpless shrug. "I want to know all of you, Blu."

"I don't want to explain things, because it's too…odd. And truthfully? I'm not completely sure of it all. The wolf mind overwhelms the human mind, you know? Suffice it to say, I'm different from the males. During the full moon, they wolf out and become a beast that seeks to hunt and have sex. Me, well, I sort of go into heat."

"You need sex?"

"Yes," she gasped as the imminent orgasm crept slowly through her body. "And no. It's like I want it, but I don't either. It's the only day during the month that a female can get pregnant. And yet, she doesn't like to make it easy for any male."

"I'll be here for you. Unless you…need a wolf?"

"I don't know. I've never had a vampire lover before. I suspect the werewolf part of me won't be too thrilled with you. Ingrained aversion to longtooth, you know."

"Do you change? Become something that isn't like you now?"

"Not like the males. They get all stretched and muscled and hairy."

"You said you liked hair."

"I've had a change of heart." She stroked his smooth jaw, and he kissed above where his finger still fondled her clitoris. "But it's definitely a different part of me. I know what I am at that moment, and yet, the werewolf takes over and well…I've never gotten all the way."

"You mean…?"

"I mean no werewolf has ever brought me to the edge during the full moon, so I'm not really sure what happens then. You'll just have to see. And I want you to see. I need you to see."

"I wouldn't be anywhere else."

"Promise me you won't be offended by whatever I do or say. My werewolf may not like you at all."

He kissed her mons and resumed a steady pace. "Promise."

"Oh, Creed."

Blu succumbed to a quiet climax that wilted her and made her liquid like the steam dribbling down the walls.

ALEXANDRE AND CREED shared a beer and whisky as Blu sashayed down the stairs. She kissed her husband and wandered into the kitchen.

She easily heard Alexandre. "She's so hot, man. Seriously? A werewolf?"

"You should try new things," Creed said. "A change of breeds might surprise you."

Wearing a proud smirk, Blu took the milk from the fridge and tilted the carton back, gulping the cold liquid.

"You know I love Veronica, man," Alexandre said. "We've new information on the rescue the other night."

She paused. Creed had mentioned rescuing vampires from blood matches, and that he had killed a wolf.

What pack was holding blood sport in the cities? Couldn't be hers. Her father would flip.

"We got a name on the one who put the match together. Near as I can figure, he's responsible for the last three matches we've rescued for."

Blu crept to the swinging kitchen doors, milk carton tucked to her chest. Closing her eyes, she tilted her head to listen.

"You're not going to like it," Alexandre said. "It's Eugene."

Squeezing the plastic carton exploded milk from the spout. It splashed her leg and toes. Blu swore.

"Something wrong, Blu?" Creed called out.

"Yeah." She fisted the door, stalked out and slammed the carton on the bar. "You two talking about Ryan?"

"Eugene Ryan," Alexandre said. "He's been organizing the blood matches around town."

"No way. My father would never allow it. The Northern pack does not run blood sport, they just don't."

"We received trustworthy information on this guy."

"He wouldn't." She looked to Creed for rescue from the other vampire's insidious accusations. "You've got the wrong wolf. Ryan may be an uncouth behemoth, but he doesn't do the blood sport."

Alexandre thumbed his chin. "How many werewolves are named Eugene, Lady Saint-Pierre?"

"Blu, the information comes from a reliable snitch," Creed explained calmly.

She tugged from his touch. What was Ryan up to? And how could her father not be aware if he were running blood sport?

"So what are you going to do?" she asked softly. "Kill him?"

"We don't murder wolves, Blu." He met her defiant stare. Earlier he'd confessed to that very wicked deed. "Not unless given no other option. We rescue the vampires your pack has starved for months and forces to fight for their lives."

"Not my pack. His information isn't right. I know it. Ryan would never—" She hated the condescending glare Alexandre pinned on her. And she, looking a pitiful mess with the milk all over. "You can't hurt him, Creed."

"I'm not sure what we're going to do yet. Can we discuss this later? Alexandre and I have strategizing to do."

At once, she felt small and controlled. A familiar feeling she had thought to abandon living with Creed.

She pushed past him and rushed up the stairs.

"Touchy," Alexandre said. "Must be that time of the month. Oh, right, the full moon soon. Yikes, man."

Bastard. Blu slammed the guest bedroom door shut and beat the bed and muffled a scream into the pillows.

Had she given Creed her trust too quickly?

AFTER ALEXANDRE LEFT, Creed was heading up the stairs to check on Blu when the doorbell rang. He redirected his path. The air-conditioning technician had arrived to install his goods. Creed took him around back and they found the best place to locate the unit. He left the technician in the basement, tinkering with the ventilation system, and caught Blu as she was walking out the front door.

"Do you mind if I take the BMW?" she asked, dangling the keys she could have only taken from his top desk drawer.

"Of course not, but I wish you'd told me you were going somewhere. You might be followed."

"Nah. I'm good at the evasive."

She was dressed unusually today with a straight peach wig and subdued gray skirt and white blousy top. She looked ready to sit behind a computer and type away the day—if not for the fishnet stockings.

"What's up?"

"Hmm? Oh, I'm headed to the mall. Need some new

things. I suppose I should break in that shiny black credit card you gave me."

"I thought you wanted to talk about Ryan?"

"I do, but it can wait until later. Is Alexandre still around?" A glance outside spied the technician's van. "Oh, the air-conditioning guy is here! I'm so ready for some cool air." She leaned in to kiss Creed's cheek. "See you later, lover."

Creed puzzled why her exit was rushed, almost evasive. She'd gone from raging over his knowledge of Ryan's involvement in the blood matches, to a shopping frenzy.

"Women."

CHAPTER THIRTEEN

THE STRIP MALLS IN this suburb offered nothing of interest to Blu. For maximum shopping pleasure, she'd have to drive to Minneapolis to satisfy her fashion cravings on Nicollet Avenue. But she didn't have cravings today.

At the edge of the Otsego suburb, a line of two-year-old condominiums fronted in redbrick, each with two-point-five trees per yard and bright red flowers near the steps, advertised idyllic domestic life.

Boring stuff, but the perfect hideout for a werewolf.

Parking the BMW before the condo with the weeds growing knee-high in the front yard, Blu marched to the door and knocked. She scanned the neighboring houses, alert for twitching curtains. No one watched.

For Sale signs dotted every other yard. The housing crisis had hit the newer developments hard. She stood in a literal ghost town.

It took a while before she heard thumps inside. Someone stumbling out of bed, stubbing his toe on the stair rail and swearing loudly.

Nothing had changed in the weeks she'd been away. He'd always been a late sleeper, and ever lazy about tending the yard. Had she actually mowed the lawn for the guy?

The door opened to reveal a man she couldn't muster a smile for now. Try as she might to summon an iota of lust for the muscled physique and ripped abs, she couldn't do it. She had no interest in Eugene Ryan. Save getting to the truth.

"As I live and breathe," Ryan said. He shoved a hand over his bald head, then slid it down his rock-hard abs. "Blu Masterson. You finally find your way from that longtooth's lair? Come here."

He reached for her, but reared back and snarled viciously. "You smell like a fucking longtooth."

"Yeah? So what did you expect?" She strolled inside and he stepped back out of disgust. "I do live with the guy."

The real disgust was this condo. She didn't remember him being such a sloth. Of course, she had done the laundry, vacuuming and all the cooking.

"You reek like vampire. Hell, sweetie, come upstairs and take a shower with me."

"Don't think so. I'm not here to suck face."

"Blu, what the hell?"

He grabbed for her arm, but she dodged him and pressed her back to the wall. Growling lowly, she surprised herself with the evasive reaction. Two weeks ago she would have endured Ryan's machismo.

"What's with you? Don't tell me you like the guy?"

"Creed is not the topic of this conversation," she said. "The fact that you've been going behind my father's back and organizing blood matches is."

"What? Where'd you hear something whacked like that? Blu, that's not my scene."

"Isn't it?"

She roamed her gaze around the room. The distinct odor of blood put her off. It was not a scent she expected in a werewolf's home. She didn't want to believe he was involved, but why would Creed lie to her?

"You've been talking to Dean Maverick's pack?" she asked.

"You know I have. It's for the both of us. Your father will never step down and allow me to lead."

"And Maverick is thinking of going lone wolf on his pack?"

"In a few months." Not a very sure answer. "We'll be made, Blu. I'll become leader of the Western pack, and you'll be my girl."

"But I'll reek of longtooth. How will you have me then?"

"Sweetie." He tugged her to him and she stood in his arms, mostly because he was too strong for her to struggle free. "Where's a kiss for the only man who loves you?"

"I thought my smell disgusted you?"

"I don't notice it much now. Come on, kiss me."

She put up her fingers to block his kiss, which was the wrong thing to do.

Ryan could slip into rage mode in half a second. He shoved her against the wall and pounded the wall above her shoulder. Fangs descending, he snarled.

"I gotta know you still love me, Blu. Don't do this to me. You'd better not be sleeping with that vampire."

"Sleeping? Not so much." Who had time when sex lasted through the night?

The punch to her gut was not unexpected. Blu took it and rolled aside, putting distance between them by stepping around behind the easy chair. "I don't like being your punching bag anymore, Ryan."

"Blu, I'm sorry. I didn't mean to. You know how to push my buttons."

"Yeah, like the homicidal maniac button?"

"I hate you like this! If I see that vampire…"

"You'll what? Chain him up and starve him? Force him to the blood match?"

"Maybe I will!"

"You bastard, you *are* involved in the matches."

He fisted the wall, putting another hole below the first. "Only because your father ordered me to."

"What?"

"Oh, get over yourself, Blu. You're playing the blind fool as usual? The spoiled and naive princess act is growing old. You know damn well Amandus has his hands in every down and dirty dealing this side of the Twin Cities."

"My father would never participate in the blood sport."

"Of course not. He's got me as his proxy for that. But he's a heavy dipper, let me tell you. Takes fifty percent of the profits. That's why I gotta get Maverick to bite the big one. Once I'm pack leader, all profits will be mine."

Bite the big one? As in…die?

Blu clung to the wall, her fingernails digging into the cracks. Her father had ordered Ryan to run the blood matches? Since when was Ryan so power hungry? Would he really murder Maverick to gain position as a principal?

This was not the kind of man she could ever care for. "Were you doing this when we were together?"

"It's not often, Blu. Hell, it takes a couple months to get them ready for the fight anyway. Unless the UV sickness sets in—then it speeds up the process nicely. Oh, don't give me that look. They deserve it! My grandfather's generation was entirely wiped out due to the longtooths hunting us. Turnaround is a bitch!"

"But my father didn't ask you to do this until…"

She couldn't decide what was worse, having cared for Ryan or learning that her father was more evil than she'd suspected.

"There's so much you don't know about Amandus. It would spin your head, little Miss Princess."

She didn't like it when he called her that. It was always in a mocking tone.

"What else is there to know?"

Ryan punched a fist into his palm. "You really want to know? How's about a kiss to loosen up my lips?"

"Just tell me!"

"Don't think so. Not without a little lovin' to show me you're still my girl."

Blu bowed her head and fisted her hands. She could not do it. She would not approach him in any way that would encourage his misplaced lust. He was so…uncouth.

Had she changed so drastically since that first night when Creed had labeled her the same?

Yes, I think so. Good for me.

"You thinking about whether you want to do it upstairs or right here on the landing, sweetie?"

"Don't call me that. I'm leaving." She swung around

and marched to the front door. Before her fingers touched the knob, Ryan called out—

"He killed your mother!"

Blu's jaw dropped. She palmed the wall to steady herself. Her father had— No. No, it couldn't be. Drawing up courage, she sucked in a breath and straightened. She approached Ryan. "You lie."

"Not about that, Blu. I'd never make up such a cruel story. I heard Amandus was in such a rage after finding out your mother was screwing a vampire he ripped her head clean from her neck."

"A—a vampire?"

Bile rising in her throat, Blu ran for the door, but he caught her by the wrist. Rage widened Ryan's pupils to devious darkness. "You're not going anywhere."

"I shouldn't have come here." She was assailed by images of her mother…her father…

Her mother had had an affair with a vampire?

"You know what else?" Ryan's colorless eyes searched hers. He stood so close she could taste the beer on his breath. "I'm guessing this whole 'let's kill all the vampires' rant of your father's is revenge. Pure and simple. He's going to stake every damn longtooth because his wife fucked one of 'em."

"Stop saying that! You know nothing."

"And now his daughter is doing the same damn thing."

"No." The denial squeaked out. He had drained her resistance.

"Seriously? So you're not fucking the vamp?"

She kicked, but her heel only managed to slide down his thigh. Ryan grinned and caught her ankle. "Let's put all that nastiness aside. You're here now. Let's get busy, for old times' sake."

"Never! The things you've told me—"

"Your father wouldn't like hearing I said anything about your mother." He dragged his tongue up her cheek. His eyes, which she'd once thought caring, now glinted with madness. "What will you force me to do to keep you silent?"

She didn't want the hurt he could give her. It wasn't right. She didn't have to take the pain to feel loved. Creed had taught her that.

"I won't say anything. Let me go, Ryan, please."

She struggled free. Palms slapping to the wall behind her, she spread her legs, maintaining a ready stance. Her heart pounding against her ribs, she eyed the door.

"Yeah? Maybe I believe you, maybe I don't. Your longtooth is the one who heads that inane rescue team. Did he send you here?"

"No, he thinks I'm shopping. I swear it. Ryan, I won't tell. I just... You have to stop this. It's not right. We'll never have peace—"

"Don't give me that bullshit. You buying into the fantasy now? Blu, you know your father never intended for your marriage to result in peace. It's a bait and switch for the big assault. You haven't told the vampire about our plans, have you?"

"No." She looked to the door. Ryan's aggression crept like dirt across her skin. How had she ever tolerated him as a lover?

Because she had known nothing else—until now.

"Blu, are you lying to me? You look me in the eye and tell me the vampires aren't aware of the pack's plans. This is big, Blu. If you know something, your father has to know, too."

He swung her about, his grip pinching her flesh. The man's eyes were frenzied. He looked near to shifting. She hated his werewolf. It always hurt her.

"I would never compromise the pack," she said calmly. "I swear it to you."

She heeled him on the shin and broke away. Tugging open the door, she gasped in the fresh air before turning to him.

"I can't love a man who murders for sport. Goodbye, Ryan."

SHE PERCHED AT THE pool's edge, the peach wig tossed to the side and a scatter of dark hair spilling across her shoulders. The sunshades had been rolled back hours earlier, and now the starry sky twinkled about the moon, which looked deceptively round. In another evening it would be completely full.

She hadn't carried in a single bag from the so-called shopping trip. Creed hadn't suspected she was in a shopping mood. Now, he could verily feel the sadness waft from her as if heat waves whisping from sunbaked sand.

Kicking off his shoes outside the sliding glass door, he padded across the cool patio stones and sat beside her on the towel. Just like her, he dangled his feet in the water.

The stars twinkled in her gray eyes, focused above the treetops. He didn't say anything for a long time. They simply sat there, admiring the sky.

He briefly wondered about tomorrow night. She couldn't become a monster, not his wife. And even if she did shift and alter shape, he was a big boy; he could handle it. She wanted him to see her. It would be good. He would make it so.

Her profile glittered under the moonlight. No faery dust tonight, just soft sensuous skin and wide, bright eyes.

Had he ever shared silence with another person and felt it deep in his being? Blu's heartbeats filled him. She had become as much a part of him as possible. Had he bitten her and tasted her blood, their heartbeats would synch.

Soon. He prayed for that. It would bond them as he'd never been bonded to another.

Yet now he sensed her misery. It felt dark and cold.

When she tilted her head to look at him, grief clutched his heart. She still did not speak, but her eyes asked him for forgiveness.

"You went to see him?" he guessed.

She nodded.

"Because of what Alexandre reported?"

Please let it be because of that and not because she missed her lover.

Blu took his hand and kissed the palm. She traced her finger along his lifeline and pressed her face into it. Teardrops moistened his flesh.

"Ryan told you the truth?"

"I didn't think he was like that. Bloodthirsty," she whispered. "And not like you, because you need it. Ryan's thirsty for sport."

"He confessed to you?"

"My father ordered him to set up the matches."

Creed sucked in a breath.

"I promised him I wouldn't tell you."

"Well, I already know. And you didn't really tell me. I guessed, so you're safe there."

"I don't want to do anything to please Ryan anymore. I hate him. I don't understand how I could have ever thought he cared for me. He cared to screw me, that's all it was. And because he was less vicious than the others, I accepted him. I was the only reason he ever became scion."

Creed tucked her head against his shoulder and stroked her hair.

"We won't move in on him. As I've said, we don't use force unless confronted."

And if the Council could just get behind that...

Hell, was he being truthful with himself? He'd already admitted he loved taking off wolves' heads. Blu had split him neatly, filling half his ego with the desire for peace, while the other half could never completely abandon the vengeance and survival tactics that ran through his blood.

"Best scenario would be to get a man on the inside to infiltrate and notify us where they keep the vampires," he said. "If we could raid and rescue their stock, we might have some success in stopping the blood matches."

"Creed, please don't think I approve of the matches."

"I know you don't."

She shivered. Tears rolled down her cheek. "There's something else. Something so horrible Ryan told me."

He hugged her to him when she broke down, sobbing loudly. Whatever it was, it clenched about his heart. He hated that anyone could hurt Blu like this. That so many had used and abused her. How had she survived all these years in the pack?

"My father," she said between sniffles. "Ryan said he killed my mother. I never knew that. I thought she'd left him years ago, and no one knew where she was. But Ryan confirmed she had an affair."

"I'm sorry."

"With a vampire."

"What?"

"My mother. Supposedly she had an affair with a vampire."

She found his gaze and Creed felt her need clutch at his soul. He hugged her closer to him. "How does that make you feel?"

"I don't know what to think. It's insane to consider. And if it is true, why would my father push me into the arms of a vampire just like his wife had done? It makes so little sense."

"I have no explanations. Life never goes the way we believe it should. That's the thrill of living it, I guess."

Her body shook against his. "Creed, all I've ever wanted was to have my mother in my life. And now to find my father killed her? I have no one."

Having no one was a familiar habit he'd learned to live with. Until now. Loneliness had fallen off his radar. And he didn't want to return to the feeling again.

Kissing her forehead, he held her, taking her pain. "You have me."

She sobbed quietly in his arms for a long time. Creed had rarely known tears. But tonight, he cried.

CHAPTER FOURTEEN

CREED LOOKED UP FROM his desk when Housekeeper popped her head in the office through the open door. "Yes?"

"You didn't hear the front doorbell? Must have been because I am vacuuming," she said. "There are two people here to see you. A man and a woman. The man looks scary."

"So you let them in?" He shook his head at her frantic nod, then reminded himself to add "don't let in strangers" to his list of training requirements for housekeepers. "Thank you, Housekeeper."

He sensed the female visitor before he entered the foyer. A witch. Creed could sniff out a witch half a state away thanks to the witch magic ingrained in his blood. But he had to purposely scent one out. She could be standing right next to him and if he wasn't on super-witch-sensory mode, he wouldn't notice her.

He checked himself, recalling how often he'd used

magic lately. Not enough to leave a noticeable residue on his aura. She would never know.

He recognized Abigail Rowan and returned her acknowledging nod as he approached the landing. Slender and elegant in pale pink satin pants and top, curls of strawberry hair spilled past her elbows. She was gorgeous, but Creed respected her power.

The other man, tall and bald, with a skull covered with tribal tattoos, smiled warmly and shook Creed's hand. The shimmer—an innate feeling vampires felt when making contact with one another—confirmed the visitor was a vampire.

But Creed knew that before even touching him.

"Drake, good to see you."

Nikolaus Drake was a newer vampire—had lived about three decades as a blood drinker—and led tribe Kila. A very peaceable tribe, thanks to Drake's doing. His love affair with a witch a few decades earlier had turned his head three-hundred-sixty degrees. He sat on the Council, along with Abigail and a half a dozen other local representatives of the paranormal nations.

"Abigail." Creed offered her a nod, but knew that witches had a problem with him. Even after the Protection had been lifted, he represented the original bane to them. One who would enslave them and steal their magic.

He hadn't done that for centuries.

"I had thought the wife and I were supposed to parade ourselves before the Council in a few days for approval," Creed said. "Why the visit today?"

"We've had some disturbing news," Nikolaus said as he stepped down into the living room and wandered before the bar. "Of all people, Creed, I thought we could trust you to keep a low profile during this period when we most need to show a good face to the werewolves."

"But I have—"

"You killed two wolves the other night during your rescue mission."

"A necessity," Creed countered the witch's vitriolic remark. "While my men and I attempt to go in and retrieve the imprisoned vampires with as little collateral damage as possible, sometimes it is unavoidable."

"You should have let the vamp die," Abigail said.

Creed flashed a glare at her and noticed Nikolaus did the same. The woman held her stance, a force neither wished to challenge.

"What she means," Nikolaus said, "is that now might not be the best time for your rescue efforts. We appreciate what you have done with the Rescue Project, but really, Creed. We, as vampires, must show the wolves we will not react to their violence with return violence. Who can be the better man?"

"That is insanity!" Creed shouted. "You sacrifice our own by sitting on your hands and turning a cheek."

"Is it no more insane to rescue a half-dead vampire and leave him to suffer for the rest of his short life?"

Creed twisted to Abigail, who had put out the challenge. Indeed, he was aware the vamp they'd rescued was so sick with UV poisoning that he had probably a fortnight of life, and that was if he were given blood daily, and could even stomach it. It would be a miserable death. A stake would have been more kind.

"Perhaps I was mistaken," he conceded.

"You were not," Nikolaus said. "The wolves forced your hand, Saint-Pierre. I cannot conceive of telling you to stop the rescues. The project is too valuable to the vampire community. But I must ask you to at least stay out of the fray until some kind of peace agreement is met. You are our representative."

"Yes, yes, please accept my apologies." Creed swiped a hand over his face and paced behind the sofa. His proximity to the witch made him uncomfortable. He sensed she looked right through him, seeking the truth of him. "And extend my apologies to the entire Council. I chose to step up to represent the vampire nations. I will not let them down." He shoved his hands in his pants pockets and allowed a little smile to break his stern expression. "You will be pleased to hear the princess and I are getting along well. I can't imagine the nations not believing we two are in love, because in fact, I can honestly say we are."

"Congratulations," Nikolaus said with a glance to Abigail. She offered lackluster congratulations. "I knew it was possible. I am the perfect example of that."

Indeed, Drake had married a witch decades earlier at a time when the Protection had made them enemies.

"Love was not a requirement," Abigail said, "biting her was. Have you bitten her, Saint-Pierre?"

"Still working on that one, but I feel sure it will happen. Perhaps a celebratory drink is in order." Creed aimed for the bar but Abigail slunk into his path. Leaning against the bar, one elbow sliding onto the stone counter, she tilted her head in a challenge. Creed sensed this discussion was nowhere near the celebratory stage. "Not thirsty?" he asked the witch, but knew the answer.

"A rumor has come to our attention."

Turning to Nikolaus, but keeping the witch in his peripheral view, Creed splayed his hands to appear as agreeable as possible.

"Please tell me tribe Nava is not plotting against the wolves," the vampire said.

Well, there it was. Creed would have to face the accusation. And he wouldn't try to dance around the truth. But it had become complicated since Blu had teased him away from the vanguard with her allure and honesty.

"And the werewolves," Abigail added, "are plotting against the vampires. We understand this marriage is being used as a ruse to soften the opponent's defenses. Is that true, Saint-Pierre?"

"Yes." Creed rubbed his palms together. He was glad Blu was out on a run. She didn't need to defend herself when she was merely a pawn in the game. Nor did he wish her to see him grilled by the Council. "Yes, it was our intent as I entered into this agreement. Nava and Zmaj had decided this would be a way to lull the werewolves so we may then attack. I have only recently come to understand the wolves were plotting the same."

Drake stepped up to him. The man was half a head taller, and imposing, even to Creed with all those tattoos marking his scalp. Though Creed knew he was a gentle man, he also knew Drake would do anything to protect his tribe and defend the nations.

Creed lifted his chin to meet the vampire's stare. Standing so close, he sensed the shimmer, but it worked a wicked tingle on his veins, tightening them. He had betrayed the brotherhood of blood that united them, no matter their separate tribes.

"Plans have changed," Creed offered. "On my part."

Drake maintained his menacing stare.

The man had once died after being doused with witch's blood. Yet he had risen as a phoenix to again walk the earth. There was nothing he had not seen, no challenge he had not accepted in his short life as a vampire.

"I love Blu," Creed put out there. "I would not dream of destroying her family now."

"Does your tribe agree to the same?" Drake asked.

"I haven't spoken with them yet."

"It must be done, Creed. I will not allow any tribe to provoke the wolves to war."

"I understand. I will do what I can to make it stop."

"Do I have your word?"

"Of course." He clasped a hand high on Drake's arm and, with his other, shook his hand. "You have my word."

The witch appeared beside the two of them, her green eyes fierce. "If you do not stop the imminent war, you will be punished for rousing anarchy within the tribes. The Council will make an example of you."

"Fair enough." Creed stepped back and bowed, conceding to the witch. Now he couldn't stomach a celebratory drink.

He'd just agreed to call off his troops. Which meant he would have to confess his love for a wolf to them all. And he had no problem with that. He just wasn't sure it would be as easy convincing the Northern pack that war was no longer an option. That a vampire had fallen in love with a werewolf. Especially after Blu had revealed her mother had had an affair with a vampire.

Amandus Masterson was not going to like this at all.

AMANDUS MASTERSON LOUNGED before the pool outside the pack compound. He wore trousers and a long-sleeved shirt. He sat beneath a beach umbrella and eased at his aching toes through the athletic sock. If any in the pack knew he was developing arthritis, he feared a mutiny. Or worse, Ryan would take him out and claim the principal status.

Idiot whelp. There was simply no way the scion would take over the reins, even if Amandus were to suddenly die. Which he didn't intend to do anytime soon. But he'd have to make sure a new scion was put in place, sooner rather than later.

As an interesting suggestion to his thoughts, Ridge strolled out onto the pool deck. He wore but jeans and sunglasses, and did not sit but instead stood near Amandus's chaise, his focus constantly sweeping the perimeter.

Good man, Ridge. He was calm, decisive and strong. And not easily riled. An excellent choice for scion.

"Who was lost?" Amandus asked.

"Anderson and that new guy from Montana, Hecker. Both from the splinter pack that wanted to join with us."

"Damned vampires." Amandus squeezed the wood chair arm and it cracked in his grip. "How do they always manage to find the location of a match? We must have a spy in our ranks."

"I've already begun questioning pack members," Ridge said. "I suspect the same. Don't worry, Principal Masterson. I will find the culprit, and after information has been exposed, I'll rip his head off."

"See that you do."

"Anderson didn't die right away. He managed to tell me something you may find interesting."

"Yes, what is it?"

"The vampire lord. Saint-Pierre. Anderson believes he might have used magic against Hecker. He made a move during their battle that was impossible. Didn't even touch him, yet sent Hecker flying from the roof of the van."

"I thought the elder vampires had been shackled of their magic?"

Ridge shrugged. "I don't know much about that."

"The witches demanded it of the elders after the Protection was put in place. Hmm…this information could prove useful. Especially if it can destroy that damned vampire. Thank you, Ridge. Good job."

The young wolf flexed his shoulders, displaying the muscles that rippled across his back and down his lats. He was a force not to be toyed with. A faithful right-hand man. Amandus trusted Ridge would suss out the duplicitous wolf before the full moon hung in the sky tonight.

Thinking of which, he wondered how Blu would handle the moon tonight. He entirely expected she would wander out and seek a wolf to mate with. He prayed it was with someone from the Northern pack. Likely Eugene Ryan.

The scion was better than the vampire lord any day.

His daughter had been insistent about not taking the vampire's bite, but now Amandus felt if they truly wanted to show allegiance it would be wise if Blu did. It was a sacrifice that clawed viciously at his memory. His daughter would commit the same sin as her mother, no matter that she was forced.

He'd already dismissed her anyway. She would serve the pack in acting the happy wife to a vampire, and then her task would be complete. Amandus had to reconcile that he'd already lost his only daughter to the enemy.

He could do that, because the prize gained for such a sacrifice would appease his aching heart far more. Unless he could use this new information about Saint-Pierre instead of sacrificing his daughter.

Either way, if Blu were to somehow survive the upcoming debacle and return to the pack he must consider what to do with her then. She would be tainted but not entirely useless.

"Ridge, if I made you scion of the pack, would you take my daughter as your wife?"

The man turned a shocked gaze on him. "Principal?"

"You heard me. I've offered my daughter to you many times, yet each instance you refuse. Why is that?"

"Er…"

"Don't you like her?"

"The princess is very beautiful, Principal. A fine prize for any wolf."

"Yet you've shown no interest. I've not seen you with a woman at the compound, come to think of it. Maybe you're one of those homosexuals." He pronounced the word with vitriol.

The wolf growled lowly, exposing his front teeth.

"Well, what is it then? Is it that she'll be tainted by the vampire if she returns?"

"I respect her. That is the reason."

Amandus got up from the chaise and shuffled for his sunglasses in a front shirt pocket. "Respect? What sort of nonsense is that? You show your respect for me by accepting what I offer you. Perhaps I was too quick to consider you become scion."

"Eugene Ryan is already scion, Principal."

"Things change, Ridge. Expect change. Always."

Amandus shuffled off the pool deck and into the shade of the entertainment room that edged the compound. The insolence of the man to refuse to take Blu as his wife.

He kicked open the swinging doors and marched through. Diaz walked ahead of him and swung to offer the appropriate bow and silent acknowledgment.

"Diaz." Amandus paralleled him. "What do you think of Blu?"

"Your daughter? She's hot."

"Yes. Exactly. Good answer."

CHAPTER FIFTEEN

BLU PACED THE BEDROOM FLOOR. She glanced at the clock. Eleven-thirty.

It seemed odd the werewolf didn't come upon her until *exactly* midnight. That should be stuff of fiction. After all, the moon was already high and it was freaking huge.

That was the way it worked. The chime of twelve effected the change.

Nervous, she paced to stem some of her frantic energy. Creed's bedroom was three times the size of a normal bedroom, and the soft, antique rug beneath her bare feet felt like silk. As she paced, she couldn't help but think.

She and Creed had lingered by the pool last night for hours. In silence. Just knowing he wanted to be there, holding her, meant the world to her. And she didn't feel so alone now.

What her father had done to her mother was unspeakable.

All this time she'd thought her mother had abandoned her, walked away without looking back. Instead, something truly evil had taken her from Blu's life.

She wanted to approach her father about it, to seek the truth from him, but he intimidated her. What had compelled Persia Masterson to seek another man? Likely she had been treated the same way Blu had been by Amandus.

But Blu couldn't wrap her mind around it right now. And she didn't need to. Creed was here to protect her. From all things.

Good ol' Creed.

He'd gone to pour a glass of whisky. She'd suggested, only half jokingly, he drink the whole bottle.

He meant to leave her alone until she called for him, or he sensed it okay to come looking for her.

Hell, she wouldn't call for him. She'd howl.

Blu didn't know what she would do with a vampire when she wolfed out. And that was the hard part.

Her rational human brain was about forty-percent present when in werewolf form. But that forty percent was easily muted as she surrendered to the beast's need for whatever it was she desired. There was no keeping the beast back, or denying it.

She prayed she didn't hurt Creed. Or scare the crap out of the vampire lord who was accustomed to taking off werewolf heads with his sword.

"LET'S HOLD OFF ON approaching Ryan," Creed said to Alexandre over the phone. "He's aware we're onto him now. I suspect he might scuttle out of sight for a while."

"I'm surprised at the order," Alexandre said. "You're becoming soft, man. Are you losing focus on the goal?"

How to explain the conversation he'd had with Drake and the witch? And also to explain that indeed his heart had altered since before the wedding. He was fully on board with the peace pact now.

"I know what I'm doing, Alexandre. We're not letting the wolf walk away. I want to keep a thumb on him. I don't want that bastard making a move without us knowing about it."

"So we plan a raid on their warehouses?"

"Have we a location where they're keeping the stock?"

He hated using that word to describe his fellow vampires, but it was a means to distance himself from the horrendous suffering and to focus on the mission.

He could never completely distance himself. Vivid memories were impossible to erase. Rachel he had loved, not deeply, but sweetly. He had known her but three months, but that was a long time for Creed. The day he'd gotten the call from Alexandre had been the worst he could recall for centuries. The wolves had kept her in chains for weeks. Creed had believed her away on a trip to visit her brother in India. When Alexandre had reported a rescued female vampire near death and un-identifiable, Creed had known before going to identify the body, it had to be Rachel.

"Yes, I'm sending out scouts to verify," Alexandre said.

"Good." Creed shook off images of the beautiful blonde vampire he'd buried only a decade earlier. "Report back in the morning."

"Will you be answering in the morning, old man?"

"What do you mean by that?"

"Full moon madness. Anything going on at your place tonight?"

"*Bonsoir,* Alexandre." He hung up and tilted back the two fingers of whisky.

The golden liquid slid smoothly down his throat. This stuff never burned. It was that good. Smirking at Blu's suggestion he drink the whole bottle, Creed thumbed the label.

That she was nervous about the change made him anxious.

He was in for the ride now. Completely. He'd married a werewolf out of contract, but now he took the vows seriously. He wanted to know his wife wholly.

But would tonight forever change his mind?

Maybe after a little moonlight madness, he'd be all for a war against the wolves. Would his wife become his lover as well as his destroyer?

Pouring another two fingers of whisky, he set it back with a swallow.

Rachel would have approved of Blu. The vampiress had been quiet and demure, but her secret fantasy had seen her fearless and insatiable.

"To Rachel," he said, and tilted back another drink.

Above, at the far end of the house, a rangy howl echoed. He moved abruptly to the bottom stair. It was such a familiar call. So…wrenching. It stirred memory. Flashes of a walk through the forest one midsummer medieval night choked the breath from Creed.

"Mon Dieu."

The wolf's howl was very distinctive, and there were many kinds of howls, he knew, each meaning something different. This one he had only heard once before, and only now did he understand the horrible crime he'd committed.

He clutched his chest and huffed out his breath.

She sounded like a wild wolf he'd once seen in the snowy forests of Blois. Creed remembered pausing to watch as the wolf passed before him, leery and revealing teeth. It had not attacked.

Perhaps it had sensed he wielded a wolf-killing battle sword.

And yet, he had advanced. He'd slain the wolf after tracking the same longing howl through the forest. The wolf had growled at him. He'd thought it a male wolf. Well, he'd never seen a female before so hadn't thought it anything but. And then he'd taken off its head.

"*Her* head. She'd been in heat," he said now. "Not a threat to me. Christ, Saint-Pierre, you bastard."

He sank to his knees on the bottom step.

The howl came again, skittering across his shoulders and down his spine. There, it dug in, clutching his bones and rattling them.

What kind of monster would slay a female? A werewolf who had only been craving love, connection, the basic needs of sexual congress. Blu would be horrified if she ever found out.

Would he be compelled to harm the werewolf tonight? An innate reaction to an enemy so ingrained he might not be able to see past the creature and to the woman he now loved?

You have changed since then. You have. Use it.

Creed nodded. "I will prove to them all I can be trusted, and as a representative of the vampire nations, that we can all be trusted."

He stood and ascended the stairs, following the echoing howl.

His wife waited.

DARKNESS FILLED THE open doorway at the end of the long, upper floor hallway. Even as Creed approached with sure strides, he could scent the musk in the air. Not offensive, yet he did recognize it as a mating scent.

Vampires had no such inclination to seek and bond with one mate, nor did they go through extensive rituals finding that mate—beyond ensuring that the mate took their bite. The bite was key. So he wasn't sure how to approach tonight.

Since they were different species, it wasn't a bonding ritual from Blu's point of view, nor from his. But this coming together of two species might bond them in ways neither could anticipate.

She howled again, another low, mournful tone.

The low-pitched howl again cracked the darkness. Was she feeling confrontational?

How dared he have slain the wolf in the woods. And yet he'd been blind to all but the blood and the power of his sword back then.

Creed quickened his steps.

No battle sword was required this night. He would tame this beast with kisses and love.

He stepped into the bedroom—and was knocked to his back, arms splaying across the ancient rug. Something thumped his chest and crouched upon him.

The loose red dress she'd worn earlier stretched tight

across her breasts. Wild dark hair dangled in his face. Wicked fangs had cut through her bottom lip. A drool of blood trickled down her chin.

Still her features were human. Nothing wolfish. Yet.

Blood scent tingled in Creed's teeth. Now would be the worst time for his fangs to come down. He didn't want her to think he was trying to be aggressive. He imagined her werewolf saw him only as a longtooth, the enemy.

"Just walk in on me then?" she said on a growl. Her voice was deeper, throaty. "No man for me."

A hand swiped him at the shoulder, lifting Creed and tossing him against the wall. The icy sting of a cut opened flesh and blood seeped from his shoulder. A good thing for his wanting blood hunger, because his own injury would mask the scent of her blood until he healed, which wouldn't be long.

The werewolf waved a hand at him, long talons slashing the air. "Hey, big boy? Wanna take me on? You're going to have to do better than that."

She sliced a claw down the center of her dress, cutting it open to reveal her gorgeous breasts. Her muscles were tight, her abs firm and strong. Her skin glistened with perspiration. But he sensed she was *more* somehow.

Creed splayed his hands. "I don't want to harm—"

He didn't see the attack coming, she moved so swiftly. Putting him up against the wall, Blu held Creed under the throat, her stretched hand tight against his Adam's apple. His feet dangled above the floor.

She cracked a menacing smile.

Now she was making him angry.

With but a flick of her wrist, she sent him flying toward the bed. He twisted midair, his back connecting with a bedpost. It splintered and broke as he went through it.

"Oh, yes!" Blu tore off the damaged post and wielded it high. She stabbed at him, missing.

Creed managed to twist the makeshift stake from her hand. "We're not going to stake the vampire tonight."

A slash of talon cut through his chest and tore the shirt down one arm. Her eyes glittered. "My bad."

It was apparent this werewolf had only dealt with the alphas from her pack. Creed had to set aside his need to be gentle with her—or take a stake to the heart.

He would need more than just cunning tonight.

A breath stirred his air magic and whipped the stake through the room. The serrated wooden tip speared the wall.

"Tricky," she cooed. "Is that all you got?"

Swinging an arm around, he clocked Blu under the chin and thrust her across the bed. Springing on top of her, he pinned her shoulders. "You want to get laid, wolf?"

Her growl could be construed as a sexy plea. Or a pissed-off warning.

She tussled beneath him, but he sensed she did not use her full strength. She'd thrown him to the wall once already; she was no pup.

"Let's do this," she said on a wicked snarl.

She gripped his hair when he kissed her. Their mouths bruised one another, their fingers and limbs moved with intention, forcefully and not gently. Every movement was extreme. She kissed him wildly, demandingly, as she pumped her hips against his, bucking and asking for what she wanted.

But when he reached between her legs, she snarled and then chuckled loudly.

"Not so fast, longtooth." In less than a blink it was he who lay beneath her, pinned by the shoulders. "You gotta earn this one."

"I'm assuming that means you want me to get rough with you?"

She bit his lower lip and tugged. "Just try to keep up, big boy."

She scampered off the bed and he followed, finding her mood more playful now than violent.

Had her flinging him against the wall been mere play? His shoulders still ached. And while the bite hadn't broken skin, it had certainly amped up his hunger for rough play.

Time to get into super werewolf sex mode.

Twisting his head and cracking his knuckles, Creed crouched and caught his charging wife as she collided with his body. Claws tore through his deltoids, painfully opening the muscle.

Her fangs gnashed the air, but he knew that teasing smile.

How would he keep up with a moon-frenzied were-wolf? Foreplay had become rousing real play with a dangerous edge.

Raising a hand, Creed flicked his wrist, directing his magic at her. It overtook the were and slammed her against the wall. She struggled against his unseen hold and then let out a howl. Through it all, she grinned.

Creed released his hold. She charged him. He flew out of the way and ended up on top of the dresser. She lunged for him and he jumped, leaping high and rolling midair to land on both feet.

"Nice magic tricks," she said. "Dodge this, vampire."

She charged. When he feinted to the left, she matched the deceptive movement and collided with him. They landed on the bed. The mattress slid, and Creed lost footing. He went down with a painful twist to his spine.

Blu's face tilted horizontal to his. "Gotcha." She kissed him quick, then licked her tongue from his nose up his forehead. She dashed into the darkness, leaving him groaning.

He slapped a hand over his chest, feeling the muscle already knitted back together. Hell of a way to seduce a man.

"I want to go out and run!" Blu declared.

A run? That was a big no-go. A werewolf on the loose wouldn't sit well with the neighbors.

"Thought you wanted to have sex?" he called. Easing upright, he winced at the stunning pain strafing his back. The woman was strong. And he dared not use all his strength, no matter what.

"You can't keep up."

"I'm still alive. That's got to count for something."

He moved through the darkness, pinpointing her panting breaths. And there, the dark sweetness of her blood. With a twitch of his fingers, Creed stirred the air into a whirl and wrapped it about his wife's body. So he could never give up his magic for personal use. Drawing her to him with a command, she landed in his arms roughly.

"Gotcha."

The wolf growled and struggled, surprised at the sneaky move. "That's not fair."

"All's fair." Creed kissed her until she succumbed and whimpered for more.

When she bashed a fist behind her into the wall, the drywall shattered.

Blu chuckled freely. She swaggered in his embrace

and shoved him hard. He landed on the mattress, angled half on and half off the bed.

It was going to be a long and adventurous night.

Fitting his leg between hers, Creed managed to flip the powerful wolf to her back. He pinned her by the wrists. Blu met his gaze with a defiant stare. So bold, her gray eyes. Trusting. He could not consider harming her, as he'd earlier worried. She did not struggle. He sensed she was giving him some slack.

Or else she was plotting new ways to overthrow him.

"I love you, Blu," he said, and licked up the side of her neck to bite the lobe of her ear not too gently. His fangs were down, he now realized, but he cautioned himself not to break skin or draw blood. Never without her permission.

She arched her chest up to nudge against his and he palmed her breasts. The werewolf's legs snapped about his hips and slammed his groin against hers.

"Let me get my pants off," he said.

"You're too slow." Claws ripped down the each side of his leg, releasing him from the clothing and drawing blood at the same time. "Did I hurt you? My bad."

"The pain you give me hurts so good, lover." He kissed her breasts, holding her firmly because she was all energy and movement and he didn't want her to slip away this time.

But she did not. She was ready for him. The vampire had tamed the wolf.

Entering her was like being overwhelmed by bliss. Creed gritted his teeth and his body shuddered as her sweet warmth clutched him tightly. He wasn't sure, but he thought her inner muscles were even more powerful in her current state.

"*Mon Dieu,* Blu. I won't last long. You're so…hot."

"Not this way." She shoved him off her—and out of her—with a firm palm.

Lying back on the pillows, Creed wasn't about to let her keep fighting. He wanted her. He needed her. Now.

She knelt on all fours on the bed beside him and wiggled her sweet derriere. "Now," she whispered in a voice that was all sexy, teasing Blu.

So the wolf liked to do it doggie style? That made sense.

Hugging her against his body, Creed entered her from behind. He found a rhythm that made her whimper sweetly, and accompanied the friction by rubbing his fingers across her clit.

He could sense when his wife neared the edge, because he raced alongside her to that same precipice. They came together, she crying out in a feminine sigh that rose to a low and satisfied howl.

Creed shouted and spread out his arms. He thrust back

his head and shoulders, still firmly hilted within her, riding the luxurious orgasm his wife had granted him.

His werewolf wife.

Blu's howl suddenly cracked. She reached back and smacked him on the shoulder, which effectively shoved him off the bed.

And then he heard a sound with which he was dreadfully familiar. The subtle cracks and uncomfortable moans as bone redesigned within skin and grew, changing, altering…

Blu flipped about on the bed. A long-taloned paw snapped out and slashed Creed across the chest, sending him colliding against the wall. He touched the deep wounds that revealed bone. Blood gushed over his fingers.

Before him stood a completely shifted werewolf.

CHAPTER SIXTEEN

THE CREATURE STANDING before the wall bled. The scent frightened her, and at the same time, it seemed familiar. How could that be?

He held out a hand, coated with blood, entreating. Blu sniffed. Did he want her to slash the hand from his body?

Straightening her spine and putting forward her ears, she sniffed the air intently. Hackles bristled. The atmosphere was familiar, as well. But this was not a natural surrounding. The earth and fauna scents were missing.

Where was the pack? The aggressive scent of her males was not apparent.

"Blu, it is me," the creature said in a calm voice.

She tilted her head, processing the familiar tones. It was human-speak. She understood some of it.

A *whuf* came up in her throat. She sniffed again and

leaned forward, towering over the creature who wasn't quite man. He smelled…different.

"Your husband."

The words made little sense. A simple bark or howl was all she required to communicate. Her muscles were lax, and she understood now she had just mated with this one. And it had not been unpleasant.

Perhaps he was trustworthy.

Stepping forward, she brought her muzzle up to sniff along his face. His blood scent was sweeter this close. She lashed her tongue up his cheek, tasting salt and perspiration and some blood. Why the blood?

Baring her teeth, she growled lowly. *Longtooth.*

The man remained perfectly still. She could not sense his heartbeat, but the warmth of him told her he was alive. Unafraid. And had not made a move to harm her.

It is safe here. She innately sensed that.

And with that reassurance, Blu stepped back until her legs collided with an object, and she toppled on the soft surface as her body began to shift. Fur receded and bones changed. Skin moved. Her face ached the most where her muzzle shortened and she became completely human. The shift from werewolf to were was painful, but forgotten as quickly as it occurred.

Her arms stretching out and legs bending up to her stomach, Blu curled up and closed her eyes. She shivered as her wolf body gave way to bare flesh. All parts of her ached now. Her memory was not complete, but she sensed she must have been fighting.

She felt the tender trace of Creed's fingers along her torso.

"Love you," he whispered beside her ear and, moving behind, he nestled his body next to hers.

BRIGHT SUNLIGHT FILTERED through the skylight. It didn't fall directly on Creed, so he figured it must be after noon. He'd never worried for the sun before. Soon he'd have to move as the sun tracked the sky.

If he could move. His muscles were lax, his entire body warm with satiation. All energy was drained after a night of insanely acrobatic and intense lovemaking.

He stared at the skylight from the island of mattress that had found its way to the corner of the room. He crooked a brow. There was a pillow stuck in the crystal chandelier.

To his left, the Louis XIV chair was stuck in the wall by two legs, its watered silk cushions shredded. A slash through the wallpaper left hanging wisps of flocked emerald velvet. Two makeshift stakes—bedposts—were stabbed into the walls. The rug was bunched near the door. Feathers from the pillows snowed across the box spring, angled on the bed.

And at his side, a small warmth curled snugly against

his aching ribs. Her hair spilled across his chest like black silk. Her fingers, now sans claws, were wrapped about his semisoft cock.

Like a peaceful kitten, she purred in sleep. Or was that a worn-out puppy?

Creed stroked her hair, but she didn't stir. How could she after the night they'd had? She'd revealed herself to him. And there may have been a few moments when he'd considered retreat.

Yes, even this former battle-hardened warrior had been shocked at the change in his petite princess. She'd become feral and wild, wary of submission, and not about to be pushed around. Wanting, needing and eager to take what she desired by tooth or claw.

Her werewolf had put her claws through his chest and broken ribs. He stroked a palm across his chest. He was healed now, but the bones yet ached.

He did not regret a single moment of it. Everything about Blu he accepted. Feisty, playful, daring, unwilling to settle when she could design her own way. A woman who had learned it wasn't right for men to treat her cruelly. A woman who had lost all family, and found solace with him, a man not even her own species.

A woman like no other.

"I love you." He hugged her warmth to his side. "So much."

BLU ATTACKED A HUGE bowl of cereal with vigor. She was always famished the day following her shift. She'd need another bowl, or two, but they were out of milk. She had to find Housekeeper and send her to the store.

A delicious masculine scent perked her senses and she lifted her head to watch Creed enter the kitchen. He wore loose jeans that hugged his hips and revealed the dark hairs below his belly button. The precise cut of his abs made her go loopy with visions of frenzied sex, hips pumping against hers and body parts sliding slickly across one another.

Blu dashed out her tongue to catch the milk drooling down her chin. Her husband smiled at that.

She'd beat him to the kitchen after waking in the bedroom disaster, uncertain about confronting his dismay. Now it was inevitable.

His easy smile went a ways in alleviating her worry.

"How you feeling this morning?" He kissed her at the corner of her eye and hugged her from behind. Resting his chin on her shoulder, he reached around and flicked a stray chocolate crunch piece into the bowl. "Exhausted?"

"Elated actually. And hungry."

"I see you got the Count Chocula."

"Yummy chocolatey goodness served up by the Count. You, um…okay?"

"Tired, but elated also."

She scooped a spoonful into her mouth and crunched quickly. A faint red line running from the center of his chest and across his shoulder revealed a healing talon wound. Oops. "You're not upset?"

"About what?"

Seriously? "The room?"

"It needed redecorating. It'll give you a chance to break in the credit card."

Whew. Could the guy be any nicer?

"What about the talons? I'm sorry. I delivered you some good ones."

"I heal." He palmed the red mark. "Some slower than others. This was a deep one. Cut through some ribs."

Digging the spoon into the cereal, Blu flicked a pale brown marshmallow onto it. No raging? No angry rebuttal to her wild need to push him away and then grab him back? Not an admonishment for the wounds she'd given him?

"Why are you so good to me? I could have killed you last night, you know."

He nuzzled aside her jaw and kissed the milk trail from her chin. "If that's what the dangerous werewolf wants to believe, I'll give you that. But you wouldn't have."

"I remember holding a stake."

"You wouldn't have used it," he whispered at her ear.

No, she wouldn't have. Her werewolf liked to play,

to tease, to coerce and, yeah, even claw, but she did not take life. What a hell of a way to get laid. But he'd been a sport about it. Heck, the guy deserved a trophy or something.

"I can't be responsible for my actions when the moon is full."

"No wonder you were pushed," he muttered. "Glad you landed on my doorstep."

"Even if I'm wolfed out? I mean…can you deal with that?"

"Each and every full moon."

She smirked. "You talk as if we'll be together many moons."

"I hope so."

She did, too. And how cool was that? The vampire and the werewolf getting it on and living in some kind of crazy harmony.

"Mmm…" Creed slipped his fingers between her legs.

"Seriously?" she said. "Because I'm eating breakfast here."

"Give me one good reason to stop, and I will."

Blu crunched furiously, her brain searching for a reason as her body thrummed at her lover's masterful touch.

"I'm waiting," he said with a flick of his forefinger.

Blu tensed at the delicious sensation. "I'm thinking."

"Just one reason. I'll stop."

She arched her back, giving him easier access.

"What do you say?"

She stabbed the spoon into the bowl. "I got nothin'."

She was on the verge of climax when an angry shout echoed down from the upper floor.

Creed slipped from her, and Blu cursed Housekeeper as her burgeoning orgasm slipped away.

"I'll handle this," she said, and made a furious beeline for the stairs.

Interrupt her morning pleasure, eh?

Stomping up to the bedroom, Blu arrived upon a frantic maid mumbling something in Spanish, which she didn't understand. Housekeeper flung her hands about before her to punctuate her frenzied tirade. She thrust a gesture toward the destroyed bedroom, then made an I-don't-understand gesture.

"I think I got it," Blu said. "You can't figure how that happened?"

Housekeeper rambled off a litany in Spanish.

"How 'bout this?" Blu bared her claws before the woman.

Housekeeper peeped to an abrupt silence. She gaped at sight of the claws, then fainted.

"Oops." Blu teased the tip of her little finger into her mouth and gave the approaching vampire her best innocent flutter of lash.

Creed strode down the hallway and bent to lift the prone woman over one shoulder.

"That's why I call them Housekeeper," he said. "They never last for more than a few weeks. Sometimes it's shock, sometimes it's—hell, it's blood loss. So I'm not a saint. But this time," he admonished with a waggling finger, "it's entirely your fault, wolf. Welcome to the family."

Giving him a catty snarl, she clawed playfully at him. "You gonna come back and toss me over your shoulder when you're finished with her?"

"Get undressed. I won't be long."

"Mmm, goodie."

THE WHELP HAD THE audacity to stare straight into Amandus's eyes. Eugene Ryan hadn't so much as offered a hello or what-did-you-need-me-for? He simply stood like some roughhousing bar bouncer waiting to be challenged. The muscles strapping his biceps were so big he couldn't even relax his arms aside his torso.

Amandus bristled and stood fully, bringing his stature only an inch higher than Ryan. "You," he muttered in the whelp's face, "are out."

Ryan gaped. He clenched fists before him, but didn't strike out.

"You've a spy amongst your men," Amandus continued. "Those bloody longtooths have found the past three sporting events you have overseen. It is utterly senseless the depths of your idiocy."

Amandus stepped back two steps until he felt the stolid presence of Ridge at his left shoulder. He glowered at Ryan, waiting for him to babble out some excuse for his ineptitude.

"Out." Ryan nodded, shaking his head at the same time. "So just like that, then? First you take away my fiancée and now I'm out of the pack? I've served you well, Principal Masterson. I've kept your involvement in the sporting warehouses quiet—"

Amandus lashed out, his claws striking Ryan across the face. Four lacerations opened across his cheek, eyelids and forehead.

The wolf yowled, and punched a fist into his open palm. "I don't need this headache! And I certainly don't need to follow your weak ass around anymore." He stepped back, putting up his palms when Ridge moved to parallel Amandus. "If you didn't have him to loom over you like a carrion-hungry crow, I'd take you out, old man."

Amandus smirked. "Get out of here before I command my crow to do the same to you."

Lifting his chin in abject disobedience to the leader, Ryan backed toward the door. He fisted an angry gesture at them both, then stepped quickly out of sight.

"You want me to follow him? Tie up loose ends?" Ridge asked.

Sucking in breath through his nose, Amandus shook off the acrid odor from the defiant wolf lingering in his senses. "Not yet. We must play our cards right. The Council watches us too closely right now."

CHAPTER SEVENTEEN

CREED DROPPED HOUSEKEEPER at her apartment in the city. She was still under his persuasion and would wake in a few hours with only a distant memory of a short gig for an eccentric man out in the country who made major messes. He left a generous cash severance on the kitchen counter, then headed home.

Tucking his sunglasses in a front pocket, he followed the thumping beat of music down the hall. The theater-room doors were open, and he saw Blu's feet bob to the tune. She turned her head before he gained her side, smiling up at him. She wore red lace this time, to match the red wig.

Mercy.

He twisted the chair—the aisle seats were rotating rockers—and she clasped her legs about his neck as he squatted before her. Her red spike heels clicked behind his head.

"Adam Ant?" he asked of the music he'd never admit to liking in the eighties.

"'Desperate,'" she sang, and tickled her fingers through his hair, "'but not serious.'"

"Desperate for a little of this?" He nudged her barely there panties aside with his nose. Dashing out his tongue, he speared her wetness. The taste of her hardened his erection instantly.

"Mmm, you'll make me howl," she teased.

"I love to make the wolf howl."

Tearing away the insignificant bit of lace, Creed ventured deeper; his prize, the wolf's sexy howl of encouragement. She spread out her legs, and he ran his palms along them, worshipful in his pose.

It would be another month before he could dally with the werewolf who preferred him scratched and bleeding before having sex. He looked forward to that adventure again.

But even with her claws sheathed, Blu filled his thoughts, his senses, his desires. Not in nine hundred years had he met his match.

The wait had been worth it.

Fingernails dug into his hair and scalp and she tugged as climax fluttered panting whimpers from her lips. He loved when she came softly like that. His fangs were already down. He'd not noticed that.

He should have come to expect it by now. He would be careful with his teeth not to cut her.

Hours later, Creed sprawled on a cozy leather theater chair, one foot propped on the seat before him, the other leg stretched in the aisle. Blu sat on him, her stomach and breasts crushed to his bare chest, her cheek nuzzled against his neck, quiet in her satiation.

His cock was still inside her. This was the place he'd never found over the centuries. A place of comfort. Equality. Acceptance. And now here he sat. Blissfully satisfied.

The red wig was tilted on her head. He gave it a tug, and she reacted.

"What?" She lifted her head. "Oh, I think I dozed off a bit. Mmm, lover, you make me come so much, I have to take naps to recover. Maybe you could float me upstairs to the bed for a while?"

"Float you?"

She lifted her head and kissed him. Brilliant eyes danced with his. "Like you did last night. You moved me. With wind or air, or something. It's your magic, right?"

"I have air magic, yes. Also earth, water and blood magic. You promised you weren't going to tell."

"And you said you were not going to use it."

"Yes, it is the one vow I find I cannot keep. And it's stupid, really, the minute things I use it for. The witches fear I would use it to control people or have the advantage in a battle against them. That was why I took the vow. Also to atone."

"Tell me about it, Creed. It's a part of you I still haven't learned. Did you steal your magic from a witch?"

This was a conversation he'd never purposefully bring up, but he could not deny her the truth of him. It wouldn't be fair after all they'd been through. She'd opened up to him. He could spill a secret and know she would not judge him for it.

"I did. Long before the Protection spell was cast."

She nodded and laid her head on his shoulder. Red hair plushed across his cheek. Her tongue dashed out to lick his chin before she said, "I know a little about the war between the vamps and witches."

"It ended decades ago."

"Right. But you were there for the beginning. Something like a thousand years ago?"

"Eight or nine hundred years."

"So you kept the witch enslaved to drain her of her magic?"

"That's how it worked."

"Tell me."

"Very well." He hugged her head aside his chest and tangled his fingers in the glossy wig. "After the Capetians' rule ended and the House of Valois began to reign in France, I left the vanguard. Well, I hadn't much choice. I'd been changed to vampire against my will. And while much war is fought during the night, I simply could not function as a soldier in the king's army, you understand."

"Lucky for you."

"Not really. I enjoyed battle." Still did. But not so much when Blu was lying in his arms. He snuggled her close, feeding on her delicious warmth.

"I resisted joining the tribe that changed me, even though at the time, the tribes were almost as war-hungry as the mortals. I used the excuse I wanted to learn things on my own, to go out and experience the world. The tribe ousted me, which suited me fine. I had grander plans. I would gain magic and become a force to be reckoned with."

It was uncomfortable to confess to his past indiscretions, but Creed wanted her to know the darkness that still resided within him. He owed her that much after all she and her werewolf had revealed to him last night.

"I stole air magic from a witch who I seduced. Told her I loved her, but really, I was focused on obtaining her magic. For a vampire to steal magic from a witch he has to have sex with her. It's a blood sex magic thing."

"Sounds sexy."

"It was calculated."

She wiggled upon him, and his cock enlivened within her. "I like that you're so honest with me. I find that sexy."

That comment bolstered him and his growing erection.

Creed continued. "The witch can grow very weak, I learned, and literally becomes enslaved to my bite and my selfish need to draw out her magic. When I saw she was becoming too weak, and felt I'd drawn enough magic from her, I abandoned her. On to the next witch. I was determined to gain all the elemental magics."

"Air, earth, fire and water?"

"Yes. Earth was next. I remember that I had some feelings for that witch beyond the desire to steal what I could from her. When she was close to death, I couldn't bear it, so I stopped having sex with her. But she insisted, saying she would rather die making love to me than be burned at the stake."

"You must have been quite the macabre Casanova."

"Must have been?"

She smiled against his chest and rocked her hips slightly.

"I obliged her, and she did die. She'd requested I burn her body and return her ashes to the earth, from which her magic had originated. Using air magic, I spread her ashes through the sky and then settled them upon a lavender field."

"That sounds pretty."

The depth of his depravity wasn't quite permeating her brain.

"But I would have so kicked your ass if it had been me," she added. "Those poor women."

So maybe she did understand what an asshole he'd been.

"Yes, well, the water witch nearly succeeded in doing just as you desire. I rescued her from a dunking chair. It's strange, in medieval times they used to dunk supposed witches in water. If they drowned, they were innocent— but then also dead. If they did not drown, they were accused as witches—and then killed. Dead either way. It made little sense. And honestly, no talented witch would have ever got caught in such a predicament. Except Celia."

"Was she not so powerful?"

"She was the most powerful witch I have known. Yet her downfall was her heart, as it is for all of us." He kissed the crown of Blu's head. "She fell in love with a witch hunter, and found herself bound to a dunking chair. I rescued her, and…"

He thought back to that escapade. Celia was so angry after he'd rescued her she was literally spitting water. She fought him so much he'd had to rebind her wrists and carry her over his shoulder to his home. Once there, he'd fed her, asked her nicely for her magic, and when she refused, well…

"The seduction was short, abrupt, and she did eventually agree, but I think I was a rebound guy, to use today's terms."

Blu shifted against him, working her hips lazily. It was growing more difficult to concentrate on his tale as his mind threatened to play mutiny and let the cock do all the thinking, but he continued.

"I took what I could from her, but she fought me tooth and nail. And I learned one must never get too close to large bodies of water when in the presence of a water witch. She nearly drowned me in the Seine. Fortunately, vamps don't drown easily. I gave up after she pinned me to the bottom of a full well for a fortnight. I have just enough water magic now to be a menace."

"What about fire?"

"Never found a fire witch. They are rare. Fire is the one thing that can kill a witch, so you don't often find practitioners in that element. Though, they are out there. After Celia the Protection was put into place. She was one of the original spell casters."

"I've heard about the Protection, but never met someone directly affected by it. So the spell made all witches' blood poisonous to vampires?"

"Yes. One bite, and the vampire is ash. It's not an easy thing to witness. And I have a few times. Should a vampire survive a witch's blood attack, he becomes a phoenix. There is a Council member who is a phoenix."

"Yes, Nikolaus Drake. I've heard of him. But you are immune?"

"Only because I've witches' blood from before the Protection in me." He tapped the ring on her finger. "Still, I don't trust that."

"I won't wear it anymore. Promise." She took it off and tossed it across the aisle to land against the iron base of a chair. "You've changed a lot, Creed."

He traced a thumb along her satin-smooth back. "I have always taken what I wanted. I'm not sure I can change that."

"You have changed. I mean, look at you, sleeping with a werewolf!"

"Yes, well, I suppose."

"But once, you enslaved someone not like you for your own benefit. Kind of like how the wolves enslave the vampires for blood sport. I'm not trying to compare them. Maybe I am. I know you're different now, and couldn't imagine you bringing harm to anyone who didn't deserve it. But I can't help but wonder what those witches experienced as you drained the magic from them."

"Blu, so many centuries ago I was a man who took what I wanted, when I wanted, from whomever I wanted. I won't apologize for what I did. Hell, I had a chip on my shoulder after being changed to a vampire against my will. They were impressed with my werewolf-killing skills and wanted me on their side. But so you know, I haven't stolen anything from a witch in centuries."

"What does that do to your magic?"

"It certainly doesn't help matters. I can feel it wane each time I use it. I believe I've one good wallop left in me before it is completely depleted."

"So you need to have sex with a witch to keep it strong?"

"Yes. But there's not a witch who would offer, I'm sure of that. I can survive without magic. It doesn't serve me beyond enhancing my daily life. It comes in handy during battle. But as I've said, I strive not to use it as a means to show the witches I am no longer a threat."

"Yes, but what if you were desperate? If magic was the only thing that could help you out of a situation? Would you sleep with a witch again?"

"I would not have another woman now, because that would be cheating on my wife."

"You really mean that."

He stroked the hair from her face. Her skin was softer than silk. The finest luxury he'd ever experienced. "I am yours, Blu. Faithfully. Can you accept the things I've done to survive? That was me then. This is me now."

She toyed her forefinger across his chest. The beat of her heart matched his, relaxed and heavy. If he were to drink her blood, then her heartbeat would synch with his and he could track her anywhere in the city. They would always have a means to find the other.

He could wait. But if she balked at accepting him now it would destroy him. But he must acknowledge any reluctance she may have.

"I can more than accept you," she whispered. Tilting her head, she kissed him under the chin. "I love you, Creed Saint-Pierre, and I'm proud to be your wife."

She pressed up, her palms to his chest, and began to rock upon his hips.

THEY STOOD AMIDST THE carnage, having ransacked the closet for a few items of clothing that hadn't been torn or shredded the night before. Blu had found an old frock coat of Creed's from the eighteenth century and it hung on her shoulders now, the heavy damask engulfing her.

The chair stuck in the wall had slowly worked its way forward, till it let go from the drywall and tumbled across the mattress.

It felt good to laugh. Blu shook her head and slapped a palm on the skewed box spring mattress. "I hope that chair wasn't an antique."

"Vintage seventeenth century. Once held position in the queen's apartments at Versailles."

"My bad?"

"Very naughty," he said, and followed with a blown kiss.

He accepted her as she was—all wild and wicked.

And she accepted him. He'd led an unsavory past as a battle warrior, bounty hunter and witch enslaver, to name a few. But as he'd explained, he was a different man now than he had been then.

Everyone changed.

Blu felt the changes within herself since she'd married Creed. She was calmer now, not so skittish around men, and the need to put on a costume and act aloof was no longer there.

Okay, so costumes were sort of her thing. And what a delicious find in the old steamer trunk at the back of Creed's closet.

She tugged the coat about her, delighting in the patterned damask fabric. Wide cuffs, softened with age, spilled past her hands. The buttons were real diamonds, and though the lace was frayed, she could easily imagine Creed seducing a poufy-skirted demoiselle into his arms.

"Here." He tossed her something and she caught it with both hands. "I don't want it—it's yours. Use it as you wish."

She pressed the pink cell phone to her lips. "I thought for sure you'd change your mind about me," she said, "and leave for the banquet by yourself."

"Are you insane? I want you by my side always. Silly

werewolf." He displayed the titanium ring. Blu had retrieved hers from the theater room, and they'd both put them on for the evening. "I'm going to throw this away after tonight. I don't want to worry about it ever accidentally spilling on you."

"I'm doing the same, though I understand now this blood wouldn't harm you."

"I guess it will either take away my magic or renew it."

"Then why not slurp it down? Doesn't sound too devastating either way."

"But what if it does not? What if there was the slightest chance that blood could harm me? Fry me to ash?"

She tucked the ring against her stomach. "Nix the slurping. I'm not willing to take that chance. Hey, I know. Why don't we do a ritual at the bridge on the way home?"

"Repeat our vows?"

"Yes, and make them our own this time," she offered. "Something simple like 'I promise to love you always. No matter what.'"

"That works for me. Always. No matter what."

He kissed her and while Blu wanted to peel away his shirt and lick his chest—among other things—she knew they had to get this over with. Tonight all eyes would be on them.

All the scheming, plotting eyes that expected them to play the pawns.

She was nervous about looking her father in the eye. Her father—the man who had murdered her mother. But she wouldn't lie about her feelings for Creed.

"Let's do this," she said.

CREED PARKED THE CAR. Before he could rush around to open Blu's door, she stepped out. An exotic princess with blue hair, she wore a deep violet top and long skirt with blue spangled beadwork on it. The fabric was layers of sheer stuff that made him itchy to stroke and try to figure how to make it reveal the skin beneath.

"Is this some kind of Indian dress?" He glanced his fingers over her breasts. "It's so sexy, especially your bare tummy hidden behind this see-through stuff."

"It's a sari, and yes, it's traditional Indian garb. My mother was born in India. She used to wear these all the time. Though I've taken the top up and the skirt down a bit."

A bare leg slipped from the skirt's front slit, and he brushed his fingers over her thigh. "You quicken me, werewolf."

"Are your fangs showing?"

"Not yet, but I won't be surprised should they make a visit if I'm to look upon you all evening without being able to make love to you."

"Soon, lover. Patience is a virtue."

"It's also a bitch."

He touched the diamond choker she had worn that first night. Actually it was rhinestones. She'd revealed she wasn't into fancy jewels, only fancy wigs. He suspected it was because she'd never had her own money to spend on fine things.

He couldn't wait for her to put a dent in that credit card.

"Do you think they'll suspect we're trying to hide something?" he asked. "Put one off on them?"

"Not if we're truthful and tell them we haven't gone that far yet."

She meant the bite, not the sex. "Will we ever go that far?"

She kissed his mouth and tapped it with a delicate fingertip. "I think we may."

"You make me mad with the anticipation."

"Good mad?"

"Very good mad."

Creed slipped her hand into his and led her inside.

A MORE DISCREET LOCATION had been chosen this time than the Landmark Center in St. Paul. A country club at the edge of the northern suburbs hosted the evening's soiree.

Curious vampires and werewolves formed the crowd.

It was very dark. The chandeliers were hung high in the three-story building, and their glow was dim.

"I think I'm going to grab a drink right away," Blu said to Creed, but she didn't slip from his side. Instead, her hands gripped tightly about his upper arm.

"Creed Saint-Pierre."

He turned to find Abigail Rowan waiting. Adorned in pale green satin, she radiated no warmth. She was flanked by the witches Evangeline Perry and Niall Eston.

"We need to talk," Abigail said.

"But we've just arrived," Blu said.

The witch nodded toward a room attached to the main ballroom. Her gaze avoided Blu. "Right now."

Blu clasped his hand and accompanied him. She sought an answer in his eyes, but he had none. Three witches wanted to talk to him? A tendril of anxiety crept about his neck. Could they know?

They entered a deceptively large room that was two stories tall and lined along one wall with windows. Dark wood paneling and brown carpeting gave it a somber look. Inside stood a dozen Council members in a line. None smiled to greet Creed.

Blu's grip grew fierce. Creed lifted it to kiss her knuckles.

"What's this?" Creed asked. "An interview? My wife and I would be very happy to answer any questions."

"Creed," Nikolaus Drake said from the line of condemning gazes. "We've learned something just this morning that must be addressed before we present you and your wife to the tribes and packs."

Abigail pressed a hand to her hip. "You've used magic against the werewolves," she announced. "Do you deny it?"

Lifting his chin, Creed took a moment before speaking. Someone had revealed his secret. He felt Blu's hand slip from his. She had betrayed him?

"I didn't say anything," she whispered. "I swear it. I didn't even know—"

"I am this man's accuser." Amandus Masterson walked to stand beside Abigail. Creed hadn't noticed him in the group. Had he walked in behind him? "We received information the elder used magic to slay one from my pack."

Yes, because that bastard wolf had participated in torturing a vampire. Creed held back the need to protest. He knew he was in the wrong.

"It is true," he offered. "I have used magic on occasion since giving my vow to the witches of the Light."

"Then you must be shackled," Abigail said, not hiding her cutting satisfaction.

"No!" Blu clutched Creed's arm. "He was rescuing a vampire the wolves had forced into blood sport!"

"Silence her," Abigail hissed.

"Blu, please." Creed, maintaining a steady gaze on the

Council before him, wrapped an arm about Blu's shoulders and pulled her against his body. "I am in the wrong."

"But they'll shackle you."

Surely she hadn't a clue what that meant, but probably guessed it involved pain, which it would.

"How dare you?" she shot at her father. "You care little about Creed."

"You were ordered silent," Amandus snapped at her. "Shall I take her from the room?" he asked Abigail.

"It is her choice to remain or leave. Creed, step forward."

Blu clung to him. "Perhaps you should leave," he said gently.

"No, I'm not going anywhere. They can't do this to you."

"If I do not take the punishment, I am no man. Blu, please."

He hated to do it, but he gave her a gentle shove and she stepped away from him. Avoiding her father, who stepped aside as the Council formed a circle, Blu moved to the wall. Tears glistened in her eyes, and each one felt like a razor-edged diamond chip cutting down Creed's heart.

He could have accepted the shackles upon his magic centuries ago. Then he'd been too proud, too arrogant. He'd been determined to keep his vow, but somehow he'd decided a little bit would harm none.

The culmination of many little bits had become his right to use magic as he saw fit. It was wrong.

He would take the shackles.

He just wished it was not before Amandus Masterson. The principal would enjoy every moment of this.

He must not balk. He'd show the old wolf what a real man was made of.

Creed stepped forward, and the Council members, hands joined, closed the circle behind him. He was aware of Blu's heartbeats. As well, the wickedly pleased thud of Amandus's heart. If the wolf thought this would change his and Blu's relationship, he was dead wrong.

"Take off your coat," Abigail said.

He did so, and tossed it outside the circle. Unbuttoning a few top buttons of his shirt and his cuffs, Creed then worked his shoulders and neck, loosening the muscles in preparation. He'd seen this spell enacted. It wasn't pretty.

Abigail stared directly at him. She could not hide the slightest curve at the corner of her mouth. Finally, she had the opportunity to make an example of him.

He would not fault her.

"Under the order of the Council, representative of the nations of the Light and Dark," she recited. "We hereby shackle Lord Edouard Credence Saint-Pierre from using stolen magic."

She thrust out her arms to each side, and the other two witches joined hands. They began to chant in the creepy, slippery tones that Creed associated with nightmares from the Middle Ages after he'd spent dozens of hours marching the vanguard and drawing his sword through so much flesh and bone.

The Council members joined hands, closing the circle. The witches' voices dispersed, becoming one and so distant.

Creed was seized by invisible claws that wrapped about his body from shoulder to ankle. He shouted as the grip tore into his flesh, yet he knew it was only a feeling, not reality.

Electric currents traced his nerves, biting into his veins and muscles with razored teeth. Eyes closed, he groped for…nothing. His fingers in claws, he could not move, save that his muscles reacted to the fiery currents.

Somewhere at the edge of the horrific pain he heard Blu's cry. Her voice bolstered him. Perhaps it was best that he'd taken the shackles only now. For now he had a reason to endure.

Hard iron shackles clamped about his ankles, invisible, but very tangible as they cut through his flesh and the icy chill of the iron burned him. Another set clamped about his knees, pressing his bones tightly together. At his hips, he felt his pelvis break.

Creed cried out from the pain of it.

His elbows were shackled tightly behind his back and his shoulders were bound. And then the heavy scalp cap lined with iron spikes crushed about his skull. Blood poured from the pierce holes, soaking Creed's vision, though it was all a hallucination.

His body lifted from the ground. Immobile and shackled, Creed hung there briefly, and then dropped. He landed on his knees and palms. The intense crush of the iron shackles went away.

The spell had been placed.

"These shackles bind the stolen magic within you," he heard Abigail recite over his gasping breaths. "Should you attempt to utilize it even once your bones will be crushed and the shackles will bleed you dry. And it will not be a hallucination. Go in peace, Creed Saint-Pierre. The Council convenes."

The circle of people moved away from him. Creed heard someone shout, "Let's give him a few moments before we make the announcement that the newlyweds are coming along well, shall we?"

The soft tickle of a blue wig dusted his cheek. Blu knelt beside him. Her fingers tentatively touched his shoulders, but he flinched. "Creed?"

"I'm sorry," he managed. It was difficult to catch his breath. He still felt the minute tingle of the shackles pressing upon his nerves. It twitched his muscles. He couldn't stop the jerky movements. "Give me a moment."

"I'll give you the rest of my life."

And like that, the pain went away.

A ROUND OF APPLAUSE introduced Blu and Creed as they entered the ballroom. Blu clutched Creed's hand as if to let go would send her reeling away into a black void.

He'd promised her the pain was all gone, yet she still felt the tremble in his palm. His muscles twitched. He was not fine.

Damn her father. He'd been gone from the room by the time Creed had stood up. She suspected Amandus thought he'd castrated her husband, in a manner.

Perhaps he had. She couldn't know how the shackles would affect Creed. If only they had a moment to themselves.

The wolves bowed on one knee as Blu walked by. All eyes fell upon the blue-haired princess. That was usual. Yet for the first time in her life she found it hard to hold up her chin and simply be admired.

For they did not admire. They judged. They preened over her. They whispered and conspired. Together she and Creed had entered the lion's den. Pray, they exited with hands joined as tightly.

Nikolaus Drake had promised Blu no one outside of the room would know what had just been done to Creed. So they would smile over their grimaces and pray the night passed quickly.

She tugged the swath of sheer purple fabric over her shoulder, wishing she'd have gone with the black velvet dress that covered more skin. She'd chosen the dress specifically for when she stood before her father.

A peripheral scan sighted the bar on the opposite side of the room. She wondered if Bree was wielding a chocolate martini with a welcoming hug.

"Darling." Her father approached for a hug.

Darling? That was one she'd never heard before. He acted as though they'd not just watched her husband's torture.

"All eyes are on us," Creed whispered at her ear. "Go to him."

Blu dropped Creed's hand, reluctantly, and stepped in for the awkward embrace with Amandus. They weren't a touchy-feely family. She could count on one hand how many times he'd hugged her in her lifetime. Rough squeezes and shoves, on the other hand, had been all too common.

Disengaging from the weird touch, Blu cautioned threatening tears. She could get beyond what he had just done to Creed. Even Creed admitted it had been a deserved punishment. But Amandus had killed her mother in a rage. Had she suffered? Ryan had said he'd taken her head off.

"You're looking lovely, daughter," Amandus said in a loud voice, obviously so others would hear. "Though the hair is over-the-top, as usual."

Blu looked aside. *Don't cry now. He wants to see you weak. It's what gives him control over you.*

"Lord Saint-Pierre." Amandus offered a hand to Creed, who shook it, even as he managed to slide his other hand around Blu's waist.

Claimed once again, Blu straightened and lifted her chin. She only ever wanted to stand in Creed's arms. For only in his arms could she be the princess she was meant to be.

Together they were strong.

"Now that the nasty business is aside," Amandus said with a vicious smirk, "there's no reason we can't all raise a glass, eh? I see you and my daughter are getting along?"

"Very well, sir." Creed hadn't used the respectful address for Amandus. "I can honestly say I love your daughter."

Her father's brows rose. He looked to Blu for confirmation.

She nodded. "We're in love. I know it's more than the Council had hoped for. But that's a good thing. We've become the perfect example for the Light and Dark nations."

"Well." Not exactly the joyous reaction most would have upon hearing wonderful news. Amandus wasn't playing this skillfully. "Isn't that wonderful. I'm sure Lord Saint-Pierre's people will be glad to hear of this. Will you let me steal my daughter from your arms for a moment, my lord? We've much to talk about."

"Certainly." Creed kissed Blu at the corner of her mouth. "But don't stray far, Blu. I want you in my eyesight."

That statement infuriated her father, for Blu saw the rage lift in his gold eyes. Score one point for the vampire.

"I'll stay close," she answered, and reluctantly parted from his warmth.

"Are you serious?" her father started immediately. Anger tensed his muscles and made his gaunt jowls puff up when he spoke. "Or are you a far better actress than I could hope for?"

"You always did rant against my dramatic streaks, Daddy dearest, but this time it is for real." She tracked Creed's casual strides through the mixture of the nations. *Turn back to me.* "I love the vampire. I consider Lord Saint-Pierre my husband in every way."

"In *every* way? Are you saying— Ah! I do not want to hear it. No matter what you have done, it will not change our plans."

"I know that. But can we have peace this evening, Father? You've had your fun, now allow Creed and I to step away from what just occurred and enjoy the rest of the night. This is a celebration of two people coming together. Maybe if you step back and look at Creed and me you'll see it is possible. We really do love one another."

"Yet you haven't taken his bite."

"No."

"Good. Then you can't really love him. I was worried for a moment. No daughter of mine will be lost to the longtooths."

"But you've already thrown me to them. And you insisted I take his bite after the vows were spoken. What's changed now?"

"You are tainted, that's for certain. I had to play the role so you wouldn't give yourself away while in the vampire's home. But if you haven't been bitten, then after this charade has come to a head, I'll find a suitable partner for you when you return to the pack."

"Return?"

As in, after the werewolves had defeated the vampires? She didn't want to imagine what might happen. Amandus would go after Creed first. That was fact.

"Yes, return."

"What of Ryan?" she asked softly.

"What of him? I've ousted the whelp from the pack. What do you know about his liaisons with the Western pack?"

Blu sucked in her lower lip. A lot. But it wasn't her place to condemn her ex-lover. She wanted him out of her life, but never dead. Amandus had kicked him out of the pack? That relieved her only until she wondered who her father had in mind to replace him.

"I haven't spoken to Ryan since the marriage," she

offered. "I know as much as you do about the blood sport."

Amandus's brows shot up on his forehead.

"I know, Father. You've been skimming money from Ryan's matches. How dare you?"

"What? Skim money, or see the vampires punished for their extermination of our breed? I don't like what you insinuate, daughter."

"Don't call me daughter. I hate you."

He gripped her upper arm. His nails were sharp and they cut through the gossamer fabric. "You will regret your words when the vampires are begging for mercy and your husband is dead."

She had guessed right. Creed would be her father's first target.

"How dare you wear that dress," he said with a sneer.

"It reminds me of Mother," she said softly, losing the courage to confront him. She would not. It pleased her though that it bothered him. "I should get back to Creed."

"Yes, yes, run along and cozy up to the bloody long-tooth. Make it look good for the Council. As soon as we're assured the vampire nations have accepted your marriage we'll begin to enact our plans."

A bloody slaughter.

There was nothing one small female wolf could do to

prevent any of it. And she'd been truthful with Creed. He expected exactly as Amandus planned.

"Promise me one thing, Father."

He studied her briefly, sneering as he cast his eyes over her hair and dress.

"I know I've no say in pack politics."

"Damned right."

"And I would not presume to sway your thinking. Whatever happens is going to happen." A war neither she nor Creed could prevent. "Will you spare Creed? Please?"

"You are mad. And I will not be defeated because your heart plays to the enemy. If the love you confess is true, then you have betrayed me, and you are no longer my daughter. And if we are to make an example of them, he must be the first to die."

"Haven't you hurt Creed enough? Please, I'll do anything. I'll marry whomever you chose for me. I'll have babies and supply the pack with females."

"You would do that?" Again those surprised brows. "You've always been dead against becoming a breeding female. How you've ranted against the mere suggestion of serving the pack."

They'd had the discussion at least once a year. Her father had insisted she support the pack by becoming a sort of broodmare. She had screamed and complained that her life would be over, and she'd sooner kill herself than sacrifice her very body and soul.

"It would be humiliating and I'd hate it. But if you will promise to spare Creed's life, I will do it. I'll mate with any wolf you designate."

As the only breeding female in the pack, she would be valued—but used constantly in an attempt to repopulate the lacking females.

Blu would rather die.

"I was thinking Ridge would make an excellent stud for you."

Blu breathed out. At least that werewolf she could stomach. "I will do it. For Creed's life. You must promise."

His bloodshot eyes traced hers. Was that the look her mother had stared into before breathing her last breath?

You've done what you swore you would not. You are doing as Amandus wishes. Crumbling before him.

To save Creed.

"Very well." Her father snarled. "The longtooth's life for your commitment to the pack. I swear to it."

She nodded.

"I didn't hear that."

Her heart dropped to her gut. "I promise you my submission."

Amandus stepped away.

There was no means to change what she'd agreed to. The

war would happen. And she would be saddled as a literal slave and mated to the strongest and most virile of wolves.

Blu turned to track her husband. He stood across the room talking animatedly to his friend, Alexandre.

She'd saved his life. And because of it she would lose him forever.

CHAPTER EIGHTEEN

CREED JOINED ALEXANDRE at the edge of the ballroom. A residual bite from the spell tweaked at his neck and he flinched.

"You are acting strange, man."

"If you'd just been through what I have, you'd be flinching, too."

"Yeah, I saw you talking with your wife's father."

Creed smirked. No reason to explain he'd just been magically shackled, which had felt as if he'd been shoved into the devil's iron maiden torture device.

"Is Eugene here this evening?"

"Haven't seen him." Alexandre kept a keen eye, constantly sweeping the room. "You'd think that bastard would stick out like a cue ball racked among eight balls."

Both men gauged the atmosphere as more tense than it had been the wedding night. All eyes were on Creed and Blu. The Council—peopled with vampires, witches and a few faeries—was chatting up Blu at the moment. She smiled and shook their hands, courteous and cordial.

Creed wondered where the werewolf representative from the Council was. There had been one at the wedding.

This didn't feel right. What perfect timing for Amandus to sic the Council witches after him.

"Her father is smiling through his vitriol," Creed commented. "They're plotting against us as we speak. Something is going down. I don't want this to turn into a bloodbath tonight."

"Not with the Council here. No one will dare," Alexandre said. "But after? I'm going to be the first to smash Ryan's face into a brick wall and rub it off."

"You think he was the one who ordered your capture?"

"Can't be sure, but Eugene the Scapegoat works for me."

"Hold back your need for revenge, my friend. This can still work. The nations can come together."

"Are you serious, man? You saw the vamp we rescued the other night. He was half-mad with UV sickness and vomiting black blood. He'll never be the vampire he once was. It would have been far better to kill him than to force him to exist now. Tell me you're doing the act about the princess. You don't love her."

"Sorry to disappoint." Creed countered Alexandre's

angry slash of hand with a calming one. "I know that was the original plan, but I hadn't expected to genuinely care for her. I am in love, Alexandre."

"Love? It is lust." He bowed his head to Creed's and said lowly, "There's nothing shameful about succumbing to her allure. But do not lie to yourself about that surface attraction."

"I would die for Blu."

Alexandre winced. "The tribe will shun you."

"I am their leader. They will do as I command, and if that is to respect the werewolves, then so be it."

"Yeah? You've never been starved for months, then forced to suck blood from your own kind to survive."

His second in command exposed his teeth, and the fangs were down. "Alexandre?"

"I'm shocked, Creed. This is not what a leader does."

"A leader guides his tribe toward peace."

"A leader stands for what is right. And if that is vengeance then you should be leading us to it."

"Alexandre, calm yourself. There will be no fighting tonight. We will put a stop to the blood matches, but we cannot expect the wolves to lay down before us without some sacrifice on our part."

"We've given blood."

"As have they."

The werewolf hunting had occurred seventy years ago,

yet Alexandre had lived during that time. Why could he not relate? Creed had seen the werewolf pelts strung along cabin walls, and the vampires who had laughed at their hunting success. He'd never participated in a hunt, but he'd known those who had.

"I need to join my wife," Creed said. "If you disobey my orders, I won't hesitate to banish you from Nava."

The vampire bowed his head, but Creed sensed his ire would not be so easily tamped down.

"How DID IT GO with your father?"

"Probably as well as it went with your tribe," Blu said. "Are they happy for us?"

"Grimacingly so." Creed lifted his champagne goblet to a passing couple, vampire male and female, arm in arm. They nodded cordially. The female's smile revealed fang. "Your father is looking a bit too frowny for my taste."

"He's always that way. He doesn't believe I love you. He can't accept his daughter has finally found happiness. He'll do anything to take it away from me."

"Did you confront him about your mother?"

She clutched Creed's arm to steady herself against the sudden wooziness.

"Are you all right?" His dark eyes searched hers, his compassion obvious. "Your father upset you. Perhaps it's time we leave."

"No, I'm fine. I didn't want to bring my mother up tonight. This is supposed to be a celebration. And every time I say it, it still is impossible to buy into."

"My heart celebrates you," he whispered into her ear. "Know that, Blu."

She did know that. And Creed's love went a long way toward bolstering her waning confidence. "Are you okay?"

"Just a few twitches still. Do you notice them?"

"No, you look fine on the outside." She kissed him. "I want to get you home, to kiss every part of you, and make you forget the pain."

He brushed a hand across her breasts, but her nipples were already hard.

"But we shouldn't rush away," she added. "I want to talk to Bree. I know she's here somewhere. I'm just…so happy. Honestly. And it's hard to be so when I know the world doesn't wish it for me."

"I wish it. I won't let them take away our happiness, Blu. No matter what happens, I will be here for you."

"What if we're ostracized?"

"It's a fate I can accept."

"Honestly? But you're the tribe leader. I can't imagine the stigma—"

"No worse than a werewolf wearing a vampire's bite," he said quickly.

She nodded, then stroked her neck uneasily.

Together they stood as the room moved about them, the partygoers slashing at them with visual daggers and cursing them under their breaths. What hypocrites. They were the ones to demand she and Creed marry and now they would condemn them.

"This really is playing like the Catholics versus the Huguenots. I don't want to play the game anymore, Creed. I wish you could make it stop."

He sighed and tilted her head to nestle against his neck. "Let me think on it some more. If you wish me to make it stop, I will do everything in my power to make it happen. There are some tricks I've up my sleeve yet."

"You can't use your magic. I heard what the witch said. Your bones would really be crushed."

"Don't worry." He studied her gaze, stroking a thumb along her jaw. "If magic would have served, I would have wielded it decades ago. We'll talk about it later, I promise."

"Is it going to freak me out?"

"I hope not. But then I know you like the freaky stuff."

"You do. Sadist."

He grinned. "Masochist."

"Wolf lover."

"Longtooth's bitch."

"Oh, bite me."

"Ah?" His eyes glittered expectantly.

"I mean…I didn't mean that literally. I can't believe I said that."

"You were teasing, lover. Though, I wish you were not." He kissed her forehead. "Okay, you run off and find your friend before I'm forced to sneak you off to the coatroom and have my way with you."

"You've given me a new option. Chat with Bree or make out in the coatroom?"

He waited for her to decide. It shouldn't be a hard decision, but Blu found moving one step away from her husband felt like a mile.

"I'd better find the faery. She'll never forgive me if I missed her. Though, trust me, Bree would be pleased to hear about an adventure amongst the coats. Find you in half an hour?"

"I'll miss you every minute you're away." He bruised a kiss to her lips and she took it with a regretful sigh. "Love you."

CREED OBSERVED ALEXANDRE mooning over his pretty lover, a vampire slayer with no tallies to her credit who he had changed to vampire less than a year ago after a vacation in Paris.

It hurt him that his second in command wasn't on

board with the peace pact. Not that Creed had bought into it originally. Now that his mind had taken a three-sixty, he needed to bring the rest of the vamps with him. If Alexandre didn't get behind him, convincing the rest of the tribe wouldn't be half as easy as it should be.

But he would never force the man to something that went against his principles. Once forced to fight another vampire to survive, while vicious werewolves looked on, Alexandre would never, and must never, be expected to want to embrace them and call them friend.

He'd stopped flinching, but he still felt a strange pressure about his temples. It had been too real. The blood had dripped from the pierce holes in his skull, hot and thick. He didn't ever want to know that pain again. It was a great deterrent against using magic.

Creed tossed back another glass of champagne and decided a breath of air would clear his struggling thoughts.

The parking lot was lined with Escalades, Jaguars and BMWs. Funny how you could pick out a werewolf from his black gangsta SUV and a vampire from his more refined choice in vehicles.

Yet the two species were more alike than different. Both lived, loved, struggled, rejoiced and, yes, hated. They had dreams and desires, regrets and suffered grief. They clung to humanity for it was the only means to survive in this mortal realm.

Blu had taught him much in the short time he'd known her.

He'd spent decades, nay centuries, hating the wolves, designing ways to overcome and defeat them when needed. Wolfsbane had killed many. Now Creed could honestly look back over those times with regret.

What a waste of time battling against the werewolves had been. It had gotten him nothing. It had served the vampire tribes no boon. War was merely aggression, a flip of the finger to the opposition.

If only he could have met Blu centuries ago, and she could have turned his world on its head then.

Perhaps though, it was best he only met her now. Her lifespan was but two or three centuries. He was glad she was still young, and he had many years to look forward to with her.

His wife had changed him at a visceral level. He may have been going through the motions by standing up for the peace pact and the rescue team, but only now did he truly understand the devastation such animosity toward one another caused.

Passing a group of male vampires who hung at the corner of the building sharing clove cigarettes, Creed nodded to a few members of Nava. They addressed him as "my lord," which he thought now was over-the-top.

Why had he insisted on the title? He'd used it since

the late fifteen hundreds. If he truly desired respect he needed to step down to their level. Or rather, simply join them and not put any on one level or another.

Things would change within Nava. He'd see to it immediately. Perhaps it was time to hand the reins over to Alexandre, let the youngblood take command. It would give him more time with his wife, and Creed liked that idea.

He saw vampires from Kila and Zmaj and others here. It was good the various tribes were getting along. One less thing to worry about.

But he had no doubt they relied upon him to signal the beginning to this war. Out of eyesight of the Council, the tribes were as hungry for blood as were the packs.

Would they listen if he announced they should step back, let the werewolves have their territories and just shake hands and make up? Old habits died hard.

This marriage alone could have never facilitated something so immense. While he'd initially played along, since falling in love with Blu he'd developed hopes it could have at least started something, the way a small spark often became a fire. Wouldn't a wave of peace be insanely fine?

He was an old man. He wanted to settle into life and love his wife for days innumerable.

Up ahead he noticed a group of weres restraining one particular wolf. He looked drunk, but as Creed paused on the curb to observe, he realized the wolf was frenzied, in a rage. Shoving at his cohorts and tugging down his red plaid shirt, he tried for a modicum of calm, but something kept pressing him to shout and swear loudly.

"That's him," one of the wolves said acidly.

The entire group looked to Creed.

Shit. He could take a were or two, but a whole group? Good thing a few tribe members stood close.

Creed approached the weres. "Evening, gentlemen. You here for the banquet?"

"You're Lord Saint-Pierre?" the one they'd been restraining asked. He was brawny and huffing, having exerted himself greatly already. His bald head sweated.

"I am. And you are?" But Creed knew the answer quickly after asking.

"Ryan."

"Ah, yes. Eugene, isn't it?"

"The werebitch's presumed mate," the wolf spat.

"Yes, she mentioned you once or twice."

The wolf fisted the air. His buddies had the wherewithal to secure him at the arms, but not tightly.

"If you have laid a single tooth to her I will rip your head off!"

"No teeth. Not yet," Creed said calmly.

He was baiting the beast. But he wouldn't back down from the rabid thing. Who had let him on the property in the first place?

"I'll thank you to keep your thoughts from my wife, wolf. She's mine now. Find yourself another dog to shove around."

"Why, you bloody flesh-pricker!"

The wolf's cohorts let go of him, laughing and ribbing him on.

Ryan lunged at Creed. They went down on the tarmac, the man growling and punching Creed in the gut. He knew wolves fought dirty, and if he gave the man a chance to wolf out, he'd never match him.

Kneeing his opponent, Creed kicked him off and jumped up to follow through. Suit coat tight across his shoulder, he shrugged it off.

The werewolves circled the fight with interest, but did not interfere. Creed sensed the vamps moving in, quieter than the wolves, but keenly interested.

He did not require a tribe member to step in, but he was glad to have them close.

He'd imagined the things he'd like to do to this bastard wolf in repayment for the pain he'd caused Blu and countless vampires. But he would not deliver a mortal wound, not here on designated neutral ground.

Vengeance in his wife's name demanded he kill the wolf; honor insisted he not.

Dodging a punch, Creed noted the wolf was slow because of his upper body. There was a point a man could develop too many muscles. He came up and elbowed the bruiser in the ribs. The move didn't even force a gasp from the wolf.

Blood spilled down the back of Creed's throat. The wolf had crushed his nose with an iron fist. He spit to the side.

"Had enough, longtooth?" Ryan barked. "Some tribe leader you are. Can't even stand against one wolf. And I'm not even breaking out the big bad yet."

Creed spit again, and the wolf dodged to avoid the bloody spittle. He used that moment of inattention to kick him high at the shoulder. The move sent the wolf flying against the brick wall twenty feet away.

"Nice one," a vampire called.

Yes, but Creed could have laid him out if he'd the power of his magic behind the kick. The shackles were yet too apparent, though, to consider such a stupid move.

The wolf shook off the hit and growled, flexing his arms in a he-man pose. And then he began to shift.

Not good. A vampire never liked to take on a werewolf without proper weapons. Yet Creed did not wish for Wolfsbane. No, that would only serve as the rally to battle.

Somewhere at the club's back door, a female yelled. A flash of violet skirts distracted Creed momentarily.

"Stay back!" he shouted to Blu.

She'd rushed out the back door and barged through the

clutch of vampires. Making eye contact with Alexandre, Creed nodded once.

Alexandre secured Blu.

"Call off your thug," Ryan growled, mid-shift. "Let her go!" His face elongated and it grew caninelike. Fangs descended. His shirt ripped down the seams. Hair sprouted across his shoulders and down his arms.

Creed willed down his teeth and lunged for the wolf. If he were close, it would be more difficult for the beast to lash out with those deadly talons. What werewolves lacked in agility, vampires made up for with speed and stealth.

Besides, he'd had a crash course avoiding claws just last night. He was up for this.

The enraged werewolf howled to the sky. The entire pack answered with short, yipping howls. Completely shifted, Ryan now stood two heads higher than Creed. His shoulders had broadened and dark hair covered his body. He stomped, flicking his head back and howling— and eyed Creed.

Creed raised a fist, and connected directly with Ryan's jaw. Bones cracked.

As did glass.

Spatters of liquid silver beaded in the air. The world seemed to slow as Creed withdrew his fist. But the wolf didn't snap at him with an angry growl. Instead, a silver bead hit the werewolf on the bloody snout and it yowled, slapping at the contact.

"Hell's mercy." Creed flipped over his hand. The ring had broken, spattering liquid silver into the air.

"It's silver!" one of the wolves shouted. The pack dispersed but did not go far.

"Bastard's not fighting fair!"

"No, I…" Creed looked to Blu. He could not hear her over the growls and wild yips, but her mouth was open wide, screaming.

For him or her lover?

The werewolf dropped, convulsing before him. The silver would track his veins and explode the beast from within.

"He's killed him. Take the longtooth!"

At Blu's father's direction the pack moved in for the kill. Wolves charged Creed and others went after Alexandre. The vampire was no match for the pack. Blu, too, was taken and wrangled by wolves.

A fist to his jaw sent Creed stumbling. A kick to his shin dropped him to his knees. Blood dribbled down his chin. The talon slash across his chest was only half-healed and hurt like hell.

"Take his head!" Amandus announced.

"No!" Blu raged, struggling against her captors. "You promised!"

The father looked to his struggling daughter and nodded.

"Wait," Amandus shouted, as a wolf transformed, talons growing out its fingers. "Leave that longtooth alive."

The last thing Creed remembered was a foot connecting with his jaw.

CHAPTER NINETEEN

"YOU MADE YOUR BARGAIN," Amandus said to Blu as she was secured in the back of the waiting SUV.

Silver shackles about her wrists—lined on the interior with leather—would not harm her, but would drain her energy. She couldn't struggle if she wished.

Indeed, she had made a deal with the devil to save Creed's life.

"You go back on the bargain," she screamed at her father, "and I'll come after you myself."

The old man smirked and slammed the door shut.

Blu shuffled into the darkness but was grabbed by two strong hands. "Welcome home, Princess. Your father thinks I've potential in the pack. We'll be seeing a lot of each other is what I hear."

It was not the familiar Ridge who grabbed her, but the creepy, lecherous new recruit, Diaz.

CREED DRAGGED HIMSELF up by the brick wall. Blood filled his mouth—his own. He spit to the side.

All about him chaos reigned. Vampires fought werewolves. Bladed weapons were slashed through the air, and wooden bullets were fired at the vampires. The occasional splash of holy water only burned flesh if the vampire had been baptized. None in Nava had been, but there were other tribes Creed worried about. A baptized vampire could not survive a holy wound.

Remarkably, no weres came after him. They must think him already dead.

The last thing he remembered was Blu shouting and struggling with her father's men.

Had they taken her?

He raced inside and toward the banquet hall, shoving aside werewolves and vampires alike. The very war they'd tried to prevent had been set loose tonight.

Because of him.

He'd not thought about the ring when he'd been fighting Ryan. It was too insane that it had broken. Of course, the glass wasn't as strong as titanium. He hadn't wished the wolf dead, no matter his vicious attack, or his fronting the blood matches.

If Blu had for one disillusioned moment loved Eugene Ryan, he would never kill him. Beat the crap out of him, sure, but not kill him.

"She must hate me. Where is she?"

Havoc bustled inside the ballroom beneath the grand chandeliers. Vampires went after werewolves, fangs bared. Weres shifted and slashed out with talons. Through the darkness and sparking lights, Creed spied Amandus. The old man observed the chaos from the edge of the room, peering around the doorway.

Creed crossed the room and shoved the man across the hall and into a dark corner. "Where is she?"

"Safe from you. Unhand me, longtooth."

The old man's eyes glowed yellow. Did he think to shift before Creed? Bring it on.

"I'll see to Blu's safety," Creed hissed. "She could get hurt in this havoc."

"She is secure. And she is no longer yours."

"No longer—? She is my wife!"

"Drop the game, Saint-Pierre. You put up a good show, but you are released from your vows. I'll burn the marriage contract. I'll not see any daughter of mine wed to a vampire."

"Too late, old man. You were the one to push her into my arms. I love her. I'll treat her far better than you ever could. Why didn't your men finish me off?"

Her father grimaced and spat. "She begged for your life."

"What? When?"

"Earlier. She knew this would happen. Just as you

have known it would, so drop the act. We've both now got the war we have strived for."

"Not my war," Creed said through clenched teeth. "Nor is it Blu's. Where is she?"

"On her way to becoming a broodmare for the pack. As she should be. Idiot bitch. To think she was in love with a longtooth?"

Creed fisted Amandus at the jaw. The wolf groped for a hold, but slid down the wall. Gripping him by the neck, Creed lifted him and leaned over his face.

"She told me how you treated her. How dare you? She is not a commodity to hand out as a prize to your warriors."

The wolf cracked a smirk and Creed squeezed his neck. The vein pounded against his palm. His fangs lowered.

"No wolf will ever again use Blu, do you understand that?"

"If you go to her, longtooth, the bargain she made with me is broken and you're dead."

Creed squeezed harder until his thumb broke through flesh. Hot blood spurted across his face. "You first."

He lunged to bite the wolf's neck.

CREED FOUND ALEXANDRE bent over outside behind a garbage Dumpster. His throat had been slashed, exposing muscle and spine, yet no vampire was going to die that easily.

He couldn't talk until the gaping wound healed. Creed shucked off his bloodied shirt and tied it about Alexandre's throat.

"They've got Blu," he said. "I suspect they've taken her to the Northern pack's compound. That's about an hour drive beyond my estate. I'm going after her."

Alexandre gripped his forearm and shook his head violently.

Creed pressed firmly against the makeshift bandage. "Don't move so much. Let the wound heal."

"Just…let me die."

Creed swallowed back an angry refusal. He'd said the same thing after Creed had rescued him from the blood match.

"No. I will not let you die. You are a good man, Alex. You've far too much to live for. What about Veronica?"

Alexandre winced but nodded. Creed could feel the man's flesh knit together beneath his touch as he held the wound closed.

Alexandre managed to whisper. "She's not worth it."

"Veronica?"

"No. Your wolf."

"Not worth sacrificing my position with the tribe? Not worth my being ostracized?"

"Exactly," Alexandre croaked.

"Alexandre, think about the women you have loved. What of your beloved wife?"

The tattered vampire nodded his head. "Maria."

The reason the man was a vampire was because of the woman he had loved so long ago. His wife had been raped, tortured and murdered. Alexandre, in a rage, had taken his revenge, knowing the hangman's noose would be his reward. He'd done it out of love. Vampires, excited at the mortal's revenge, had claimed him after that.

"You are fortunate to have known love, Alexandre, and to have it once again. It is a reason you must not ask for death now."

The vampire nodded, conceding weakly.

"I have lived almost a thousand years, can you imagine? This is it, Alexandre. Love. And I'm not going to lose it. And if Blu does choose to return to her pack and abandon me, I won't let it happen until I know she is safe. I'm going. When you are able, you gather as many from Nava as you can and retreat. We aren't prepared for this battle. We have to regroup and strategize."

"Not alone," Alexandre managed, though his words gurgled with blood.

"Yes, alone. It's the safest way without drawing attention. I'll find her, or die trying." He slapped Alexandre on the shoulder and took off across the parking lot.

A wolf, half-shifted, lolled by the trunk of a Mercedes

as he neared the BMW. Creed approached, prepared to kill it, but when it looked up at him, Creed saw one of its eyes had been torn out.

"I had no idea my men had become so vicious." He backed away and got in the car. "They've become blood crazed. This fight will escalate to war if we don't stop it."

Backing from the lot, he peeled onto the road. There was no time to waste. He stopped at his estate, ran inside and grabbed Wolfsbane. He made the drive to the compound in a half hour and parked two miles out on a dark gravel road.

SWINGING WOLFSBANE through the cool evening air, Creed stalked down a ditch and across a barren field. The wolves would smell him coming. He was covered in wolf blood, his own and, as well, Alexandre's. Would they scent their principal's blood on him, too?

He swiped a palm over his bloodied chest, but it would do little good. He should have washed before coming here. He hadn't time now.

He had to reach the compound quickly, and without being noticed. A spell to summon the wind would keep his scent hidden.

He began to summon, and the first pinch of iron to his skull stopped him cold. Creed fell to his knees. "Fuck."

No magic. Not ever again.

He shook off the nerve-abrading pain and stood. "Guess I'll have to do things the old-fashioned way."

He'd charged vanguards many times. Usually with dozens of soldiers flanking him. Pray tonight the vanguard was all sleeping inside the compound.

Breaking into a run, he dashed across the lumpy field. Chunks of dried earth made footing difficult, but his steps were so quick he barely touched ground before pushing off in another stride. Beating a fierce pace, he gained the massive cement compound.

Entering at ground level would be suicide. He sighted an iron ladder attached to the side of the compound and leaped for it, landing five rungs up. Climbing quickly, he hurdled over the roof edge and landed on the flat roof with a roll, but did not come up on his feet. Instead he crouched beyond the demarcation where the security light beamed.

Taking the cement roof ledge in careful steps, he avoided the light as it flashed around again. He couldn't scent Blu as easily as a wolf could.

If only he'd bitten her. With her blood in his system, his heartbeat would synch to hers when she was near. He would know her presence.

A rustle behind alerted him. Creed slipped noiselessly up against a tin chimney flue. So they did have guards outside. Smart. He hoped the guard wasn't in werewolf form. The moon was officially still full, even though it was waning, and that made the enemy formidable.

"Who's there?"

The unseen enemy was not in werewolf form, else he wouldn't have been able to speak.

Creed jumped to the top of the chimney. The wolf looked up, still unable to pinpoint the intruder. Creed sprang, landing on his opponent on the shoulders and bringing them both down on the loose-pebbled rooftop.

They grappled, but Creed didn't take any chances. He slashed Wolfsbane across the wolf's throat before he could cry out and alert others. The foul scent of wolf blood permeated the air. Blood pooled on the pebbles and Creed stepped away so he would not leave tracks.

Drawing tall, Creed relished the adrenaline rush of success. He liked taking off werewolf heads. And defeating an enemy that should rightly have more strength.

How could his wife ever love him? He knew well he could act on the outside, but inside he would always be her enemy.

"No," he whispered. "Never."

Blu was not the enemy. And he had begun to change, thanks to her.

Creed stepped back, wiped the blade across the wolf's pant leg, then tilted his head to listen. No others on the roof.

Without Blu's scent or the blood bond, he would have to listen for the heartbeats below. Already he sensed two, perhaps two stories below him. Calm heartbeats. Walking farther, he paused as each new heartbeat pulsed a message to him. Most were calm, some aggressive, a few sleeping. He counted eight so far.

And then he sensed the erratic pulse of fear. "Blu."

Whispering her name, Creed wished he could use magic to send it below to his wife, but perhaps their bond would reassure her. "I'm coming for you."

"I'M COMING FOR YOU."

She heard the voice in her head, thought it was Creed, but didn't dare to dream.

Whimpering at the aches pulsing in her muscles, Blu nuzzled her face into the scratchy straw barely covering the cement floor. It was cold in the basement, and her dress was gossamer thin. The skirt was made from yards of fabric, but she wasn't able to utilize more than the long loose end designed to sweep over her arm and wrap it about her shoulders.

Her ankle pulsed madly. It must have twisted when Diaz had shoved her from the van. Normally a minor injury would heal within minutes, but shackled in silver, as she was, the injury might grow worse.

If she could shift to wolf shape, she could slip from

the shackles and scamper out of here. But again, the silver kept her weak.

She prayed this was not how her father intended to keep her now. Surely he would allow her to return to her private quarters and live as she had.

Not like this.

She was not an animal.

When Creed looked at her, all he saw was his wife. His lover. He made her so proud to stand at his side. And now she would never see him again.

They'd both been shackled tonight. What a sorry end to the relationship. Yet she would shackle herself to Creed for the rest of her days if she were able.

"Oh, Creed."

Footsteps descending the stairs alerted her. Blu was too drained to scent who was coming. It was probably Diaz. The wolf had manhandled her down the stairs and she'd feared rape, but after chaining her to the plumbing pipe, he'd merely cracked a wicked grin and promised to return.

If Amandus gave her to Diaz to mate with, she would sooner rip out her heart.

"Oh, *mon Dieu.*"

That voice! Diaz's voice would not make her heart flutter. Blu wanted to lift her head, but she couldn't muster the strength.

"Chains and shackles? No, no, Blu. Can you hear me?"

"Creed?"

"We must be quick. I don't think I alerted the guards, but they will scent the blood on me soon enough. My love, I am so sorry for this. Had that fight not started you would not be here right now."

He lifted a shackle and Blu moaned as the numbing ache prickled through her body. "Silver?"

"Yes. I'm too weak to struggle out. Please, Creed, get out of here and save yourself. There are too many wolves. You can't fight them all. Not without magic."

"I'd die without you, Blu. I'm not going anywhere unless you're in my arms."

She heard the sound of metal scraping across the cement. The glint of a blade made her wince. "You brought Wolfsbane?"

"Have a problem with that?"

"Swing to your heart's content, lover. I'm so over the pack's nasty dogs."

He wrenched on the shackle about her wrist. "I can't use the sword. I don't want to cut you. But the silver is soft. I can snap it. Your wrists are so delicate—"

"Just do it. Ouch!"

The torn silver abraded her flesh, but did not draw blood thanks to the leather lining. What silver could do to a werewolf— Oh, Ryan. She'd watched her lover die tonight, unfeeling and almost relieved.

Creed kissed her free wrist, imprinting his warmth on her skin as if a brand. Clasping it to his cheek, he held her there, safe and loved. She shuddered at the tender touch.

A kiss to her mouth stole her breath. *Take it all,* she wanted to say. *Take me into you and protect me.*

He bent and broke the other shackle, and again he kissed her wrist, tendering the bruise carefully. Blu slid her fingers through his hair, madly relieved to have him here.

"How did you find me?"

"Your blood was outside and on the steps. I'm going to kill any wolf who has caused you to bleed, I vow that."

A thank-you was all she could manage. She was too weak, and getting weaker. Her father's men would not think twice about killing Creed. They were likely looking for him right now.

"Can you walk?"

"If I can shift, I can lead us out of here. I'll have more energy in wolf shape."

"Shh."

With a staying touch to her shoulder, Creed stood and pressed his back to the wall. He loomed over her, Wolfsbane held before him with two hands.

Then she heard it. Footsteps clattered down the hallway, followed by a menacing voice. "Your loverboy is coming for a kiss, Princess!"

Diaz. Let the vampire take care of his nasty ass. She had more important things to manage.

Blu groaned and pushed herself onto all fours. She closed her eyes and concentrated on the shift, safe in knowing Creed would take care of the wolf. As her body began to change, her fur was spattered with Diaz's blood. A head rolled to the edge of the straw.

Blu yipped as the shift ended. Gossamer fabric puddled beneath her four paws and a blob of blue wig lay nearby. Now in wolf shape, she was only half-sure of the tall man standing over her.

Friend or enemy?

WHEN A WERE SHIFTED to animal shape, Creed knew they only partially possessed their human mind. It was similar to when she'd shifted to werewolf shape the other night.

A long-legged wolf with fur so black it gleamed blue stood before him. Was that the reason for her name? he wondered. She was gorgeous. The darkest fur outlined her eyes and muzzle. Her canines were brilliant against the darkness.

He remained still so as not to scare her. They must both be sure of the other.

She sniffed at the were's decapitated head, licked the

blood, then snarled and backed from the thing. Whining, the wolf bowed her head and stepped aside. She wiped a forepaw over her muzzle, as if to clean away the nasty blood.

Creed couldn't know if she would see him holding the bloody sword and immediately place him as an enemy. Did the animal form of Blu know what swords were? Or did she merely mark the world by scent, and the form standing there was taller and towered over her, so he must be feared?

He glanced down the hallway toward the stairs. They had little time before the rest of the wolves realized what was happening and came down to investigate.

"Hey, lover," he called to her as he carefully put out a hand and squatted before her.

If he could put himself at eye level with her, she may not deem him a threat. He set the sword behind him. He'd once faced her werewolf. This could prove more harrowing though because she was completely animal now. Her instincts about him could be different than when she was half woman.

"Blu, do you know me?"

The wolf growled lowly, baring her teeth. Obsidian-dark ears flicked back against her head. Lowering her head and sniffing, she then snapped her head up, sniffing the air curiously.

"I'm your husband," he offered. "I love you."

He extended his arm, tilting his palm up and opening his fingers.

Please, Blu, know me.

Cautious, the wolf stepped forward. She growled and barked. Creed wanted to shush her, but dared not.

Surely her bark had alerted the others. It took remarkable control not to grab her and dash out of here. The wolf could rip him to shreds with her teeth.

Sniffing, she dragged her nose to the tips of his fingers. Wary gray eyes dashed to his, then down. Her wet nose moved across his palm and wrist.

Creed held his breath. Perhaps his heart stopped. The world grew still. Nothing mattered but the two of them.

He had to get her out of here. They would treat her as an animal. No one would put his wife in chains ever again.

Face-to-face, she sniffed at his jaw. She had to scent the wolf and vampire blood on his bare chest. But then, the wolf's tongue lashed out and licked him on the face. She pounced on him, paws to his shoulders and licked him on the cheeks, nose and forehead.

"Okay, okay, I think I passed muster." He ruffled his fingers through her silken fur. "My gorgeous werewolf princess. Did I mention how much I love your natural hair color? Or rather fur?"

She licked his nose, then bounded playfully and yipped.

"Quiet, lover." He gestured down the hallway. "Can you lead us out of here?"

She scampered into the hall and looked back to him. A wag of her tail spoke volumes.

Creed grabbed Wolfsbane. "Right behind you."

He kept her pace as she loped the dark twisting halls. The entire compound was constructed from cement, a windowless and seemingly endless labyrinth. It reeked of mildew, which made it difficult for Creed to scent anything beyond that. He would rely on the wolf's keen nose.

Blu paused and growled. Stepping nervously, she looked to him. She must sense danger, or smell others of her kind. She signaled him with a high-pitched whine.

"I got it. Stay right here."

Just ahead, the hall turned a corner. Ruffling his palm over her head as he passed, Creed took the darkness carefully, knowing he would not see the threat until it was too late.

Ahead he sensed one frantic heartbeat. The were had to smell him. Would it be in four-legged wolf shape when Creed turned the corner or as the ferocious werewolf?

A werewolf would not be so quiet and stealth. It would have charged him by now.

Lunging forward, Creed swung Wolfsbane and it found a solid target. The man had no time to howl. Still in human form, the body split from shoulder to hip, it collapsed.

Creed stepped over the carnage. Blu sniffed at the body, stepping wide to avoid the rapidly pooling blood. A growl revealed her fangs. She snapped at the fallen wolf, then passed him by and loped ahead.

She pawed at the steel door, her claws scraping the old paint job, whining to get out.

"You and me both," he said. "This leads outside?"

Blu yipped.

Creed kicked the door down.

A werewolf lunged inside, fixing its talons into his chest, and slicing his ribs neatly.

Creed choked on the blood rising in his throat. He slammed the beast against the wall. Blu latched on to its leg, tearing at the sinuous muscle. It provided a distraction Creed needed. A slash of Wolfsbane opened the creature's chest.

Creed patted Blu on the head. "One point for you, wolf."

She shook her head, flicking off blood. A yip accepted the battle point.

Outside, the grounds were clear. Deceptively so. Blu did not pause, only took off across the midnight-dark field, but angled toward the edge of a forest that backed the property.

"I'm right behind you," he muttered, clutching his bleeding chest. His ribs had taken a beating lately.

Gasping for breath, Creed took off at a run. Half a

mile later, he charged to a halting stop at the top of the roadside ditch.

Blu waited, stepping anxiously at his arrival, and yipping a greeting.

He nodded down the gravel road. "There's my car."

The rangy howls of an angry pack quickened his steps. He reached the car, opening the passenger door to let in Blu. She leaped inside and he slammed the door shut. Sliding across the hood to his side, Creed shoved the sword inside and fired up the engine.

Something landed on the roof, denting it above the passenger seat. Blu yipped and pawed at the cloth ceiling.

The pack circled the car, in four-legged wolf shape, all of them.

Whatever crouched on top was much bigger.

Creed slammed a foot on the accelerator, clearing wolves as the car charged ahead, and spewing gravel from the spinning tires. Above them metal creaked. Blu barked louder and more frantically.

He wanted to put some distance between them and the pack but before he could the windshield shattered as the roof was peeled from the car like the top of a tuna can. Accelerating to sixty, Creed shouted for Blu to get down on the floor.

Somehow she understood, tucking herself under the dashboard and curling her head against her body.

The roof flew away.

Creed slammed on the brakes, and the werewolf that had taken off the roof soared onto the gravel road in front of the car, rolling over and over.

He grabbed Wolfsbane. "Stay inside."

Stepping on the seat, he was halfway through the roof when the werewolf landed in a crouched position on the hood. A fearsome growl preceded a slash of talon. It cut open Creed's cheek. He swallowed blood.

A swing of the battle sword stretched the muscles at his shoulder and biceps. Hot blood spattered his face and neck. Blu barked madly, pouncing on the seat and whining.

He hated that she had to see the carnage, but he could do nothing about it.

After returning to the driver's seat, he rocked the car to remove the halved werewolf from the hood. It was remarkable the engine still turned over for the healthy dent in the hood.

"I'm sorry." He peeled from the gravel road and onto a main highway. "I didn't mean to kill your lover outside the ballroom. It was an accident."

She barked, yet wagged her tail.

"We're home free. For now."

CREED SLOWED AS THEY passed his estate. Flames lit up the sky. Three fire trucks parked along the outer gates, and another had parked inside on the cobbled driveway. Heavy streams of water sprayed onto the property but did little against the flames.

He couldn't feel much sadness for the loss. The only thing that mattered to him sat on the passenger seat, transformed to human were shape, huddled under a suit jacket he'd scavenged from the backseat.

Cruising slowly by, he took an abrupt turn to avoid the police car ahead. He wore no shirt, was covered in blood, and a naked woman sat beside him. To top it off, there was no roof on the car.

The officer gave his tattered wreck of a car a double take, but then turned to the more important job.

It had begun. And if the werewolves wanted a war, he would give them one.

SHE STIRRED AS HE LIFTED her into his arms and carried her to the parking garage elevator. After washing off the blood using a chamois from the trunk, Creed had gone inside the hotel to rent a suite, and now he returned for Blu with his suit coat.

Clutching him fiercely, she shuddered, naked beneath the coat. "Has it begun?"

"Yes," he answered staunchly.

"Don't let it happen," she whispered weakly. "Please, Creed. For us."

He swallowed the need to shout to the heavens, to demand explanation for this insane battle. To beg to turn back the clock and leave that damned silver-loaded ring at home.

And to never have to find his wife in chains.

Now all she asked was that he stop what he wanted to rush head-on into. He wanted to take werewolf heads from their necks with a slash of Wolfsbane until their blood flowed like a river.

Blu shuddered again. "I love you. I know you'll make things right."

And there it was.

He could no more draw Wolfsbane against the enemy than he could set down this gorgeous princess and walk away from her right now.

"I will make this right," he vowed.

And this vow he would honor.

CHAPTER TWENTY

CREED MADE CALLS ALL through the early-morning hours while Blu slept. He connected with every Council member he could think of who would have the vampires on their side.

He didn't want to exclude a werewolf representative; there were simply none currently standing on the Council who made themselves available.

He was learning. He had to control his anger toward the werewolves and find less violent means to handle that aggression. Whatever the Council asked of him, he would now do without ulterior motives. It was what had been originally expected of him.

But more so, he just wanted to prove himself to Blu. How could she love him when he relished killing her kind? Blu had seeped into his pores and under his skin.

Just being in her presence changed the air around him and made him want to be better. And he would do so.

Alexandre had successfully gathered the remaining Nava members—two had been murdered at last night's banquet—and they convened right now across the city.

The order was rapidly spreading for the vampires to stand down. They were not to make a move until the Council could be brought in. Yet Creed tensed with the need to avenge his fallen tribe members.

Now he stalked the penthouse suite, shades drawn against the noon sun. His fists coiled in a permanent clench. Those bastard wolves!

With a glance to the sofa, where a swath of sheer violet fabric had been abandoned, he was reminded of the wolf lying in the bedroom, and his anger ebbed.

Do it for her. Change. You can be better.

He wondered if he should wake Blu up. She normally didn't sleep so long. Yet she had been put through a lot. He hoped the silver shackles he'd torn away from her wrists would not have a lasting effect on her body.

He would take the invisible magical shackles over and over again to save Blu from any discomfort.

The penthouse elevator rang, and he buzzed in the guests from a control box on the kitchen counter.

"Lord Saint-Pierre, long time, no see," Nikolaus Drake said as he strode without grandeur into the room.

Behind him a short, slender woman in motorcycle leathers and dark sunglasses nodded acknowledgment and sauntered in.

"My wife, Ravin," Drake said.

"We've met," Ravin said with a sneer. She tucked her shades in the front pocket of her leather jacket. "Sixteenth century, wasn't it?"

"About then," Creed replied. "Long time, no see." *Witch.* But he'd moved beyond prejudices. Though he sensed she might still hold a grudge.

"Still wielding magic?" she asked.

"I was just shackled last night."

"Serves you right," the witch said on a sneer.

"It is difficult to resist the urge to use magic at times," Nikolaus added, much surprising Creed.

He and Nikolaus both possessed magic. Creed had stolen it; Nick had drunk his wife's blood—accidentally, of course. And then after he died from her blood, he rose like a phoenix. He was now one of the strongest vampires alive, if you didn't count his son, Ivan.

Creed still held the record for oldest.

"But you always resist," Ravin said to her husband.

"I'm pleased you've come on such short notice," Creed said. "No doubt, you are aware of what's gone down."

"Reports say the fight began when you killed a

werewolf." Drake eyed him fiercely. "I thought we'd come to terms about this, Saint-Pierre."

"We have. You can trust me, Drake. What happened last night was self-defense and pure accident," Creed offered. "I was wearing a ring with liquid silver in it. I hadn't expected it to break."

"Yeah?" Ravin looked him up and down. "Then why wear such a thing?"

"It was my wedding ring, given to me by my werewolf bride as a show of trust. She, in turn, wears a ring with witch's blood inside. From before the Protection."

"Don't the wolves realize that blood has no effect on you?"

Creed shrugged. "It could cripple my magic, or maybe increase it. Doesn't really matter anymore, does it? Listen, here are the facts. The Northern pack is on a rampage against the vampires. My man in charge has secured the Nava tribe, but there are others out there still unaware. We're trying to contain the outbreak but I feel it'll quickly widen through the city. The wolves are re-lentless."

"News of the attack has spread like wildfire," Drake added. "Wolves in California and New York have already begun attacking vampires."

The witch said snidely, "I wouldn't be surprised if it hops the continent before evening."

"Christ." Creed swiped a hand across his jaw. "This marriage was supposed to be a means to bring the nations together."

The witch slapped her arms across her chest. "Good going, longtooth."

"Ravin," her husband admonished.

"What? Just because I married a vampire and gave birth to one doesn't mean I have to like all of them."

"I've given you no means to favor me," Creed assured her.

He faulted no witch the right to hate him. After all, he was responsible for their suffering so many centuries ago.

"Truth is," Creed said to Ravin, "tribe Nava went into this alliance with ulterior motives. I was to play the loving husband, convince the wolves we could get along with their kind, and see them lay down arms first. Then we intended to attack."

Ravin whistled lowly and looked to her husband. "How come I didn't hear about this?"

"We just found out about it," her husband said. "Creed has agreed not to go through with the attack."

"Sorry." Creed offered a head bow to Ravin. "We purposely made sure no Council members were aware, or your husband's tribe. Kila has set a peaceable example. It seemed a wise plan at the time. But then I learned the werewolves had the same hidden motives."

"Where'd you learn that?" Ravin asked.

"From me." Blu appeared from around the corner. Her sleep-tousled dark hair hung over one shoulder. The terry-cloth hotel dressing gown wrapped about her figure made her look so frail.

"Good afternoon, Princess," Drake offered with a half bow.

"This is the werewolf princess?" Ravin said. No respect in that tone. "What did you do, Saint-Pierre, kidnap her? Are you holding her hostage?"

"Hostage?" Creed kissed Blu's brow, tucking aside the long strands that had slipped into her lashes. "I love Blu. She is my wife. And nothing is going to change that."

Drake and his wife exchanged looks. It was Ravin who finally shrugged and offered, "Sounds like we've work to do. Who else is on their way?"

At that moment the elevator rang. Creed buzzed in the occupants. Ravin hugged the man who stepped into her arms. He lifted her feet from the floor and swung her about.

"Mom, it's been a few months. Are you getting shorter?"

"You're getting taller, Ivan. Will you ever stop growing? And, Dez, so good to see you."

"Ivan Drake," Creed said to Blu, wrapping an arm around her waist. "Nikolaus and Ravin's son. And his wife, Dez. I called as many members of the Council as I could manage."

"Good plan." She nestled her head against his chest.

"How do you feel?" he asked.

"In need of a shower, but otherwise fine. You're all healed?"

He kissed the crown of her head. "Well enough."

Truth was, his heart ached far more than any talon slash or broken bone could.

"I wish we had a few minutes to ourselves," she whispered. "I need to wrap myself about you. Just…feel you."

"When they leave I'm all yours."

Ivan approached and shook Creed's hand, and he made introductions to Blu.

An hour later, the penthouse was filled with a dozen vampires and witches, and the one token werewolf, Blu. She had excused herself to take a shower. Ravin and Dez, along with Lucy Stone, the paranormal debunker from Venice, mixed drinks in the kitchen.

Truvin Stone was absent, which Nikolaus had intimated was a good thing. Some differences died hard.

"I'm not sure what we can do. This is huge," Ivan announced as he accepted a whisky Coke from his wife. "But I made some calls to the European tribe leaders on the way here. It's not gone that far, nor will it. They will not tolerate anarchy. The *loup-garou* across seas are much more refined."

"I thought you came from France," Ravin said to Creed. "Guess European *savoir-faire* doesn't apply in your case, eh?"

Her husband silenced her. "Ravin, leave the man alone. It was an accident that started this."

"I cannot deny Nava's intent to dupe the wolves. My apologies to the Council." Creed faced the tribe leaders. "Tribe Nava has always stood at the edge, apart from the others."

"Putting on airs and following their own law," Ravin muttered.

Ignoring the spiteful witch, Creed asked, "Have we sent out spin?"

"We've a team rallying in the city," Dez reported. "Lucy and I are heading out soon. Already there's been a news report about a savaged body found in downtown Minneapolis. It's one of our own. Our insider at the Associated Press is prepared to suppress anything that comes over the wire. We'll take care of this."

"Will your wife communicate with the wolves for us?" Ivan asked Creed. "She may be our only hope."

"No, I will not ask it of her. Her father abuses her, and the pack hierarchy does not allow for a woman's voice to be heard. She would be in great danger were she to have contact with the pack now. Besides, I may have seriously injured Amandus, the pack principal. Have we no wolves on the Council?"

"Just the one. He'll never show."

BLU LISTENED BEFORE QUIETLY entering the room again. Creed had injured Amandus? She clutched her throat and waited for the tears to come. But they did not. The title *father* did not demand respect. She knew now respect must be earned.

The only man who had earned her respect was Creed.

Now dressed in a simple black T-shirt and skirt, and her natural hair, she remained by the wall, at a distance. The men converged on the other side of the room near the grand piano, while the women chatted over drinks in the kitchen of the huge open floor plan penthouse.

She approached the women tentatively. She'd never had girlfriends, beyond Bree, and so wasn't sure how to engage with a group of them. There wasn't a wolf in the house, and that made Blu uncertain about interaction.

Sliding onto a stool next to the woman with long red hair, she offered a smile. "Lucy?"

"Yes, Lucy Stone. I do damage control and PR for the Light and Dark nations. How are you feeling? Sounds like you and Lord Saint-Pierre had a time of it last night."

Ravin Drake eyed her with an intent gaze as she leaned

onto the counter, waiting for her reply as if Blu needed to prove herself.

"I'm fine. It was a shock that everything happened as it did. We had thought everyone would see we were truly in love.... I guess that was foolish."

"But Creed said the wolves had been planning to attack, too," Ravin shot out. "So you must have known something would go down."

"It wasn't supposed to happen last night. Creed and I were merely there to put on a show that we could live together peacefully. Except we are in love, so it wasn't a show. I hate what's happening now."

"Yeah, well, the webs we weave."

"Ravin," Dez admonished.

Ravin touched her black spiky hair, unaffected. "I don't like Creed Saint-Pierre. Never have, never will. I would have left him to burn last night if it had been my choice."

"Burn?" Blu asked.

"We had to burn the banquet hall to cover evidence," Lucy provided. "The wolves went after Creed's home. We weren't a part of that."

"Creed rescued me from my pack," Blu offered quietly. "I love him for that. Aren't you a witch?" she asked Ravin. "I thought the witches and vampires had gotten over their tiff?"

"Tiff?" Ravin snorted. "Pass me the vodka, will you, Dez? Tiff." She shook her head.

"Ravin holds grudges," Dez supplied as she poured her mother-in-law a few fingers of the clear alcohol. "But we're all here to work together now. Is there anything you can tell us that may provide a means to stopping this war before it begins?"

Blu sighed. "I don't know much. My father was determined to take back the land the vampires have stolen from the wolves over the years. But our nations have been battling since the beginning of the twentieth century. Longer even, I'm sure. So many little things got out of hand."

"Yes, the vamps used to hunt wolves back in the fifties," Lucy said. When Dez shot her an impressed glance, she provided the details. "I've done my research. I may be new to the vampire thing, but I'm up on the history." Lucy said to Blu, "I used to be a reporter, now I debunk paranormal occurrences that are real. Someone's got to do spin work."

"So you're a vampire?"

"Yes, thanks to my husband, Truvin. I'm pretty new. Only a few years."

"And the rest of you are witches?"

Dez nodded. "Which goes to show—" she shot her mother-in-law the evil eye "—that opposites of any kind can attract, become friendly and even learn to love. Isn't that right, Mrs. I Married The Vampire I Once Killed?"

"Damn straight." Ravin tilted her shot glass at the women, then tipped it back.

"There's something else," Blu said slowly. "I think it's the core reason my father is so against the vampires. I recently found out my mother had an affair with a vampire. And…that my father killed her because of it."

Lucy rubbed a hand over Blu's shoulder. "I'm so sorry."

"It's always over passion," Ravin said, shaking her head sadly. "All right, I'm over dissing Creed. Let's figure a way to make things right, shall we? Because heaven knows the menfolk can't survive without their women standing behind to back them up."

The elevator rang. The doors opened, and out stepped a man Blu had never expected to show here. Especially not in a room full of vampires. "Severo."

A FEW WEEKS AGO, Blu had wanted to punch the former pack leader if she ever saw him. Now, the world, as viewed through both her and her husband's eyes, had changed.

When the vampires merely stood back, leering at the werewolf who had entered, Blu made a point of walking over and shaking his hand.

"Severo, I'm honored."

"It is I who is honored, Princess." He lifted her hand and kissed the back of it. He nodded to the Council members, and addressed a few. "Nikolaus. Ivan. Ravin."

"What are you doing here, Severo?" Creed stepped forward.

The last wolf in the world Blu expected to side with vampires was Stephen Severo. He had lost his family to vampire hunters, had watched them string his parents up as pelts, and then witnessed them shift to human shape in death. He had been enslaved by the vampires, and had narrowly escaped being bitten.

And yet, Severo's wife, a woman he'd met as a mortal, had been recently changed to a vampire.

"Most of you know I'm not much for vampires," Severo stated. He shrugged his shoulders and the leather duster coat swept about his knees. "There are precious few I trust, which includes the Drakes. Of course I love my wife. But I am appalled after hearing what went down last night. The wolves acted out of order. They are my former pack. Amandus Masterson has always had the wrong goals. I'm here to help. Tell me what you've planned."

Blu squeezed his hand and kissed him on the cheek. "Thank you."

The man was a lone wolf, not allied to any pack. What he was doing would have repercussions, but not so dangerous as if he were in a pack. He risked being shunned, but obviously he was fine tucked away sharing a life with his wife.

"We're not sure," Creed provided. "What the hell can we do?"

Severo's eyes swept the room, taking in the line of witches at the kitchen counter. "Why not a spell? It's been done before with the Protection."

"Like what?" Ravin crossed the room. "Make all werewolf blood poisonous to vampires? That's so been done, and I don't think it would be as effective. It's not like the vamps ever try to bite the wolves. I hear wolf blood is pretty nasty."

The petite witch didn't so much as flinch when Severo growled at her.

Blu decided she liked Ravin, even if the witch hated Creed. She was sure there were many who had issues with her husband. A man couldn't live for nine centuries and not gather a few enemies.

"A spell might work." Ivan Drake put a finger to his lips in thought. Tallest in the room, and once the devil Himself's bounty hunter, the man's commanding mien drew attention. "But not the blood. Something subtler. Dez, what do you think?"

"I can consult the Book of All Spells. If there's a base spell, something we could use to begin with, I can then master a greater spell. If you'll let me use the bedroom,"

Dez said to Blu, "I'll call up the Grande Grimoire and look through it."

"Come with me." Blu led the witch toward the bedroom. She grabbed the wet towels from the bed and tossed them in a pile near the chair. "Where is it?"

"The book?" The witch waited at the end of the bed, slender fingers folded together. "It's out there—" she looked up and aside "—in the otherworld. It's where I keep all my important stuff. I won't call it to me until you've left the room."

"Oh. Sorry." Starting for the door, Blu paused. "You married your enemy?"

"Ivan's a complicated bit of man," she offered. "He was born to a witch and a vampire, so he's never known prejudice against my kind. I can't imagine how hard it's been for you, being forced to marry your enemy."

"I didn't like it at first, but I love Creed. The whole drawing a line in the sand because someone is different than you seems so silly now."

"It is silly." She approached Blu and touched the ends of her hair, still wet from the shower. "But you still fear him. There's something about Creed you're not completely sure about."

Blu looked down. "It's just all men in general."

"I don't know him," Dez said, "but I get a feeling for him when standing close. He's strong and proud. A hard man to change. But he genuinely loves you. I feel that, too. Don't be afraid of the things he can give you, Blu. And in turn, you give him what's for, too. Okay?"

Blu nodded and smiled. "Thanks, Dez."

An hour later, while waiting for Dez's research to pan out, Blu had learned a few interesting bits from Ravin over shots of vodka.

Ravin had crossed Creed's path in the sixteenth century. He had returned to France from a sort of crusade against werewolves who'd frenzied across Germany, killing mortals inflicted with a vampire bite. It had been a bizarre quest, Ravin remembered Creed telling her. He'd been dirty, bloodied and not at all genial to her.

He'd downed half a dozen ales with her before he realized she was a witch. Then, he'd hit her with some of his air magic, slamming her against the wall, and had strode out as if he were too good for her.

Didn't sound like the Creed Blu now knew. He had changed over the years. It was all good now. Or as Creed would say, *très bien.*

"I would like to have known him in an earlier time," she said to the witch. "Perhaps in a wilder time. A freer time."

"He would have slain you," Ravin said bluntly. Then she studied Blu for a while, a smile creeping onto her lips. "Or maybe not."

With a rallying whistle, Dez called everyone into the bedroom where a huge book was spread open on the bed. "I think I have an idea."

CHAPTER TWENTY-ONE

CREED BID DEZ AND Ivan goodbye, the last guests, and went in search of his shoes. He'd been conversing with the Council members in his bare feet. He'd had the hotel order clothing for them both, but the shoes had only been delivered an hour ago.

"Blu?"

She sat on the bench before the glossy, black grand piano. He hadn't noticed her there, so quiet and small. Without a bright wig, she blended into the surroundings.

"I'm off to supervise the spell," he told her. "They plan to begin at midnight."

"That's three hours from now." She propped an elbow on the piano. "Do you think Dez's idea will work? That the spell will end the fighting instantly?"

"Sounds like it might. It's worth a shot, Blu. I don't want this to go any further than it has."

"Come sit by me." She patted the bench.

He had things to do. There were nations to save. But Blu's pale entreating eyes obliterated those nations with a flutter of lash. How could he possibly concern himself with all that when the only thing that mattered to him was right here?

He slid onto the bench and pulled her into a hug. "*Ma chère,* you feel so good. When this is over I'm going to hold you all day. All night. Weeks on end."

"Hold me now. We've time before you need to go. Give me one hour?"

"Anything for you." He dipped his head aside her neck and her hair swept over his face. "I love when you adorn me with your tresses."

She giggled. "You say such romantic things, vampire."

"I'm an old softy at heart, I guess."

"Old, yes. Soft? You have your moments." She slid her hand across his lap and he reacted to her touch. "But I wonder how hard I can make you?"

"Blu, now's not the time."

"Now is the only time, lover. I want to make love with you. Before the end comes."

"It will not arrive."

"You don't know that."

Her fierceness reminded him of the proud wolf who had

led him from the compound. And of the woman who had begged him to make things right. He hadn't done that yet.

"What if you leave and never return?" she asked. "What if the spell doesn't work?"

"Then I'll not stop until it is right. I made a promise to you."

"Give me what I wish this one time."

He should not think of sex at a moment like this. But he could not deny that her strokes across his lap were getting a rise out of him. The woman was insatiable. And he adored her for that.

And what if…?

It could go badly for him this evening. He had no idea where the Northern pack was, if Blu's father was plotting against Nava at this moment. Amandus could be looking for Creed. For Blu. There was so much to worry about.

It was now or possibly never.

"You want to stop the world and get off for an hour?" he wondered aloud.

"Yes, please."

He lifted her into his arms and strode into the bedroom.

Her robe spilled from her shoulders and she sat naked and proud upon the bed, his princess of the daylight. She entreated him to enter her kingdom with a crook of her finger. Creed shed his clothes and she stroked him hard. As he slid inside her, the world did slip away.

Only two. Entwined tightly. Breaths gasping and muscles tensing.

Skin brushed skin, gliding on the silk sheets, and shivering when bruised by the air.

Hair so black it was blue slithered across Creed's arm and shoulder. He pushed his fingers through her dark veil and pressed his mouth, teeth bared, against her neck.

Together they climaxed. It was sweet, slow, yet intense. Blu's body arched above his, giving of herself completely.

And when he thought she would slide from him and begin to dress, she straddled him and tucked her head beside his.

"I love you more than I've loved before," she said. "This is the first time I've ever known romantic love. It is a true love that spreads from my heart through my bones. I didn't think anything like this was possible, Creed. You fill every part of me."

Every part of her body hugged his. Her breasts were heavy against his arm and chest, her leg draped across his hips, her mouth whispering against his neck.

This was his world. He would allow nothing to take her from it. Nothing.

"Lover?"

"Yes, Blu. My princess, my heart, my death and my life."

"I want something from you. Something I want more than anything else in this world."

"Ask," he whispered, "and I'll fight every pack on this planet to get it for you."

"Fighting isn't necessary. You just need to kiss me."

"A kiss? Is that all my werewolf princess desires?" Dazzled by her sparkling gaze, he sighed.

Blu's lips parted, her tongue teasing the bottoms of her upper teeth. "A kiss…and then…a bite."

Creed's heart thudded. Could she be asking…? Granting him permission to do the one thing he most desired?

"Bite me, lover. Make me yours completely."

"Truly? It's only because we're so unsure of what will happen—"

She pressed two fingers over his mouth. "I've never been more sure in my life. I need to surrender to you. I want to wear your mark. It would be finer than anything I could buy with that pretty little credit card."

"B-but the blood hunger?" They both knew werewolves did not take blood for survival. But once bitten by a vampire? That would change.

"If you can do it, I can." She licked along his jaw. "Don't deny me. You know you want to taste my blood."

She made her tongue firm and teased the vein on his

neck. She knew what that did to him, how it made him ache. Creed's teeth tingled, but they didn't automatically descend now. Curious.

"Show me your teeth, lover," she whispered.

"Blu, tell me you know what you're saying."

"You know I do."

He rolled her onto her back and knelt over her. The penthouse looked over the city and it was dark twenty stories up in the sky. But Blu's eyes glittered for him like two stars he could kiss and possess without fear of being burned. Her mouth pursed and she coyly tilted her head aside.

He stroked her neck, the vein warm and pulsing expectantly. Never had he been so desirous of the bite.

He would not question again. This gorgeous princess always knew what she wanted, and did not toy with her demands. If she wanted something, she took it. Or asked for it.

The world was falling apart, and the only thing he wanted was to gather her into his arms and sink his teeth into her flesh, and lose himself in the blood bond.

"I love you," she whispered. "Bite me."

His canines descended. Creed parted his lips to display them to his wife. She touched them, not showing the fear she'd once had for them. He didn't require the stroking of his teeth to increase his arousal. The fact that she accepted him excited him like nothing he could ever imagine.

"I will wear your mark proudly," she whispered.

Mon Dieu.

His teeth pierced her fine skin and glided into the vein. Blu's body arched against him, her nipples skimming his chest. He stroked one, but his focus remained on the blood easing from his wife's vein.

Wine and whisky and centuries of liquids drank and sloshed and spilled and devoured—nothing compared to this. To the hot elixir flooding his mouth and sweetening his tongue.

Fangs retracted, he sucked at her neck. Her hand slid across his back and fingernails drove softly into his skin. Heady, the drink. His, only his. His werewolf princess, the wild-haired sex-kitten who growled rather than purred.

Devour was a poor word to explain how he sucked at her neck. He consumed her. Surrounded and dove deep and *became* her.

He slipped his other hand between her legs. She cried out as he found her clit and slicked across it masterfully. Her arms sliding across the wrinkled sheets, Blu tried to anchor herself to this world.

He wouldn't allow it. They had gone beyond. Nothing held them down now. He could drink from her ever after and never satisfy his thirst and, yet, he drowned in the splendor of her life.

Blu cried out, a blissful and aggressive declaration of climax.

Creed took his mouth away, gasping for air but needing little. Red jewels spilled down her neck and glittered. He licked the blood trickles away.

Still she came, an amazing swoon that now captured him.

Better than orgasm, it was the wide and spacious world opening up to him. And he needed more.

Clasping her throat with one hand, he again drove his fangs into her vein below the previous bite. Blu convulsed in pleasure. He sucked a short drink, then dragged his fangs down her flesh.

The hot mound of her breast beckoned. So soft, aching for his intrusion.

"Yes," she gasped. "Take me there. Please."

Just above her nipple, he sank his teeth into the generous, firm flesh. He drank a little there. And below the other breast, on the underswell where it was so hot and smelled like the hotel's tangerine soap. Mmm, blood oranges?

He could not determine where one climax ended and the other began. Together they built their own world, topped by a constellation of unending orgasm.

Gliding his palm down her stomach and following with his mouth, Creed sunk his teeth in the backside of her hip, there, where her bottom gently curved. But when he tickled his tongue across her thigh, he avoided the artery. There was no danger this night, only pleasure.

Kissing her clit, he dashed his tongue to taste the sweetness of her climax. She was so wet and throbbing for him. There, he did not use his teeth; instead he impaled her with his tongue until she cried endlessly with pleasure.

Her fingers twined into his hair and she pulled him to her as she sat up and kissed him on the mouth, fangs still down. He pricked her lip and blood trickled across his tongue.

"You wear my mark now," he murmured. "You've given me a gift, Blu."

"That was incredible. I don't know why I didn't let you do that sooner."

"You needed to trust."

"And to love. I'm yours. Always yours," she said. "No matter what."

"In body and blood."

CHAPTER TWENTY-TWO

CHOOSING THE CORRECT SPELL was paramount. They could not make werewolves' blood poisonous to the vampires, or vice versa. There was to be no violence this time, as there had been during the war between the witches and vampires. None from the two nations must suffer because of the spell, or the Council would not condone it.

A love spell was out of the question. That would be the utter opposite of a poison spell like the Protection, and could have more dire results. Manipulating the wills of either werewolves or vampires was also too malicious to consider.

Dez and Ravin finally came up with a sort of repellent spell. When a vampire or werewolf approached the other with hatred or violence in mind, an auralike field would form around both, repelling them from each other.

Neither would be hurt. They could make a go at each other yet never succeed in violence. Once the repellent spell touched them, their anger would dissipate. It wouldn't change the opposing parties' minds about the other; it would simply make them indifferent.

It was manipulative, but the least of all evils they had considered.

That also left the floor clear for attraction. The spell would not affect those whose feelings were amorous or even simply friendly toward one another. (They highly doubted that would occur.)

It also would not detect falsehoods, one who purposefully chose to deceive, but that was a glitch that could not be avoided.

Dez was elected the witch to perform the spell. She had eight centuries on her, and was the keeper of the Book of All Spells. Her magic was powerful, the kind needed to encompass the world.

They'd chosen a field twenty miles from the nearest suburb and miles from any home. It edged an Indian reservation, yet was not held by a private owner, as far as Lucy's research of city records showed. The grounds needed to be neutral.

Ravin first blessed the grounds with a simple spell, then stepped back to join the others around a great bonfire, to wait.

Dez conjured and whispered for over an hour.

Creed arrived, and was greeted with hopeful wishes for the spell. He fixated on the burning pyre, yet his heart beat with the vivid memory of Blu in his arms. In his blood now. He could still taste her, feel her rush through his veins. What a gift she had given him.

When the blood hunger struck her she need only drink from him. She need not seek others; he would not have it. Blu would be relieved surely.

When finally Dez spread her arms and commanded it so, the night fell still. All Council members turned to the witch to see what would happen.

Flames burst fifty feet into the air, sending sparks across the field. Like fire sprites, the sparks danced through the plowed dirt as if live entities.

"Is that supposed to happen?" Ivan called to his wife.

"Not sure," Dez said, joining the group, spell book tucked under an arm. "There's…someone out there?"

Indeed, from amidst the fire stepped someone—or something.

"Ah-ah-ah, my pretties." The dark figure stomped toward them in a flaming veil that formed from its very body. Black horns curled tight against its head. Fire sprites congregated around the beast in dancing reverie. "It's not going to be so easy as all this."

Ivan was the first to recognize it. "Oh, hell."

"I'm not even going to look," Dez said. She squinted at her husband. "Is it?"

Ivan nodded. "Himself."

BLU HUNG UP THE PHONE just as Creed walked into the bedroom and hugged her. She could feel his strength claim her, yet also his exhaustion in the sigh that whispered over her ear.

He shivered as he sucked in a breath. "Didn't work," he said.

"What happened?"

"Himself paid us a visit. He has an interest in keeping the nations at odds."

"The devil Himself."

Blu had only been told about the prince of darkness, and how he appeared to others. When one not attached to Himself looked at him, they saw their greatest temptation. "What did he look like to you?"

He smoothed a hand over her hair and kissed her eyelid. "Like you, my love. With the violet wig." He brushed aside the hair from her neck to inspect the wound he'd left behind.

"And you said black was your favorite color. I think you have a new one."

"Actually, I do have a new one, but it's not violet."

"Hmm, you like green?"

"Nope. I prefer Blu."

She pouted prettily and touched the bite marks on her neck. "How does it look?"

"Angry, actually. But it'll heal."

"And scar. And then the whole world will know how much I love my husband." She toppled him on the bed then showered him with kisses.

Could it be so simple as this? No cares, a laughing tumble in his wife's arms? Creed wanted it desperately, but it seemed the world—and the very devil—would conspire against him.

He stroked the fine, silken column of Blu's neck. "Do you have regrets?"

"Never," she said proudly. "I've been checking it in the mirror. And when you touch it now, it sends shivers through me. Good ones that tingle in my breasts."

He dashed his tongue over the reddened pierce marks. Blu moaned appreciatively. "I can feel your heartbeat as my own now. We're in synch."

"Is that sort of like me having your scent in my nose?"

"Yes. I could find you anywhere in the city if I needed to."

"So we've got our own sort of GPS on each other now. Cool. How soon before I'll want to take blood?"

"Not sure. You worried?"

"Not if you're the guy I get to suck on. Can we do it that way?"

"I wouldn't have it any other way, lover. You must bite only me if you feel the craving for blood. I am your willing donor."

She rolled her eyes at the euphemism.

Creed noticed the pink cell phone lying on the nightstand. "You were talking to someone?"

"Believe it or not, that was Severo on the phone as you walked in. He's offered to speak to my father."

"That's quite an offer from the werewolf, but it won't be necessary. I had a good think on the way here after the spell failed. I'm going to speak to Amandus."

"No!" She reached for him as he tugged his shirt off and sorted through the newly purchased clothes scattered on the bedroom chairs. "You can't go to my father after rescuing me. He'll kill you, Creed. We broke the bargain I made."

"Then we've nothing to lose, yes?"

"But…" Her eyes widened with unloosed tears.

"It needs to be done. We won't get anywhere trying to concoct spells if Himself continues to negate them."

"Why would you do this?"

He snapped out a black button-down shirt and slid his arms through the sleeves. "Because I love you."

"And loving me means committing suicide? Leaving me alone forever?"

"Blu, I don't intend to die."

"Of course not, but you will! One lone vampire against an entire pack of wolves—"

"I'll keep a keen eye for wooden stakes and holy water."

"You're not baptized!"

"Sorry, just trying to keep things light." Holy water wouldn't harm him, they both knew.

She shrugged from him when he tried to pull her into an embrace. "This isn't funny. Amandus wants your head now."

"Blu." This time he wouldn't allow her to shuffle away, and secured her with a tight hug from behind. He hated that she wanted to push him away, when they both needed this contact so much. "I have to try."

"My father is unreasonable. He'll lie right to you, and then knife you in the back when you turn away."

"A knife will do little but piss me off."

"Be serious, please. What will you say to him?"

"I'll think of something when I get there."

"You're being foolish, vampire." She lifted a defiant chin. "You would never step into the fray without focus and careful strategy, like you always say."

"Blu, sometimes we *think* different than we *know*. There's no other course but to go to your father, the leader of the pack determined to head this battle."

"Don't do it. Not for Amandus. He's a bastard. And I

don't want you to kill more wolves. If we're going to sacrifice, then bring me back and let me serve as the breeding wolf he demands of me."

The stroke of his fingers across her lips served as a wicked soothing to Creed's troubled soul. Yes, he had a soul. It belonged to Blu now, as hers belonged to him. The blood bond had done that for them, mingled their souls in a manner.

"Don't do that." She shrugged from his touch. "I don't want your tenderness now. You have to be smart. To stand for what you believe in, like the tribe and all those vampires my kind has killed in the blood sport."

"I am doing just that!"

"But why must you sacrifice your life for it?"

He gripped her wrists. Her gray eyes flared and glinted with the vicious warning he'd seen on the night of the full moon. The proud werewolf princess had emerged from hiding to shine. That was why he loved her.

That was why he must protect her.

"No one will ever harm you again, Blu. As long as I breathe, I will protect you. You asked me to end this? I will."

"Stupid alpha male."

He chuffed out a smirking breath. "Gorgeous werewolf princess."

"Idiot longtooth."

"My heart."

"Suicidal maniac," her voice cracked.

"My wife."

"Oh, my love."

CREED STRODE ACROSS THE shadowed carport. It wasn't hard to locate his car. The black BMW was now a convertible. The roof had been tossed somewhere west of the city. A trail of blood smeared across the dented hood.

He should have abandoned it in the countryside, but Blu had been so fragile; he'd needed to get her to safety. Now it sat here, hidden behind the huge SUV he'd rented to take him to the spell site earlier.

Flipping open the cell phone Blu had insisted he bring along, he called cleanup to dispose of the BMW. Then he tossed the pink bit of plastic and electronics into the backseat. He'd get her a new one and ensure the faery's phone number was in it.

Reaching in the front seat, he drew out Wolfsbane, surprised it was still there.

"We've been through a lot, haven't we? Fighting for kings, bounty hunting for the tribe. Slaying the enemy."

An enemy he now regarded with abiding love. An enemy with brilliant gray eyes, a sexy smile and an appetite for Count Chocula and barely there lacy things.

An enemy who was no longer his enemy.

Be that as it may, he was not required to love the family or the pack because he loved Blu. Blu had made it clear Amandus was no real father. What he had done to his daughter and wife was not the way of any pack. And Amandus had known about Ryan's involvement with the blood sport. The pack principal was corrupt.

Creed should have killed him when he'd had the chance at the banquet. But that would have put him on the same level as Amandus. He'd stopped himself short of drinking the wolf's blood as the fight had raged around them. He hadn't wanted that nasty taste in his mouth. Nor did he wish to go against Council wishes.

He should talk to Severo and allow the wolves to handle this amongst themselves. But it was too late. Amandus had pushed him too far.

Creed slashed Wolfsbane through the air. It cut without a sound, and he could feel the air molecules scream as they were parted. He'd not once swung this blade without wounding. Not once had he regretted a swing.

But Creed could no more kill Amandus now than he could kill any werewolf simply because he had once labeled them enemy. His opinion of their species had altered.

Most important, his wife had asked him not to kill another wolf.

He would do what he could to bridge the gap between the nations. For Blu.

He tossed Wolfsbane into the backseat and turned to stride away.

THE MOMENT HE SLAMMED into Park and stepped from the rental SUV, half a dozen wolves surrounded Creed. Musk sharpened the still night air. The pack members snarled and shouted obscenities at him.

Yeah, so he was a bloody longtooth. Wasn't it time they got a new oath for the vampires?

"I walk peacefully," Creed called. He held his arms out to reveal he bore no weapons. "I wish to speak to your principal, Amandus Masterson."

"No vampires on the premises," said one who wielded a machine gun with more piercing vitriol than a bullet. "You've got five seconds to get off the property, longtooth."

Creed put up his hands in surrender. "I merely wish a talk." Seriously? An assault rifle?

As a wolf charged him, Creed braced for impact. He took a head and shoulder to his gut, which toppled him to the ground. Dust rose about them as the wolf pounded his chest with rapid, lung-bruising punches.

"Cease!"

The attacking wolf whipped around his head to whoever had made the command.

Creed spit and leaned up on an elbow.

"Bring him in!" called a voice from the compound's dark interior.

The wolves glanced from one to another, not at all pleased with the order.

"Diaz, off him!"

His punisher, with one last kick to Creed's side, jumped off. Creed stood, questioning the wisdom he'd employed in coming here alone, but knowing this was the only way to do it.

He hoped to survive to see Blu again. But if he did not, he would go down ensuring her safety.

The one called Ridge patted Creed down, hands tracking his sides and legs. He fisted Creed in the ribs. The impact took his breath, but Creed merely winced.

"You must have a death wish," Ridge muttered, and shoved him forward.

AMANDUS MASTERSON STOOD ten paces from Creed in the massive room that looked like an emptied factory. Tumescent duct piping ran two stories above the cement floors. Glass block windows set high in cement walls let in little light. Shoved against the far wall were old machines that looked pre-twentieth century for the huge gears and leather pulleys.

Congregating behind the pack principal stood eight

wolves, each a physical specimen of strength and seething anger. A riot of musk and aggression tainted the air. If he so much as flinched, Creed suspected one of the dogs would growl.

Their numbers were large for a pack. On average a pack was six or eight males strong, though he'd known the rare pack to be as large as twenty. And he had killed three in the compound last night. Obviously the wolves had not suffered so much as they wished the vampires to believe.

But the fact remained, there were no females. And that was directly related to the vampires hunting their breed many decades earlier.

Creed inhaled and bowed before Amandus, his hands clasped before him. "Principal Masterson. I come to you not as the leader of tribe Nava, nor as a representative of the vampire nations."

Amandus tilted a wicked sneer at him and crossed his arms high on his chest. The old wolf would not be so easily impressed. Below his Adam's apple, the flesh was bruised and scarred. Creed had begun to rip the old man's throat out at the banquet, but he couldn't complete the job. He was Blu's father, after all.

"I come to you as your daughter's husband. A man concerned only for her well-being."

Snorts and snickers from the wolves echoed in the

vast building. Creed did not look away from Amandus's dour sneer.

As Blu had guessed, Creed was winging this. He didn't need a plan. His heart would show him the way.

"It was you who gave her to me, Principal. You who offered your daughter to a vampire. That was a bold gesture. An immense sacrifice. And we all know neither side expected the other to submit to the pact of peace. It was a game. A stupid game."

"Not stupid," Amandus hissed.

"But certainly a folly."

The werewolf grudgingly gave an agreeing nod to the foolishness of it all. "Get on with it, longtooth. I tire of your company already. If I must endure your stench, then make it good, and make it quick."

Dropping to his knees, Creed bowed his head. The wolves had formed into a half circle before him and he could sense the curiosity over his move. As well, he could feel their bloodlust. It was so thick, he could bite it from the air and spit it at them.

At a time when he wished to wield Wolfsbane, or even magic, he could only trust his heart would lead him through this.

"I humble myself before the pack," he offered. "What has gone on for centuries between the vampires and werewolves has always been accepted as how things are.

Now I find it unacceptable. It pains me to see us go at one another with no more reason than the lust for blood and vengeance. We have, both sides, committed heinous crimes against the other."

"We have never hunted and skinned vampires alive," Amandus said sharply.

No, but they did force vampires to kill one another, which was an equally heinous crime.

"You owe us much land, vampire."

"The lands the vampires have purchased have been done so in a legal process."

"By a Council prejudice to the wolves, you know that," Amandus hissed.

That could be true. But if more wolves chose to serve on the Council— No. Now was no time for picking at stupid details.

Amandus stepped forward and bent to meet Creed's gaze. "You have tainted my daughter, longtooth."

"If you choose to see it that way, then I certainly have. If loving someone is harmful or tainted, yes, I am guilty. Do not forget you offered her in this game of deceit."

Amandus hissed. "She means nothing to me now. She has broken our bargain."

"I did that. Not her. It was I who stole her from the compound. I took her from chains." His heart ached to recall the silver shackles about Blu's wrist. "One does not chain someone they care about."

"Do not presume to tell me how to treat my offspring!"

"Of course not." Yes, he must watch his anger. This was his last hope. "I do not know the ways of the pack."

"You never will. Why try, vampire? There is no way you can make reparations for the land. For our lost generations!"

"Nor can the wolves atone for the lives they have enslaved and forced to fight to the death."

Amandus scoffed. "You *murdered* Ryan. As well as two others from my pack."

It would serve no good to explain that Ryan's death had been an accident and the others self-defense. The principal knew that.

Nava had lost two vampires during the fight. All was fair in war. As well, he would not bring up the wolf's murdered wife. That may push him over the edge. It was a crime he must answer to eventually, but now was not the time.

"Please, Principal, I sense you wish this to end, too. We've lost too many of our own." Spreading his arms to expose his heart, Creed asked, "What can I do?"

"Take his life," muttered a wolf from the pack. Another cried, "Kill the longtooth."

Amandus paced before him, his heels scuffing the floor. "I would ask for my daughter back, but as I've said, she is ruined and of no use to me now."

Interesting. Because Blu could return to the pack, mate with a wolf and have many werewolf children, Creed felt sure. That the principal put such spite to the vampire taint made him wonder about his efforts now.

"Your death would mean little. I see no significance whether you are a tribe leader or a common bloodsucker."

The wolf knew he was an elder, one who possessed magic, and should be more fearsome. He must take pride in the fact he'd been the one to see Creed shackled.

"You may have something," Amandus finally conceded. "I do wish this to settle. Losing pack numbers is difficult. We are few as it is. The River pack lost a female in the battle last night."

Creed bowed and shook his head.

"My daughter refuses to play her part repopulating the pack. Useless bitch."

Creed winced. She was the most incredible creature in his world. But a man so insensible as Amandus could never see that. Feeling his neck heat and his muscles tense, he cautioned himself against the simmering rage.

"You agree to sacrifice for peace?" Amandus said suddenly.

Creed looked at the man. What sacrifice had the man in mind?

Did it matter?

Your death will leave me alone. Is that how you show me your love?

He couldn't die, could not abandon Blu.

But he was so close. He could feel the end near. The end to battle, the killing, the war. Was one simple sacrifice all that was required?

It would never completely dissipate the hatred between the nations. But if the revered Northern pack stepped from the vanguard, other packs would follow, as well, the tribes would.

"You vow that Blu will be free from the pack to live as she chooses?"

"So be it," the principal muttered. "She is free."

"Then I agree," Creed said. Though what he agreed to, he didn't know.

Amandus whistled sharply, bringing his first man to his side. "One thousand talons!"

Ridge nodded and grinned a toothy snarl at Creed.

Others gathered in a line flanking Amandus. The wolves shifted, their bodies bulking and lengthening, talons growing from their fingers, and fur rippling across their bodies as clothing tore and fell from their furred limbs.

His own hackles prickling, Creed winced at the acrid odor of musk and aggression.

Amandus motioned Creed to stand. "You survive

this, vampire, and you have my word on peace. You will have atoned for Eugene Ryan's death and the injury you gave me. And, despite my utter disgust for your kind, you will have earned the right to call my daughter wife."

The first strike happened without warning. Icy pain cut across Creed's chest. The lead wolf slashed a talon through him.

He was immortal. A vampire who healed rapidly, and could not die unless his heart was staked and his head removed. But immortality did not mean he didn't feel pain. He felt it acutely, perhaps more than the average mortal because of his heightened senses. A cut to flesh sizzled like a hive of bee stings.

The second talon burned through the flesh strapping his abdomen, searing through muscle and meat and drawing hot blood. Creed clamped his jaw tight, fighting the need to release an agonizing yowl. He would remain standing. He must.

For Blu.

Quickly and fiercely, the wolves took turns, each of their slashes made with surgical precision. All growled wickedly to deliver the blow, and then chuckled as their evil task was completed and they filed to the back of the never-ending line.

A slash across Creed's thigh cut the artery. A talon at his cheek cut into his mouth, scratching a tooth. A bicep muscle was torn, snapping painfully like sliced rubber.

It was the most agonizing pain. It burrowed deep, electrifying his nerves. An unending pain formed from hell. Twenty times worse than the shackles.

Yet, as the twentieth and thirtieth slashes were delivered, the first slashes began to heal. New flesh was reopened and tormented over and over again.

How could he endure the one thousand talons Amandus had called for?

Creed lost count somewhere around ninety-eight. He staggered but remained standing in the blood that pooled at his feet. Occasionally he cried out. The pain was too fierce not to shout, to attempt to alleviate or redirect the fire of agony. Once he put up a hand to block a slash, and the talon cut through his palm.

When Amandus called out, "One hundred!" Creed fell to his knees.

A werewolf romped around behind him and began to work on a new set of slashes.

CHAPTER TWENTY-THREE

RIDGE DELIVERED THE five hundredth slash across the vampire's bloodied bones. How the vampire still managed to kneel on all fours was beyond him. Occasionally he'd cried out the princess's name.

Was love so powerful then?

He swung to face Amandus and shifted from werewolf form to half were shape so he could speak. Spitting away sweat and blood from his lips, he then said, "Enough. No wolf has survived this long."

"I'll say it's enough when we've reached one thousand," Amandus spit. "Insubordinate."

Covered with the vampire's blood, Ridge shook his head, flinging droplets from his soaked hair. He cast a weary glance over his comrades, all red with blood and heaving from exhaustion. Reluctant now, they all had lost the vigor for vengeance.

"No," Ridge said, and stepped to the principal. "The

vampire has proved his worth. He's survived. He does this for peace, and for your daughter."

"Do you dare to disobey me?" Amandus growled lowly. Of the wolves in the room he alone had not shifted to werewolf shape at all.

Ridge nodded. "The vampire has earned the princess. And peace between the packs and the tribes. You don't like it?"

"Not exactly—"

One swipe of Ridge's bloodied paw took Amandus Masterson's head from his neck. The principal's body slumped. And the pack nodded silently, respectful of Ridge's act.

"TAKE HIM OUT OF HERE."

Creed could barely make out sounds. Blood beat loudly in his ears, muffling the world. He could not smell anything but his own acrid, meaty blood.

A were's face appeared above him, floating, or maybe Creed could not focus. It was the one called Ridge. He was no longer in werewolf form.

"Lord Creed Saint-Pierre, you have my promise to peace. And you may call Princess Masterson your own." Ridge glanced over his shoulder. "Get this vampire gone from here! Jones, clean up this foul mess!"

The *mess* must be the thick sticky liquid Creed lay in. His own blood. Half of him, surely, pooled on the cement floor.

A hand gripped him at the ankle. He screamed but heard no sound. Other hands grasped at open, seeping parts of him. They handled him roughly, as if something to discard with a toss.

So much pain. His flesh was peeled away, his bones exposed. He could no longer heal quickly for he'd been torn to shreds.

As consciousness flickered, he thought of the most beautiful color in the world. Blu. And he smiled.

BLU HUNG UP THE PHONE and then threw the whole thing against the penthouse wall. It smashed, scattering electronic bits and plastic.

"What is it?" Severo, who had stopped by after he heard Creed had gone to the compound on his own, got to her as she began to shake.

She shoved away his embrace and gripped the kitchen counter.

"Who was it? Creed?"

"Ridge, my father's second in command, who has just taken leadership of the Northern pack. He said I could pick up Creed a mile out from the compound. They laid him in a ditch. That means he's not in good shape. He could be dead, Severo!"

"He could also be alive. Let's go. He won't survive for long in this sun."

SEVERO TOOK THE COUNTRY road going ninety. His Jeep handled the road well enough, but he struggled to keep it straight on the loose gravel. Blu wanted to leap, shift to wolf shape and race across the countryside. But this way was faster, so she clutched the dashboard as tightly as her jaw.

"There are blankets in the back," he said as they rounded a curve that set the Jeep on two wheels for a jaw-tensing few seconds. "You'll need them. The compound is ahead, but I don't know where—"

"There!" Blu released the door latch and bounded out, her feet hitting the ground and racing to meet the speed of the vehicle.

The glint at the edge of the ditch was not a jewel or metal—but blood. She could smell it before she could see it. Blood and the acrid scent of smoke. The sun burned him!

She landed on the blood-soaked grass beside what must be her husband but looked like a mass of man-shaped meat. His face was flat on the ground, arms splayed and legs bent. He bled everywhere. Huge gashes cut through his back. There was more blood and bone exposed than flesh.

Why had the wounds not healed?

Because there are so many.

Blu immediately knew her father had instituted his

favorite punishment upon Creed—one thousand talons. A werewolf never survived beyond two or three hundred. One rarity had seen her father reneging the punishment after one hundred, because he wished to save his best warrior.

She pressed her palm aside the bloody mass of Creed's neck. His throat was torn, but there she felt a pulse.

Severo appeared in the ditch with blankets in hand. "Is he alive?"

"Barely."

"Cover him from the sun. I'll carry him to the Jeep."

ALEXANDRE ARRIVED an hour after they'd returned to the hotel. Blu would not answer the door and appreciated that Severo had stuck around. Nothing could make her leave Creed's side.

Piles of bloody towels lay heaped on the floor. She'd washed her husband's wounds but tearfully realized he was one entire wound. The strips of flesh that had been spared were few. The sun had burned his back and the wounds festered.

But he was in there. He must sense her presence, feel her careful touches. Touches that must pain him, and she regretted them while she knew they were necessary.

"Stop crying," she told herself. "You have to be strong for him. He did this for you."

And he was still alive. That was better than dead. It had to be.

A quiet knock at the door did not dissuade her from the task of wringing the towels in the washbasin and rinsing them for reuse.

Severo peeked in. "How is he?"

"I think he may be healing. It's hard to tell. But he moaned a few minutes ago. Alexandre, hello."

"Oh, hell." The tall vampire rushed to the bedside and held a palm over his friend's chest. He moved it over Creed's body, as if a metal detector used to determine pulse. "He will live."

"You promise?" Blu asked, tears welling much against her will. "Please, Alexandre, promise me."

"You can't kill us so easily. Unfortunately." He swallowed and looked over Creed's chest. "The heart is still pumping so it did not take the damage."

Yes, Blu had been able to peer between ribs and see the thick, beating muscle. How his heart had not been torn open was beyond her understanding. She couldn't imagine her father's men purposely avoiding his heart to keep him alive.

But what better way to prolong the torture than to keep the victim alive?

Bile rose in her throat. She hated her father and the pack so desperately. And yet, Ridge had said something else when he'd called. Amandus was dead, at Ridge's hand. He'd claimed leadership of the Northern pack.

She had lost her father and Ryan in less than twenty-four hours. Neither, however, was worthy of her sadness or tears.

"I have news," Alexandre said softly. He turned his back to Creed and spoke to Blu and Severo. "The Northern pack has burned the sporting warehouse. They've taken a step toward peace. In fact, the one who claimed leadership—"

"Ridge."

"Yes, he's offered to stand good on the peace pact. I'm having the Nava tribe's attorneys draw up contracts right now to return a portion of land to them. There is some land that we can determine, without doubt, was gained by nefarious means. It's a beginning."

"Possible only because of your husband," Severo said. He put a hand on her shoulder. Blu appreciated the steadying warmth. He was one wolf she actually trusted. He tipped up her chin. "Ah? You wear his bite."

She stroked her neck.

"You will not regret it," he offered with kind eyes. Tugging aside his coat collar, he revealed a similar scar at the side of his neck. "The bond is like no other."

"Your wife bit you? Do you drink blood?" she asked.

He nodded. "Only from my wife. It is an incredible experience. And you mustn't worry, the blood hunger will not force you to take a victim out of desperation. You'll have time to return to your husband's side."

"Thank you, Severo. For all you have done."

"We'll leave you two. If there's anything you need, Blu, you have my number."

"Yes, but I don't know what to do. What *can* I do?" She looked to both men, finding hope in Severo's eyes, but little else.

"I wonder," Alexandre said. He grabbed her hand and examined it. "Have you the ring still?"

Blu glanced to the bedside table where she'd deposited the ring last night. "What can that do? Creed believed it might take away his magic."

"Yes, and yet he also believed it could have the opposite effect."

"But at the risk he may be reduced to ash if either guess is wrong. Besides, he's been shackled. He can't use his magic without having his bones crushed!"

"I wasn't aware," Alexandre said. "When did that happen?"

"Last night. As soon as we arrived at the clubhouse. It was so awful. They bound him magically."

Alexandre rubbed his chin thoughtfully. "He needs magic, Blu. He'll heal faster if he can utilize his magic."

"Magic?" Severo asked.

"He's an elder," Blu said. "One of the first vampires who used to steal magic from enslaved witches."

"Remarkable," Severo said. "Yet the shackle spell does not take away his magic. Perhaps the Council would see to giving it back to him, just to heal. It is worth the risk to help him heal, no?"

"Death is the risk," Blu insisted.

She glanced at Creed's ravaged body. Death or what horrendous condition if she did not try to help him? Would he remain tattered and broken forever? Could he function like that? Possibly, but would he *want* to live that way?

Not forever. No man would, and most especially not this proud warrior. But she could not imagine life without him now.

Looking to Severo, she asked, "Do you think the Council would agree to giving him the use of his magic? What would he do with it? He's incapable."

"He needs air, open space, to utilize any magic he may have," Alexandre said. "And his earth magic, as well."

"*If* the blood works."

"Yes, if. Severo, will you take her to the Council?"

"No, I won't leave Creed."

"The Council will not come to you," the werewolf offered. "If you want to save your husband, you must beg mercy."

"And quickly. Take this." Alexandre handed her the

ring. "Get permission, then we'll bring Creed to a good spot. Drip the blood into his heart."

Blu held the ring before her and tapped the glass. "I'm not sure."

How could Alexandre be certain it would help him? He'd been a vampire centuries less than Creed.

Severo hugged her and examined the ring. "If you do not try it, he may never recover. The vampire is immortal, but a man can only take so much damage before his body simply gives up."

"You think he'll die if I allow him to heal without magical assistance?"

Both Severo and Alexandre nodded.

"Then let's go." She hastened out of the bedroom, with Severo behind her.

ABIGAIL ROWAN LIVED in a cottage Blu couldn't help but label quaint. It was surrounded by lush flower blooms, manicured hedges and even had Welcome scrawled across the front doormat.

Blu knocked again, this time faster, louder and more insistent.

Severo hissed. "Be careful, Blu. Mustn't do anything to rile her."

"But we can't afford to waste time. Creed is almost dead. Where is she?"

The door creaked open to reveal a thin blonde woman in white silk pajama bottoms and top. Her hair was tousled, as if she'd just risen.

"Oh, hell, no," Abigail said.

"Did we wake you?" Severo asked.

"What do you think?"

"But it's afternoon." Blu stepped forward, but the witch didn't move aside to allow entrance. "Can we come in?"

"No. You interrupted the first hour of good sleep I've had in days. What's wrong now?"

"It's Creed. He's dying."

The witch shrugged and made to close the door, but Severo blocked it with his boot.

"Oh, come on," Abigail whined. "If you need to speak to the Council there are plenty other choices than me. I'm tired."

"He needs his magic back." Blu shoved the door inside and entered, forcing Abigail to step aside. She heard Severo apologize as he entered. "My father instituted his favorite punishment of a thousand talons against Creed, and now he's near death. But Severo and Alexandre Renard both believe Creed may have a fighting chance if he can utilize his magic."

"Not *his* magic," Abigail said, her tone not so weary now. "Magic stolen from helpless witches."

"They weren't so helpless," Blu snapped.

"Blu," Severo cautioned. He bowed graciously to the witch. "It would only be until he can recover. Then you could shackle him again."

"No." Abigail paced before the glass coffee table. Even looking tousled as she was, Blu felt her power. She was no witch to mess with.

She could accept the justice meted out by shackling Creed of his magic. But that didn't mean she had to kowtow to this woman because she had a beef against her husband.

"I won't leave until you change your mind," Blu said. "I can't. He's my husband. I love him. Have you never been in love, Abigail?"

"No," she offered with disinterest. "And I can sleep with you here. Makes no matter to me."

"Please. He risked his life to end the war."

That got Abigail's attention.

"You haven't heard?" Severo spoke now. "The Northern pack has burned a sporting warehouse and the vampires are in talks to return some land to the wolves."

"Amandus Masterson allowed this?" Abigail asked.

"He's dead," Blu said.

As final as those two simple words. She would not grieve that man any longer than it took to bury his bones in the ground.

Blu lifted her head and met the witch's bold green eyes. "Ridge killed him. He refused to complete the punishment against my husband. Because of Creed the vampires and werewolves have agreed to peace."

The witch exhaled. "I don't know…"

A knock on the door startled them all.

"Oh, now what?"

"I called Ridge on the way here," Severo offered.

The witch opened the door to reveal the hulking wolf. Ridge bowed politely and stepped inside. "I've come to beg for Creed Saint-Pierre's life," he said.

"Seriously?" Abigail took in all three of them. She was stymied. And she looked small and powerless. "Three werewolves come to beg for the life of one vampire? I never thought I'd see the day."

"Please." Blu took Abigail's hand and clasped it between both of hers. "I love him."

The witch rolled her eyes and tugged away from Blu. "Fine. But he gets shackled right after his recovery. If he can recover."

TWILIGHT PURPLED THE SKY. The field out back of Creed's estate had not been touched by fire. It was private, surrounded by woods on two sides, and fenced in on the other. Blu had carefully arranged a blanket and Alexandre laid his leader down.

Abigail immediately began the spell to reverse the shackles. It was much shorter then the original spell and, with but a clap of Abigail's hands, Creed's body reacted, lifting in an arch from the ground as if he'd been hit with defibrillator paddles, then collapsed, motionless.

Alexandre grabbed Blu's hand and drew her away from Creed, leaning down to stroke the hair from her cheek. "I have never liked werewolves. I still do not like them. I was once taken captive and forced to fight in the blood sport."

"I'm so sorry, Alex, I—"

"Doesn't matter right now. What does, is that I've seen a remarkable shift of thought in Creed. And it is because of you. You are very good for him, Princess. I count you as my friend, and thank you for loving my best friend."

He bowed and kissed her on the brow then dismissed himself, along with Severo, Ridge and Abigail. The witch didn't say anything but, surprisingly, she clasped hands with Ridge as they strode across the field.

"This is it," Blu said. "I hope this works."

Unscrewing the small titanium stopper from the ring, she paused over her lover's open chest. Blood scent tormented the air. It was not an odor she could normally stomach, but after spending hours over Creed's bloody body, she had become numb to it.

The brief thought emerged: if her husband died she would be left to feed her new blood hunger alone.

"Please don't leave me, Creed. I can survive the blood hunger alone, but never without your companionship. And you heard Alexandre. He's your best friend. You don't want to leave him, do you?"

She stroked softly over the ravaged flesh and muscle. "Does my blood still flow within you? Can you feel me, Creed? You said our heartbeats were now synched. Know that my heart beats only for you."

If only her blood could bring him back now. Could it? What if she dripped her own blood onto his wounds? It was a better risk than the witch's blood.

She clicked the minuscule glass vial with a fingernail and tilted it to watch the crimson flow along the glass.

If Alexandre were wrong, witch's blood could kill Creed. But if Severo were right, he would die anyway. And really, what could a few drops of werewolf blood do for him?

Kissing the glass vial, she then carefully tipped it over Creed's heart. Five drops fell onto his beating heart and permeated the muscle.

"Come back to me, lover. We've only just begun."

Nothing magical happened. The air did not change or begin to sparkle like some grand transformation scene in a movie.

Nothing.

Perhaps the shackle spell had depleted his magic? What had she expected?

Blu sucked in her lower lip and bent over him. Closing her eyes, she began a mantra, "Please heal. Come back to me."

Hours passed. Creed remained motionless, save for a few twitches in his fingers and some moans. He was fighting to survive.

Blu continued the mantra.

Another hour later a breeze tickled the tall grasses, stirring up cricket song. Blu sensed a change in the air. She sat up straight.

A clover-sweet breeze sifted through her hair, drawing the long dark strands across her face. Air tickled her mouth, much like a lover brushing his lips over hers.

Blu closed her eyes and imagined Creed's mouth at hers. She wrapped her arms about her shoulders and, sitting at her husband's side, surrendered to the feelings of warmth and love.

"You're doing this," she whispered. "I can feel your kiss on my skin. It worked. The blood revitalized your magic. Save yourself, Creed. Come back to me."

The wind began to swirl around them in a gentle tornado. Blu spread her arms and wiggled her fingers. The air caressed her like Creed's kiss gliding over her skin.

And then a tremendous gasp of air brought him from the precipice of hell and back to this realm. Chest heaving, Creed opened his eyes and he cried out in agony.

Blu did not lunge to protect him, to try to make it better. He needed the air, so she stood and stepped back. The cashmere wrap she wore over her T-shirt slipped from her shoulder and rippled like a flag. It brushed Creed's face.

Hours passed as she watched the wounds knit together and the flesh become smooth and new. His arm, broken and distorted, mended and straightened, and his fingers clutched handfuls of grass.

When he was able to sit, naked save for the blanket across his lap, he stretched an arm, flexing the scarred muscle. He nodded, satisfied he had begun recovery.

He sought Blu's eyes, and she knelt before him and stroked his cheek. What a wonder that he had become whole. She prayed he was as whole on the inside as he appeared outside.

"My werewolf princess," he whispered.

"You did it. The blood in my ring revitalized your magic."

"But how? I am shackled…"

"Abigail removed the spell. Just so you could heal. She'll shackle you again, when you've regained your strength."

He nodded. "You give me all the magic I require. Kiss me," he murmured.

His lips trembled against hers, his sigh tickling her mouth. Then the sharpness of fang slid across her lip.

"Your fangs are down, vampire," she said slyly. "You really have recovered."

He smirked. "Again, it's you. You do something to me, werewolf. I don't know what it is, and I don't need to know. The fighting. Has it…?"

"My pack has conceded," she said, "and thanks to Alexandre the Nava lawyers are returning land to the wolves. Ridge killed Amandus."

"To save me," he managed. "The wolf stopped my torture."

She'd always known Ridge was a good man.

"The peace pact has been signed, Creed. Because of your sacrifice. I love you for this."

"I think I died in that compound, Blu. Died with every stroke of the wolves' talons. But the one thing that kept me here was you. I wanted to hold you again, to breathe your life."

She kissed him, giving him the breath he had survived for.

EPILOGUE

DEEP IN THE STORAGE ROOM, behind many steamer trunks and beneath the bored gaze of an Italian marble statue of a naked warrior, something moved.

Creed approached carefully. Without a sound he prowled over the tiled floor, avoiding boxes and the pulling snag of a wooden pallet.

A flash of green popped from behind an open steamer trunk. Gray eyes dazzled. Red lips pursed and blew him a kiss.

"Are you snooping?" he asked, pausing before a crate and crossing his arms over his chest.

A sexy werewolf princess dressed in a flouncing eighteenth-century-style Watteau dress skipped to him and, with a bobble of her bright wig, bowed grandly before him.

"I never snoop." Her wink fluttered thick dark lashes. "Why do you have a woman's dress packed away in your things?" She pressed her palms against the tight corset, pushing up her breasts saucily. "Was she a lover?"

"What if I told you that dress once belonged to Marie Antoinette?" Creed reached for a pink bow on the bodice and tugged her to him.

"You're kidding me."

How he loved the dazzle in her eyes. It had been six months since they'd wed. It had taken half as long to heal completely from the internal wounds the Northern pack had inflicted on him. Then to endure the shackle spell again had weakened him for a time. He couldn't have survived without Blu to kiss him to health and be his reason for living.

And for that precious vial of witch's blood.

Since they'd arrived at Creed's Paris estate Blu had spent her days going through it, discovering the treasures he'd collected through the centuries.

"I am kidding," he said. "It probably belonged to an acquaintance. I'm not sure where it came from, actually. I must say I've not before seen it accessorized with green hair."

"I still like my wigs even though I don't need them to hide behind anymore."

"I like them, too. Wear them whenever you wish. You would have set the eighteenth-century salons on fire,

Blu. Such a marvel you would have been. A rock star in the halls of Versailles."

"You make me wish I had lived then."

"I'll tell you all about it."

"Start with the clothes," she cooed. A twist of her hips sashayed the wide skirts across Creed's legs. "How did the men get these tight corsets off the women so easily?"

"Ah?" He crooked a finger for her to approach. "It's not so much easy, as a long and lingering pursuit for pleasure." He dipped his head to her breasts and tongued them. "Can I keep whatever I unwrap?"

"You don't know? You're stuck with me, vampire. For centuries."

"I can live with that."

"You *will* live with that."

"Don't tell me what I'll live with or without," he teased.

"I can if I want."

"Spoiled brat."

"Wicked vampire."

He lashed his tongue over her nipple. "Tasty."

"Hungry."

He bit not too gently, drawing blood. "Only for you."

* * * * *

AUTHOR NOTE

When writing I often play music in the background, and sometimes a theme song will grab me for each character, or a certain scene. By the time I'm finished with the story, I have a complete soundtrack. So for those curious, below is the list of songs associated with *HER VAMPIRE HUSBAND*.

"Big Love Adagio"—Bond—(Blu and Creed's wedding march)

"Up All Night"—Slaughter—(Blu's theme song)

"Meet Me In The Red Room"—Moulin Rouge Soundtrack—(Blu's theme)

"So Alive"—Love and Rockets—(Creed's theme song)

"Send Me An Angel"—Deadstar Assembly— (playing in club Violet)

Blu and Creed falling-in-love songs:

"Wake Me Up Inside"—Evanescence
"New Thing"—Enuff Z'nuff
"She's Tight"—Cheap Trick
"Topless"—Breaking Benjamin
"Raspberry Beret"—Prince
"Breathe A Sigh"—Def Leppard
"How Soon Is Now?"—Love Spit Love (The Craft Soundtrack)
"Wicked Game"—H.I.M. (His Infernal Majesty)
"Mad About You"—Slaughter

Werewolf/Vampire mood stuff:

"Twist"—Korn
"7"—Prince
"The Wild Life"—Slaughter
"Psycho"—Puddle of Mudd
"Ardera Sempre"—Miranda Sex Garden
"Bodies"—Drowning Pool
"The Unforgiven III"—Metallica

NOCTURNE™

Coming next month

THE VAMPIRE AFFAIR by Livia Reasoner

The world knew Michael Brandt as a playboy tycoon.
The underworld knew him as a fierce vampire hunter. Then
tabloid reporter Jessie Morgan uncovered his secret and
Michael must fight heaven and hell to protect her from
the power of the undead.

WOLFTRAP by Linda Thomas-Sundstrom

When a full moon awakens the beast within
Dr Parker Madison, he is hell-bent on finding explanations
for his new Otherworld form and his insatiable lust. Then
he saves Chloe, the girl who stirs his darkest desires and
may hold the answers he's searching for.

SINS OF THE HEART by Eve Silver

Soul reaper Dagan is on a quest to find his brother's
remains and to find those responsible for his death. Roxy
Tam is searching for the same thing but for different reasons.
When Dagan and Roxy come together for a common goal,
they must choose between honour and the
inescapable passion that binds them...

On sale 5th November 2010

MILLS & BOON

are proud to present our...

Book of the Month

Proud Rancher, Precious Bundle
by Donna Alward
from Mills & Boon® Cherish™

Wyatt and Elli have already had a run-in. But when a
baby is left on his doorstep, Wyatt needs help.
Will romance between them flare as they
care for baby Darcy?

Mills & Boon® Cherish™
Available 1st October

*Something to say about our
Book of the Month?
Tell us what you think!*

millsandboon.co.uk/community
facebook.com/romancehq
twitter.com/millsandboonuk

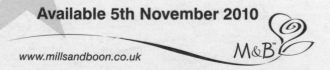

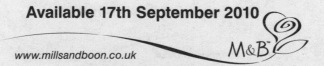

Mystery, magic and... marriage

Sorcery and seduction…
A dark and spooky night…
Trick, treat…or a Halloween temptation?

*Things are not quite as they seem on
All Hallows' Eve…*

Available 1st October 2010

www.millsandboon.co.uk

M&B

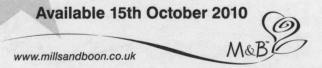

FREE BOOK
AND A SURPRISE GIFT

We would like to take this opportunity to thank you for reading this Mills & Boon® book by offering you the chance to take a specially selected book from the Nocturne™ series absolutely FREE! We're also making this offer to introduce you to the benefits of the Mills & Boon® Book Club™—

- **FREE home delivery**
- **FREE gifts and competitions**
- **FREE monthly Newsletter**
- **Exclusive Mills & Boon Book Club offers**
- **Books available before they're in the shops**

Accepting this FREE book and gift places you under no obligation to buy, you may cancel at any time, even after receiving your free book. Simply complete your details below and return the entire page to the address below. You don't even need a stamp!

YES Please send me a free Nocturne book and a surprise gift. I understand that unless you hear from me, I will receive 3 superb new stories every month, two priced at £4.99 and a third larger version priced at £6.99, postage and packing free. I am under no obligation to purchase any books and may cancel my subscription at any time. The free book and gift will be mine to keep in any case.

Ms/Mrs/Miss/Mr _____ Initials _____

Surname _____

Address _____

_____

_____ Postcode _____

E-mail _____

Send this whole page to: Mills & Boon Book Club, Free Book Offer, FREEPOST NAT 10298, Richmond, TW9 1BR